SWEET TEMPTATION

"You're beautiful, Melissa, a very beautiful, very desirable woman," Reid said in a husky voice.

When he reached up and gently cupped her face, his touch seemed to burn her skin. And as his slender fingers trailed gently across her face, she swayed toward him, her lips aching for his kiss.

As his mouth closed over hers, he was intoxicated by the sweet taste of her mouth and abruptly his kiss became more passionate, almost brutal.

The sudden change from sweet seduction to fierce possession was too quick for Melissa and she struggled, finally tearing herself away from him. "No! Stop it!"

Reid released her and smiled mockingly. "What's wrong, Melissa? I thought you wanted me to kiss you. You've been begging for it for days now. You've been flaunting that seductive little body of yours in front of me, leading me on. And you wanted that kiss all right until I started kissing you like a real man kisses a woman. And you got more than you bargained for. You're a little girl playing a woman's game. Go back and play your silly little virgin games with your stupid little boys and leave the men to the *real* women."

Captive Love

LAUREN WILDE

ZEBRA BOOKS
KENSINGTON PUBLISHING CORP.

For my son, Steve, with love.

ZEBRA BOOKS

are published by

Kensington Publishing Corp.
475 Park Avenue South
New York, NY 10016

First printing: June, 1988

Printed in the United States of America

Chapter One

From the minute she saw him, Melissa couldn't take her eyes off him. She stared at the strange man, as if drawn by some powerful, invisible force, becoming suddenly and totally oblivious to the crowded, noisy river landing beside her and the smattering of houses that sat high on the bluff above it. She didn't see the teeming mass of humanity that swirled and eddied about their boat. Nor did she notice the score or more of long keelboats, clumsy flatboats, and noisy steamers, all jostling for a position at the landing on the muddy river. To her, Vicksburg on the Mississippi had ceased to exist. She wasn't even aware that her heart was racing and her mouth had suddenly turned dry. Time stood still, and only she and this man remained, locked in some strange vacuum of time and space.

He stood at the end of the landing, as tall and proud as the majestic oaks on the riverbank behind him, his muscles rippling sinuously beneath the buckskins that molded his broad shoulders, muscular arms, and long, whipcord legs like a second skin. The soft breeze ruffled his chestnut hair about his deeply tanned face, the reddish glints catching the sunlight from above.

Nature had been extremely generous to this man. Not only had she endowed him with a tall, commanding physique and rugged, exceptional good looks, but she had given him something much, much more. There was a compelling, almost savage, virility about him; the air around him fairly crackled with the force of his dynamic presence.

Melissa watched as the stranger walked across the landing, easily shouldering aside the crowd of men around him, his long-limbed walk lithe, lazy, catlike. Her breath caught in her throat as she drank in the sheer animal beauty of him. He looks like a lion, she thought, with his broad shoulders and slim hips, his tawny coloring, his proud carriage. Even his eyes were feline, flickering, alert, golden-colored.

How can I get him to notice me? Melissa wondered. Then, her beautiful turquoise eyes sparkled. Of course, she thought, by making every other man on the landing take notice.

Discreetly, she unbuttoned the first three buttons on her bodice, revealing a tantalizing amount of cleavage. She leaned across the railing, pretending to be straining to see something far off to the side of the steamboat, her most dazzling smile pasted on her face.

"My God! What *are* you doing?" a shocked voice asked from behind her.

She whirled around, a guilty look on her face, and then her eyes glittered angrily. "What are you doing here? Snooping on me again?"

Instantly, her sister Ellen knew she had made a mistake. Sharp words only made Melissa more stubborn, fueling her fiery, rebellious nature.

"I'm not snooping on you," Ellen answered in a soothing voice. "I just happened to walk up and saw what you were doing." Ellen shook her head in exasperation. "Whatever made you expose your bosom like that?"

Melissa tossed her head, sending her lustrous black curls bouncing around her small shoulders. "I'm *not* exposing myself. I was hot and just thought it would be cooler if I loosened a few buttons. Besides, our ballgowns show more bosom than this."

"But we're not in a ballroom, and those are hardly gentlemen down there," Ellen answered, casting a wary look at the tough-looking frontiersmen and the rough-talking roustabouts that were swarming all over the landing below them. "Now, please, button up your bodice," she said in a placating voice, "before they mistake you for some brazen hussy."

Melissa pouted, her jewellike eyes still glittering rebelliously. Then shooting her sister a murderous look, she buttoned her dress. When she was finished, she flipped her head again and turned once more to gaze out over the landing, her small chin

7

raised defiantly.

What am I going to do with her? Ellen thought in despair. Melissa was always doing the most outrageous things. Even as a child, she had been uncommonly curious and overflowing with energy. No wonder their flighty, high-strung mother couldn't handle her. Of course, their father spoiling her so rotten hadn't helped, either. No, as much as she loved her sister, Melissa was undoubtedly the most willful, stubborn, and spoiled person she had ever known. Trying to protect her from herself and act as a buffer between her and their mother had been a formidable task for Ellen.

Ellen's baby-blue eyes narrowed as she saw the rapt expression on her sister's face. Ellen knew that look only too well. Undoubtedly, her sister had spied another man to work her charms on, one more conquest to add to her long list of broken hearts. Yes, besides being willful and spoiled, Melissa was also a notorious flirt.

Ellen glanced down at the river landing. She had no trouble finding the man her sister was staring at in the crowd. He stood out from the others — a man any woman, regardless of her age, was bound to notice, a man whose masculine sensuality was so powerful it stripped a woman of her thin veneer of civilized respectability, leaving only her primitive instincts in acute awareness that he was male and she was female. Even Ellen felt drawn by his overpowering sexuality.

Ellen frowned, noticing his buckskins for the first time. This was no man for Melissa to play her games with. No placid gentleman she could lead around by the nose. He was a frontiersman, a breed of man who played by no man's rules, a law unto himself, a man who shaped his own destiny, a man often as savage as the Indian he fought the land for, a man who took what he wanted. This was no man for her flirtatious sister to play her childish, teasing games with. This man was dangerous! Her sister could very well be hurt.

Fear for her sister made Ellen's words sharper than she intended. "My gracious alive, Melissa! Stop gawking at that man like that!"

Ellen's tone of voice broke the spell Melissa had been under. She bristled. Her turquoise eyes flashed as she retorted hotly, "I've no idea what you're talking about! I'm not gawking at anybody!"

Melissa glanced back down at the crowded river landing, wondering how Ellen could have known she was staring at one particular man. Unless—unless Ellen had noticed him, too. The realization that her straitlaced sister had not been immune to him tickled Melissa's fancy.

In an abrupt change of mood, she turned back to her sister. "Oh, Ellen, isn't he the most beautiful man you've ever seen?" Her eyes sparkled.

Ellen was used to Melissa's mercurial moods. She smiled, "Men aren't beautiful, Melissa. They're handsome. And we knew men just as handsome as him back in Carolina," she said in a patient voice.

"Oh, I'm not talking about his face," Melissa replied. "I mean the rest of him. He's so strong looking. So exciting. So . . . well—so *male!*"

Ellen flushed, remembering only too well her own awareness of his masculinity. But southern ladies of quality didn't use that shocking word, male. It was crude, much too descriptive. "Manly is the word to use," she corrected gently. "And besides, ladies don't notice such things."

Melissa sighed in disgust. She loved Ellen, even more than she did her father, who spoiled her rotten. No one was as patient with her as her calm, sweet, gentle sister. And Melissa knew Ellen had appointed herself as her protector, her guardian angel. But why did she have to be so perfect all of the time? So chaste and ladylike? Didn't she ever think a wicked thought? Do anything wrong? Wasn't she even curious to know what really happened between men and women in the marriage bed? What all the big mystery was about? She wondered what Ellen would think if she knew Melissa had let one of her admirers touch her breasts. Oh, not for long. Just a mere touch. Or that she actually let another put his tongue in her mouth, an act that had repulsed her instead of exciting her. But now she longed to tell her sister about it, just to see the shocked look on her face. Only the realization that such a confession would lead to more lectures on ladylike behavior kept her from it.

"Well, maybe *you* don't notice such things about men, but *I* do," Melissa said in an irritated voice. "And so do other girls. And I still say he's the most beautiful man I've ever seen!"

Melissa tossed her head and looked defiantly

back down at the stranger on the landing, daring her sister to say more. The man was directly below them now. Sensing someone watching him, he stopped and looked up.

Melissa's breath caught as those golden, feline eyes looked up into her own. Once again, she was caught in his hypnotic spell, feeling the powerful pull of that intense, magnetic gaze. Dumbly, she stared at him.

Who was that beautiful creature staring at him? Reid wondered. His tawny eyes flicked over her, noting her expensive clothing. She was obviously quality. But surely, no lady would stare at a strange man so boldly, almost brazenly. Was she one of those high-class courtesans from New Orleans?

Reid's eyes slowly raked her body, lingering over the curve of her proud, young breasts and the swell of her hips. His sensuous lips slowly curved into a seductive smile.

Melissa felt that smoldering look as profoundly as if he had reached up and touched her, as if his hands, instead of his eyes, had undressed her and were slowly caressing her naked flesh. She had seen looks of admiration before, even open desire, but she had never before had a man's gaze affect her so strongly. Her legs felt suddenly weak, the palms of her hands turned clammy, her heart raced. She tingled all over. The new sensations stunned her, frightened her. Momentarily taken aback, she blushed furiously.

Reid saw her flush and frowned. This was no courtesan. She was just another one of those southern belles playing her silly yet dangerous games. He knew all about such women, more than he cared to know. They were spoiled, shallow women — women who had nothing better to do than flirt and tease, playing with a man's emotions, making promises they had no intention of keeping. Well, he wasn't interested in playing games with this spoiled little girl. He wanted a woman, a real woman.

Reid's look of admiration turned to one of open disgust. His smile changed to a sneer as he bowed mockingly.

Melissa was shocked at the handsome stranger's open insult. No man had ever treated her so contemptuously before. To the contrary. She was used to being worshiped. Her pride fought to the surface of her jangled emotions. How dare he! Her turquoise eyes flashed as she lifted her dark head haughtily, saying in an outraged voice, "Well, I've never — I've never seen such a rude, arrogant man in my entire life!" Then she whirled and proudly walked away.

Ellen had watched the whole exchange between Melissa and the handsome stranger with bated breath. Now she stared at her sister's back, knowing that once Melissa's temper had cooled, she would be as undaunted as ever. Yes, she knew her beautiful sister. Melissa would only take the insult as a challenge. Her stubborn sister wasn't about to be bested by any man.

Ellen glanced down at the river landing, but the disturbing stranger had disappeared. She should have felt relief, but she didn't. She couldn't shake the feeling that this was not the last they had seen of him. She knew, with an almost uncanny certainty, that Melissa had met her match — and her destiny.

Chapter Two

Melissa walked across the small deck and leaned against the railing, inhaling a long, deep breath of fresh air. She could hear the murmuring voices of the women in the small cabin behind her and knew her mother would scold her for leaving. But she didn't care. She couldn't stand another minute of their inane conversation. Besides, it was hot and stuffy in the small room, and it reeked of stale perfume and body powder.

She turned and walked a few feet away, peering out at the shadowed shore. The massive oaks with their dangling Spanish moss swaying in the breeze looked eerie in the moonlight. The sweet smell of magnolias and wild night-blooming jasmine mingled with the smell of damp earth and filled her nostrils.

At this time of night, the steamboat moved upriver slowly for fear of hitting snags or submerged sawyers. She could barely feel the vibrations from the engines, vibrations that shook the little steamboat at full speed so badly she feared it might break apart. Nor could she hear the engine noises that were so deafening during the daytime that the passengers had to shout to be heard over them. Even the birds that nested at night on the small islands in the river were quiet. It was a relief, for they were usually so noisy that one could hardly sleep because of them.

After the women's incessant chattering in the cabin, the soft night sounds were soothing to Melissa's nerves. She stood listening to the gurgles and soft sucking sounds of the water against the riverbank, the steady swish, swish, swish of the paddles against the water, the crickets' chirrups, and the frogs' croaks. Somewhere in the distance, a bull alligator bellowed and an owl hooted.

She glanced down at the lower deck where the deck passengers were already bedding down for the night, some with blankets, some just rolling on their sides and into tight balls. Most of the "deckers" were men, riverboat men who were returning north, or frontiersmen, who slept with their muskets by their sides. She wondered if the man she had seen on the landing that afternoon was down there? A small thrill coursed through her. Despite the fact that he had angered her, she hadn't been able to get him out of her mind. All afternoon, she had secretly hoped to get a glimpse of him on the deck below. She knew he wouldn't be on the upper deck, for that was reserved for the first-class passengers. But then, maybe he wasn't on this boat at all. Maybe he had taken another steamer, or was on his way south, instead of north, like her. A sudden feeling of disappointment filled her at that thought.

The sound of a child crying drew her attention back to the lower deck. A man and woman and their three children sat huddled in a corner, the woman rocking and crooning to the smallest child. A farmer and his family going west, Melissa thought.

West. The thought of it excited Melissa. When her father had announced the decision to move west, Ellen and her mother had wept at the loss of their beautiful plantation home. But not Melissa. She had been utterly bored with her life there. Her social contacts had been limited to the families of the other plantations that surrounded theirs. Even the balls that had once excited her had lost their appeal. The same people came; the same subjects were talked to death; the same music was played; the same dances were danced; even the food was the same. The monotony had extended to her suitors. The young men's names changed, the color of their eyes and hair, but underneath, they were all the same—boring. The thought of moving to a new location and seeing new, exciting places and meeting other people had fired Melissa's imagination and appealed to her restless nature.

She smiled, remembering her trip thus far. On the coastal steamer from Charleston to New Orleans, her mother and sister had stayed in their cabins, both suffering from seasickness. But Melissa had not been the least bothered by the dip and sway of the ship. She had seized the opportunity to be out from underneath their watchful eyes and roamed the ship at will, meeting new people whose backgrounds were so different from her own, watching the sailors at their work, badgering the captain and first mate with incessant questions, questions that reflected her keen intelligence. She had been so engrossed that she hadn't even noticed the young men watching her with admiring, and often hungry, looks.

Even the last day, when the storm had hit, Melissa had refused to give up her new freedom and retreat to the safety of her cabin. Much to the disquietude of the captain, who had feared she would be swept overboard, she had stubbornly remained on deck, reveling in the buffeting wind that whipped her clothes and hair about her, in the rain pelting her face, in the smell of salt and ozone in her nostrils.

Then they had docked in New Orleans, the queen of the Mississippi, that exciting city unequaled by any other in America with its continental air and unique mixture of Spanish and French culture. Melissa had fallen in love with the city, admiring its lovely homes with their wrought-iron grillwork and courtyards, enjoying its theaters, its luxurious hotels and fine restaurants. The city had been so different from Charleston. Even the Creole cuisine had been unusual, exotic, and spicy, like the city itself.

The only disappointment in her trip thus far had

been not being able to visit Natchez. She had been titillated by the whispered stories of the notorious Natchez-Under-the-Hill, sin city of the Mississippi. But the packet had not stopped there. Instead, it had passed it at night and stayed well in the main channel of the wide, somnolent river. The only thing she had been able to see were the lights in the distance. But even then, the sounds had drifted across the still water, the tinny sound of a piano, boisterous male laughter, the reports of several pistol shots. The sounds had only teased her curiosity, adding to her frustration and disappointment.

And now, standing on the dark deck, Melissa was again bored. She glanced back at the women's cabin, knowing she should return before her mother noticed her absence. She was sure she hadn't missed anything. Undoubtedly, the women were still discussing the new fashions, a subject they had been at for hours.

The sound of muted male voices drew her attention to the men's cabin farther down the deck. Each day, after the evening meal, the women withdrew to their cabin for conversation, the men to their cabin for drinking and gambling. Melissa knew their conversation would certainly be more stimulating than the women's, perhaps even risqué. Curious, she wondered what the men's cabin looked like. She knew it was forbidden territory to the ladies. Were the men hiding something? Were the walls covered with pictures of half-nude women as she had heard they were in some gambling dens?

Melissa's thoughts were interrupted by her mother's shrill voice as she and Ellen rushed out of the women's cabin. "Oh, there you are, Melissa! Land's sake, child, you frightened me to death when I looked up and saw you were gone. Whatever are you doing out here all by yourself?"

"It's hot in the cabin, Mother," Melissa replied defensively. "I only stepped out for a breath of fresh air."

"Well, you could have at least told me where you were going, instead of scaring me half out of my wits," Mrs. Randall snapped. "Goodness, child, you have absolutely no consideration for your poor mother at all!"

Melissa sighed. What did her mother think could possibly happen to her while she was standing less than twenty feet away? Did her mother think an Indian would sneak over the rail and kidnap her daughter?

"I'm sure Melissa didn't mean to worry you, Mother," Ellen said in a soothing voice. "And she's right. The cabin was unbearably hot. Why, I thought I might swoon from the heat myself," she added in hopes of distracting her mother's attention from Melissa.

Mrs. Randall looked at Ellen with alarm. This golden-haired, blue-eyed beauty was her favorite. Ellen was so sweet and serene, so well mannered. She never gave her mother any trouble, like Melissa did. "Swoon? Are you all right, child?"

"I'm fine now, Mother," Ellen replied. "All I needed was some fresh air, too."

Mrs. Randall delicately fanned her face with her

handkerchief. "Yes, it's terribly hot here, isn't it? Even hotter than back home. Do you think it will be this hot in Missouri?"

Ellen smiled in amusement, thinking how easily her flighty mother's thoughts could be sidetracked. "The humidity here makes it so hot, Mother. I'm sure Missouri will be much cooler."

"Oh, I do wish your father would reconsider this move," Mrs. Randall wailed. "I miss our home and all my friends so much. Do you think Mildred's daughter has had her baby by now?"

Melissa rolled her eyes in exasperation. If her mother had asked that question one time in the past week, she had asked it at least a hundred.

"I'm sure she has by now, Mother," Ellen answered sweetly.

"It's disgraceful," Mrs. Randall said in a disgusted voice. "Imagine! Two children within two years. Her daughter's husband must be an animal."

Melissa frowned. She had often heard her mother and her mother's friends refer to men as animals. Something to do with that mysterious marriage bed again. Melissa wondered just what the men did that was so animalistic? And if it was disgusting, why did the women allow it?

"Well, come on, girls," Mrs. Randall sighed. "It's time to go to bed."

Go to bed? Melissa thought with disgust. At nine o'clock? Why, she wasn't even sleepy. Then she sighed with resignation. What difference did it make? She could just as easily be bored lying in bed as standing out here. At least in her cabin, she

20

wouldn't have to listen to her mother's silly prattle.

As the three women walked toward their cabins, Mrs. Randall said, "Well, thank goodness we don't have to sleep in the women's cabin. Mrs. Clemmons told me that Mrs. Sims snores. Just like a man! Isn't that disgusting?"

"Yes," Ellen replied, "we're fortunate that Father insisted we wait for one of these new packets that have a few private cabins. Doubly fortunate that we were able to get two of them."

Mrs. Randall stopped, frowning and fumbling in her reticule.

"What's wrong, Mother?" Ellen asked.

"Your father forgot to give me the key to our cabin," Mrs. Randall answered. She shook her head in disgust. "That man! Once he gets his mind on drinking and gambling, he forgets everything else. Now what will I do?"

Melissa saw her golden opportunity. Before her mother could think of a solution, she said, "Don't worry, Mother. I'll get the key from Father."

Quickly, she turned and hurried away, hearing her mother's voice calling to her, "Come back here, Melissa. You know you can't go into the men's cabin—Melissa! Do you hear me?"

Melissa raced to the men's cabin and stepped into it, still half afraid her mother would catch her and snatch her back out before she got a chance to get a good look at it. The room was hazy with smoke and reeked with the strong smell of cigars and whiskey. Melissa glanced at the walls, feeling a keen sense of disappointment at finding them bare.

21

In fact, the men's cabin was an exact duplicate of the women's cabin. Built-in cots lined the walls, and the only furniture was a round table surrounded by chairs, at the back of the small room. Except for one man, who was sleeping on one of the cots, all of the men sat at the table, so engrossed in their card game that they hadn't even noticed Melissa.

Melissa squinted, her vision being hampered by both the smoke and her watering eyes. Finally spying her father, she walked across the small room and laid her hand on his shoulder.

"Father?" she said quietly.

Mr. Randall startled and looked up in surprise. "Good heavens, Melissa!" he said in a shocked voice. "What are you doing here?"

"I'm sorry, Father," Melissa said sweetly, "but you forgot to give Mother the key to your cabin, and she wishes to retire."

For once, Mr. Randall was truly irritated with his daughter. He knew damn well his wife hadn't sent her into the men's cabin to retrieve the key. No, undoubtedly that had been Melissa's idea. And what would the other gentlemen think of his headstrong daughter? Feeling acutely embarrassed, he stumbled to his feet and fumbled through his pockets for the key, wondering what possible excuse he could give the men for his daughter's invasion of their privacy.

Sensing her father's thoughts, Melissa glanced down at the men sitting beside him. They looked absolutely shocked. But Melissa wasn't worried.

After all, they were only men. She knew she'd have them wound around her little finger in no time at all.

She turned to them and smiled sweetly. "Heavens, gentlemen, I shudder to think what you must think of me, barging in on you like some brazen hussy. But my dear mother was feeling indisposed. This terrible heat, you know." She blinked back imaginary tears. "I was so afraid she would swoon before I could even find the captain." She hung her head, managing to look very small and helpless. "I hope you will forgive my indiscretion."

Melissa's little act had the exact results she knew it would. Instantly, the men were scrambling to their feet, flushing and apologizing to *her*. All except one, who seemed reluctant to rise.

Melissa glanced at the offender as he slowly rose to his feet, towering over the other men and dwarfing them with his exceptional breadth of shoulders. She barely suppressed her gasp of surprise. It was *him,* the same man she had seen on the landing that afternoon. Her heart quickened with excitement.

He had changed his buckskins and was now dressed as the other gentlemen at the table. Strangely, he looked just as at ease in the elegant clothing as he had in the frontier dress, and he had lost none of his magnetic sensual appeal in the transition, either. Melissa looked up into his golden eyes and felt that same pull, those same peculiar feelings stealing over her. Then she noticed the amused glint in his eyes. Well, she wouldn't be humiliated by him twice, she thought angrily, jerking her eyes away.

She found herself facing two other young men, their eyes filled with admiration. Aware of the handsome stranger's gaze still on her, she deliberately gave the two young men a small flirtatious smile and a smoldering look from the corner of her eye. Predictably, the men's expressions turned to one of open desire. See, Mr. Cat-eyes, Melissa thought smugly, all men aren't immune to my charms.

Mr. Randall interrupted Melissa's game. "Here's the key."

Melissa turned and took the key from him, knowing that her father had already forgiven her by the loving glint in his eyes. She stood on tiptoe and kissed his cheek. "Good night, Father."

"Sleep tight, Princess," Mr. Randall replied, patting her back tenderly.

Knowing every male eye was on her, particularly that obnoxious stranger's, Melissa turned and said, "I'm sorry I interrupted your game, gentlemen. Thank you for your indulgence. Have a pleasant evening." Then she gave them a dazzling smile, turned, and walked toward the door.

Mr. Randall chuckled silently at the enraptured looks on the men's faces. He should have known that Melissa could handle the situation. As usual, she had captivated her audience. He didn't notice the scowl on one man's face, the man with the strange golden eyes.

Melissa walked away, hearing the sound of chairs

scraping as the men reseated themselves at the table, feeling very proud of herself. She was determined she wouldn't look back at the handsome stranger. But despite her resolve, she stopped at the door, sneaking a last look at him.

He sat at the table, his long, slender fingers lazily shuffling the cards, his feline eyes still watching her intently. Their eyes met and locked across the hazy room. Then his sensual lips curved into a knowing smile, a smile that told Melissa that he was well aware that she couldn't resist one last look.

The smile infuriated Melissa. Why, that conceited bastard! she thought angrily. She gave him a go-to-hell look, and, for the second time that day, turned her back to him and flounced away.

Chapter Three

The passengers paced the deck impatiently as the steamer's crew loaded wood from the riverside woodyard. This was their third stop for wood today. Not even the hot, resinous pine, the engineer's favorite firewood, could satisfy the little steamer's ravenous appetite for long. Finally, the gangplank was pulled up, and the steamboat chugged away amidst cheers and sighs of relief from the impatient passengers.

At this point on the Mississippi, the river was wide, silent, and deserted. Not a hint of civilization had been seen for miles and miles. Immense trees lined the river's edge. The underbrush beneath them was thick, dense, and tangled with vines, some of which were blooming profusely, others heavy with wild purple grapes. From the deck of the steamer, one could see an occasional alligator sunning himself on the bank or spy a fleeting deer.

Melissa, standing with her sister and parents at

the rail, lifted her face into the slight breeze as the steamer picked up speed. The breeze was a relief from the hot sun beating down on them. But the reprieve was short-lived, for the heat of the boilers was soon added to that of the sun, as they sent red-hot cinders from the smokestack swirling around the steamer. As the paddles spun faster, the vibrations increased and the noise rose to a deafening pitch, only adding to her discomfort.

The packet's shrill whistle blew, signaling the approach of a riverboat. Another steamer, its decks piled high with crates and barrels, chugged past. Its smokestack added even more smoke and hot cinders to the clear Mississippi air. Behind it floated a flatboat, its tattered sail billowing in the breeze.

Melissa was fascinated with these flatboats, these floating shanties, for invariably, in the middle of the boat, a shabbily constructed loghouse stood, with a clothesline strung across its roof. Off to one side was a pen with chickens and pigs and, occasionally, a lowing cow. As they passed the flatboat, the big raft bobbed precariously in the waves caused by the steamer's wake, and Melissa smiled as the flatboat's resident dog barked furiously at the offending waves.

Thirty minutes later, the packet pulled to the side and stopped again. An audible groan of disgust was heard from the passengers.

"What are we stopping for this time?" Mrs. Randall asked her husband testily.

Mr. Randall looked around. "I don't know, my dear. I don't see another woodyard anywhere near."

Melissa turned and leaned over the rail, searching the riverbank with her eyes. Behind her, she heard her father saying, "Oh, excuse me, Mr. Forrester, but do you know why we're stopping this time?"

"Probably to clean the mud out of the boilers, Mr. Randall," a deep male voice answered. "You realize they use river water in them."

"Yes, I know," Mr. Randall answered in an irritable voice, "but they just cleaned them yesterday."

"And they'll stop and clean them tomorrow, too," the man answered dryly. "Usually they're cleaned once a day, sometimes twice. Otherwise, we'd run the risk of an explosion."

Melissa was captivated with the man's deep, melodious voice. Goodness, she thought, if the man was just half as attractive as his voice . . . Smiling her best flirtatious smile, she turned and found herself facing a pair of broad shoulders. Her beautiful turquoise eyes widened with recognition. She didn't even have to look up into his golden eyes to know it was *him*. Her smile froze on her face as she thought bitterly, She should have known. Naturally, his voice would be just as sensual as the rest of him.

Mrs. Randall stared at the stranger, wondering how she could have possibly missed noticing this handsome young man among the other male passengers. She studied his well-tailored and obviously expensive frock coat approvingly. What a fine catch he'd make for one of her daughters, she thought, a sly glint flickering in her eyes.

She turned to her husband. "Goodness, Jacob,

where are your manners? Aren't you going to introduce us to this young man?"

Mr. Randall frowned. He knew exactly what his wife was thinking. When he had met Mr. Forrester the previous evening, he had been impressed with the young man, too. Because of the man's well-tailored clothes, gentlemanly manners, and knowledgeable talk of growing cotton, Mr. Randall had assumed he was a planter traveling the river on business. But as the night had progressed and the young man had steadily and methodically fleeced everyone sitting at the table, Mr. Randall had begun to suspect he might be one of those river gamblers everyone was warned about, a new breed of men who traveled the steamboats and preyed on migrating planters and businessmen. No novice at gambling himself, he had watched the man carefully, but detected no sign of cheating. Either the man was very skillful or very lucky at cards. But not knowing which, Mr. Randall was reluctant to introduce his daughters to the man, particularly since Mr. Forrester was a man the ladies obviously found very attractive.

Mr. Randall could feel his wife's eyes glaring at him and sighed in resignation. It seemed he had no choice. "My dear, this is Mr. Reid Forrester. And this, sir, is my wife and daughters, Ellen and Melissa."

Reid smiled, saying pleasantly, "My pleasure, Mrs. Randall and Miss Randall." Then turning to Melissa, he bowed slightly, saying, "I believe we met last night."

29

Melissa colored hotly, thinking, Well, he might look like a gentleman, but he certainly didn't act like one. No gentleman would remind her of her indiscretion last night, particularly in front of her mother. Why, he made it sound so intimate, as if they had had an assignation or something.

"Last night?" Mrs. Randall asked in a shocked voice.

Melissa saw Reid's eyes glittering with amusement. And he's laughing at me, she thought. *Again!* How dare he!

She shot Reid a murderous look. "Mr. Forrester was in the men's cabin last night when I went to get your key, Mother," she said in a tight voice.

"Oh, I see," Mrs. Randall answered nervously. She was shocked by her daughter's rudeness to the young man. What was wrong with her? Usually when such an attractive young man was around, Melissa was all charm. But she acted like she couldn't stand the man. But then, there was still Ellen.

Mr. Randall hadn't missed Melissa's hateful look, either. Well, he thought, at least I don't have to worry about her becoming infatuated with him. She obviously disliked him, and Ellen would never be swayed by a man's good looks. She was much too sensible. Feeling more at ease, he said, "Mr. Forrester, are you familiar with this river?"

"Yes, sir."

"Could you tell me how much farther it is until we reach Missouri?"

Reid looked out at the riverbank beside them.

"Actually, we've already reached Missouri. This is the state's southernmost tip, commonly called the bootheel."

Mr. Randall looked out at the swampy wilderness beside them. The area was filled with grotesquely shaped cypress trees and cottonwoods. "It looks awfully low," he remarked.

"It is," Reid answered. "This is the part of Missouri that sank during the New Madrid earthquake." He motioned to the opposite bank. "And that part of Tennessee, too."

"Earthquake?" Mrs. Randall gasped. "There was an earthquake here?"

"Yes, ma'am, there certainly was," Reid answered. "A very powerful earthquake, powerful enough to make the mighty Mississippi flow backwards for several hours and overflow its banks, flooding everything around it for hundreds of miles. The most destruction occurred at New Madrid, just a few miles upstream."

Mrs. Randall's face turned ashen. "How often do these earthquakes occur?"

"As far as I know, it's the only one that ever hit this area," Reid answered.

"Were you in this area at the time?" Ellen asked.

"Yes, I was, Miss Randall. At the time, I was working on a keelboat on the Mississippi. We were just a few miles north of Cairo when the quake hit."

Mr. Randall frowned at Reid's words, "working on a keelboat." My God, he thought, was this man one of those wild "Kaintuck" riverboat men, men

who claimed they were half horse and half alligator, who bragged they could outdrink, outcuss,
outfight any man alive? He glanced at Reid's broad
shoulders. Undoubtedly, the man could hold his
own in any fight. But still, the rest didn't fit. His
speech and manners were too gentlemanly. "You're
from Kentucky?" he asked in a suspicious voice.

Having guessed Mr. Randall's thought, Reid's
eyes twinkled with amusement. "No, I'm originally
from Savannah, Georgia. I came west back in '10, by
way of the Natchez Trace, or 'The Devil's Back-
bone', as the frontiersmen call it."

The Natchez Trace? Mr. Randall thought. He
had traveled across that lawless pathway? Why,
even Meredith Lewis, famed frontiersman that he
had been, had been murdered in a crude wilderness
inn on that notorious trail. "If you crossed that
trail, then you're lucky to be alive, Mr. Forrester."

"Yes, I am," Reid answered. "As a matter of
fact, the party I was traveling with *was* attacked by
bandits. We considered ourselves lucky that we
were just robbed and not murdered, too. Which is
why I was forced to work on a keelboat."

Mr. Randall noticed Reid's pointed explanation
and flushed in embarrassment. My God, he
thought, can the man read minds, too?

"And you were lucky enough to survive the
earthquake, too," Ellen remarked. "It must have
been a terrifying experience for you."

"It's not a day I'd care to relive, Miss Randall,"
Reid said dryly.

Melissa frowned in concentration, then said, "I

32

seem to remember reading a newspaper that said something about a small steamboat traveling the Mississippi and going through an earthquake. Do you suppose it was the same one?"

Reid's eyebrows rose in surprise. He wouldn't have expected this spoiled flirt to even look at a newspaper, much less read one. "Yes, the *New Orleans* was the first steamboat to travel the Mississippi and it *did* go through the earthquake. And considering that the boat was hardly more than a raft, with a paddle on the side and a boiler and smokestack in the middle, it was a remarkable feat." He chuckled. "It also added a touch of humor to the whole miserable situation. You see, the Indians had never seen a steamboat before. They called her, 'Penelore', the 'Fire Canoe', and they were terrified of her. A few days after the earthquake, a group of Chickasaws saw the steamboat chugging down the river. They decided that the steamboat was what had caused the earthquake and all the aftershocks they were still feeling. They thought if they destroyed the 'Fire Canoe', everything would return to normal. They chased the steamer in their canoe for miles and miles, but the *New Orleans* outran them."

Ellen noticed her mother had been exceptionally quiet. She glanced over and saw she looked alarmingly pale. "Are you all right, Mother?" she asked with concern.

All the talk of floods, earthquakes, and Indians had upset Mrs. Randall. For the first time, she was sincerely afraid of this hostile country her husband had brought their family to. "To tell you the truth, dear, I'm not feeling too well. I think I'll go to my cabin and lie down for a few minutes."

"I'll go with you, Mother," Ellen said kindly, leading her mother away.

"I hope you get to feeling better soon, Mrs. Randall," Reid said.

After they had walked a few steps, Mrs. Randall turned and asked, "Aren't you coming, Melissa?"

Melissa really didn't want to leave. She still wanted to try out her charms on this handsome, exciting man.

"Melissa?" her mother asked in a querulous voice.

"Yes, Mother," Melissa replied in an irritated voice. Then she turned to Reid and said, "Good day, Mr. Forrester," smiling her prettiest smile.

Reid looked her directly in the eye and nodded. Melissa felt herself drowning in that golden gaze. Reluctantly, she turned and hurried away, feeling a keen sense of disappointment.

Over the next two days, Melissa saw Reid often, but he made no attempt to approach her, even when she made it obvious that she would welcome his company. She tried to attract his attention in an oblique way, chattering gaily, laughing, flirting with the other young gentlemen when she knew he was within seeing and hearing distance, hoping he would join the circle of admiring men as the young men back in South Carolina had always done. But much to her chagrin, he acted as if he didn't know she existed.

On the third day, she stepped out of the cabin and saw Reid and Ellen standing by the railing talking. She was shocked at the wave of jealousy that swept over her. The feeling was totally alien to her, never having been on the receiving end of that ugly emotion before.

Smiling her prettiest smile, she walked over to them, intent on casually joining in their conversation. but when Reid saw her approaching, he abruptly excused himself and, giving her a curt nod of his head, walked away. Melissa felt the rebuff as keenly as a slap in the face. Feeling half hurt and half angry, she thought, Who in the devil did he think he was? He had no call to be so rude.

That evening, Melissa was in a brooding mood and, wanting to be alone, again slipped away from the women's cabin. This time she walked back to the stern of the steamboat and stood at the railing, looking out over the water. A brilliant full moon hung low in the dark sky, bathing the landscape in a soft white light. She smiled, thinking the wide, gently curving river looked like a huge silver ribbon that some goddess had carelessly tossed away. She was so awed by the beauty of the night that she didn't even notice the tall man standing farther down the rail.

But Reid had seen Melissa immediately. The little flirt had been trying to gain his attention for days, practically throwing herself at him. And now, had she deliberately followed him out here? Christ, she was a bold one, he thought with disgust. And so positive of her charms.

His eyes narrowed as they swept slowly over her soft curves. He had to admit she was a beautiful and very desirable young woman, and he was a man with a healthy sexual appetite. He should take what she was so freely offering, except that he knew she wasn't serious. She was undoubtedly a virgin, just teasing him, still playing her childish games. What she needed was a lesson, a good scare, and he was just the man to give it to her.

Melissa didn't hear Reid when he walked up behind her. What a little actress she is, Reid thought. Well, I'll play her little game with her—for a while.

"Good evening, Miss Randall," Reid said in a quiet voice. "It's a beautiful night, isn't it?"

Melissa startled at that deep, familiar voice. She turned. "Goodness, you frightened me, Mr. Forrester. I didn't hear you walk up."

Reid hid his smile of amusement. "Please, call me Reid. And I hope you'll allow me to call you Melissa."

Melissa was totally dumbfounded. Why, he hadn't even been civil to her, had repeatedly been rude and insulting. And now he was so charming. Suspicious, she looked up into his eyes, expecting to see that mocking glint in them. His look of open admiration stunned her.

"Yes . . . of course . . . of course you may," she stammered, confused by his sudden turnabout.

Reid's eyes slowly drifted over her features. Her dark hair waved softly about her face and, in the moonlight, emphasized her creamy, flawless complexion even more than usual, giving her an almost ethereal appearance, and those eyes, he thought, his breath catching in his throat. Framed by her thick, dark lashes, they looked like two shimmering turquoise jewels nestled in a bed of black velvet. His eyes continued their rapt exploration, moving across her pert little nose and then lingering on the small mole that sat just to the side of her soft, sensuous mouth. He wondered why he had never noticed that enticing little beauty mark before, a mark that drew a man's attention to a mouth that begged to be kissed. Yes, she was beautiful, he admitted, conscious of her sweet scent and of her full, soft breasts rising and falling just inches from his own chest, seeming to tease of their own volition, daring him to touch them, taste them. She was a woman who could make any man's blood boil. It would be so easy to play her game.

Melissa was mesmerized by that golden gaze, by his overpowering presence that seemed to tower over and surround her. Ordinarily, she would have preened under such a bold, admiring look. But Reid was no ordinary man, nor were her reactions to him the usual ones. Never had she been so aware of herself. It seemed as if every nerve ending in her body tingled, that every muscle was tense with expectation, waiting for something. She was acutely conscious of her heart pounding in her chest, her breasts rising and falling. He stepped closer, and Melissa could feel the heat radiating from his body, smell his exciting masculine scent. Mutely she watched him, falling even deeper into the hypnotic spell he was weaving.

"You're beautiful, Melissa. A beautiful, very desirable woman," Reid said in a husky voice.

The timbre of his deep, rich voice sent tingles racing up her spine and put goose bumps on her skin. When he reached up and gently cupped her face, she flinched at the sudden contact of flesh on flesh. His touch seemed to burn. And then as those long, slender fingers trailed gently across her face to her chin, lifting it, her bones seemed to melt. She swayed toward him, her lips aching for his kiss.

As Reid's warm mouth closed over hers, skillfully playing and coaxing, Melissa lost all presence of mind. She melted into him, her arms twining about his broad shoulders. Reid crushed her to him, molding their bodies tightly together. Melissa had never been kissed so masterfully, so totally. When Reid's tongue glazed her bottom lip, then her teeth, she opened to him instinctively, wildly excited, as he plundered her mouth, his tongue dancing around hers. She wiggled even closer to his hard body.

Reid was intoxicated by the sweet taste of her mouth, her exciting womanly scent, her incredible softness against him. Feeling himself becoming aroused, his manhood hardening and rising, he forced himself to remember his purpose — to frighten her. Abruptly, his kiss became strongly passionate and his tongue thrust ruthlessly, almost brutally. Deliberately he forced her groin into his, insinuating himself between her thighs, grinding his hips into hers.

The sudden change from sweet seduction to

fierce possession was too quick, too soon for Melissa. Feeling that hard, throbbing part of him against her, enormous and frightening, seemingly scorching her right through their clothing, Melissa finally heard the warning signals that her mind had been sending.

She struggled, and finally managed to tear her mouth away. "No! Stop it!"

Reid released her. Looking down at her, he smiled mockingly. "What's wrong, Melissa? I thought you wanted me to kiss you. You've been begging for it for days now."

Melissa flushed, knowing that what he said was true. She had wanted to attract him, had wanted him to kiss her. But not like *that*. Not so . . . so passionately. "You had no right to take such liberties," she retorted.

"Oh, I see," Reid replied in a deceptively silky voice. "You only wanted a few compliments and a chaste little kiss. Is that it?"

"No!" Melissa denied hotly.

In a lightning-flash move, Reid caught her arms, his fingers biting into the soft flesh as he shook her angrily. "You little liar! For days now, you've been prancing about, flaunting that soft, seductive, little body of yours in front of me, smiling at me, leading me on. Oh, you wanted that kiss all right. And you liked it well enough at first. In fact, you couldn't get enough of it, pressing your body even closer, opening to me willingly. Until I started kissing you seriously, like a real man kisses a woman. Then you got more than you bargained for, so now you deny it. You're a spoiled child, Melissa. A little girl, teasing and flirting, playing at a woman's game. Hell, you don't know the first thing about pleasing a man. Go back and play your silly little virgin's games with your stupid little boys." His golden eyes glittered, his sensuous mouth curved into a sneer. "Leave the men to the *real* women."

Reid threw her away from him with disgust, turned, and walked away without a backward glance.

Melissa stood on the empty deck, stunned by his words. Then reaction set in, as her body began to tremble with rage, her eyes blinking back angry tears. How dare he! How dare he call her a silly child! Why, she was just as much a woman as any!

If Reid thought he had frightened her away, he didn't know Melissa. To her, his insulting taunts were like a gauntlet thrown down in open challenge. And Melissa wasn't about to run away like a frightened rabbit.

She'd show him, she fumed silently. She'd show him what a woman she was. His sudden passionate overtures had only taken her by surprise. She had never gone that far before. But now that she knew what to expect, she'd be ready for him the next time, and *she'd* be in complete control. And there was no doubt in her mind that there would be a next time. She'd see to that! Oh, she'd show him she was a woman, all right. She let him take all the liberties he wanted—until that last final one.

She frowned. She wasn't sure just what that last ultimate step was. That frustrating mystery again!

Undaunted, she raised her chin stubbornly. She'd know when the time came. Her instincts would tell her. She'd lead him on until he was mindless with passion, begging and pleading. And then she'd tell him no and laugh in *his* face for a change. Oh, I'll show you, Mr. Cat-eyes. I'll make you pay! she swore to herself.

But then she remembered that she would never have the opportunity to get her revenge. Tomorrow morning they would reach St. Louis, where they'd go their separate ways. New tears of rage and frustration stung her eyes. "Damn him," she sobbed. "Damn him!"

The next morning, Melissa deliberately dawdled, hoping Reid would be gone before she went on deck. She couldn't stand the thought of facing his taunting eyes and mocking smile and knowing she'd never have the chance to pay him back. When she could delay no longer, she finally squared her shoulders and walked out of her cabin. A quick glance told her that Reid was nowhere in sight. Sighing with relief, she relaxed and looked about her with curiosity.

St. Louis sat on the crescent-shaped bend of the Mississippi. The center of the town was dominated by the old French fort and its stockade, and surrounding it were smaller log homes. After seeing the beauty of New Orleans, Melissa was sorely disappointed.

Her attention was drawn to the crowded, noisy river port that was bustling with activity. Steamboats tooted warnings to get out of the way to the

41

keelboats trying to dock, and the riverboat men on the latter cursed and shook their fists in return. At one end of the landing, flatboats were lashed together to form one big island, where boatmen went from one craft to the other, singing and carousing. The levee was swarming with people rushing about their business.

Despite her earlier disappointment, Melissa was filled with a new excitement and the air seemed to crackle with it. The excitement of the frontier, filled with the promise of adventure, the challenge of facing danger and the unknown, surrounded her.

Her mood was shattered by her mother's querulous voice. "Oh, there you are, Melissa. We've been looking everywhere for you."

Melissa turned to face her parents and Ellen. "I'm sorry I was late, but I couldn't seem to do a thing with my hair," she lied glibly, patting her lustrous locks.

Her mother glanced up at Melissa's hair before snapping. "Well, it looks fine to me." She looked about the river port with disgust. "I hardly think it matters here, anyway. I've never seen such a primitive, uncivilized place."

Melissa saw her father looking about thoughtfully. Was he thinking the same thing? Was he going to change his mind? Take them back to South Carolina? She held her breath.

Then, spying someone, Mr. Randall smiled, saying, "Oh, there he is. I was afraid I had missed him in all this hustle and bustle."

"Missed who?" Mrs. Randall asked.

"Mr. Forrester," he replied. "I wanted to ask him about the packet services on the Missouri."

Melissa froze for a split second, then glanced down at the levee. Her heart sank. It *was* him. He towered over the crowd, his chestnut hair gleaming in the morning sun. He was deeply engrossed in a conversation with an older man standing next to him.

She studied the second man. Dressed in buckskins, a coonskin cap covering his long, sandy hair, a long musket clasped casually in one hand, he looked the typical frontiersman, tall, lean, and rawboned. She looked closer at the man's face, much of it obscured by his bushy beard, and noted the dark, leathery skin, the squint of an outdoorsman. Standing next to Reid, still dressed in his elegant planter's clothing, the pair looked incongruous, ill-matched.

"Come along now, before he gets away," Mr. Randall said impatiently as he hurried off.

Much to her horror, Melissa had no choice but to follow her parents and sister down the gangplank and across the crowded levee. When they reached the two men, Melissa lifted her chin haughtily and pretended deep interest in something taking place across the landing from her. She wouldn't give him the satisfaction of even looking at him, she vowed silently.

"Excuse me, Mr. Forrester," Mr. Randall said.

Reid turned, a surprised look on his face. Then he smiled. "Good morning, Mr. Randall." He

43

nodded politely to Mrs. Randall and Ellen and said, "Ladies." His eyes coldly raked Melissa, still standing with her back pointedly to him, the obvious snub observed by the frontiersman standing next to him. "What can I do for you?" Reid said, directing his attention back to Mr. Randall.

Mr. Randall glanced curiously at the strange frontiersman. Seeing his look, Reid said, "Excuse my manners. Mr. Randall, this is my partner, Nathan Edwards. He and I trap furs together. Nathan, this is Mr. Jacob Randall and his wife and their two charming daughters, Ellen and Melissa."

Melissa had no choice but to turn and acknowledge the introduction. She shot Reid a quick, murderous glance and then smiled sweetly at his partner, chorusing with her mother and Ellen, "How do you do, Mr. Edwards."

Nathan's quick eyes didn't miss Melissa's hot look at Reid. Now I wonder what's going on between them, he thought. First Reid's glaring at her, and now she's glaring at him. Why, the air fairly sparked with the animosity between them.

Mr. Randall's eyebrows had risen at Reid's introduction. "Your partner?" he said in a surprised voice. "But I thought you said you worked on a keelboat."

Reid laughed. "I did for two years. Then I met Nathan here." Reid decided not to mention that he had met his partner in a barroom brawl. Had Nathan not clobbered the man who was fixing to smash Reid's head in with a chair while his back was turned, Reid would probably not be alive to-

44

day. "Nathan's partner had just left him to return to Montreal, and when Nathan offered to take me on and teach me the fur trade, I jumped at the chance."

Nathan chuckled. "After poling that keelboat for two dollars a week, and with prime beaver going for eight dollars apiece, you'd better believe he jumped."

"Eight dollars a pelt?" Mr. Randall asked in an astonished voice. "I had no idea trapping was such a lucrative business."

Nathan chuckled again. "It sure is. Why, a good freeman, an independent trapper like Reid or I, can easily make two thousand dollars a year. A lot of French *voyageurs* got downright wealthy doing just that. Bought themselves big, expensive homes back in Montreal."

"But what would they want a big, expensive home for, if they were trapping furs most of the year?" Mr. Randall asked.

"Why, for their white wives and family, naturally," Nathan replied.

"White wives?" Mr. Randall asked in a suspicious voice.

"Yep. You see, most of them had Injun wives back in the fur country."

Bigamy? Mrs. Randall thought with horror. How disgusting! This was certainly no conversation for her daughters' delicate ears. She cleared her throat loudly, signaling her husband to end this disgraceful conversation.

Mr. Randall heard his wife's signal, but his curiosity had been aroused. "But surely you must mean the more disreputable men."

"Nope. They all did it," Nathan answered, his black eyes twinkling with glee at Mrs. Randall's outraged look. "Why, even Manuel Liza, who was part owner of the Missouri Fur Company, had him two wives. A white wife here in St. Louis and a handsome Omaha wife back up at Fort Liza."

Mr. Randall was well aware of his wife glaring at him, but he couldn't resist asking, "And what do the wives think of this arrangement?"

"Why, I don't reckon it bothers the Injun women," Nathan answered. "They're used to their husbands having more than one wife. And as for the white wives," he chuckled, "well, I don't reckon they know about the others. I heard when Liza took his white wife up to visit his trading fort, he sent word ahead to keep his squaw away from the post."

Despite himself, Mr. Randall had to laugh. So did Reid and Melissa. Nathan looked at Melissa in surprise, having expected her to look as primly outraged as her other and sister had. Now here's no mincing powder puff, he thought with admiration, noticing her intelligent eyes for the first time. Not only was she a real beauty, but she had a sense of humor, too.

"Come, girls," Mrs. Randall said in a tight, angry voice, "let's leave your father and these . . ." she shot Nathan a furious glance, saying sarcastically, ". . . gentlemen to their business." With a haughty flip of her head, she turned and walked away, Ellen following dutifully along behind her.

But Melissa lingered. A sudden horror had occurred to her. She had assumed Reid was unmarried because he was traveling alone. She wasn't worried about an Indian squaw. She knew those weren't real marriages. But did Reid have a white wife someplace? Despite her anger at him, even if she never saw him again, she had to know.

She looked Nathan directly in the eye. "And tell me, Mr. Edwards, what do your wives and families think of your being gone so much of the time?"

Nathan was no fool. He knew exactly what she was asking. Did he and Reid also have two sets of wives? He grinned. "No, little missy, I'm not married. The only kin I've got is a sister back in Kentuck. As for Reid here . . ." He hesitated, aware of his partner's piercing golden eyes on him. "Well, he . . . he ain't got nothing holding him here, either," he finished lamely.

"Melissa!"

Melissa and the three men all flinched at the shrill voice of Mrs. Randall. Sighing with exasperation, Melissa turned and hurried off, calling ahead, "Coming, Mother."

Nathan chuckled as Melissa walked away. Now she was a bold one, he thought with renewed admiration. As highspirited as any thoroughbred filly he'd ever seen. And as stubborn as a mule, too, he'd bet.

"Now, Mr. Randall," Reid said. "What was it you wanted to ask me before we got sidetracked?"

"I was wondering if you could tell me which

steamboat companies have packets going up the Missouri River?"

Reid frowned. He knew Mr. Randall was considering buying a plantation in Missouri. He had assumed the plantation was in the eastern part of the new state, somewhere around St. Louis. "Just where is this plantation you're planning on buying, Mr. Randall?"

"The man who is selling it to me said it was located in western Missouri, somewhere north of the Missouri River and east of the Platte Country."

"The Platte Country!" Nathan exclaimed in a shocked voice. "Hell, mister, that's Injun territory!"

Mr. Randall looked confused. "I don't understand. The man assured me it was part of Missouri. Naturally, I wanted to be positive of that, since I'll be using slave labor."

"Yeah, it's part of Missouri, all right. Just barely," Nathan said in a disgusted voice. "Where did you meet this man, anyway?" he asked bluntly.

Mr. Randall didn't like the older trapper's attitude. It made him feel like a little boy being reprimanded. "In New Orleans!" he snapped.

Reid sensed Mr. Randall's indignation at being asked so many personal questions, but the man obviously had no idea of what he was getting into. That portion of Missouri was still wild and sparsely populated. It sat on the very edge of the frontier, even past Franklin, which was the last outpost of civilization. And as Nathan had said, the Platte Country was still Indian territory, filled with roving

48

bands of Kiowas, Cheyennes, Arapahoes, Pawnees, and Sioux. It certainly wasn't the kind of country a man would take his family into, especially one as pampered and genteel as his.

Reid rubbed his chin thoughtfully. "If it's cheap fertile land you're looking for, Mr. Randall, the government just opened more Indian lands for settlement in Mississippi. There's plenty of land all along the Yazoo River. It's good land for raising cotton, particularly the new variety of long staple cotton that was just recently introduced from Mexico, the Petit Gulf."

Mr. Randall frowned at Reid's words. Once again the young man sounded like a knowledgeable planter. Just who was this man, anyway? "I'm a tobacco man myself, Mr. Forrester. I'm afraid I don't know a damn thing about growing cotton."

Reid shrugged. "It's good, fertile land. I'm sure tobacco would grow just as well as cotton."

Mr. Randall sighed deeply. "I'm not just looking for land. I'm too old to start over from scratch. In fact, I wouldn't even consider this move if I hadn't been almost wiped out for three consecutive years by the tobacco worm."

Reid nodded in understanding. The tobacco men had their worm, the cotton men their boll weevil. Both fought a constant battle.

Mr. Randall continued. "This Mr. Jamison, the man I talked to in New Orleans, came out here when the country was still in Spanish hands. His plantation is already established. The fields are in and producing well. The main house and slave cabins are already built. He's selling the whole thing—land, buildings, household furnishings, and slaves. Do you have any idea of how much it would save me, not having to pay to transport my slaves and furniture?"

Reid doubted very much that the plantation would be what Mr. Randall was expecting. Oh, the land might be fertile enough and producing well, but he certainly wasn't going to find any plantation house like he was used to, not way out there in that wilderness. And the cost of transporting his tobacco down the treacherous Missouri River would eat up any savings he'd make on not having to transport his slaves and furnishings. Still, Mr. Randall wasn't a young boy. He was a mature, grown man, a businessman. Surely, when he saw it for himself, he'd change his mind. Besides, it wasn't any of Reid's business, he decided.

"I see," Reid remarked noncommittally. Then he continued. "About that first question you asked me, Mr. Randall. There aren't any packets going up the Missouri. The only steamers going up the river are owned by the fur companies. They're cargo ships, carrying supplies up to the settlements between here and Franklin and bringing furs back on the return trip. They do take some passengers. But let me warn you, the accommodations are pretty crude."

Mr. Randall frowned and said thoughtfully, "I realized the steamers only went as far as Franklin. Mr. Jamison told me that. But I just assumed some steamboat company would offer a regular passenger service." Then almost as if he was thinking out loud, he muttered, "We're supposed to meet Mr. Simpson in Franklin a week from tomorrow. What if I can't find a steamboat going upriver before then?"

Both Reid's and Nathan's heads snapped up at the word, *"we're."* They exchanged looks of disbelief before Reid asked, "What did you say?"

"What?" Mr. Randall asked in a distracted voice. "Oh, yes, I said, what if I can't find a steamer going upriver before then?"

"No, before that."

"I said, we're supposed to meet Mr. Simpson in Franklin a week from tomorrow. Then we'll go by keelboat on up the Missouri to his plantation."

"You ain't planning on taking your womenfolk with you?" Nathan asked in a shocked voice.

Mr. Randall shot him a resentful look. "Of course, my family is going with me."

Reid was just as shocked as Nathan. "Mr. Randall," he said in what he hoped was an inoffensive manner, "I know it's none of my business, but considering the poor traveling accommodations and the wild, dangerous country you'll be going through, don't you think it would be wiser to leave them here in St. Louis for the time being?"

Mr. Randall glared at the two men. They had no right to invade his privacy, question his decisions. All he'd asked was if there was a packet service. "I'm afraid that's impossible!" he snapped. "I promised my wife and daughters before we left South Carolina that I wouldn't buy anything until

51

they had seen it and approved. And I have no intentions of breaking my word to them."

Reid couldn't really blame the man for being resentful. He wouldn't appreciate someone sticking their noses into his business either, no matter how good their intentions were. In hopes of soothing the man's ruffled feathers, Reid said, "You're absolutely right, Mr. Randall. A promise must always be kept. My apologies for offending you."

Nathan followed Reid's lead and offered his own brand of apology. "And if it would relieve your mind, the Missouri Fur Company has a steamer leaving for Franklin tomorrow morning. As a matter of fact, Reid and I were planning on walking over there and buying our passages when you walked up."

Reid winced at Nathan's words. He wished his partner hadn't been quite so helpful. He didn't like the idea of spending another week in the company of that little flirt, Melissa.

"You're going to Franklin, too?" Mr. Randall asked in a surprised voice.

"Yep," Nathan answered. "We're heading back north."

"But I thought trapping was winter work."

"It is," Nathan answered, then added with a shrug, "But we've got repairs to make on our cabin, and this is the best time to do it. Besides, it will take a month of steady paddling to get to our cabin on the Yellowstone River."

"A month?" Mr. Randall asked in an astonished voice. "Where *is* this Yellowstone River?"

52

"Off the Missouri River, not too far from the Canadian border."

"My God, that far?" Then Mr. Randall laughed and said, "And you accuse *me* of going off into the wilderness?"

Nathan smiled, but thought, There's a big difference in you and us. We ain't packing womenfolks with us, and we know how to take care of ourselves in the wilderness.

"Would you like to walk over to the fur company and book passage with us?" Reid asked politely, secretly hoping the man would decide to take another boat.

Mr. Randall glanced over his shoulder at his wife and daughters, standing several yards away in the hot sun, waiting impatiently. "No, I think I'd better get the ladies settled into a hotel first. Where can I find this Missouri Fur Company?"

"On Chestnut Street, right here on the levee," Reid answered.

"What's the address?"

Nathan laughed. "You don't need no address. You'll know the place. It's a big stone warehouse with furs stacked outside, all over the levee, and stinking to high heaven. Just follow your nose."

"Well, thank you, gentlemen, and I'll see you tomorrow," Mr. Randall said, then turned and walked away.

As Reid and Nathan turned and walked off in another direction, Nathan spat, "Damned fool! Taking his womenfolk into dangerous country like that."

Reid shrugged. "It really isn't any of our business, Nathan. Besides, I have a feeling that once they get past Franklin and see what a deserted, wild country it is, they'll turn around quickly enough and hurry back east."

"Yeah, I guess you're right. I reckon he's just one of those men who has to see for himself."

Nathan looked back over his shoulder as Mr. Randall and his family left the river landing. "One thing I'll say for him. He sure has got himself two pretty little girls there." He chuckled. "That little black-haired missy. Now, ain't she something?"

Reid's look hardened. "She's a spoiled little flirt!"

Nathan's bushy eyebrows rose at Reid's angry words. "Well, that ain't nothing new," he replied in a calm voice. "All those southern belles are little flirts. But everyone knows it and no one takes them seriously. And as for being spoiled, well I reckon if I had a little gal that pretty and had the money to do it with, I'd spoil her, too."

Reid stopped in his tracks and glared at his friend. "Dammit, Nathan, don't tell me about southern belles. I know all about them. She's just like Valerie—beautiful, spoiled, shallow, and weak!"

So that was it, Nathan thought. She reminded Reid of Valerie, and he still hadn't gotten over his hurt and bitterness. Well, that little black-haired gal was certainly as pretty as Valerie had been. No, even prettier, Nathan decided. And as for spoiled, Nathan sensed what Reid had meant was that she was used to having her own way. That didn't surprise him. He had seen the stubborn streak in her right off. But then Reid was an obstinate cuss himself. Now Valerie had been more selfish than stubborn. And as for shallow, he figured that little gal's feelings ran deep, real deep. But one thing he was damned sure of. She wasn't weak. No, beneath her soft, feminine exterior, there was a core of iron in that little gal. He'd stake his life on it. Yep, unless he'd missed his guess, there was a hell of a lot of woman there.

Reid was still glaring at him. "You fancy the little blonde, then?" Nathan asked.

"I don't fancy either one of them!" Reid snapped. "But I can tell you one thing. *If* I was a man considering marriage, which you know damned well I'm not, I'd pick the blonde."

"Why?"

"Because she's what a woman should be. She's sweet and gentle and dependable. There's a serenity about her that soothes a man, relaxes him."

Nathan almost snorted out loud. Why, a wife like that would be as ill-matched to Reid as a plow horse to a thoroughbred racehorse. His friend would be bored to death within a week. No, what Reid needed was a woman as strong, spirited, and adventuresome as himself, a woman who would keep him on his toes. And that little filly back there was just the gal to do it.

As they continued to walk down the levee, Nathan studied his friend from the corner of his eye. He wondered at Reid's almost violent dislike for

Melissa. It had been a long time since he'd seen his partner be anything but indifferent to a woman, particularly a lady. The other kind, he took, used, and promptly forgot. Was he really attracted this time and fighting it? And what about the little gal? She seemed to dislike him just as much. Well, something was going on. Nathan could almost see the sparks flying between them. Whatever it was, it wasn't indifference, and that was a beginning. Yep, this next week was gonna be mighty interesting.

Chapter Four

Melissa walked out into the bright morning sun, the light in her turquoise eyes rivaling that great orb in the sky. She could hardly contain her excitement. It bubbled in her, threatening to burst loose at any minute. Her family thought it was her adventuresome spirit rising to the surface, that her excitement stemmed from her anticipation of beginning their trip into the wild, unknown frontier. However, it was nothing as simple as that. What fired Melissa's soul was the promise of revenge.

Ever since her father had announced they would be traveling up the Missouri River with Reid Forrester and his partner, Melissa's busy little mind had been bustling with plans for how she would achieve her revenge. With the methodical precision of a military strategist planning his campaign, she had plotted the arrogant frontiersman's downfall.

She had decided to use a different approach this time. Instead of openly flirting with him, she

57

would be much more subtle, attract him insidiously, reel him in slowly. And her first line of attack would be to act as if nothing unpleasant had ever happened between them. She knew he was expecting her anger, but she would be coolly pleasant. By being just the opposite of what he was expecting, she could place him off guard. Then she would gradually become more charming, slowly weaving her web until she had him exactly where she wanted him. After all, she had plenty of time. A whole week. Yes, the next time Mr. Cat-eyes kissed her, she'd show him what a woman she was! And this time, he wouldn't be able to accuse her of being a flirt, of deliberately throwing herself at him. He'd never even realize he had been caught in her silken web.

Melissa never stopped to consider what a dangerous game she was playing. There was a big difference in planned seduction and innocent flirting. Deliberately planning to inflame a man's passion and then reject him was courting disaster. Nor did she consider the volatile nature of the man she was toying with or her own vulnerability to his considerable masculine charms. This time, she was playing with fire.

When Melissa saw the small steamer they would be traveling on, she was even more delighted. With the entire center of the deck loaded high with cargo, leaving only a small walkway around the rails, there would be no way Reid could avoid her company, no place for him to hide. Now, it would be even easier to make him very much aware of her, without arousing his suspicion that she was pursuing him. In that close confinement, all she had to do was simply be there. She almost laughed out loud with sheer pleasure at this unexpected boon.

While her mother and Ellen were voicing their disgust and disappointment over the small steamer, Melissa took the opportunity to search the deck for her prey. He stood at the stern of the boat with Nathan, apparently engrossed in a discussion concerning the paddle wheels they were examining, totally unaware of her presence.

Melissa was glad, for it gave her the opportunity to feast her eyes on him without him realizing it. He was dressed in his buckskins and deerskin boots again, except this time he carried his long, twin-lock rifle, and from his belt hung a wicked-looking skinning knife and—a tomahawk! A bullet pouch hung from his neck, and across his broad chest was a thin rawhide sling carrying his powder horn, bullet mold, ball screw, wiper, and awl.

As handsome as he had been in his tailored clothes, Melissa thought the buckskins were much better suited to him, enhancing his strong masculinity and animal sleekness and grace. Her eyes drifted hungrily over his wavy, chestnut hair, his rugged, deeply bronzed face, and on his broad expanse of shoulder. In the hot sun, he had left the drawstring on his tunic untied, and she could see the dark hairs in the vee there on his tanned chest. Her eyes continued their pleasant wandering. Because of the heavy tomahawk, Reid had buckled his belt tighter, causing his tunic to ride higher. The

59

tight buckskins stretched over his muscular thighs, and Melissa allowed herself to admire those powerful legs—then froze. His legs weren't the only thing the buckskins molded. Despite herself, Melissa stared at that bold outline of his manhood, for obviously nature had been as generous *there* as she had been with the rest of him. Melissa remembered only too well what *that* had felt like pressing against her. A warmth suffused her and she jerked her eyes away as if burned.

Stop it! she scolded herself harshly. Get control of yourself! Have you already forgotten how he laughed at you, insulted you? If you aren't careful, he'll make a fool of you again.

Yes, she would have to remember her plan for revenge. Concentrate on that. Steel herself against his powerful, magnetic attraction. But, she admitted wryly, it wasn't going to be easy.

She discovered there was only one central cabin on the small steamboat, miserably cramped and crude, shared in the daytime by all the passengers and the crew and, at night, by the women and children, the men sleeping on the open deck. The only other passengers, besides the Randall family and Reid and Nathan, were two French trappers, who, either because of the language barrier or because they were naturally taciturn, stayed to themselves.

As soon as they had settled their possessions in the small cabin, the Randalls headed for the deck, where it was cooler. While her parents and Ellen watched the gangplank being pulled in and the preparations for departure, Melissa wandered to the back of the ship where Reid and Nathan stood, determined to put her new plan in action.

Smiling a harmlessly friendly smile, she said in a pleasant voice, "Good morning, gentlemen."

Nathan turned, his genuine pleasure at seeing her lighting his face. "Well, howdy, little missy."

Reid frowned before turning reluctantly, fully expecting to see Melissa glaring at him. But to his surprise, she was smiling as if nothing unpleasant had ever happened between them. His brain sent out warning signals. He looked at her suspiciously. Surely, she wasn't flirting—again! But there was nothing flirtatious about her decorum, only friendliness, as if they had been casual friends for years. Now what was she up to? He gave her a wary look and said, "Good morning."

Melissa knew her ploy had worked. She had disarmed him, at least temporarily. The knowledge buoyed her self-confidence and, glancing at their weapons, she said cheerfully, "Well, it looks like you're ready for the frontier."

"Can't be too careful once you leave St. Louis," Nathan replied.

At that minute, the paddles behind them began to turn. Knowing they would soon be splashed with water, they moved to the front of the boat, where the vibrations and noises from the engines were less. Melissa elected to stand beside Nathan, rather than Reid, having decided that the best way to make her presence felt to the handsome trapper was to become friends with his partner. That way, he couldn't accuse her of flirting with him, and he certainly wouldn't think she was flirting with Nathan, a man old enough to be her own father.

As Melissa directed her conversation to Nathan, seemingly unaware of Reid standing at his other side, Nathan chuckled to himself. He knew exactly what she was doing, but he didn't mind. It wasn't often an ugly, old coot like himself had the company of such a pretty young thing. Besides, he was enjoying her fresh enthusiasm.

As the steamer paddled up the Mississippi, Nathan pointed out things of interest to Melissa. Soon, Melissa was so engrossed, she actually did forget Reid was standing next to them. But Reid was aware of her, much too aware. He was standing downwind from her and could smell her sweet scent. It brought back memories of the night he had held her in his arms and kissed her, memories that were so vivid they were beginning to arouse him all over. He longed to move farther away, but with all the passengers lined up on the narrow passageway by the railing, that would be too obvious and awkward. So he stood and glared at the river beside him, silently cursing her.

Melissa noticed a change in the river a few minutes later. Where before it had been turbid, it seemed to have divided into two distinct bands of color, a reddish, muddy color to the left side and a clear blue-green to the right. Even more peculiar, the left side of the river, the muddy side, seeming to be running faster. She had never seen anything like it before.

"What happened to the river?" she asked Nathan.

He chuckled. "The Missouri River has entered the Mississippi. That reddish section is the Missouri, Old Muddy, the Indians call it, coming in from the west and carrying all that silt and mud with it. The clear water is the Mississippi, coming from the north."

"You mean, they're actually two separate rivers flowing side by side and sharing the same riverbed?"

"Yep."

Melissa looked to the western bank to see where the Missouri entered. She strained her eyes, but all she could see was a solid line of trees.

"If you're looking for the mouth of Old Muddy, you're in for a long wait," Nathan said, his eyes twinkling. "It's twenty miles upstream."

"Twenty miles!" she gasped. "These two rivers flow side by side for twenty miles without merging?"

"That's right."

Melissa stared at the two rivers in disbelief. Then she laughed. "They look like they're deliberately ignoring each other, snubbing each other."

"Yep, they're just like people in a way. You know, the riverboat men have a saying about them. They say the Mississippi is a high-class lady and the Missouri, he's a rough western man. At first, they go side by side, ignoring each other. Then the roughneck starts wooing the lady, but the lady doesn't want anything to do with him. She stays

63

cool and aloof. Then finally she relents and they marry, becoming one, mingling their waters to become one mighty river."

"Yes, I can see it," Melissa answered. "They are almost like people."

Yep, they sure were, Nathan thought, chuckling to himself. Just like these two people standing next to him. Melissa acting cool and aloof, and Reid seething just below the surface. Hell, standing where he was, he could feel the currents passing between them, just as below the surfaces of those two rivers undercurrents were undoubtedly flowing.

They entered the mouth of the Missouri River that afternoon. The river was wide, but shallower and more turbulent than the Mississippi, bordered with high bluffs.

Feeling a little braver, Melissa stood between Nathan and Reid. But much to Melissa's frustration, Reid directed his attention to Ellen, standing on the other side of him. Again, Melissa felt that pang of jealousy and wondered, with horror, if he was attracted to her sister. After all, Ellen was a beautiful woman, and some men did seem to prefer her. But even if he wasn't attracted, just being friendly, Ellen was going to be a problem. How was she going to catch Reid's attention and get her revenge if he should decide to spend his time with her sister?

Aware that Nathan was watching her thoughtfully as she observed Reid and Ellen, Melissa jerked her eyes away from the couple. Her gaze fell on the paddle wheels, churning the water and leaving a frothy wake on the river behind the steamer. The deck by the wheels was sopping wet from water being thrown by the spinning paddles, and Melissa was tempted to get closer and let the water splash on her. Even as muddy as it was, it would be a relief from the heat.

"Better stay away from those wheels, little missy," Nathan said as if guessing her thoughts. "Those blades can break a man's arm or completely sever it from his body."

Melissa smiled. "Well, Mr. Edwards, you'll have to admit that splashing water looks cool and inviting."

"I wish you'd call me Nathan."

Melissa frowned. It was one thing to call Reid by his first name, but Nathan was an older man. That simply wasn't done in her social circle. "Oh, I don't think I should."

"Well, I'm right sorry to hear that," he replied in a disappointed voice. "I was kinda hoping we'd be good friends."

Melissa did want to be friends with Nathan, and not just to give her an excuse to be around Reid. She had discovered she liked the older trapper for himself. "But we can be friends."

"I never heard of any good friends calling each other mister and miss. At least not where I come from."

Melissa laughed and replied, "All right, I'll call you Nathan."

Nathan grinned, his black eyes twinkling. "And I'll call you Missy. Melissa is too fancy a name for an old Kentuck backwoodsman like myself. That is, if you don't mind."

Melissa thought about it. If Reid called her Missy, she would be furious, knowing he would be ridiculing her, calling her a child again. But she didn't mind it from Nathan. She knew that from him it would be just an affectionate nickname. "No, I don't mind."

When she entered the cabin that night, her mother gave her a hard look and said in a stern voice, "Melissa, I don't want you to spend so much time with Mr. Forrester and Mr. Edwards. It's unseemly for a young lady like you to socialize with the likes of them."

"What's wrong with them?" Melissa asked hotly. "You seemed to like Mr. Forrester well enough when you thought he was a wealthy planter." Her turquoise eyes flashed dangerously. "Is that it? They're not wealthy enough to suit you?"

Ellen moved in to soothe both antagonists. "Oh, Melissa, I'm sure Mother doesn't think that. She wouldn't be that unfair. And Mother, with the boat being so small, it's impossible not to talk to them. I'm sure you wouldn't want us to be rude to them. You've always told us a lady is always gracious and always polite. And besides, they've both been so helpful and well mannered."

Mrs. Randall was perplexed, not knowing what to say. She sputtered impotently, then said, "Well, I wish you'd stop asking so many questions."

"How am I ever going to learn anything, if I don't ask questions?" Melissa snapped back.

"Ladies don't constantly ask silly questions, particularly about men's business. Men don't like that. A lady is supposed to sit and listen. She should be seen, not heard."

That night, Melissa lay in her cot railing silently at her mother. Ladies should be seen and not heard, she thought with disgust. Like some pretty, inanimate object? Well, she'd be damned if she'd sit by like some piece of furniture, or play that silly mindless-creature woman's role either. If the men didn't like it, that was just too bad!

And she could see her family was going to be a problem. With Ellen around to distract Reid, and her mother objecting to her spending too much time with him and Nathan, getting her revenge was going to be even harder. Now she would have to juggle her family as well as manipulate Reid into the position where she wanted him.

The next morning, three new passengers came on board. The new arrivals introduced themselves as Mr. and Mrs. Jacobs and their son, Mark. Mr. Jacobs explained that he was a planter on a little vacation, traveling up the river to visit his other son, who had just recently married and moved to Franklin.

Mark Jacobs was a handsome, personable young man. He took one look at Melissa and was immediately attracted, but the presence of the tall, fierce-looking man standing next to her made him hesitate. If that formidable-looking man had already staked his claim on the beauty, he wasn't about to interfere. No, that was one man he wouldn't want to tangle with, regardless of the prize. Then he discovered Ellen. Although she didn't look nearly as exciting as her sister, she was certainly just as beautiful, and he was quite contented to take second choice.

Melissa was extremely pleased with the new passengers. Since both men were planters, with similar interests, Mr. Jacobs and her father were soon deeply engrossed in conversation. And now her mother had someone else to occupy her attention, another woman just as snobbish and flighty as herself. Even the threat of Ellen disrupting Melissa's plans had been erased, for Mark Jacobs had zeroed in on her like a honeybee to a flower. Now Melissa could concentrate on Reid without any interference from her family. She almost laughed out loud with relief.

But that was a long, tiresome day on the river. Because the Missouri carried more mud than the Mississippi, it was necessary to stop more often to clean out the boilers. And because the engines had to work harder to turn the paddles in the thick water, the wood supply was more quickly consumed. To make matters even worse, there were no woodyards on the Missouri. The wood had to be chopped by the crew. To Melissa, it seemed it would be easier and faster to get out and push the steamer upriver.

On the fourth stop that day to clean out the boilers, Melissa looked down at the muddy river with total disgust. Even their drinking water, also obtained from the river, refused to clear, no matter how long you let it sit, whereas on the Mississippi, if allowed to sit for 24 hours, the mud would settle to the bottom, leaving the clear water on top. "I think the Missouri is more mud than water," she said to Nathan with a sigh.

Nathan laughed. "You're not the first person to get disgusted with this river. Why, there're more jibes about this river's mud than probably any river in the world. Like the recipe for the liquor the mountain men sell the Injuns. It calls for one quart of pure alcohol, one package of black chewing tobacco, one bottle of Jamaican ginger, one handful of red pepper, one quart of molasses, and Missouri River water. Now the mountain men insist the Missouri water is the most important ingredient. They swear that's what gives it its kick."

Everyone laughed.

"Boat comin'!" one of the crew called in an excited voice.

Everyone turned and looked upriver in anticipation. The sight of another river boat relieved their boredom and the monotony of the scenery.

The traffic on the Missouri had been much lighter than on the Mississippi. In the last two days, they had seen only four other boats, all traveling in the opposite direction and piled high with furs, the stench drifting across the waters and filling the air.

As the new boat approached, Melissa frowned. Instead of the inevitable furs, the flatboat carried a big log house, and behind it were several pens with

69

chickens, pigs, and turkeys. A clothesline hung across the front of the boat, and from it dangled scores of colorful sunbonnets. Who in the world could use that many sunbonnets? she wondered.

Seeing her puzzled look, Reid said, "See that calico flag flying over the boat? That's the mark of a 'store boat.' You don't see too many of them on this river. It's too sparsely settled. But you'll find them all up and down the Ohio and Mississippi Rivers, traveling from settlement to settlement peddling their wares."

At the next stop for wood, Reid and Nathan decided to join the woodcutting party, as much for the exercise as to be helpful. Melissa could understand. She was beginning to get restless herself, confined to the small steamer. She imagined that confinement was even worse for them, men accustomed to hard, physical activity.

Melissa knew she should turn her back as the other ladies were doing as the men stripped off their shirts in preparation for the hot, strenuous work. Instead, she averted her head, sneaking a look at Reid as he bared his broad chest. She stared beneath lowered lashes at that expanse of bronzed flesh with its dark chestnut hair that tapered to a fine line at his belt, her eyes feasting on the muscles rippling in the sunlight.

As the gangplank was lowered, the engineer called to the wood party, "See if you can find some oak or hickory this time. That damned cottonwood burns up too fast."

The men nodded, then hefted their heavy axes,

and climbed up the steep river bluff to the woods above. Melissa watched as Reid chose his tree and then attacked it with an expertise as good or better than the riverboat men, his movements fluid, graceful, perfectly timed. Even when the other men stopped to take a breather and wipe the sweat from their brows, Reid continued, his ax blade biting deeply into the hard wood, seemingly unaffected by the hard labor and the hot sun beating down on him. Melissa was amazed at his strength and endurance.

Why does he have to be so blatantly male, so perfectly shaped, so good at everything he does? Melissa thought bitterly. She could still feel his powerful magnetism drawing her to him. Every time she looked at him, she felt that warm curl deep in her belly.

With supreme will, she reminded herself of her vow for revenge. Today, Reid had been more relaxed around her, as if he was accepting her friendship and had buried his animosity toward her. He was totally unsuspecting now. It was time to move to stage two of her scheme for his downfall.

The next morning, Melissa convinced her mother to let her wear one of her lower cut, lightweight dresses, arguing that the heat had been so oppressive the day before she had almost swooned. She was also successful in leaving behind her bonnet. Even her mother had readily agreed that the hat offered no protection from the sun and served only to hold in the heat.

Dressed in one of her prettiest sprigged muslins,

and with her hair pulled back and up on the top of her head in a tumbled mass of shining black curls, Melissa knew she looked very pretty. She stepped onto the deck. Spying Reid and Nathan standing by the rail, she threaded her way around the cargo until she stood behind them.

Smiling prettily, she said gaily, "Good morning."

Reid and Nathan turned. Melissa hid a smug smile when she saw the brief but blatant look of admiration in those golden eyes before Reid jerked his eyes away.

"My, you're looking fetching this morning, Missy," Nathan said. "As cool and pretty as one of those little violets that bloom in the spring."

"Well, thank you, Nathan," Melissa replied.

Melissa wasn't disappointed when Reid didn't compliment her. She hadn't expected it. And she knew she would have to move very carefully today, or he would get suspicious. Today was just for looking.

And when Reid thought Melissa wasn't noticing him, being engrossed in conversation with Nathan, he did just that. From his height, he had an excellent view of the tops of her soft, ripe breasts and the tantalizing valley between them. His eyes had a hard time trying to decide whether to feast on those luscious mounds, or on her soft, creamy shoulders, or her lustrous, black curls, or her sweet, vulnerable nape that he ached to kiss.

Feeling the heat rise, he swore silently to himself. Damn the little bitch! Was she flirting with him again? His golden eyes narrowed suspiciously, but he could detect nothing flirtatious in Melissa's behavior. Why, she hadn't even smiled at him, except for that brief smile when she greeted them. He stood by, feeling his sexual frustration growing and puzzling over why she was almost ignoring him today.

The next day, Melissa deliberately brushed against Reid several times. On the crowded boat, it was easy to do, and Melissa knew Reid was well aware of those "accidental," brief encounters of their bodies. Her sharp eyes didn't miss the small jerk in his jaw or the tensing of his muscles beneath his buckskins. When he glanced at her suspiciously after each brush, Melissa was careful to look very innocent, meeting his eyes with a totally candid look, as if she was completely unaware of their bodies touching.

On the fifth day, Melissa donned her prettiest dress, a frothy bit of turquoise muslin that matched the unusual color of her eyes. When she stepped onto the deck, Reid had to fight to suppress his groan of frustration.

But Reid wasn't quite successful in hiding the small moan, for Nathan, standing next to him, heard it and chuckled to himself. He hadn't been fooled for one minute by Melissa's innocent little act. He had been secretly delighted with her antics, hardly able to wait from day to day to see what she would pull next. Not knowing that she was deliberately trying to attract Reid to get revenge on him, Nathan assumed she was stalking him as marriage prey. And Nathan heartily approved. He liked the spirited girl and felt his partner had been lonely for too long. There were some men, like himself, who could go a lifetime without marriage and never be lonely or feel that something was missing from their lives. But Reid was a man who needed a woman by his side, a woman as strong, as passionate, as vital as himself.

Nature aided Melissa in her ploy that day. Late that afternoon, a sudden storm swept down on them. Seeing the angry, threatening thunderclouds and zigzagging flashes of lightning, all the other passengers and crew fled for the safety of the cabin, all except Reid and Melissa.

They stood on the deck as the wind whipped around them, as lightning flashed and thunder boomed in their ears, as the small boat rocked wildly from the waves on the river buffeting it. It was an exciting, exhilarating feeling, as if the electricity of the storm was charging their own bodies with its power.

Melissa laughed with pure glee. "It's beautiful! Wonderful!" she cried.

Reid looked away from the fascinating, exciting panorama around them and down at Melissa. With the wind whipping her dark hair around her face and molding the frothy dress to her womanly curves, her face alight with joy, her eyes glittering with excitement, he thought her the most beautiful thing he had ever seen.

Suddenly, the rain came, a torrential downpour that soaked them to the skin before they could dart under the tarpaulin that flapped and twisted wildly in the wind. For a minute, they huddled under the canvas covering, laughing like two children who had just committed some naughty trick and gotten away with it.

Then, glancing down at Melissa, Reid sucked in his breath. The thin, wet muslin hugged every curve and hollow of her body, leaving nothing to his imagination. His eyes drifted over her slender, shapely legs, lingered on the slight mound above her thighs, and then locked on her full breasts, rising and falling in her excitement, the nipples rigid from the cold.

Melissa was totally unaware of her exposure and of Reid's smoldering gaze. She laughed. "Oh, that was exciting!"

Reid tore his eyes away from those luscious mounds and looked into her face. Her hair hung in wet curls about her face, and her thick, sooty eyelashes were spiked with glistening raindrops, looking like glittering diamonds surrounding her jewellike eyes. Reid watched, mesmerized, as a small drop slid down her cheek, past the enticing mole beside her mouth, down her soft throat, to disappear finally in the valley between her beautiful breasts.

A sudden, powerful wave of desire swept over him, so urgent and intense it shocked him. He wanted her. Now! Here! Desperately, he fought the urge to grab her, bring her to the deck with him, kiss her until she was breathless, make passionate love to her, take her as fiercely and savagely as the storm that still raged about them.

"Melissa! Are you still out there?" Mrs. Randall shrieked from the cabin.

At that moment, Reid could have gladly throttled the woman. His whole body was on fire, his manhood straining at his buckskins, throbbing and aching for release. "Damn that woman," he muttered between clenched teeth.

Melissa glanced over her shoulder nervously. "Oh, dear, now I'm in for it. When she sees my wet dress, she'll have a fit."

Reid glanced back at Melissa and realized that everyone would see more than Melissa's wet dress. They'd see just exactly what he had seen. He remembered the looks of admiration he had seen in the crew's eyes when they gazed at Melissa, looks they sneaked when they didn't think anyone was watching. And that Mark Jacobs, too. Even though he was obviously courting Ellen, Reid had caught Jacobs's admiring glances at Melissa. A fierce possessiveness rose in Reid. Well, he'd be damned if he'd let them ogle her lush curves, lusting after her, raping her with their eyes.

As Melissa turned away, Reid caught her arm roughly. "Wait a minute!" he said in a harsh voice.

Melissa turned back, surprised at both his tone of voice and the angry look on his face. Reid bent, picking up a crumpled blanket left by one of the men on the deck, and tossed it over her shoulder. "Here, you'd better put this around you, before you catch cold."

Melissa pulled the blanket around her thankfully, realizing for the first time that she was cold.

But, before she could thank him, Reid had stalked away, leaving her feeling puzzled and strangely frustrated.

The last night on the steamer, the passengers sat around on the small deck, the women lingering to enjoy the cool air before going into the stuffy cabin and the men conversing congenially in muted tones. Nathan, his back propped against a crate and his long legs stretched out before him, brought out his harmonica and began playing a soft tune.

Everyone stopped talking to listen, enjoying the soothing music. Then much to everyone's surprise, the French trappers began to sing along with the music, and although the words were French, everyone was amazed that these tough-looking men could have such beautiful singing voices.

Reid leaned forward and said in a low voice to Melissa, "The *voyageurs* love to sing. They sing while they're walking through the forests, while they're setting their traps, while they're paddling their canoes."

When the song finished, Mr. Randall looked at his two daughters fondly and said, "Why don't you sing a song for us, girls?" He turned to the others, saying in a proud voice, "They harmonize so beautifully."

Even Mrs. Randall was feeling mellowed by the soft music. She turned to Mrs. Jacobs, saying, "Everyone back home loved to hear them sing. They'd beg for more and more."

Ellen flushed. "Oh, I don't think we should," she said shyly.

Even Melissa was reluctant, aware of the crew's and trappers' eyes on them. It was one thing to sing in front of people you had known all your life in the privacy of your own drawing room, but to sing in front of a group of tough riverboat men and frontiersmen was another thing. Surely, they wouldn't appreciate the sisters' pitiful little harmonizing. No, undoubtedly, they liked their songs bawdy and lusty.

It was finally Nathan who convinced them to sing. "I know you're used to a more genteel audience, ladies. Like the Jacobs family, here. But it's been a long time since us old, tough cusses have heard the sweet sound of a woman singing a soft tune. Why, I haven't heard that since my ma sang to me, when I was a little boy at her knees."

Nathan picked a well-known tune, and as the two girls sang, everyone marveled at how well their voices did harmonize, Ellen's voice a sweet, lilting soprano and Melissa's a deep, rich contralto.

But Reid's ears heard only Melissa's voice. The husky, seductive sound sent warm waves of pleasure coursing through his body. And when the song finished, amidst much clapping and pleas for more, Melissa glanced at Reid, her look sultry and inviting.

Reid's heart raced at that look, his heat rose. Dammit, he could almost swear she was deliberately trying to seduce him. Not just flirting or teasing him, but actually trying to seduce him. And there was a big difference between the two. He studied her thoughtfully as she sang the second song. Had he been mistaken about her? Maybe she wasn't a virgin, after all. Surely, no virgin could be so subtle, so artful, and she seemed very adept at getting out from under her mother's watchful eyes. Had she already had a lover back East? But if she wasn't a virgin, why had she acted so outraged, so frightened that night he had kissed her? Then he remembered that he hadn't been exactly gentle at the end. In fact, he had been deliberately rough, almost brutal. And even experienced women liked to be wooed and coaxed.

And so, because he wanted her so badly, Reid convinced himself that Melissa was an experienced woman, a woman looking for a brief, casual fling. And he would be more than happy to satisfy her and quench that fire she had lit in his blood.

That night, Melissa lingered after the other women had left, deliberately wandering to a deserted section of the boat. She had been acutely aware of those golden eyes on her while she sang. She sensed a change in Reid's attitude toward her. Tonight, she thought, her heart racing with anticipation. Tonight, he'd kiss her, and she'd have her revenge.

When Reid appeared at her shoulder, she wasn't the least surprised. She turned and smiled up at him seductively.

That smile almost undid Reid. For the second time, he clenched his teeth, fighting down the urge to take her in his arms, smother her with kisses until she was weak, take that sweet, tempting body she was offering him. But he knew this wasn't the time or the place. He didn't want any quick, hasty coupling. He wanted to savor all of her delights to the fullest, taste and enjoy all of her sweet secrets, bring them both to complete fulfillment. No, it would have to wait. He didn't even trust himself to kiss her, for fear his control would shatter.

Melissa stood and waited in breathless anticipation, drowning in that smoldering golden gaze. Without realizing it, all thought of revenge had fled. She ached for his kiss, his touch, the feel of his body against hers. Waiting was almost unbearable—sheer torture—and she would have thrown herself in his arms if Reid had not said in a husky, curt voice, "Good night, Melissa."

Melissa watched dumbly at Reid walked away. Disappointment flooded through her as her mind reeled in confusion. What had happened? She could have sworn he was going to kiss her. Surely she couldn't have imagined that look of desire in his eyes. Then why hadn't he kissed her? Had she done something wrong?

The next day, Melissa was more determined than ever to bring Reid to his knees. In the cold light of day, Reid's sudden turnabout the night before had rekindled her almost-forgotten anger at him.

But Reid didn't give Melissa any opportunity to work her wiles on him, much to Melissa's frustration. He deliberately avoided her, volunteering for every wood detail, then helping in the boiler room, where even *she* didn't dare to follow.

As the day wore on and he continued to elude her, she began to worry that he suspected her plot and was determined to foil it. Had she given herself away in some way? If so, how? And when? Everything had seemed to be going beautifully until last night.

Reid never suspected a plot. He avoided her simply because his body was at the breaking point and the hard labor gave him some release from his sexual tension. But even then, he was aware of her, too aware of her. He could hardly wait until they reached Franklin and could get off the boat. Then, it would be just a matter of waiting for the right opportunity.

That night, Melissa stood on the porch of the small inn they had checked in to after docking in Franklin. She completely ignored the crude log building behind her, a building she would normally have found quaint and been eager to explore. She didn't care about the soft feather mattress that graced the bed in the room upstairs, either. As exhausted as she was from the trip up the river, sleep was the last thing on her mind. Her eyes were glued to the path in front of the inn, a path that led to the small settlement above her. She knew this was the only way to reach the inn. She also knew that Reid and Nathan planned to stay here tonight, and she was determined to see Reid. *He won't get away from me this time,* she thought with a determined gleam in her eyes. *Not unless he crawls through a window,* she added wryly.

Melissa had been dismayed when Reid and Nathan had hurried away almost as soon as they had docked in Franklin. Something about business,

Nathan had called over his shoulder as they rushed away. Now, as she stood waiting for their return, her emotions were tangled and confused. She felt angry, bewildered, and hurt by Reid's earlier behavior and his deliberate shunning of her. But even more puzzling was her own behavior now. She wasn't sure just why she was waiting for him, what she wanted him for. It wasn't her desire for revenge that motivated her, for, strangely, that had faded away, like a puff of smoke in the wind. No, what drew her was some other emotion, some shadowy emotion she couldn't put a name to, didn't understand.

Ellen and Mark Jacobs walked out of the inn door. Seeing her, Ellen said, "Mark and I are going to take a walk through town. Would you like to join us?"

Melissa saw Mark frown at Ellen's words. His courting had turned very serious the past few days, and Melissa suspected he was going to propose tonight. She could certainly understand his not wanting Ellen's little sister tagging along.

Melissa smiled. "No, I really don't feel like walking. I think I'll stay here, but thanks anyway."

As Ellen and Mark walked away, Melissa studied the young man critically. He was handsome, she admitted. A week ago, she might have been interested in him herself. But after knowing Reid, all men seemed pale and dull. After that magnificent lion of a man, all others seemed like mere cubs.

Melissa watched as two new figures moved down the path toward the inn. Even in the dark, Melissa knew that one was Reid. No one else had that lithe, catlike walk or those broad shoulders. She waited, her heart thudding in her ears, feeling the ridiculous urge to turn and run, yet also feeling rooted to the spot.

"Well, hello there, Missy," Nathan said when he recognized her. "Sure is a right pretty evening, ain't it?"

"Yes . . . yes, it is," Melissa answered, very aware of Reid's eyes on her.

Nathan glanced at Reid. Hell, he thought, Reid looks like he's gonna eat her up. Never saw a man look so hungry. Nathan chuckled. "Well, I'm for an early bed. That hard deck can get to an old man's bones. See you two in the morning."

"Good night," Melissa muttered as Nathan walked past.

"Would you like to go for a walk, Melissa?" Reid asked quietly.

Melissa looked at him in surprise and then melted under that warm golden gaze. She searched frantically for words, but her mouth was suddenly too dry for words. She nodded mutely.

Reid took her arm and guided her up the dark path. But when the path forked, instead of taking her toward the settlement, he took her along the path that followed the river.

Melissa looked down at the placid water below them and then at the sliver of moon that hung over it. The soft rustling of the cottonwoods overhead and the lapping of the water against the riverbank soothed her ragged nerves, lulling her. For a few minutes, she forgot who she was with. And then, as he stepped closer to her, she became suddenly and shockingly aware of his presence. She glanced back and realized for the first time how far they had wandered from the inn.

"Don't you think we'd better go back?" she asked in a nervous voice.

"Do you really want to go back, Melissa?" Reid asked in a low, husky voice.

It was too late for Melissa. The warm tone of his voice sent delicious ripples running up her spine. His male scent filled her nostrils, exciting her. The heat from his body seemed to undulate from him in warm waves. Once again, she had fallen under his hypnotic spell. The world seemed to spin around her as her legs turned weak, threatening to collapse under her weight.

Reid cupped her face in his warm hands and lifted it for his kiss. His lips grazed her forehead, her eyelids, her cheeks, before stopping to nibble at that enticing little mole beside her soft, sensuous mouth. And then with a groan, he pulled her body into a tight embrace. His warm mobile mouth covered hers, tasting, teasing, tantalizing, before he kissed her hungrily, his tongue greedily ravishing her mouth. Only when he felt Melissa sag against him, heard her throaty moan in his ears, did he break that long, searing kiss and sweep her up into his arms, carrying her under a huge, spreading oak that sat on the very edge of the river bluff.

Melissa loved the feel of Reid holding her in his strong arms, holding her tightly against his hard chest. With the sound of his heart thudding steadily against her ear, she felt so safe, so secure, so protected. And when Reid gently laid her down on the soft grass, she was still floating in a warm haze.

Reid lay down beside her and looked into those jewellike eyes, eyes that smoldered with promised passion. He bent his dark head, nibbling at her throat, then placing a trail of fiery kisses up her chin to her temple.

"You want this just as much as I do, don't you, sweet?" he whispered in her ear.

Want what? His kisses? Melissa's passion-dulled mind asked. "Oh, yes," she breathed.

Reid smiled a small, triumphant smile. "Then you'll have it, my little seductress. Everything that sweet, tempting body of yours is craving — and more."

Seductress? Melissa thought, still in a daze. But before her muddled mind could think any further, Reid was kissing her deeply, passionately, as his hands swept over her soft curves, exploring and caressing with deft expertise. That warm curl in Melissa's belly grew, spiraling outward, as she lifted her arms to embrace Reid, her fingers tangling in the soft curls at his nape to pull him even closer.

When Reid's lips left her mouth, she whimpered in protest and then gasped in pleasure as he dropped searing, nibbling kisses down her throat and across her shoulders to the rise of her creamy breasts.

"God, your breasts are beautiful," Reid muttered.

Breasts? Melissa glanced down and saw her bodice was completely opened and her breasts totally exposed to Reid's hungry gaze. She watched in total horror as his long, tanned fingers curled around one creamy mound, cupping it, lifting it as his head descended. No! her mind screamed. And then as Reid's tongue flicked at the sensitive nipple, then rolled it around before his mouth completely closed over it, her mind did a complete turnabout. "Oh, yes, yes," she moaned pulling his head ever closer, wanting to hold him there forever, never wanting these wonderful sensations his warm lips and skillful tongue were invoking to stop.

And Reid had no intention of stopping. Never had a woman fired his blood the way this one did. He was intoxicated by her scent, the feel of her silky skin, her incredible softness. He pulled her into an even tighter embrace, moving his body half over hers, molding them together, pressing that rigid, throbbing part of him against her.

Melissa felt that hard, swollen man-flesh against her thigh. But this time, she wasn't afraid of it. She wanted to get closer to it. Instinctively, she squirmed closer, caressing that long, hot ridge with her thigh.

Reid groaned and lifted his head. One hand cupped the back of her head to hold it firmly as he kissed her deeply, thoroughly, his mouth grinding on hers, seemingly bent on branding her for life. Melissa was feeling breathless when his mouth left hers to again explore the soft sweetness of her throat and breasts.

She was floating on a golden cloud as Reid's fingers stroked her thigh, slowly inching upward until they tangled in the soft curls between her legs. Melissa's eyes flew open in disbelief at his boldness. But before she could even whimper in protest, Reid's subtle fingers were working their magic, gently exploring the aching lips before separating them to stroke that tiny bud, that most sensitive spot on her body.

Melissa gasped as shock wave after shock wave of sheer sensation coursed through her.

Reid's fingers continued their sensual assault as Melissa moaned and arched her hips, pressing her womanhood ever closer to those deliciously tormenting fingers.

God, Reid thought, as he stroked her wet, throbbing flesh, she's so soft. And inside, what would she feel like? Like warm, wet velvet? His fingers slipped deeper, gently exploring. Then, feeling that thin, yet undeniable membrane, he froze.

A virgin? Godalmighty! He jerked his hand back as if he had been burned. What kind of a crazy game was she playing? What was the little bitch up to?

Roughly, he pulled away from her embrace and, in one lithe movement, was on his feet, glaring down at her. "Get up!" he snarled.

Melissa was still spinning in the maelstrom of sensations Reid had invoked in her. She looked up at him through dazed eyes. "What?" she mumbled.

"Dammit, I said get up!"

Reid reached down and jerked her to her feet, his

fingers biting into her soft shoulders as he shook her angrily. "What kind of game are you playing? What are you up to?"

Melissa shook her head in confusion.

"Don't lie to me! Dammit, I might be a fool, but I know deliberate seduction when I see it. What I want to know is, why? What are you plotting?"

Plotting? Melissa's eyes flew open in surprise. He knew. He knew she was plotting revenge. But she had completely forgotten that. "No, I . . ."

"Cut out the act!" Reid snapped. "You look as guilty as hell. Now answer me!" He shook her again. "Why did you deliberately seduce me? And how far would you have gone? All the way?"

Melissa was stunned by his anger. She stared at him dumbly.

Reid pushed her away with disgust and paced angrily. She was plotting, all right. She'd looked as guilty as hell when he'd accused her of it. But what? Why would a virgin plot to deliberately seduce a man? Then a suspicion took hold and grew. Of course, that was the only explanation.

He whirled and caught Melissa roughly again, glaring down at her. "Have you got some crazy idea in your head that you want me for a husband? That if you let me take your virginity, I'd do the honorable thing and marry you?" Reid laughed, a harsh, ugly laugh. "Well, you can forget it!"

Marriage? Melissa thought in total astonishment. "No, I didn't plan that. I . . ."

"Oh, I see," Reid interjected. "You planned to run to your father when it was all over. Tell him I'd compromised you, ruined you? Well, that wouldn't work, either. Your father couldn't force me into marriage. No one could. Because it's entirely out of the question. Even if I was crazy in love with you, I wouldn't marry you."

Melissa was reeling under his hateful accusations. She had to get away from him, so she could think. She turned, intending to make a run for the inn.

Before she took two steps, Reid caught her and whirled her around. "Oh, no you don't, you little bitch. You're not going back there looking like that. Cover yourself!"

Melissa looked down and gasped in horror when she saw her breasts were still bared. Blushing furiously, she fumbled with the buttons, her fingers trembling badly.

"Dammit," Reid growled, pushing her hands away and rebuttoning the bodice himself. Then he straightened her clothes and pushed a lock of hair back in place. He looked at her for a minute, critically, and then snapped, "Come on!"

Melissa had no choice but to try and run to keep up with his quick, angry strides as Reid almost dragged her back up the hill to the inn.

When they reached the clearing, he roughly spun her around. "I once called you a spoiled little tease, Melissa. Well, I misjudged you. You're much worse." He sneered. "You're a lying, scheming, conniving bitch. And I hope to God I never lay eyes on you again!"

He gave her one last disgusted look, turned, and

walked away, melting into the dark forest.

The next morning, Melissa lay and stared up at the ceiling above her bed. She had spent half the night cursing Reid, and the other half crying. Now, she just felt weak and drained.

He was right, she admitted. She had been a silly child playing games. And she had certainly been no match for a man like Reid, a man who was obviously very experienced with women. She remembered only too well how his skillful mouth and hands had worked their magic on her. She blushed with shame when she remembered how wanton she had been.

Yes, she felt ashamed of herself, not only for her wanton behavior when he made love to her, but for the way she had deliberately led him on. No wonder he made those vile accusations. After her bold pursuit of him, what else could he think? And now she had no one but herself to blame. She had brought her humiliation on herself.

She remembered the look of complete disgust on his face when he had left her. Now he hated her, and that hurt, hurt deeply. She fervently wished she could undo it all. Go back to the beginning and start all over. Maybe then . . .

Melissa's thoughts were interrupted by a knock on the door. "Melissa? Are you awake?"

Oh, God, Melissa thought. I can't face Ellen now. I can't face anyone. She remained silent, hoping her sister would leave.

The door opened, and Ellen walked in. "Oh, you're awake after all," she said with a smile.

"Goodness, I was worried. It's not like you to stay this late in bed."

Melissa turned her head away so Ellen couldn't see her swollen, red eyes. "I'm really not feeling well, Ellen," she mumbled. "I have a terrible headache."

"Oh, dear, I'm sorry to hear that. Then I don't suppose you'll feel up to going downstairs to tell Mr. Forrester and Mr. Edwards good-bye. They've decided to leave today, instead of tomorrow as they had planned."

Leaving? Melissa's heart rose to her throat, and she knew why they were leaving early, she thought bitterly. Because Reid couldn't stand the thought of looking at her again.

"Do you want to tell them good-bye?" Ellen asked gently.

Melissa really wanted to tell Nathan good-bye, but she couldn't face Reid and his accusing eyes. "No. No, I really don't feel up to it. Please, tell them I said good-bye and good luck."

Ellen frowned. Something was wrong. Terribly wrong. Melissa had never been sick a day in her life. Then as Melissa moved to her side, Ellen caught a brief glimpse of her swollen eyes. So, what she had feared had happened, Ellen thought grimly. Melissa had played with fire and been badly hurt. Ellen's heart filled with compassion, but she knew better than to try to comfort her sister. Melissa was much too proud for that.

"I'll tell them for you," Ellen said, walking to the door. She turned at the doorway. "Why don't you stay in bed today? You're probably just exhausted from the trip."

"Yes, I'll do that," Melissa muttered.

For some time after Ellen had left, Melissa lay in the bed, stunned by the news of Reid's abrupt departure. Then she jumped from the bed and peeked out the window, seeing Reid and Nathan as they pushed their canoe into the muddy waters of the Missouri.

She watched, her eyes glued to Reid's back as the canoe glided farther and farther down the river. He's leaving, going out of my life forever, she thought numbly. Then a pain replaced the numbness, building, filling her completely, so great she didn't think she could bear it.

She slumped, leaning her head against the windowpane. A single tear slid down her cheek as she sobbed quietly. "Oh, God, why did I have to fall in love with him?"

Chapter Five

"Stand to your poles and set off!"

The cry awakened Melissa, just as it had every morning for the past week since she and her family had left Franklin. She opened her eyes and stared at the rough-planked ceiling, wondering how she could endure three more days on the crowded keelboat.

She glanced to her side, watching the other women as they rolled from their hard wooden cots, groaning from their stiff muscles and rubbing their aching backs. Sighing in resignation, she swung her legs off the cot and sat up, feeling her own sore muscles objecting to her movements.

"Good morning!" a cheerful voice said.

Melissa glanced up to see Hannah Jones smiling down at her. A tall, rawboned woman with dishwater-blond hair and a mass of freckles on her face, she looked as tough as her backwoods husband. Melissa looked at her weathered skin and wondered how old the woman was. She suspected that Hannah wasn't more than thirty, but that hard life in the Kentucky hills had aged her prematurely.

"Good morning," Melissa muttered.

"Looks like it's gonna be another scorcher," Hannah remarked.

Melissa didn't bother to answer. She stood and tried to smooth out her wrinkled dress. In the small, cramped cabin, the women didn't bother to change into nightwear. They slept in their clothes. Besides, on the crowded boat, with the door to the cabin left open and the wooden flaps on the windows tied up for ventilation, privacy was of a minimum. Changing clothes had to be done behind a blanket, while two other women held it up to prevent the men on the deck from seeing.

She glanced across the cabin and saw her mother and Ellen getting up. They looked just as rumpled and haggard as she did. But we still look better than the other women, she thought.

Like Hannah, the other three women were farmers' wives, all worn down from trying to scratch a living out of the poor, rocky soil in the Kentucky hills. Except, unlike Hannah, who was always smiling and cheerful, they were sour, dreary women, as taciturn as their husbands.

Melissa had been surprised when she had boarded the keelboat and found this tight-knit group of backwoodsmen and their wives. Hannah told her they had all been neighbors back in Kentucky, and were moving to the new fort where the Kansas River joined the Missouri in hopes of finding more fertile land. They had loaded all of their meager possessions into one wagon, and now that wagon sat on the keelboat deck, along with four mules, one scrawny cow, and a crate of cackling chickens.

Melissa wandered out onto the deck, enjoying the cool morning air, air that by noon would be scorching hot, drying their skin and parching their lips. The smell of bacon frying wafted in the air, and she glanced up to the cabin's roof where one of the crew was cooking over a fire that sat in a box of earth. Already, the farmers were lining up to wait for their breakfast.

But, as usual, she wasn't hungry. She seemed to have lost her appetite the past week. She walked listlessly across the deck and sat down on a keg of cider, watching the crew heaving the heavy cordell which was attached to the mast and then to a huge tree farther upstream. Pulling on the heavy rope, while the other crewmen pushed with their long poles from behind, the keelboat moved forward at an agonizingly slow rate of speed.

She remembered that Reid had once worked on a keelboat. Had he been like these men, rough-talking, hard-drinking, swaggering and boasting, always looking for a fight? Somehow, she couldn't imagine him like that. For all of his rugged toughness, there had been nothing coarse about him. The memory of him brought on a fresh wave of pain. Oh, God, would she never forget him? Would she always feel this void inside her, this aching emptiness?

Mr. Randall stood farther down the deck, watching his beloved daughter with a worried frown on his face. He had noticed the change in her. Her sparkle, her zest for life that made her so unique, so special was missing. Was she ill? Had she picked up some insidious fever from drinking the river water? Or was she just discouraged and disappointed, like he was?

His eyes wandered over the windswept landscape. He had no idea it would be such a wilderness, so lonely and isolated, so untamed. This was no place for his family or himself, for that matter. Reid and Nathan had tried to warn him, but like a fool, he had refused to listen. Well, he had gone this far. He at least owed Mr. Simpson the courtesy of looking at the plantation. But he had already decided not to buy. No, he would go back to eastern Missouri and look into that land Mr. Jacobs had told him about. With Ellen seriously considering young Mark's proposal, it would be perfect to have their plantations so close, and he knew Ellen was anxious to get back to Mark.

War Eagle lay on his belly and looked over the bluff to the river below, his alert black eyes slowly following the keelboat as it moved upriver. His heart was full of bitterness. Already, the white man had pushed his people, the Allied Ones, from the land east of the Father of the Waters. And now the whites were invading this land, too, pushing their way up the Big Muddy, reaching out their greedy hands.

They said they wanted the land. Fools! Didn't

they know men couldn't own land? No more than he could own the water or the rivers or the sky above them. Those things belonged to the Great Spirit. He only allowed man to use them.

But these white men had something War Eagle wanted. Firesticks. These were not the firesticks the trappers traded with. Those were weak, snapping like twigs, jamming, shooting fire the wrong way, blinding and maiming a man. No, these were white men's firesticks. Superior, solid firesticks.

War Eagle's thin lips curved into a smile. His chief would be pleased if he brought back such an unexpected prize. Two months ago, he had sent him with twenty braves to raid their enemies' camps. "Bring back many horses, strong horses," he had said. War Eagle and his raiding party had swept south, then east, hitting the Pawnee and Ki-owa camps by surprise, snatching their horses from under their noses. Now they had fifty new mounts, and it was time to return to their camp. Both the braves and the horses would be needed for their annual buffalo hunt, but first, they would capture the firesticks.

War Eagle's black eyes narrowed as he studied the keelboat. Ever since his scouting party had brought back the news of their discovery two days ago, he had watched the boat carefully, stalked it as he would have stalked an animal that was his prey, observing until he knew its strengths and its weaknesses. Now he was ready to move. He would attack right before dawn, while the boat was still anchored close to shore. Everyone except the two guards would still be asleep, and even the guards would be nodding their heads, knowing that their watch would soon be up. Yes, that was when they were the most vulnerable, at dawn.

War Eagle nodded his head decisively, then shimmied backwards on the cliff until he was certain he was well out of sight of anyone on the keelboat. Then, crouching, he ran to another Indian who waited behind a huge boulder with their horses.

War Eagle mounted his horse in one swift, graceful movement. He looked down at the other brave, his back eyes glittering, "At dawn — tomorrow," he said.

Melissa was awakened by a cry of pain, followed by another cry. "Injuns!"

Dazed, she sat up in her cot and looked about in the dim light. The Kentucky women were already rolling from their cots to crouch on the floor, while Ellen and Mrs. Randall sat bolt upright, their faces ashen and their eyes filled with terror. An arrow whizzed through the open window and hit the cabin wall behind her with a dull thud. Melissa stared at the quivering shaft with shocked eyes.

"Get down! Get down on the floor!" Hannah yelled, pulling Melissa down with her on the floor.

Then all pandemonium broke loose. Blood-curdling war whoops mixed with the riverboat men's roared oaths and the frontiersmen's bellowed curses, as gunshot after gunshot shattered the pristine, early morning air. Two of the Kentucky farmers rushed into the cabin, pushing women aside to get to the window that faced the riverbank where the attack was coming from. One at each corner of the window, they half crouched, pointing their long Kentucky rifles out and firing at the Indians. The guns roared, the sound reverberating in the small cabin with an ear-splitting, deafening noise. Ice cool, the men crouched on the floor, swabbed their barrels, poured in their powder, inserted their patches, put in a ball, tamped it down, rose, took aim, and fired again. Over and over and over.

More arrows flew through the air, their whizzing flight drowned out by the noises of the guns and the men's yells. Soon the cabin was filled with the blue haze of gunsmoke, stinging their nostrils and making their eyes water. Melissa cringed on the floor, choking and fighting for air. And then as the smoke suddenly thickened, she looked and froze in horror, seeing the cabin roof on fire.

"Get out!" one of the farmers yelled. "The cabin's on fire!"

He turned, pushing one of the women from the floor and toward the door, then froze, a look of surprise on his face before he crumpled to the floor. An arrow protruded from his back.

Panicked, the women ran to the door, pushing and shoving to be the first out of the burning cabin. In the mad scramble, Ellen was knocked down, and Melissa bent to help her up. A new sound echoed off the cabin walls, the hysterical wail of Mrs. Randall.

"Shut up!" Hannah yelled, shaking the screaming woman to shock her from her hysteria. When the surprised Mrs. Randall quieted, Hannah led her to the door, while Melissa pushed Ellen through the blinding smoke.

Once on deck, Melissa gulped in huge lungfuls of blessedly fresh air and then looked with horror at the scene before her. The boat was littered with dead bodies; some were sprawled spread-eagle on the deck, others hung limply over the barrels piled in the center of the boat. All were riddled with arrows. The sickeningly sweet smell of fresh blood mixed with smoke gagged Melissa. She fought down the bile that rose in her throat.

Gunshots still rang loud and clear as the rest of the men grimly fought on, crouching behind anything they could find for protection. The mules, frightened by the noise and smoke, brayed and kicked at the pen that kept them from escaping, while the terrified chickens squawked, adding to the terrible din. And behind them, the fire crackled ominously, casting an eerie, rosy glow over everything.

"We've got to get off this boat! It's a death trap!" Hannah yelled above the noise.

Melissa, holding a sobbing Ellen by the shoulders, headed for the gangplank, following the other women.

"No, this way!" Hannah called, leading Mrs. Randall, who stumbled behind in a daze. "The Injuns are coming from that direction."

Hannah led them to the back of the boat, away

from the side facing the riverbank where the Indians were already swarming over the low rails and up the gangplank.

"Jump in and swim for shore." Hannah instructed. "Head for those boulders over there and hide. It's our only chance."

Cool and composed, Melissa nodded and watched as Hannah jumped into the water, pulling Mrs. Randall with her. She waited until the two surfaced. The shock of the cold water had snapped her mother from her dazed state, and now she stood in chest high water, sputtering indignantly.

Melissa turned to Ellen. "Jump!" she shouted.

Ellen stood on the edge of the boat, frozen with terror. "I can't swim!"

"You don't have to swim. See, they're standing up."

Ellen shook her head dumbly, and Melissa, very aware of the fierce hand-to-hand combat going on behind her, pushed her sister into the water and jumped in after her.

The four women waded to the riverbank, Melissa dragging Ellen behind her, and Hannah pushing Mrs. Randall in front of her. Their heavy skirts impeded their movements as they stumbled on partially submerged rocks and slipped on the muddy river bottom. They were almost bowled over by one of the frightened mules as he swam for the safety of the shore, his eyes wall-eyed in terror.

When they reached the bank, they ran for the boulders, but when they were halfway there, Mrs. Randall turned. "My husband! I can't leave my husband."

Before Hannah or Melissa could stop her, the woman was racing back down the riverbank to the burning boat, shrieking, "Jason! Jason!"

Melissa darted after her mother and, just as she had caught her, gasped in disbelief as an arrow pierced her mother's chest and she crumpled to the ground with a low groan of pain.

She knelt beside her mother and, gathering the limp body in her arms, stared in shock at the arrow and the bright red blood staining her mother's bodice. She looked down into her mother's face and saw her glazed eyes, the eyes of death.

Suddenly, Melissa was jerked roughly to her feet and whirled about to face an Indian. She looked at his thin, sneering lips and his black, glittering eyes. Was this the man who killed her mother? Rage, like none she had ever known, filled Melissa. She sprang at him like a lioness, clawing and snarling, her fingernails raking his face and chest.

Two Feathers grunted in pain and surprise. He had expected the girl to cower, tremble in fear before him. He had certainly not expected this vicious attack. He fought back, struggling with the girl, amazed at her strength and wiriness. Finally, he spun her around and locked an arm around her neck, squeezing the breath from her until she sagged, then collapsed in a heap at his feet.

When Melissa regained consciousness, she was laying facedown on the ground, gasping for breath. Her throat ached, her vision was blurred. Now that the fight was over, the only sound was the crackling of the fire. She turned her head and looked at the burning cabin on the keelboat. Indians were still swarming over the boat, collecting scalps and guns, their half-naked bodies glistening in the firelight.

"Thank God, you're alive," Hannah said beside her. "I thought that buck had choked you to death."

Melissa's head jerked up in surprise. She had not realized that Hannah and Ellen were beside her. She glanced at her sister. Ellen knelt on the river-bank, her arms locked tightly around herself as she rocked and sobbed quietly.

"Is it over?" Melissa asked in a hoarse voice.

"Yep, it's over," Hannah answered in a grim voice.

Melissa looked back at the boat. "My father?"

"He's dead, honey," Hannah answered in a gentle voice. "They're all dead. All except us."

"Your husband, too?" Melissa asked, wondering how she could feel so much compassion and yet feel so empty herself.

"Yep, him, too," Hannah answered in a flat voice.

Melissa sat up and looked about at the Indians. They seemed to be totally ignoring the three women huddled on the riverbank. "What will happen to us?"

"I reckon, since they haven't already killed us, we're to be taken captives," Hannah answered.

Ellen was more alert than Hannah or Melissa had thought. Her head snapped up. Her eyes had a wild look about them. "Captive?" she screeched.

"No! No, they can't!"

"Sssh," Hannah cautioned.

"But don't you understand? They'll ravish us. I'd rather be dead!" Ellen wailed.

Ravish, Melissa thought. Another one of those words whose meaning was vague, shadowy. What did it mean? She knew it was something a man did to a woman, something horrible, and that in some way it was connected with those other mysteries she had puzzled over. Oh, why hadn't her mother explained more of those things to her and Ellen? Melissa knew Ellen didn't know any more about it than she did. Like her, Ellen only knew that ravishment was something terrible, some form of horrible punishment, something that she'd rather die than have happen to her.

Ellen was still raving hysterically. "Why didn't they kill me too? I'd rather be dead! I hate them! Beasts! Savages!"

Melissa glanced around nervously and saw several of the Indians glaring at Ellen. If she didn't shut up, they'd kill her, she thought. She shook her sister roughly. "Stop it, Ellen! Stop it!"

But Ellen still raved, screaming even louder. Fearing for her life, Melissa slapped her—hard. "Shut up! Do you want to get us all killed? Shut up!"

Ellen was stunned by the slap. She looked at her sister in disbelief. Before she could get hysterical again, Melissa said in a soft but determined voice, "We're going to get out of this, Ellen. We'll find someway to escape. Someway—Somehow."

"But . . . but . . . "

"Sssh, don't worry," Melissa soothed. "I'll take care of you. I won't let anyone hurt you. I promise."

Melissa glanced over at the ground beside them and, seeing a pair of moccasins, looked up into the face of the Indian she had attacked. Several vivid red scratches ran down his face and naked chest. Melissa took grim satisfaction in knowing she had put them there.

He reached down and pulled her to her feet roughly, glaring down at her. Two other Indians pulled Ellen and Hannah to their feet. Melissa jerked her arm away from her captor, lifted her chin stubbornly, and glared back at him, her turquoise eyes spitting pure hate. The Indian looked surprised at her defiance, then with a guttural growl, he grabbed her arm, twisting it painfully. Melissa flinched at the pain, but stubbornly refused to scream.

A fourth Indian walked up, and Melissa knew from the others' deference that this must be their leader. Taller, more leanly muscled, and yet of broader shoulder, he stood proudly before them, a fierce look in his black eyes. A commanding air seemed to surround him, one that demanded respect, and Melissa admitted reluctantly to herself that there was a savage handsomeness about him.

War Eagle looked at the three women with disdain and said, "Why do you want these women?"

"They are our captives. They will be our slaves. They will help our wives with their women's work," one of the Indians replied.

"They are white women," War Eagle spat. "They are weak. They cannot do an Indian woman's work.

"Then, to warm our pallets," the Indian holding Ellen's arm answered with a leer.

"This one is mine," Two Feathers said in a possessive voice, pulling Melissa closer. "I captured her myself. I share her with no other brave."

War Eagle looked at Two Feathers with contempt. He had seen him struggling with the woman while he and the other braves fought hand-to-hand combat with the white men. That was why Two Feathers had no red hand painted on his body or his horse. He had never killed a man in hand-to-hand combat. Nor did he wear any coup marks and the only feather he wore was a red one, signifying he had been wounded. Even worse, Two Feathers was no better hunter than he was warrior. He had never killed a buffalo. He was a "tail tier," one who tied a knot in the tail of a buffalo another had shot to claim the hindquarter. Two Feathers was a coward.

But War Eagle was a warrior and a hunter. He wore four red hand marks on his body, and after today, could add two more. His face and body were slashed with white marks, his coup marks. He wore six golden eagle feathers upright at the back of his head, first coup feathers, and others hung from his braids, all symbols of his brave exploits. And War Eagle had never killed less than three buffalo in a hunt. War Eagle was not a coward.

War Eagle turned his dark eyes to the young white woman Two Feathers claimed. She glared up at him defiantly, her turquoise eyes glittering. This one was no coward, either, he thought with a hint of admiration. He had seen her fighting Two Feathers. She had been as fierce as that big she-cat he had once seen in the mountains, and now she stood before him as proud as an eagle.

But still, as brave as she was, she was a white woman, weak, unused to hardships. These women would slow his party down, and he was anxious to get back to camp. But then, he couldn't refuse to take them either. Two Feathers and the other two braves were within their rights. These were their captives.

"It will be your responsibility to see that these women do not slow us down," War Eagle told the three braves in a stern voice.

The three Indians nodded eagerly. Then Two Feathers looked down at Melissa. His cruel lips curved into a sneer, his look lustful.

War Eagle saw his look and it disgusted him. "And remember your vow!"

Two Feathers flushed, remembering the vow of celibacy he had taken with the others before leaving camp. Sexual intercourse was strictly forbidden on raiding parties. Not until they were safely back in camp could a brave rape his captive.

War Eagle looked at the three braves coldly. "No one will dishonor this raiding party. If you do not remember your vow, I will kill you myself," he said in a low warning voice.

Two Feathers watched with hatred in his eyes as War Eagle walked proudly away. From the time they were boys, Two Feathers had resented War Eagle. He had always excelled in everything he did, while he, Two Feathers, seemed doomed to failure. As they had grown older, Two Feathers' resentment had turned to hatred.

But now he had something to be proud of, Two Feathers thought smugly. He had a captive, his own personal slave. Now the villagers would notice him, and for once, his wife would be pleased with him. Yes, the other women would envy his wife for having a slave to help her with her work, and the braves would envy him for having her in his pallet. Two Feathers looked down at Melissa, his eyes again filling with lust. Oh yes, the other braves would envy him, for this women would light a fire in any man's loins. But only he could have her.

War Eagle drove his raiding party hard, ruthlessly, the next few days, following the Missouri west, then north. Because they were driving a herd of captured horses, fresh mounts were never a problem. And for this reason, the captives were allowed to ride by themselves. Not that that was any consolation to Melissa. She had never ridden astride, with only a buffalo hide thrown between her and the horse's back. By the end of the first day, the inside of her legs were raw, and every muscle in her body screamed in pain. That night she collapsed on the ground, totally exhausted, not even bothering to eat the piece of jerky Two Feathers tossed to her. She fell asleep, totally oblivious to the hard ground beneath her or the cold night air around her.

It wasn't until the third morning that Melissa noticed Two Feathers filling his waterskin in the muddy Missouri, then cutting a fleshy stem from a nearby cactus, stripping it, and placing the stem in the water-skin. The strange act aroused her curiosity, and she could hardly wait until they stopped for their noon meal—more jerky. She watched as Two Feathers removed the stem, threw it away, and then drank before tossing it to her. Melissa couldn't believe it. The water was perfectly clear. The cactus stem had absorbed all of the mud.

She laughed, the first sound she or Ellen or Hannah had made since the first day, all being too exhausted to talk.

Hannah looked at her as if she had gone berserk. "What are you laughing at, honey?"

"Us."

"Us?"

"The white man," Melissa said, still smiling. "Do you know, we went down that damned Missouri, stopping every few miles to clean the mud out of the boilers and drinking that horrid, dirty water, when all the time the solution to our problem was sitting right there on the riverbank beside us. The whole length of the river is studded with cactus plants."

"Cactus?"

"Yes, cactus." She pointed to Two Feathers. "I saw him putting a piece of cactus in his water-skin this morning and—look." She handed the water-skin to Hannah.

"Well, I'll be damned. Now that you mention it, the drinking water *has* tasted fresh. I was just too whipped to notice where they got it from."

Melissa looked down at the clear water in the bag. "It's amazing."

"Look, honey," Hannah said, "don't ever get the idea Injuns are stupid. If you watch them real close, you can learn a heap of things from them. They have uses for almost everything nature had given them, uses you or I would never dream of."

"You sound like you know something of Indians."

Hannah shrugged. "A bit. There was a tribe of them close to where we lived in Kentucky." She looked around at their captors. "But they were pretty tame, compared to these."

From that time on, Melissa was more aware of her surroundings, and, after three days of near stupor, that first awareness shocked and frightened her. She had not realized the state Ellen was in. Not her physical condition, for all three women were bedraggled and exhausted, their faces sunburned and their lips cracked and bleeding. It was Ellen's mental state that alarmed Melissa. Her sister was almost catatonic, moving like a speechless, mechanical doll, her eyes dull and lifeless, staring into space. The horror of the Indian attack and seeing her parents killed had thrown her into a deep, profound shock. She had retreated completely into herself.

Now, their positions were reversed as Melissa

110

protected and cared for Ellen. It was Melissa who coaxed her sister to eat and drink, who rode by her side to make sure she didn't fall off her horse, who bathed her dust-streaked face and arms and hands. At night, Melissa held her sister in her arms, protecting her from the cold, for the Indians lit no fires for fear of attracting an enemy raiding party. They would take no chances of having their rich prize, the herd of horses, stolen from them.

Once, when Ellen's captor became impatient with her and looked as if he was going to hit her, Melissa flew between them, baring her teeth and nails. The Indian backed away. The only thing he had ever seen look that fiercely protective had been a she-bear protecting her cubs, and he still carried on his arm the scar that resulted from that confrontation.

They traveled up the Missouri and crossed it when they reached the Platte River, following the new river westward. The area was swampy, full of mud flats, the river shallow and broken by sandbars.

One day when they stopped for their noon break, Melissa led Ellen down to the shallow river. Setting her on a low rock, she said, "Wait here, Ellen. I'll wet a piece of my petticoat and wash your face for you."

Melissa and Hannah walked down to the river, knelt, and began washing their faces. Neither noticed Ellen when she rose and walked toward them, stumbling in her dazed state on a rock and then falling against another pile of larger rocks.

111

Melissa heard a rattling noise, followed by a hissing, then a scream, and the sound of something whizzing through the air. She jerked her head to the side and saw the snake just a few feet from her, its head smashed and buried in the sand by the heavy war club, its fist-sized body still slithering, its tail still rattling. She stared at the snake in frozen terror, not even realizing that Ellen had been bitten, momentarily deafened to her sister's screams.

"Melissa! Help me with her!" Hannah called.

Melissa turned and saw Hannah trying to hold Ellen down. Her sister, who had been so docile, so silent, was now thrashing wildly and screaming hysterically. Melissa hurried to the two women.

"Be still, Ellen! Be still! All that thrashing will only make it worse!" Hannah yelled at Ellen to be heard over her screaming.

"Get me something sharp. Something to cut with," Hannah told Melissa as she knelt beside them.

Melissa looked about her wildly, unable to see any stone that looked sharp enough to cut with. Seeing a pair of moccasins, she glanced up and saw War Eagle standing over them, his black eyes watching impassively. He must have been the one who threw the war club, Melissa thought. She glanced down, and her eyes locked on the bone knife he wore strapped to his breechclout.

She stood before him and pointed to the knife. "Your knife, I need your knife."

The other Indians, observing the scene curiously, gasped at the woman's audacity to ask a brave for

112

his knife. She was a captive, a mere slave. War Eagle stood and stared at her with stony eyes.

"Please," Melissa whispered, her eyes teary and imploring.

Without taking his dark eyes from her, War Eagle unstrapped the knife and handed it to her. Another gasp came from the braves, this one of surprise.

Melissa snatched the knife and turned, crouching beside Hannah and Ellen, who was still thrashing wildly. She looked down and saw the wound that Hannah had bared on Ellen's left shoulder. The ugly bite was already swollen and discolored.

Hannah took the knife. "Try and hold her still. I've got to get that poison out," she ordered.

Melissa fought to hold Ellen's twisting, bucking body while Hannah cut crosses over the fang marks and then lowered her head to suck out the venom. Over and over again, Hannah sucked and spat out the poison on the ground beside them, sucked and spat, while Melissa tried to calm her sister with soothing, crooning sounds.

Ellen's thrashings gradually began to weaken and finally stilled. It took a minute for Melissa to realize her sister was too still. She glanced up and saw Ellen's glazed eyes, then stared at them in horrified disbelief.

Hannah sat back on her heels and wiped her mouth. "I'm sorry, honey. I tried to save her. But the bite was too close to the heart and all that thrashing . . ."

Hannah rose and walked to the stream, kneeling

to rinse out her mouth. Melissa sat cradling her dead sister in her arms, still staring at her face in stunned belief. Then a low, mournful wail began deep in her throat and rose to an ear-splitting pitch, sending shivers up the Indians' spines.

Melissa crushed her sister to her, rocking her limp body, tears streaming down her face as she sobbed. A few minutes later, Two Feathers stalked to her side and impatiently jerked her to her feet. Melissa whirled on him, and Two Feathers, momentarily stunned by the wild look in her eyes, backed off a few steps.

Melissa stood in a half-crouched fighter's stance, her eyes shooting furious sparks. "No! I won't leave her! Not until she's buried!" she screamed.

For a minute, all the Indians seemed stunned by her fierce look. All except War Eagle, who still watched with impassive eyes. Hannah held her breath.

Then Two Feathers grunted an oath and started to grab Melissa's arm again. A sharp command from War Eagle stopped him. Two Feathers looked at his leader in disbelief, then reluctantly stepped back. The other Indians grumbled in protest, but one look from War Eagle silenced them.

Hannah looked around nervously, then touched Melissa's arm, "Come on, honey. If we're gonna bury her, then we'd better get a move on. I don't think that big buck is gonna give us all day."

Melissa looked around, spying a grassy knoll a few yards away. Hannah saw her look and said, "Forget it, honey. We'd never be able to dig up that prairie grass. Why, I'll bet it's got roots on it two feet deep. It'll have to be right here on the river-bank."

"But the grave will wash away the first rain," Melissa objected.

"We'll put rocks over it when we're through. It's the best we're going to be able to do."

Melissa nodded in resignation, and the two women knelt and began digging, scooping the dirt out with their bare hands. For over an hour, they labored in the hot sun, the sweat trickling down their faces and between their breasts, their hands scraped and bleeding and fingernails broken from digging out the small rocks that were embedded in the soil.

When they were about three feet deep, Hannah sat back and wiped her face with her arm, "We're gonna have to stop here, honey. We've hit bedrock. Ain't no way we're ever gonna be able to dig any deeper."

Wearily, they climbed from the grave. When they were standing beside it, Hannah said, "You get the feet and I'll take the head."

Melissa looked at the shallow grave and then back at her beautiful sister. She hated putting her in there with no coffin, or anything. She looked over at War Eagle's horse, standing just a few feet away, and gazed wistfully at the spare buffalo hide thrown across it.

Hannah guessed her thoughts. "Forget it, honey. He may have loaned you his knife, but there ain't no way he's gonna let you have that hide. I'm still surprised he's even letting us bury her."

But this was for Ellen, and Melissa was willing to take the risk of incurring the warrior's wrath. For the second time, she turned to War Eagle. He stood, as he had the entire time they had been digging, with his arms folded over his broad, bronzed chest, his look inscrutable. Melissa pointed to the buffalo hide, then to her sister, and then made a rolling motion with her hands. A brief look of disbelief crossed his face before he glared down at her.

But Melissa refused to be intimidated by that look, a look that would have sent the other braves scurrying. She met his look bravely, her chin set at a defiant angle. For long minutes, they stared at each other, their eyes fighting a silent battle of wills. Finally, War Eagle gave a curt nod.

Hardly believing what she saw, Melissa hesitated. War Eagle grunted and impatiently jerked his head toward the skin. Quickly, Melissa ran to the horse, whipped the skin from its back, and ran back to where Hannah waited.

As they knelt to wrap Ellen's body, Hannah muttered, "Well, I'll be damned. That buck is just full of surprises, ain't he?"

After they had covered the grave with rocks, Melissa found two sticks that she fashioned into a crude cross and forced between the stones on the grave. Hannah looked around nervously, aware of the other braves' muttering and impatient pacing.

Melissa knelt by the grave and bowed her head to pray. Two Feathers again stalked to her side to pull her away. For the second time, War Eagle barked a sharp command at him.

Two Feathers glared at War Eagle. Twice, War Eagle had overridden Two Feathers' authority with this slave. Two Feathers added this to his long list of resentments, and his hatred for the warrior leader grew.

Melissa rose from the grave, then, spying the knife War Eagle had loaned her, picked it up and walked back to him. Her arms were dirty to the elbows, her dress was torn and tattered, her smudged face was streaked with tears, but she stood before him proudly and looked him in the eye boldly. She handed the knife back, saying, "Thank you."

War Eagle watched her intently as she walked away to her horse. No, this beautiful white woman was not weak, he thought. She was strong and proud and brave, a kindred spirit. She was a woman for a strong warrior, not a weak coward like Two Feathers. She was meant to be a wife and bear strong sons and beautiful daughters. No, this strong, courageous, desirable woman was meant to be War Eagle's woman, his mate for life.

When the river forked into the North and South Platte, the raiding party turned directly north into the prairie, a windswept land covered with a tall, luxuriant grass, a virtual sea of grass, waving and undulating in the breeze. Only an occasional, singular tree could be seen, looking as if nature had misplaced it and then forgotten where she had put it.

They continued north into a land where high buttes could be seen for miles around. The air was more arid here, but still the grass grew, only shorter and browner. The summer days lasted sixteen hours, and they rode from dawn to dusk.

To Melissa, the memory of her previous life seemed like a dream, as if the gracious life, with its balls, parties, and luxuries, had been some figment of her imagination, some fantasy. It seemed as if she had spent her entire life racing across this endless grassland under a cloudless blue sky with the hot sun a glaring white orb above her, and that she would continue to ride for an eternity, or until she rode off the ends of the earth.

She became as brown as the Indians, as lean-muscled, as adept at stripping the fruit of a prickly pear cactus and handling her mount as any of them. She learned to ride from sunrise to sundown without a drink of water, chewing on a sagebrush leaf to cool her mouth. And when they finally reached their destination, five weeks after her abduction, Melissa was a different person. The spoiled, pampered, flirtatious southern belle was gone. In her place was a woman with a core of finely tempered steel.

Chapter Six

Melissa looked about the Indian camp curiously. Nestled against a bubbling, sparkling stream lined with elm, ash, willow, and rustling cottonwood trees, it was much larger than she had expected. Well over a hundred tepees graced the area, all facing east, their buffalo hides painted with colorful symbols.

As they rode through the camp, men, women, and children converged on them from every direction, calling greetings and chattering excitedly. Camp dogs ran behind them, barking and snapping at the horses' hooves. The Indians stared at Melissa and Hannah with open curiosity, for they had never seen white women before. A few pointed and giggled at them.

War Eagle rode up to the largest tepee, gracefully dismounted, and stood, tall and erect, waiting patiently for his chief to come out and welcome him back. The chief's standards stood at both sides of the entrance, the eagle feathers fluttering in the breeze. The flap of the tepee opened, and a white-haired, shriveled old man emerged, a buffalo hide thrown over his skinny, stooped shoulders.

Piercing black eyes looked out of a weathered, leathery face. "Roaring Thunder welcomes War Eagle."

"War Eagle and his raiding party have done as Roaring Thunder commanded," War Eagle told his chief. "We have brought back many horse, fifty strong horses."

Roaring Thunder's eyes lit up with pleasure. "War Eagle and his raiding party have done well."

War Eagle's thin lips twisted into a little smile. "We have brought back more than horses, Roaring Thunder. We have brought back eight white man's firesticks. Good firesticks, not trading firesticks. And three kegs of black powder."

A flicker of astonishment passed through the old chief's eyes. "This is good. This is very good for our people."

War Eagle nodded, not disappointed at Roaring Thunder's failure to praise him. He knew that would come later at the victory ceremony.

Roaring Thunder's eyes scanned the raiding party, then froze. "War Eagle has brought back captives?"

"Yes, two white women. Two Feathers claims one. Bear Claw the other."

Roaring Thunder stared curiously at Melissa and

Hannah for a minute, for he had never seen a white woman, either. Then he said, "Roaring Thunder has heard that white women make poor slaves. They are weak."

"These two are not weak. They are strong."

Roaring Thunder accepted War Eagle's word, then dismissed the captives from his mind. "How many braves have returned with War Eagle?"

War Eagle's eyes filled with sadness as he answered, "All but Raindancer and Strong Beaver have returned."

Roaring Thunder was surprised. With such a successful raid he would have expected the losses to be much higher. But then, he shouldn't have been surprised, he reminded himself. War Eagle was an exceptional warrior-leader, his best.

"War Eagle has brought back Raindancer's and Strong Beaver's scalps?" Roaring Thunder asked.

"Yes," War Eagle answered, his look grim.

Roaring Thunder turned to the excited, babbling crowd of Indians. Suddenly, the crowd hushed, the air around them filled with expectancy. "Raindancer and Strong Beaver have gone to the Great Spirit," Roaring Thunder announced. "Their scalps will be given to their women so they can protect them from the evil spirits."

Immediately, every woman in the camp began to wail, the high, keening noise making a terrible din and raising goose bumps on Melissa's skin. And then, to her amazement, several of the women began to rip their clothes, tearing out their hair and clawing their faces and arms.

Roaring Thunder turned back to War Eagle. "Our people will have four days of mourning, then the victory ceremony."

"And the captives?"

"They are a part of the spoils. Two Feathers and Bear Claw must wait until then to claim their slaves. Put them in a tepee under guard."

War Eagle nodded and turned. He walked to where Melissa and Hannah still sat on their horses and said something to Two Feathers and Bear Claw, holding out his hand.

Bear Claw looked resigned and handed the tether to Hannah's horse to War Eagle. Two Feathers glared at War Eagle angrily before tossing Melissa's horse's tether to the warrior-leader. As War Eagle led away the two women on their horses, Two Feathers scowled at his back.

Melissa and Hannah were taken to a small tepee at the back of the camp and put into the care of two fierce-looking guards. After the guards had pushed them into the tepee and secured the flap firmly, Melissa said to Hannah, "What will they do to us now?"

Hannah sighed and sat down on a buffalo pallet. "I don't know, honey. I ain't ever been an Injun captive before."

"But you said you knew something about Indians!"

"I said we had some back in Kentucky," Hannah replied in a patient voice. "But they were tame Injuns. They didn't take captives. Of course I've heard stories, but I ain't sure how much of them are

122

true."

"What stories?"

"Well, some say the Injuns rape their women captives."

"Rape? What's that?"

"Well, I reckon you polite ladies call it ravish. But it don't matter what you call it, it's still the same thing."

Melissa's heart was pounding in fear. She longed to ask Hannah just what the word meant, yet was afraid to know.

Hannah continued. "Then some say that ain't true. They say the Injuns just make the captives their slaves. And others claim the captives are turned over to the women to be tortured to death."

Tortured to death? Melissa was so horrified by that possibility that rape and slavery seemed insignificant. Surely nothing could be worse than being slowly tortured to death. All afternoon and most of the night, she waited in tense expectation for the Indians to come for them, the wailing from the village only adding fuel to her grizzly imaginings of what horrible tortures the Indians might do to them.

The time passed slowly in the small tepee for the two women. Despite her dread about what their fate might be, Melissa was curious about the Indians. One day, she said, "I wonder what tribe of Indians these are?"

Hannah shrugged. "Don't see how it makes much difference."

"But if we knew what tribe this is, we might get

123

an idea of where we are."

"Still don't see what it matters, but if you want me to, I'll ask the guard."

"Ask the guard?" Melissa said in a surprised voice. "You speak Indian?"

"I know a little Injun sign language. Enough to ask that buck out there what tribe he belongs to."

When the guard entered the tepee that night, his face covered with ashes to show he was in mourning, Hannah stood and spoke to him in sign language, her big, bony hands fluttering with quick movements. The guard looked surprised that Hannah knew the sign language, then grunted, making a slashing motion across his neck. Not knowing what Hannah was asking the guard, the abrupt motion terrified Melissa. Oh, God, she thought. They're going to slit our throats.

After the brave had left, Hannah said, "He says they're Sioux."

"Sioux? When did he say that?"

"That's what this means in Injun sign language," Hannah answered, making the same motion across her throat.

Melissa felt weak with relief, then asked, "Then you know where we are?"

Hannah shook her head. "Nope. Haven't the slightest hint. Those Sioux roam all over the west. All I know is we're somewhere east of the Missouri River and west of the Rockies, and that covers a heap of territory."

The next day, to relieve their boredom, Melissa and Hannah took to speculating about the drawings painted on the tepee's hide walls. Melissa pointed to one picture that baffled her. "What do you suppose that one means?"

Hannah pushed a limp hank of hair out of her freckled, rawboned face and creased her brow thoughtfully. "I reckon that's a picture of one of them platforms the Injuns bury their dead on. Some Injuns don't bury their dead in the ground."

Melissa looked at the picture of the platform thoughtfully, wondering why, if the Indians didn't bury their dead in the ground, the warrior-leader had allowed her to bury Ellen? Had he just been curious to see how white men disposed of their dead, or had he been showing his respect for the dead? She sensed it was neither of these reasons, particularly not the second, since the other Indians had disapproved of his actions. Melissa never guessed that War Eagle had allowed her to bury Ellen because he respected her personally, because he admired her courage and fierce determination.

On the afternoon of the fourth day, the wailing stopped. To Melissa and Hannah, the silence was ominous. Then that evening, the drums began beating, followed by loud whoops and hollering. The din was even worse than the wailing had been.

Both women sat and waited in tense expectation, both sensing that the drums had something to do with them and dreading what it might be. When the flap to the tepee was abruptly flung open, they both jumped in fright, their hearts racing.

Two Feathers entered, followed by Hannah's captor, Bear Claw. They motioned for Hannah and

Melissa to follow them.

"Well, I reckon this is it," Hannah mumbled in a grim voice as she rose.

Melissa was terrified, but she was determined not to let the Indians see her fear. She set her chin bravely and rose proudly, walking from the tent and looking much too stubborn to Two Feathers. He still smarted under War Eagle's interference with his slave, thereby humiliating him in front of the other braves. He blamed Melissa's stubbornness in insisting she be allowed to bury Ellen for this humiliation. He was determined to subdue her, break her will, and humiliate her in return. And he knew just how to do that—and satisfy his lust at the same time.

Two Feathers pushed Melissa roughly into his tepee and closed the flap. Melissa looked around fearfully, then saw an Indian woman in the shadows cast by the flickering firelight. She was a short, dumpy woman, with plain features and a sullen mouth. There was something about her eyes that disturbed Melissa. They had a cruel look about them.

Little Crow looked at Melissa with disgust, saying to her husband, "She is too little and skinny. She will not make a good slave. Why did you not bring me the big, strong one?"

Little Crow's complaint angered Two Feathers. She was never satisfied with what he did, always complaining, always comparing him unfavorably to the other braves. "Be quiet!" he snapped.

Little Crow looked at him sullenly.

126

Two Feathers glared at her. "It is late. Go to your pallet."

"Where will *she* sleep?" Little Crow asked.

A smirk crossed Two Feathers' thin lips. "In *my* pallet."

Little Crow saw the look of lust in her husband's eyes when he looked at the white-eyes. She knew he was going to rape the captive. That didn't bother her. The white-eyes was a slave. She deserved to be punished. But what worried Little Crow was the slave was beautiful. What if she should please Two Feathers? What if she should please him so much he would make her his second wife? That would never do. She wouldn't tolerate any interloper usurping her authority in this tepee, particularly not a white-eyes.

Little Crow gave Melissa a hateful look and walked sullenly to her pallet at one side of the tepee. She lay down and rolled, placing her back to Melissa and Two Feathers.

Melissa sensed the Indian woman's dislike. She glanced back at Two Feathers. His half-naked body was still painted from the ceremony he had just left, and in the firelight, he looked menacing and much bigger than he actually was. His black eyes glittered with naked lust, his thin lips curved into an ugly sneer.

Melissa knew something terrible was going to happen to her. She gasped when Two Feathers removed his breechclout and tossed it aside, horrified by what she saw. She knew with a certainty that this ugly, swollen thing was to be his weapon, that

127

somehow he would hurt her with it. Despite her vow not to show her fear, she cowered, and when he pounced on her, she screamed in terror.

She fought, not only from fear, but from revulsion. As Two Feathers ripped her clothes from her body, she fought with a strength born of desperation. She clawed and twisted, bucked and kicked. Two Feathers was shocked at her strength, angered and frustrated by her wildly thrashing legs and bucking hips that prevented his penetration. He slapped her face viciously, and, even though she was reeling from the blow, Melissa managed to rake her nails across his face and chest.

Two Feathers knew his wife was watching from across the tepee and, undoubtedly, gloating at his failure to subdue the white woman. His fear of failure and being humiliated once again by this woman, made him even angrier. He shot to his feet, dragging Melissa with him, then balled up his fist and slammed it into her jaw.

Melissa went flying through the air to sprawl on the ground. She looked up through dazed eyes, her ears ringing, and saw Two Feathers standing straddle-legged over her, that horrible male weapon jutting out at her. And then she became aware of something else. In her fall, her hand had slipped under the pallet and now lay on something long and hard. Carefully, she investigated the object with her fingertips. A knife!

Just as Two Feathers started to lower his body on hers, Melissa whipped out the knife and slashed wildly at him with it, back and forth. Two Feathers screamed in pain and jerked back, crumbling to the ground.

Melissa huddled into the wall of the tepee, her eyes darting from the Indian rolling on the ground in agony to the knife in her hand. Seeing the blood-stains on the blade, she realized for the first time she had cut him. Her eyes flew back to Two Feathers. She was shocked by what she saw. She had expected to see his legs or chest lacerated, but the knife had found his ugly weapon. His hands, where he cupped himself, were covered with blood, the red, sticky liquid dripping from beneath his fingers and pooling on the ground below. Melissa stared at that pool in horror. She had never seen so much blood! Bile rose in her throat.

She jumped in renewed fright as she saw Little Crow spring from her pallet and cross the tepee. Oh, God, she thought, she'll get the other Indians and now they'll kill me for sure. But to Melissa's surprise, Little Crow knelt by her husband and pushed his hands away, looking at the wounds with an impassive face.

Melissa looked nervously at the flap, still expecting to see the other Indians rushing into the tepee, thinking they must have heard Two Feathers' scream. But as she waited breathlessly, she finally realized that, with all the whooping and hollering, they probably hadn't heard.

She turned her attention back to Little Crow and Two Feathers and watched warily as Little Crow reached for a leather pouch. Her wariness turned to fascination as she watched Little Crow take out a root, chew it, and then spread the gumlike mess over Two Feathers' bleeding, horribly lacerated organ. Then the Indian woman shredded the heads of cattails and packed them around the injured organ before bandaging it with a long strip of rawhide.

Then Melissa froze in new terror as she saw Little Crow walking toward her with deliberate, menacing steps. Her eyes locked on the wicked-looking quirt the Indian woman held in her hand, its long leather thongs trailing the ground. Little Crow's eyes glittered with cruelty, and her lips were twisted into a malicious sneer as she raised the whip.

Before Melissa could rise to defend herself, the whip came lashing down with such force it knocked the knife from her hand, her fingers stinging as if they had been burned. And then Little Crow was whipping her viciously, becoming more and more excited in her blood lust, almost frenzied. The whip tore at Melissa's naked, tender skin leaving huge red welts that burned like fire over her breasts, stomach, and legs. The whip lashed across her face, the tip of one thong grazing the corner of her eye. Melissa realized she could have been blinded and rolled into a tight ball, trying to protect her face and most vulnerable parts.

Melissa clenched her teeth, determined not to give the Indian woman the satisfaction of crying out, as Little Crow even more frenzied, beat her savagely, sadistically. God, how long can this night of horror last? Melissa thought. And then as one particularly cruel blow fell across her lower back, Melissa arched as a sharp pain tore through her flanks before she fainted into blessed, welcomed unconsciousness.

Little Crow stood over Melissa's inert body and smiled down sadistically at the angry welts on the woman's back. One lash mark, the last one, was deep and bleeding freely. Little Crow took smug satisfaction in knowing it would leave an ugly scar.

Little Crow was feeling very proud of herself. She had succeeded where her husband had failed. She had subdued the white-eyes, made her cringe in fear, broken her spirit as she had broken the skin on her back. Now the white-eyes knew who was master in this tepee.

She glanced back at her husband, noting with contempt that he, too, had fainted from pain. She felt absolutely no compassion for him. In fact, she was pleased with the way things had worked out tonight. She knew her husband was a coward. After tonight, he would be too afraid to try and take the white-eyes to his pallet again. There would be no danger of her usurping Little Crow's authority. No, after tonight, he would hate the white-eyes, give Little Crow full reign over this slave.

She looked back at Melissa and smiled smugly, thinking of how much the other Indian women would envy her, now that she had a slave. Oh, a few of the other women had slaves, other Indian women who had been captured on raids, but their slaves were not as afraid of them as she would make this white-eyes fear her. She would whip her to keep her in line. But not as hard as she had tonight. A dead or crippled slave would be useless to her. And

131

she would work her, harder than any of the Indian slaves. She would show all those women who had laughed behind her back at her weak, cowardly husband that *she* was not weak and cowardly. When she showed them how hard she worked her slave, how much the white-eyes feared her, they would show her some respect!

The next morning, Little Crow awakened Melissa with a rough shake. Melissa looked up groggily, and then as she turned, she gasped at the pain that shot up her back. Seeing the Indian woman's smug look at her gasp, Melissa vowed that was the last time the Indian would have the satisfaction of seeing her pain.

Little Crow threw a worn, moth-eaten tunic down beside her, and then a pair of moccasins, motioning for her to put them on. Melissa knew she had no choice. Her clothes were ripped beyond repair. It was that or go naked. When she slipped the tunic on, she had to clench her teeth to keep from gasping the second time as the rough skin brushed over her raw back.

Before Little Crow pushed her from the tepee, Melissa noticed Two Feathers lying on a third pallet and covered with a hide. From his deep, slow breathing, she wondered if he had been drugged.

When they stood outside the tepee, Little Crow picked up the big switch she had cut and waved it threateningly before Melissa. The switch had three forks on the end and was willow wood, the same wood the braves used for their bows, a strong, pliant wood that would bend but not break. Little

Crow knew the switch would cause pain, but not wound seriously enough to maim. Melissa looked at the switch warily, but refused to cower.

As Little Crow pushed her through the Indian camp, Melissa learned what the switch was for. If she didn't move fast enough, or stumbled and fell, Little Crow would whip her, seemingly taking pleasure in hitting her on the lower back where the pain was so much worse. So Melissa forced her body to move faster, knowing that if she didn't the pain would be worse.

That day, she learned what her chores would be. First, she collected firewood and lugged water from the stream to the tepee. Then, she spent long hours in the hot sun picking berries, wild fruit, and sunflowers. When that was finished, she spent more grueling hours on her hands and knees digging in the hard ground for edible roots.

When she and Little Crow entered the tepee that evening, Two Feathers was awake. He glared at Melissa with pure hate in his eyes, and Melissa recoiled from that look, retreating into the darkest corner of the tepee and sinking to the pallet in utter exhaustion, the cut on her lower back throbbing and stinging. From there, she watched the two Indians warily.

Two Feathers said something to Little Crow, and she knelt beside him and tossed the cover back, baring him to both her and Melissa's gaze. Melissa's eyes widened at what she saw. The binding was covered with blood.

She watched as Little Crow unwound the bloody

dressing and gasped when the slashed organ was exposed. The sight sickened Melissa, and she thought in horror, My God, I practically amputated it.

Melissa watched as Little Crow again pulled her medicine pouch to her. More gum? she wondered. Then she frowned when she saw her take a small bone needle and pull a hair from Two Feathers' head. She watched in disbelief as Little Crow sewed small stitches in the bleeding lacerations. Then the Indian woman repeated the same procedure as the night before, gum and all.

She's crazy to use his hair to stitch him up with, Melissa thought. He'll get infected for sure. She should have used thread. Then she remembered Indians didn't have thread. But from that day forward, Two Feathers healed rapidly, the slashes amazingly free from infection for such deep, ugly cuts.

When Little Crow took Melissa to the stream for their daily bath a week later, Melissa was pleased to see Hannah already in the water. She hadn't seen her since the night they were separated and had wondered how she was faring in her captivity. Melissa waited until Little Crow had disrobed and joined her friends in the water. Seeing Little Crow engrossed in conversation and ignoring her, Melissa quickly stripped and waded to where Hannah stood.

Both women had become accustomed to stripping and bathing naked in front of the Indians, but being naked in front of another white woman embarrassed them both. Hannah turned beet red, making her freckles stand out even more. Melissa turned pink under her golden tan.

"Howdy, honey. How're you doing?" Hannah said.

A sweet warmth rushed over Melissa at the words. She hadn't realized how much she had missed the sound of English and Hannah's cheerful voice. "Oh, Hannah, I'm so glad to see you," she cried quietly.

Hannah smiled broadly, knowing how she felt. "I've missed you, too, honey. I've been keeping an eye out for you. I seen you with that squaw of yours and her big stick."

The reminder of Little Crow and her switch made Melissa turn to see if the Indian woman had noticed her talking to Hannah. Undoubtedly, if she caught her talking to her friend, she would whip her again.

When she turned, Hannah saw the still-raw lash mark on Melissa back. Her eyes widened with horror. "Godalmighty! What happened to your back? Did that buck do that to you?"

"No, she did," Melissa said, facing her again.

"She did? With that stick of hers?"

"No, with a whip she has in the tepee."

"But why? What did you do to make her so mad?"

"I cut him." Melissa paled in remembrance of that horrible night. "When he attacked me that night."

"Cut him? With what?"

135

"With a knife I found, under his pallet."

"But why did she beat you? Why didn't he do it?"

"Because I really injured him. Badly." The memory of all that blood made her feel sick once again. "My God," she muttered half to herself, "I almost amputated it."

"It?" Hannah asked suspiciously. "Honey, are you telling me you cut his—his thing when he was trying to rape you?"

Melissa's head shot up. "So that's what rape is!"

Hannah looked at her in astonishment. "You mean you didn't know?"

"No. I knew he was going to do something with that horrible thing, hurt me in some way, but just what I didn't know." Melissa looked thoughtful for just a minute, then added, "I guess I still don't know."

Hannah explained, and Melissa listened, horrified. When she had finished, Melissa asked, "Did your captor do that to you, rape you?"

"Sure he did. But it wasn't too bad. Hell, I've been married. I was used to it. Besides, he wasn't cruel. I don't think his heart was really in it. I think he only raped me because it was expected of him."

Used to it? Melissa thought. Then she remembered her mother saying men were animals. She put two and two together. So that's what happens in the marriage bed. Why, it was disgusting! "Then that's what a husband does to his wife?" she asked, disgust and horror written all over her face.

"Look, honey, I think you're getting the wrong

136

idea here. There's a big difference between what happens between a husband and a wife. That ain't rape. Rape is brutal. It's done to hurt and shame the woman. And it's done against her will. Now a man loving his wife is different. He kisses her and fondles her, and it can be right pleasant sometimes."

Melissa remembered those wondrous feelings Reid had evoked in her when he had kissed her, touched her. Yes, it certainly could be pleasant. But she was jerked from her thoughts by Hannah's next words.

"And sometimes it's just tolerable. That's how it is with Bear Claw most of the time."

"You mean you *let* him do that? You don't fight him?" Melissa asked in a shocked voice.

"Sure, I let him," Hannah replied in an exasperated voice.

Melissa stared at her in horror. Hannah sighed deeply. "Look, honey, let's be practical about this. The way I figure it, we're gonna be here the rest of our lives, and I don't aim to spend the rest of my life being raped by Bear Claw every time he takes a notion he wants me. Or being a slave, either. No, I'm gonna try real hard to please that buck, both in bed and out of it. That way, I figure maybe he'll make me his second wife."

"You'd marry him? An Indian?"

"Sure I'd marry him. Like I said, Bear Claw ain't too bad. And to tell you the truth, honey, there was a heap of times my husband wasn't too good to me. He drank, and when he drank, he got real mean and ugly. He'd beat me and he'd rape me. I figure I could do a lot worse than Bear Claw."

"You'd be content spending the rest of your life married to him and living in an Indian camp? Don't you even want to escape? Go back to civilization?"

"Escape? Why, honey, civilization must be a thousand miles away. And I don't mind living here. To tell you the truth, I worked harder on that farm back in Kentucky than I do here."

"But what about his wife? Wouldn't that bother you, for him to have two wives?"

"Naw, not really. Crossed Toes and I get along passably. She's just a kid, you know. And I don't think she'd mind if he married me, either. I'm a hard worker, and I reckon she knows she could get a heap worse. He could marry some lazy squaw, and she'd still have to do all the work and wait on her besides."

"She doesn't beat you?"

"Oh, she carries a little stick, just like all the squaws with slaves do. But she ain't never used it. Shucks, none of them use their switches like Little Crow does on you. Godalmighty, honey, you sure drew the black bean when you got that squaw."

"Is that her name, Little Crow?"

"Yep. I was curious, so I asked Crossed Toes. She said your buck is named Two Feathers and that squaw, Little Crow. It's a good name for her, too. The crow is the meanest critter in this world."

Melissa walked back to the tepee that afternoon, feeling very depressed. Hannah might be content to spend the rest of her life in this Indian village, but Melissa sure wasn't. The thought of spending year after year with Little Crow's cruelty and Two Feathers raping her was more than she could bear. And there was no doubt in her mind that Two Feathers would try to rape her again once he was healed. She had seen the look of hatred in his eyes every time he looked at her. But unlike Hannah, Melissa would never submit meekly. No, he would have to kill her first!

When Melissa and Little Crow reached the tepee, Melissa was surprised to see War Eagle standing outside the tepee and talking to Two Feathers. She admired the three horses he held the tethers to, thinking they certainly looked a lot better taken care of than Two Feathers' mangy-looking horses. After a few minutes of what appeared to be a heated argument, War Eagle shot her a look and stalked off angrily. The look stunned Melissa. She had the distinct impression they had been discussing her.

Two Feathers walked back into his tepee, smiling smugly. War Eagle had tried to buy his captive, and he had refused to sell her. It had given him immense satisfaction to thwart his enemy. And he would never sell her to War Eagle, not even after he had tired of her.

Two Feathers glared at Melissa when she entered the tepee. She dog! He wasn't through with her yet. As soon as he was recovered, he would get his revenge. Except this time, before he raped her, he would stake her to the ground, spread-eagled.

She'd never get the chance to use a weapon on him again.

After the fall buffalo hunt, Melissa was given two more chores. First, she was put to work pounding the buffalo meat with service-berries and fat to make pemmican, the Indian's staple, and stored it in buffalo bladders. The second chore was a more backbreaking one. Since Two Feathers had not shot a buffalo, Little Crow made a deal with another woman whose husband had shot three. She would put her slave to work scraping and curing the three hides, if the woman would give one hide to Little Crow in return. Melissa stood in the hot sun every day, scraping the tissue from the hides, then kneeling over the staked hides and rubbing them with a mixture of buffalo brains and fat to soften them.

As totally exhausting as her days were, Melissa's nights were even worse. She would lay huddled on her pallet, aware of Two Feathers' dark, piercing eyes on her, expecting him to pounce on her at any minute and wondering if she had the strength left to fight him off. Then, as time passed and he made no move toward her, she began to suspect that she had injured him to such an extent that he was incapable of raping her. But still, she had the uncomfortable feeling that he was planning something unpleasant for her.

Two Feathers *had* been planning his revenge on Melissa. However, much to his frustration, he hadn't been able to find the means to accomplish it. He couldn't rape her. Just as Melissa had suspected, he had discovered—to his utter horror—

that her well-aimed wielding of his knife had left him with permanent damage. He couldn't get an erection! Nor could he beat her. In his tribe, it was considered unmanly for a brave to beat a woman; that's why the women carried the switches. He couldn't kill her. What excuse would he give? She was a strong and hard worker. And she hadn't tried to escape. The other Indians, who hated waste of any kind, would question why he had killed a perfectly good slave.

He couldn't even sell her without losing face, for Two Feathers suspected that Melissa was a virgin. As desirable as she was, he had no doubts that the brave that bought her would force her to share his pallet, and if that brave succeeded where he had failed and discovered she was still a virgin, Two Feathers would be ridiculed by everyone, laughed right out of the camp for not being man enough to take her. The fact that he had always bragged of his male vigor, had particularly boasted of what he would do to his new slave, would only make the discovery of his failure more humiliating.

Two Feathers knew only one warrior who would not spread the word that he had failed to force the slave to submit to him—War Eagle. War Eagle never gossiped or openly ridiculed others' weaknesses. He kept his thoughts to himself. And War Eagle still wanted the slave. He had made a second bid after the buffalo hunt, this time offering four horses and two buffalo robes—an astonishing, generous offer. But Two Feathers would *never* sell the white woman to his hated enemy. His pride would never allow it. Two Feathers was in a quandary over what to do with the white woman.

The next day, when Melissa was carrying a load of firewood to the tepee, Little Crow deliberately tripped her, thereby giving Little Crow the excuse to beat her slave. Melissa fell flat on her face, and the firewood scattered everywhere. Immediately, Little Crow pounced on her, grinning gleefully, her eyes glittering with excitement as she viciously switched Melissa.

Melissa felt the stinging lashes across her back and the back of her legs and scrambled to her feet. But when she stood, a sharp pain tore through her ankle, and she tumbled back down to the ground, clutching the injured ankle, gritting her teeth to keep from crying out as the willow bark bit into her tender flesh. Then suddenly, the lashes stopped.

Melissa looked up and saw War Eagle towering over Little Crow, his face scowling, a look of utter contempt in his black eyes. Little Crow's face drained of all color. She turned and hurried away. Then, to Melissa's further amazement, War Eagle held out his hand to help her up.

The crowd of Indians that had watched the whole scene gasped when War Eagle gently helped the white woman stand. If any other brave had done so, they would have laughed at him or ridiculed him. Warriors didn't come to the aid of mere slaves. But no one laughed at War Eagle. He was much too respected and admired. Instead, they looked at Melissa with new eyes, awed by the woman who could command such concern from such a fierce, noble warrior.

By the time Melissa was standing, Hannah was by her side to support her. War Eagle gave Melissa a strange, penetrating look, then turned and walked away.

Hannah watched War Eagle thoughtfully as he strode away. "That handsome buck is in love with you, honey," she said.

"In love with me?" Melissa said in an astonished voice. Then she laughed. "That's ridiculous. Just because he let me bury Ellen and now he helped me up doesn't mean he's in love with me. He's just being—compassionate."

"Nope, I don't think so. I've seen him watching you, a heap of times. He just stands there and watches, those black eyes of his looking like they're gonna soak you right up."

A shiver ran through Melissa. "Then he just wants my body. That's not love."

"Sure, he wants that, too," Hannah replied calmly. "He's a man, ain't he? And whether you like it or not, that goes along with the loving." Her look turned thoughtful again. "You know, if you play your cards right, he just might buy you from Two Feathers. Maybe even make you his wife. That'd get you away from that bitch, Little Crow."

"Marry me? Why, I wouldn't marry an—" Melissa's nose wrinkled with distaste—"an Indian."

"War Eagle ain't just any Injun, honey. He's a cut above the others. Even the Injuns know he's special. Many of them say he'll be the next chief."

"War Eagle? Is that his name?"

"Yep. And I think he'd be right good to you, too, honey. Loving and gentle."

"Gentle?" Melissa scoffed. "Why, he's the most ferocious warrior in this whole tribe."

"Yep, he's a strong man, all right. But strangely, it's the strong ones who are often the most gentle with their women. The weak men are the mean ones. They seem to think being mean and mistreating others make them bigger, more important."

"Well, it doesn't matter how gentle he'd be, because I'm not going to let any man do *that* to me," Melissa said in a determined voice. Reid's face suddenly flashed through her mind, and a wave of longing swept over her. "Not unless I love the man, body and soul," she added.

Hannah shrugged. "How's your ankle?"

"It's feeling better," Melissa replied, testing her foot gingerly. "I think I just twisted it. Could you help me back to the tepee?"

"Sure, honey. You just lean on me."

As Melissa limped toward her tepee with Hannah supporting her, her mind continued to dwell on War Eagle. Finally, she asked in a curious voice, "Hannah, where do you think War Eagle got those scars on his back and chest. They don't look like the kind of scars a wild animal would make."

"They're his sun dance scars," Hannah replied. "I noticed some of the other Injun men had them, too, but he's the only one I've seen who has them on both his chest and his back. Anyway, I was curious, so I asked Crossed Toes about it. She said every year they have a ceremony where the bucks dance around a big pole, staring up at the sun, with buffalo skulls hanging from their chests or backs. It's supposed to be their way of proving their bravery and their endurance. A kinda manhood test. They can't stop dancing until those buffalo heads fall off."

Melissa assumed the buffalo heads were tied on, lashed to the men's bodies. "But how can that cause those scars?"

"They tie the skulls to both ends of a wooden skewer that's been threaded under the brave's skin and through his chest or back muscles. Those skulls can't fall off until the skin and muscle tears. Crossed Toes said sometimes they have to dance all day before that finally happens."

"They deliberately abuse their bodies? But that's horrible!"

"Yep. Sent shivers up my spine when she told me that. But these Injuns have a heap of that self-abuse mixed up with their beliefs. Remember that first day when the women were tearing out their hair and clawing their faces and arms? Crossed Toes said that's the way the women show their respect for the dead, that the more they respected that dead person, the more they mutilate themselves. She said the greatest honor a woman can give a dead person is to cut off the first digit of her little finger. But she admitted not many of the women did that. They didn't have the guts."

Melissa shivered, thinking she wouldn't be brave enough to cut off a part of her body, either. No, no matter how much she respected the person, she couldn't do that!

The next day, Melissa could walk on her ankle without assistance. But it was still sore, and as the day wore on, she began to limp badly. Irritated by her slave's slowness, Little Crow began switching her again.

Melissa had tolerated Little Crow's whippings for one reason only. Not because she was afraid of Little Crow, as the cruel Indian woman thought, but because she was afraid that if she tried to defend herself, the other women would come to Little Crow's defense and pounce on her, too. She had no desire to be whipped to death or maimed for life by a bunch of frenzied Indian women. But Melissa had reached the end of her endurance. She had had enough of Little Crow's beatings. She whirled, snarling, and, in one lightning-flash movement, jerked the switch from Little Crow's hand and broke it over her knee. Then she glared at the surprised Indian woman, her eyes flashing dangerously.

Little Crow was stunned by Melissa's action. Suddenly, she realized she had lost control over her slave. The white woman had a dangerous look in her eyes, a murderous look. She looked about her frantically, her eyes beseeching the other Indian women to come to her aid.

But Little Crow was in for her second shock. During the months of Melissa's captivity, the Indian women had come to admire the white woman's strength and endurance under suffering. Little Crow, instead of impressing them, had shown her true character, that of a cruel woman who abused others for no purpose other than her own self-gratification. They stared at Little Crow, their contempt and disgust for her written all over their faces.

Little Crow knew then that the women had no intention of coming to her rescue. They felt she had brought her slave's rebellion down on herself. If she fought, she would fight alone.

But Little Crow had no intention of fighting the white-eyes. She looked too fierce and very dangerous. Terrified, Little Crow turned and fled, the women's scornful laughter in her ears.

War Eagle had stood across the clearing and watched the whole episode with an inscrutable look on his face. Then, as Little Crow ran off, his lips twisted into a smile. The white woman had sent her enemy scurrying in fear. He was proud of this woman he had come to love.

That night, Two Feathers sat in his tepee brooding. Little Crow had come to him and demanded he sell the slave, telling how she had been shamed by War Eagle's interference the day before, and then by the women's refusal to help her punish the slave that afternoon. Now Little Crow was afraid the slave might kill them both in their sleep.

Two Feathers didn't know what to do. The other Indians had found out about War Eagle's generous bids for the slave and were ridiculing Two Feathers for refusing, since Two Feathers had the least amount of horses of any brave in the village. It seemed the white woman had brought nothing but humiliation to both him and Little Crow.

And yet, he couldn't sell her, for that would bring only more scorn down on them. He didn't even dare to tell Little Crow his reason for refusing to sell her. His wife, too engrossed with her new slave, had not noticed his absence from her pallet. When Little Crow learned the white slave had un-manned him, she, too, would belittle him, as she had always taken every opportunity to do.

And so, for hours, Two Feathers brooded. Then suddenly an idea occurred to him. Yes, that was the solution, he thought, his eyes lighting up with re-lief. He would take the slave to the fall trading fair and sell her there. Sell her to a brave from another tribe, a tribe that lived far away. Or better yet, sell her to one of those white trappers. That way, he could be sure no rumors would filter back to his village.

And next summer, he would dance at the sun dance ceremony. If he succeeded, could prove his bravery, the villagers would have to respect him. And maybe the Great Spirit would be pleased with him and make his manhood rise again.

When Two Feathers told Little Crow of his plans, she was delighted. She, too, wanted the white-eyes out of the village. She wanted no reminders of her humiliation around.

But unlike Two Feathers, Little Crow had not learned her lesson. She still wanted something that would make the other women envy her. She remem-bered that only one other woman in the village had a white man's kettle, a true marvel, for it could be used directly over the fire. With a kettle, she would no longer have to put hot stones in a suspended skin pouch to cook her stews or boil water.

Little Crow smiled smugly and said, "Sell her for an iron pot. Bring me back a big black iron pot."

Chapter Seven

The long canoe glided over the placid water of the lake, then swerved gracefully, shooting as straight as an arrow toward the shore. When the bow of the canoe grounded, the two trappers sitting in it dropped their paddles and jumped from it, pulling the canoe farther up on the sandy shore.

Reid looked up and down the narrow beach of the lake where he stood. The whole lakefront was lined with Indian canoes, bullboats, and voyageurs' canoes. "It looks like there's going to be quite a crowd," he remarked to Nathan.

Nathan's dark eyes scanned the area. "Yep, the fall trading fair always draws a bigger crowd than the summer one. The Injuns have to stock up for winter just like us."

The two men lifted their long rifles from the bottom of the canoe, then ambled up the hill where the trading fair was already in full swing.

As they walked through the noisy crowd, Reid looked about him, always amazed at the variety of goods that the Indians brought to these trading fairs.

But what amazed Reid even more was that many of these tribes were enemies. If they met on the open prairie, they would be at each other's throats, not satisfied until one or the other was annihilated. Yet, at these trading fairs, these same tribes mixed congenially and bartered their goods, talking to one another in Indian sign language, a language introduced by the Kiowas, who served as the first intermediary between the northern and southern tribes.

Reid frowned as a tall, husky Indian woman shoved him aside, and then taking a second look he sneered with disgust, realizing it wasn't a woman, but an Indian dandy, a man who dressed like a woman. According to Nathan, many of the Indian tribes sent their boys approaching manhood into the wilds to fast and pray, awaiting a vision that would tell them what their future would be. These dandies claimed to have had a vision that they were women. From that day forward, they lived in a separate lodge with their own kind, dressing like women and doing women's work. The Indian women laughed at them, and the men either scorned or pitied them, but their presence was generally tolerated.

Reid watched as the dandy walked away with a mincing stride. The Indian reminded him of an overdressed, overpainted, gaudy whore. He shook his head in renewed disgust.

"Reid," Nathan said in a low, urgent voice, "look at that woman slave that Injun is selling over there."

Reid glanced to where Nathan pointed, but the woman's back was turned to him, and all he could see was a pair of long black braids and a slender body covered with a dirty, moth-eaten buckskin dress. He knew the Indians often sold their unwanted Indian slaves at these trading fairs, women that were too lazy or too old or too worn out to be good workers, or women who had proven to be barren, and therefore, in the Indian's eyes, useless.

"So what? I've seen Indian slaves before," Reid answered in a disinterested voice, then glanced away, his eyes scanning the scene in the opposite direction.

"That's no Injun woman," Nathan said. "She's white!"

A white captive this far west? Reid thought in surprise. One of the eastern tribes must have brought her here. Some poor farmer's wife whose frontier home was attacked and razed by the Indians. Reid had seen white women who had been rescued from their Indian captivity. What he had seen had sickened him, disturbed him deeply. They had all been pitiful creatures, their eyes vacant looking, as if their souls had long departed and left only their ravaged bodies behind. No,

Reid didn't want to look at the poor white woman. He hoped he went a lifetime before he had to see that again.

"Dammit, you stubborn cuss! Will you look at her?" Nathan cried, his hand tugging at Reid's sleeve.

"I don't have to see her to know what she looks like," Reid said in a tight voice, deliberately keeping his back turned. "I've seen white women after the Indians have finished using them. There's nothing left of them. They're just empty shells."

Nathan's eyes were glued to the captive woman. "Well, they ain't broken this one's spirit. Those eyes of hers are flashing like lightning in an electrical storm. And she's got her chin stuck out, defying them all." He chuckled, saying in a proud voice, "I always knew that little Missy had a core of iron in her."

Reid's head snapped up. Missy? Did he mean Melissa? He whirled and looked at the woman. Her face was thinner, and her skin was as tanned as an Indian's, but he'd recognize those turquoise eyes anywhere. No one but Melissa had such beautiful jewellike eyes. A surge of pure joy shot through him, stunning him with its intensity.

Then, remembering what a scheming little liar she was, he frowned, his golden eyes narrowing as he studied her closer. If anything, she was more beautiful; the thinness of her face only revealed more of her exquisite bone structure, and her turquoise eyes were more startling against her golden

153

tan. Damn! Did some cruel god of fate have something against him, to throw her perversely into his life again, just when he was beginning to forget her?

For months after he had left Franklin, Reid had been haunted by the memory of Melissa in his arms. At night, he had tossed and turned, remembering her sweet scent, the feel of her incredibly soft skin pressed against him. The days had been no better, for visions of her sensuous mouth with the tantalizing mole beside it and her sparking turquoise eyes had drifted through his mind. It was as if she had bewitched him. And now, when her memory was finally fading, when the fire she had lit in his blood was finally cooling, she had showed up again in his life, undoubtedly to torment him further.

"Dammit," Nathan said, "we tried to warn that father of hers. But that stubborn cuss wouldn't listen to us. Now look at the fix she's in. I wonder if her mother and sister are here, too?"

Both men scanned the area, but neither could see any sign of the two women. With their golden hair, they would have stood out in the crowd like a sore thumb.

"Well," Nathan said with a grim voice, "they're either dead or the Injuns left them back at their camp. Either way, there ain't no way we can help them."

Both men's eyes swiveled back to Two Feathers and Melissa. Melissa stood on a small stump, her hands tied behind her back. Two Feathers held one arm firmly to keep her from jumping off as he called to the crowd to come forward and view the slave he was selling. A circle of men, both Indians and white trappers, were already standing around them, waiting impatiently for the bidding to begin, their eyes raking Melissa lustfully.

"Would you look at her?" Nathan asked with open admiration. "Any other woman would be hanging her head in shame or cowering in fear. But not little Missy. She's staring them all down, as bold and brave as you please."

Reid looked at Melissa. What Nathan said was true. She stood proudly, her whole body a picture of defiance. Her eyes flashed dangerously as they flicked from one man to the next, as if daring them to touch her.

Nathan scratched his bushy beard. "I can't figure it," he said thoughtfully.

"Figure what?"

"Why that buck's selling her. Like you said, they don't usually sell their captives till they're all used up, till there ain't nothing but a shell left. Now we can both see Missy's got a hell of a lot of life left in her. So why's he selling her?"

Nathan's words, "through using them" made Reid wince. He looked back at the brave holding Melissa, knowing the Indian had raped her, taken her virginity brutally and callously in selfish lust. A bitterness welled up in Reid. The thought that this savage had cruelly taken what he had desired for himself—and turned down because she was a virgin—infuriated him. Now he wished he had taken her after all. At least he would have been gentle with her, made love to her, not attacked her. He would have brought her pleasure instead of pain. And how many others had raped her? How many of those red bastards had had her soft, sweet body between their thighs and emptied themselves into her? His fury grew. They had defiled her, dirtied her, and now she was as used as any common whore.

Perversely, Reid blamed Melissa for her downfall. If she wasn't so beautiful, so desirable they wouldn't have wanted her. Had she flirted with them, too? Led them on? Reid's thoughts were totally irrational. But in his pain, Reid wasn't really thinking. He was simply reacting. He was a man who felt that what should have been his had been stolen, sullied, and soiled, somehow cheating him and ruining it for him.

And then, seeing a trapper raise the hem of Melissa's tunic to get a glimpse of what was beneath, his emotions did a complete turnabout. A fierce wave of protectiveness swept over him. He growled and stepped forward and would have attacked the man if Nathan had not pulled him back. "What in the hell is wrong with you?"

"Didn't you see what that bastard did?" Reid ground out between clenched teeth.

"Sure I saw. It made me mad as hell, too. But, goddammit, you can't go rushing in like a charging bull buffalo. One crazy move like that, and every damned Injun and trapper that's got his eye on her will jump us. Now simmer down, before you get us all killed." He looked back at Melissa, then grinned. "Besides, she can take care of herself. At least for the time being."

Reid glanced back at Melissa. She was kicking at the offending trapper's hand. Two Feathers was having a hard time trying to keep her on the stump. Finally he pulled his knife, warning the trapper away.

"Nope," Nathan continued. "The only way we're gonna get her back from that Injun is to buy her." He glanced over at the Indians and trappers surrounding Two Feathers and Melissa, and frowned. "But that might not be so easy. If that buck over there is planning on offering that string of horses for her, we're sunk. We ain't got nothing to trade that compares to them."

Reid looked at the brave with the string of horses. Nathan was right. The eight horses were magnificent animals, and they certainly couldn't outbid that. He studied the brave closer, curious about the man who was willing to pay so much for Melissa. Instead of the lustful looks the other men were giving her, the man's eyes were fiercely possessive. The look puzzled Reid. Why would a man be possessive of a woman he had never seen before today?

War Eagle stood and patiently waited for the bidding to begin, seething inside. His anger at

Two Feathers was not because he had refused to sell Melissa, but for shaming her. War Eagle was infuriated that Two Feathers was humiliating the white woman by bringing her to this trading fair and selling her as if she was a useless thing. Even if War Eagle had not loved Melissa, he would have been angered by the insult to her. She had been a good slave, a hard-working slave. She did not deserve such scornful treatment.

When War Eagle had learned of Two Feathers' plan for Melissa, he had followed them to the trading fair. He hoped that Two Feathers would not be able to refuse his bid this time—the eight horses and his most prized possession, his white man's firestick.

War Eagle hated to give up his firestick. Three of the firesticks he had captured had gone to other Sioux chiefs to cement alliances. Roaring Thunder had kept one for himself and given the other four to his most valued warrior-leaders. War Eagle felt he had been deeply honored to receive one. He hated to give it up, particularly to a brave as cowardly and undeserving as Two Feathers.

Two Feathers signaled for the bidding to begin. Using sign language, each man made his offer, the bids going higher and higher. Melissa stood on the stump, feeling sick with shame but proudly refusing to bow her head. She watched with horror as three rough-looking trappers pooled their trading goods, knowing that if they

won the bid, they would all take their turns raping her. She couldn't fight off three men at one
time! And she had never seen such disgusting-
looking men. Even from where she stood, she
could smell their stench and see the lice crawling
through their beards and over their greasy, stringy
hair.

Hearing a deep, familiar voice, she looked
around with surprise, seeing War Eagle standing
before her. Melissa was not the only one surprised
at War Eagle's sudden appearance. Two Feathers
had not known the warrior-leader had followed
them to the trading fair, nor had he noticed him
in the crowd.

"Stop this disgraceful foolishness, Two Feathers," War Eagle said in a disgusted voice. "No
one here can top my bid. I offer eight
horses . . ."

"No!" Two Feathers yelled, his face turning
beet red. "I will not accept your bid!"

"I have not finished yet," War Eagle said in a
tight, angry voice. "I offer eight horses and my
firestick." He lifted the rifle and waved it, so
everyone would know it was part of his bid.

The crowd of Indians gasped. Surely the brave
wouldn't refuse this offer. This wasn't any trading
gun. It was a white man's gun, one of the best.
Combined with the horses, it was an impossible
bid for any of them to top.

Two Feathers looked at the gun hungrily. He
wanted it badly, twice as much because he knew

159

Roaring Thunder had given it to War Eagle as a symbol of his esteem. But Two Feathers' personal pride refused to let him accept it. He glared at War Eagle, his look full of hate. "No! I'll never sell her to you. Never!"

War Eagle was stunned by Two Feathers' look. It was the first time Two Feathers had let War Eagle see his naked hatred. Always before, he had saved those looks for the warrior-leader's back. War Eagle knew then that nothing he could offer would change the brave's mind.

When the crowd saw Two Feathers refuse War Eagle, they quickly shoved War Eagle to the back of the circle, afraid that Two Feathers would have second thoughts if War Eagle persisted. Immediately the bidding resumed, two Indians moving in front of the three trappers to present their offers first.

"Why do you suppose he refused him?" Reid asked in a puzzled voice.

"I'd say that buck has a personal grudge against the other one," Nathan answered.

"Personal?"

"Yep. Didn't you notice they didn't use sign language. They spoke to each other. They're both Sioux, and I'd guess they're from the same village. That second buck called the first one by his name."

From the same village? Reid thought. Then the brave with the horses *had* seen Melissa before today. Had he known her? If so, how well? Had the brave had Melissa's sweet body? Did he think that gave him a claim on her.

Reid was torn from his distressing thoughts by Nathan urgently shaking his arm. "What?" Reid said in a distracted voice.

"Dammit! Where in the hell has your mind gone? This ain't no time to be daydreaming. I said we may have a chance of buying Missy, after all."

Reid looked at the three trappers, who were impatiently waiting for the Indians before them to make their offers. He, too, had seen them pooling their trading goods. "Well, that brave may be out of the running, but how are we going to compete against that?" He pointed to the large pile of trading goods.

"I don't think that buck is looking for ordinary trading goods. I think he's waiting for something special."

"Special? What in the hell are you talking about?"

"Well, if I got that buck figured right, he's looking for something that will impress the other Injuns in his tribe. Something that no one else has. And I got an idea."

"What?"

Nathan reached into his shirt and pulled a chain and medal out and over his head. Dangling it in front of Reid's face, he said, "I'm gonna offer him this Saint Anne's medal my old partner gave me before he went back to Canada."

"Why would an Indian want a medal of the trapper's patron saint?"

"Hell, that Injun doesn't know one medal from another. I'm gonna tell him it's one of those Jefferson Peace Medals."

"You mean one of those medals Lewis and Clark handed out when they passed through here?"

"Yep, but they only gave them to the most important chiefs. Now, you know how fast word gets around with these Injuns out here. I'm betting that buck has heard of those medals and would give his eye teeth for one."

Reid looked at Two Feathers thoughtfully. "It just might work."

"Just to play it safe, go get that hand mirror you use to shave with out of your pack."

"Mirror? What do you want my mirror for?"

"You remember when the *Expedition* steamed up the Missouri two years ago with the president's presents for the Injuns at Council Bluffs?"

Reid remembered the great Indian assembly. Over a thousand Plains Indian chiefs had attended. "What's that got to do with my mirror?"

Nathan laughed. "Well, I heard there was a big mirror in one of the staterooms and one of the chiefs spied it. He ran off and got the other chiefs. Those Injuns went crazy over that mirror, laughing and making faces at themselves. Of course, the officials couldn't give any of them the mirror. They only had that one, and what they gave to one, they had to give to the others, too."

"And you're thinking that brave may have heard that story, too?"

"Maybe. But even if he hasn't, I'm hoping he'll be just as fascinated as those Injun chiefs were."

Reid grinned. "One mirror coming up." He turned and loped back down the hill to their canoe.

When Melissa saw Two Feathers refuse War Eagle's bid, she was bitterly disappointed. Standing on the stump and being raked over by the leering men's eyes, many of them with a cruel glint in them, she had come to realize that what Hannah had said was true. War Eagle might be fierce, but he wasn't cruel, and to follow them all the way to the trading fair, he must feel something for her other than animal lust. She *would* have been better off with him than she would be with any of these others, particularly those three trappers. She shivered with revulsion.

When the three trappers moved forward, their eyes glittering ominously, Melissa felt despair for the first time since her capture. She wished she was dead, and knew she might well be before the night was over and these men were through with her. Tears glistened in her eyes. Feeling miserable and totally defeated, she hung her head, refusing to watch the trade that would send her to her doom.

For that reason, she didn't see Two Feathers impatiently wave the trappers away, his eyes

163

locked on the medal Nathan was holding and dangling enticingly. Nor did she see Nathan handing Two Feathers the medal and mirror, using sign language to explain the medal was a Jefferson Peace Medal he had won from an important chief of a far western tribe.

Nathan had pegged Two Feathers correctly. Despite all his vows of earning the villagers' respect by proving his bravery, he was still a coward. It would be much easier to simply make them envy him. He had heard of the medals from the Great White Chief. Not even Roaring Thunder had one of those. And the piece of glass that captured his spirit? Was it magic? Could he capture others' spirits with it? War Eagle's spirit? His eyes glittered with excitement.

Then he remembered Little Crow's instruction to bring her back a big iron pot. He knew that if he didn't, he would never have a minute's peace. He looked at the two trappers, a speculative gleam in his eye. They looked very anxious. He smiled smugly, signalling he would accept their bid if they added a kettle.

"A kettle?" Nathan muttered in disbelief.

"I saw a trapper selling kettles down the hill when we arrived," Reid whispered. "Keep him occupied until I get back."

Within minutes, Reid was back, carrying a big black kettle. Grinning with self-satisfaction, Two Feathers took the mirror and medal, slipping it proudly over his head. Picking up the kettle, he walked away, completely forgetting Melissa's existence, lost in his fantasies of how the villagers would now envy him.

War Eagle had stood in the distance and watched the whole transaction with disgust. He knew the medal was not a Jefferson Peace Medal. He had seen one of them. They were much larger. Two Feathers was a fool. The white men had tricked him. With fools like Two Feathers, no wonder the white men thought Indians were stupid.

But now what would he do? War Eagle wondered. He could not buy the white woman with horses and his firestick from these men. They were trappers. They had no use for horses. They used canoes and they already had a good firesticks. His eyes narrowed. Then he would have no choice but to take her from them. With fierce determination, he turned and walked away.

Three other pairs of eyes watched Two Feathers as he swaggered away with his prizes, their eyes glittering with anger. Then as they looked back to where the two trappers stood with the white captive, their looks turned sly. They huddled together, whispering and plotting.

Melissa felt the bonds on her hands being cut and knew the trade was over. Bile rose up in her throat. She couldn't stand the thought of looking into those cruel eyes.

"Missy?" Nathan said in a puzzled voice.

Melissa's head flew up. Her eyes filled with

165

wonder. "Nathan?" she whispered in a disbelieving voice.

"Yep, it's us," Nathan said, his craggy face beaming. He reached up and helped Melissa down from the stump.

Reid stepped from behind the stump where he had cut Melissa's bonds. Melissa felt that golden gaze on her. She felt as if she had just stepped from a long, cold winter into the warm sun. Her body became suddenly alive, her heart doing crazy flip-flops as a wave of almost painful happiness washed over her.

Then she remembered the last time she had seen Reid, his terrible accusations, his last words, "I hope to God I never lay eyes on you again." She couldn't bring herself to meet his eyes. For this reason, it was Nathan's arms she threw herself into, sobbing out her relief.

Nathan held her, crooning and soothing her, filled with compassion for her, knowing that what she had gone through had been a horrifying experience. Just thinking of what those red devils must have done to her made his blood boil. "There, there, Missy. It's all over. You're safe now. We won't let nothing happen to you."

When Melissa had thrown herself into Nathan's arms, Reid had felt a sharp stab of jealousy. He scowled at them, fighting back his urge to tear her from Nathan's arms.

Melissa risked a peek at Reid and saw his scowl. He hasn't forgiven me, she thought bleakly. He still hates me. She sobbed all the harder.

When Melissa had finally regained her composure, Nathan asked in a gentle voice, "What happened, Missy?"

"Our keelboat was attacked by Indians. All but three of us were killed. Ellen and I and another woman."

Reid's eyes again scanned the crowd for a golden head. "Ellen? Is she here, too?"

Melissa totally misinterpreted Reid's look. So, she thought bitterly, he was attracted to Ellen all along. He had never cared about her. He had only wanted her body, just like all the others. "She's dead," she replied in a tight voice.

Something about Melissa's tone of voice warned both men away from further questions. Nathan said to Reid, "Why don't you take Missy up to the trading post and see if you can't haggle that Scotsman up there out of a room for tonight? In the meanwhile, I'll buy our supplies and that way we can get out of here bright and early tomorrow morning."

Reid knew what was worrying Nathan. He, too, was very aware of the angry, resentful looks the other bidders were casting in their direction. He suspected the men might try to take Melissa from them by force, under the cover of darkness. It would be easier to defend themselves in a room in the trading post than out in the wide open. But Reid didn't want to be alone with Melissa. He realized that, despite everything, he still wanted her. He didn't trust himself with her. A new anger was added to his already tangled emotions, anger at himself for still being susceptible to her charms.

"Why don't *you* take her back to the trading post and *I'll* buy the supplies?" Reid snapped.

"Well, if that ain't the stupidest thing I ever heard," Nathan retorted. "You know damned well I'm better at haggling with these Injuns than you are. Besides, they like to seal the bargain with a snort of whiskey, and you don't drink."

As far as Nathan was concerned the matter was closed. He looked at Melissa. "I'll see you in the morning, Missy."

Melissa wasn't happy at the prospect of being in Reid's company either, particularly since he acted like he couldn't stand to be around her. "Won't you be coming to the trading post when you're through with your business?"

"Afraid not, Missy," Nathan answered. "Someone has got to stay close to the canoe and supplies tonight. Otherwise they might get stolen."

After Nathan had left, Reid glared down at Melissa and said curtly, "Come on."

He turned and walked rapidly toward the trading post. Melissa had to practically run to keep up with his quick, long strides. Once they were in the log building, Reid said, "Wait here until I talk to the post manager."

Melissa stood off to one side as Reid talked to

a tall, red-haired man, feeling very conspicuous when Reid motioned to her and the man gaped in disbelief. Finally, the two men walked over to her.

"Melissa, this is Ian McTavish," Reid said. "He runs this trading post."

"I'm sorry to hear about yer misfortune, lass. Ye can have my room for tonight. 'Tis not much, but at least it has a bed in it. I'll sleep in the storeroom."

Melissa had assumed the trading post rented out rooms like a hotel. "Oh, I couldn't take your room, Mr. McTavish."

"Nonsense, lass. 'Tis my pleasure. After all, 'tis not often I have such a lovely wee guest."

Lovely? Melissa thought with self-disgust. That was a laugh! My God, she looked terrible. She was sweaty and filthy, her hair in tangles, her hands looking like a washerwoman's, her skin burnt to a crisp. It was bad enough that Reid had seen her looking so horrible, but he had also witnessed her degradation at Two Feathers' hands. Oh, that must have amused him. To see her auctioned off like some farm animal.

Ian McTavish led them to the back of his trading post, where his room was. As he had said, the room wasn't large or lavish, but to Melissa, after sleeping for months in a tepee, it looked wonderful. The only furnishings were a chest, a chair, and a big bed. Melissa gazed at the big bed longingly. It looked heavenly.

Before Ian left, Reid asked, "Do you think you

could arrange for a tub of hot water?"

Ian smiled at Melissa and said, "Aye, I think that can be arranged."

"Thank you," Melissa said to Reid after Ian had left.

"For what?"

"For asking for the bath."

He shrugged his broad shoulders. "It was for my benefit as much as yours. You don't exactly smell like a rose garden, you know."

Melissa's face flushed bright red with embarrassment. But she had had enough humiliation for one day and enough of Reid's insults to last her a lifetime. "Well, you'd stink to high heaven, too, if you'd worn the same buckskin day and night for three months and just finished a weeklong ride without enough water to drink, much less to bathe in."

Melissa turned and walked to the small window, staring out and blinking back angry tears. Reid looked at her stiff back and felt like a first-class heel, realizing what he had said had been a blow below the belt. He knew that Melissa was proud, and that she would rather be dead than caught looking like she did. He looked at the buckskin dress with disgust. Besides being moth-eaten, three sizes too big for her, filthy, and sweat-stained, it also reeked of the bear grease the Indians used on their hair. Couldn't they have found anything better than that, or at least given her a change of clothes? And what had she said

170

about riding a horse? He had never stopped to consider how the Indians had gotten her this far west. My God, they had dragged her over a thousand miles of hostile territory, an unbelievable trip for a white woman, particularly a woman brought up with all the comforts of life. How had she endured it? Christ, it was a miracle she had survived! He looked at her closer, seeing how thin she had become, noticing her raw knuckles and torn nails, and had the urge to take her in his arms and comfort her.

But Reid knew once she was in his arms, he would do more than comfort her, and that would make him no better then the Indians. Damn her! Just being around her tore up his insides. His emotions were so tangled he couldn't even think straight.

The silence hung heavy between them in the small room. Even when the Indian boys brought in a wooden tub and filled it with water, neither spoke. The boys, aware of the tension between them, cast wary glances at the two before they scurried off, glad to be away from the whites who looked as if they were ready to pounce at each other any minute.

Finally, Reid broke the silence. "I'll wait outside while you bathe." He walked to the door. "Toss out those rags when you've stripped and I'll burn them," he said quietly.

Melissa whirled around. "Burn them?" she asked, shocked.

171

"Well, you certainly don't want to put that filthy thing back on, do you?" he asked, motioning to the buckskin tunic. "There would hardly be much purpose in taking a bath."

"But that's all I have to wear!"

"I'm sure Nathan will trade with the Indians for some new clothes for you."

"But he won't be back until tomorrow morning. Can't you buy something for me to wear here at the trading post?"

"Trading posts don't carry ready-to-wear, and certainly not anything for women. They sell blankets, staples, guns, knives, powder, things like that. This isn't Saint Louis, you know."

"But Nathan won't be back till morning. What will I wear?"

"Wrap one of those bed sheets around you."

After Reid had left, Melissa quickly stripped off the filthy tunic and her moccasins and, opening the door a crack, tossed them out. She looked down at herself and thought wryly, Well, I'm right back where I started, as buck naked as the day I was born.

Melissa enjoyed the luxury of hot water and bathing in privacy so much she drew the procedure out, dallying long after the water had cooled. A knock at the door startled her.

"Did you drown in there?" Reid called impatiently.

She glanced out the window and saw it was turning dark. Goodness, how long had she been in the tub? Why, even her fingers had wrinkled.

"I'm getting out now," she called back.

Quickly, she dried off and then neatly arranged the sheet around her, tucking it firmly in at her breasts. After wrapping a towel around her wet hair, she carefully walked to the door to keep from tripping on the sheet and opened it, seeing Reid standing there with a tray of food in his hands and a dark scowl on his face.

"Food?" Melissa asked in delight.

"Yes. But don't blame me if it's cold," Reid replied sourly, pushing the door open and walking in the room. The two Indian boys hurried in behind him, having waited impatiently to retrieve the tub.

While the boys pulled the tub from the room, Reid sat the tray on the chest and lit the small lamp sitting there. He turned and looked at Melissa. She flushed under that penetrating gaze. It wasn't because her shoulders were bared to his view, though. She had worn dresses that exposed much more. It was her awareness that she was totally naked beneath the thin sheet, and the look in Reid's eyes told her he was also very aware of that fact. Instinctively, she clutched the sheet at her breasts.

Reid frowned at her protective movement, then glanced up at the towel on her head. "I'll be back in a minute."

Melissa lost no time in attacking her food once Reid had left. The stew was delicious, not watery and tasteless as Little Crow's had been. The corn-bread was sheer heaven. And for the first time in months, she had enough to appease her hunger, for Little Crow had been very stingy with her servings, apparently intent on giving her just enough to survive.

With her stomach full, Melissa suddenly felt very sleepy. She glanced over at the big bed that looked so inviting. She rose, walked over to it, and sat, intending to crawl right in and fall asleep. She startled when Reid walked back in. She had completely forgotten about him.

He tossed a comb on the bed. "I borrowed this from Ian. I thought you would like to comb your hair."

Melissa had forgotten about her hair, too. She picked up the comb gratefully, but she wasn't about to thank him. Undoubtedly, if she did, he'd have another barbed remark to make.

She removed the turban and started to comb her hair, then hesitated when she saw Reid straddle the chair, leaning over its back, his golden eyes on her. Surely, he wasn't going to sit there and watch her comb her hair, she thought in dismay. Then she realized he must be waiting for her to finish to take the comb back to Ian.

"This may take some time," she said.

Reid nodded curtly, but made no effort to get up.

Damn him! Melissa thought angrily. If he was a gentleman, he'd leave. But obviously he'd left what manners he had back in Missouri. He was just as crude as all these other men out here. She turned her back halfway away from him, determined at least that she wouldn't have to watch him while he watched her.

She glanced over her shoulder and saw his gaze had dropped. Looking to see what he was staring at so avidly, she realized with dismay that when she had turned away from him, the sheet had opened at one side and one of her legs was exposed up to mid-thigh. Snatching the sheet and jerking it over her leg, she shot him a murderous look before again turning her back to him.

Even wet, Melissa's hair was hopelessly tangled, for the crude wooden Indian comb she had used had never removed all the snarls from her long, thick hair. Over the months, they had just accumulated, and now her hair was as matted as a rat's nest in some places. She pulled and tugged at her hair, her eyes filled with tears of pain and frustration. Her haste to finish so she would be rid of Reid only made matters worse. To add to her frustration, every time she jerked on the comb, the sheet threatened to come loose, and she spent as much time tucking it back in place as she did combing.

Finally, with a muttered oath, Reid rose, walked to the bed, and took the comb from her. "I'll do it."

"I'm perfectly capable of combing my own hair," Melissa retorted, grabbing for the comb.

Reid snatched his hand away. "The hell you are! By the time you're finished with it, you'll be bald-headed."

"And you think you can do better?" Melissa snapped.

"If I can get the tangles out of a beaver pelt, I can get them out of your hair. Now, turn around," Reid said in a stern voice, pushing her shoulders around so he could reach the back of her head.

Melissa felt the dip of the bed as Reid sat down behind the bed and the tug of the sheet from where he had sat on a fold of it. Frantic, she clutched it to her breasts to hold it in place. Then she felt the brush of his hand against her neck as he picked up a wet strand of hair. She sat rigid with resentment as he combed, reluctantly admitting that he was more adept at removing tangles than she had been. He worked methodically, taking a small strand at a time, working the snarls out from the bottom up. She was amazed at his patience and gentleness. But the longer he combed, the more tense she became. She was much too aware of him, of the warm heat radiating from his body, of the tantalizing brush of his fingers against her shoulders, of his heady masculine scent, a smell that had always done peculiar things to her.

Distract yourself, she told herself firmly. Concentrate on something else. Then, for the first time, she became aware of the whooping and hollering coming from outside.

"What's going on out there?" she asked.

"It's the Indians," Reid answered. "They're celebrating and getting all liquored up. It's always this way at night at these trading fairs."

Selling liquor to the Indians was the only serious area of disagreement Reid and Nathan had. Reid was adamantly against it. Nathan argued that everyone did it and that Reid's disapproval stemmed from his own personal feelings against drinking. But that wasn't the case. If a white man wanted to pickle his brain with the stuff, that was his business. But the Indian was a different matter. He couldn't hold his liquor. A few drinks and he was roaring drunk, often turning wild and belligerent. At best, Indians were unpredictable. But a liquor-crazed Indian was downright dangerous to everyone around him, white and Indian alike.

By the time Reid had finished combing the tangles from Melissa's hair, it was late. He tossed the comb on the chest and walked to the door, "Now maybe we can get some sleep."

Melissa watched in horror as he snapped the bolt to the door firmly shut, then turned, removing his powder horn from around his neck. "You're not planning on sleeping in here with me?" she asked in a shocked voice.

Reid shot her an irritated look as he laid his rifle, powder horn, and pouch of balls carefully on the chest beside the bed. "That was the whole purpose of taking this room. To get you away

177

from that drunken rabble out there."

"But you don't have to sleep in here with me," Melissa argued, feeling panic rising. "Can't you sleep outside the door?"

"What about that window over there? What's to keep them from coming in that way?"

"But you can't sleep in here with me!"

Reid's nerves weren't at their best. All evening, he had halfway expected the Indians, becoming more and more liquor-crazed by the minute, to attack the trading post. That apprehension, combined with the sexual tension Melissa had generated in him, left him in no mood for arguing. "Cut out the outraged-virgin act, Melissa! We all know what happened to you in that Indian camp. You're hardly an innocent anymore."

Melissa was stung by his harsh words. "But I am still a virgin!"

"Dammit, you're still just as big a liar as always, aren't you?" Reid threw back. "Are you going to sit there and deny you were raped?"

Melissa remembered Two Feathers' brutal attack. Even though he hadn't been successful at raping her, just the memory of that ugly, humiliating assault filled her with shame. A deep flush rose on her face, and she ducked her head, saying in a small but determined voice, "I wasn't raped."

Reid had been waiting breathlessly, hoping by some miracle that she hadn't suffered that cruel degradation. But in his mind, her flush of shame gave lie to her words. He knew she had been raped. The Indians always raped their female captives, and as beautiful and desirable as she was, there was no doubt in his mind that she had been defiled. The Indians weren't blind, and they weren't made of stone. And no woman would want to admit to such a shameful, humiliating experience. His bitterness returned, along with his unreasoning anger. He wanted to lash out, hurt someone. Unfortunately, that someone was Melissa.

He strode to the bed. "Move over. I'll take this side of the bed," he said gruffly.

Melissa's head snapped up. "You're not going to sleep in the bed with me."

"I certainly am. I'm paying a hefty price for this damned room and I intend to enjoy this bed."

Melissa's outrage overrode her shock. She jumped from the bed and stumbled on the sheet. Jerking angrily on it, she hastily rearranged it, then clutching it tightly to her with one hand, reached for a pillow with the other. "Then enjoy it! I'll sleep on the floor," she said hotly.

"The hell you will! Get back in that bed!" Reid roared.

"I will not!"

"Oh, yes you will," Reid ground out between clenched teeth.

Melissa's eyes flashed. "You can't tell me what to do."

"I can and I am."

179

"Go to hell!"

A snarl escaped Reid's throat as he caught Melissa and threw her on the bed. When she scampered to get out the other side, frantically fighting the sheet that had twisted around her and was impeding her flight, Reid grabbed a hank of her hair and jerked her back, throwing himself over her and pinning her to the mattress with his weight. Completely forgetting the sheet, Melissa struggled, trying to claw at his face. Angrily, Reid grabbed both of her wrists in one hand and forced her arms above her head.

His golden eyes glittered as he glared down at her. "Let's get something straight from the very beginning. You'll do what I tell you to do, when I tell you to do it. Do you know why, Melissa? Because I own you now."

Melissa's eyes widened at his words. "No!" she gasped.

"Oh, yes, Melissa," Reid replied with a smug smile. "I bought you. Or have you conveniently forgotten this afternoon? You're my slave now, and you'll do everything and anything I tell you."

"You can't own me. I'm white," Melissa objected in a weak voice, the true horror of what he was saying slowly penetrating her brain.

"Color has nothing to do with it," Reid said coldly. "That rule doesn't apply out here. I should think you would know that by now. You were the Indian's slave and he sold you. If those trappers had bought you, you'd be their slave now. But I bought you and that makes you mine."

Melissa stared at him in disbelief, her eyes wide with shock.

Reid was very aware of her body beneath his. While Melissa hadn't realized the sheet had come undone in their tussle, he had. Her breasts and one leg were exposed, and Reid was very conscious of those soft breasts pressed against his chest, the length of her slender leg trapped between his long ones, seemingly burning right through his buckskins. Her scent drifted up to him, sweet and womanly, intoxicating his senses. His desire, which he had been struggling to keep at bay all evening, rose, hot and urgent.

His mouth crashed down on hers, his hard male lips grinding on her soft ones. Melissa gasped at the bruising, torrid kiss, and Reid took the opportunity afforded him, his tongue plunging into her mouth like a fiery dart, plundering, ravishing the heady wine that was uniquely hers. As his tongue slid in and out and around, Melissa was awash in sensations as waves of hot and cold rushed over her, leaving her tingling clear to her fingertips and her lungs feeling as if they had been seared. She fought against the onslaught of feelings threatening to engulf her, sensing that Reid was punishing her and not loving her, refusing to give in to the demands of this arrogant man and her own rising passion. She struggled, trying desperately to get away from the hot, passionate kiss that threatened to consume her, jerking her head from side to side, but Reid's mouth followed with fierce determination until Melissa felt weak from lack of air. She squirmed and twisted in a vain effort to escape the weight of his body and the iron-like grip on her wrists, the movements only serving to inflame Reid further, teasing and taunting until he saw a red haze behind his eyes, his pulsebeat pounding in his ears like a wild tom-tom.

Finally, he broke the kiss, his breath rasping in the air as he had said in a husky voice, "Stop fighting me! It won't do you any good." His free hand slid down one arm in a long, possessive caress, then cupped one of her bared breasts.

Melissa gasped in surprise, having not realized the sheet had come undone in their struggling. Then, as his long fingers brushed back and forth across the nipple, she was horrified as it rose and hardened in eager anticipation.

His golden eyes smoldered as he gazed down at her. "This soft, sweet body of yours belongs to me now. I can do anything I want with it. I can beat you . . ." Deliberately, he ground his groin into hers, so that she could feel the long, hot proof of his arousal. ". . . . or I can take you. With — or without your consent!"

He would actually go that far? Force himself on her? Rape her? The memory of the night Two Feathers had attacked her flashed through her mind, that and the terrible beating and pain that had followed. Her eyes filled with naked terror.

The look in Melissa's eyes was like a dash of ice water on Reid's inflamed senses, an expression of such utter fear that his mind recoiled from it. My God! What had the Indians done to her? What horrible things had she been forced to endure to cause such terror? But his body still wanted her—desperately, so much so that every fiber of him was screaming for release. He struggled for control, the man against his base, animal instincts, until, with a strangled oath, he pulled away from her and leapt from the bed, while Melissa hastily covered herself with the sheet.

Standing beside it, he glared down at Melissa, feeling frustrated and angry, a mixture of anger at himself for wanting her so badly and anger at her for making him want her. What was there about her that brought out the worst in him, the animal that lurked in the depths of every man's soul? Why was he so defenseless against her that she could strip him of all civilized trappings and turn him into a savage? The realization that Melissa held a dark power over him against which he had no defenses angered him even more. He was a man accustomed to being in complete control of his life, and yet, around her, he couldn't even control his lust.

His words were said more to convince himself than her when he snarled in a hard, biting voice, "Don't worry, Melissa. I won't force you. I wouldn't take you, even if you were willing." He leaned forward, his golden eyes glittering. "I don't want your body. I don't want the leavings of any man — particularly a dirty redskin's!"

Reid's denial was meant to punish Melissa for her power over him, and Melissa felt the brutal words like a slap in the face. None of his insults and accusations had ever hurt or humiliated her so badly. Quickly, she rolled away from him, clutching the sheet tightly around her and desperately fighting to hold back the tears that were threatening to spill from her eyes.

He had decided in his mind that she had been raped, she thought in utter misery. She had openly denied it, but he had refused to believe her, calling her a liar again. Now he thought her used and dirty. That's what he had been punishing her for. But even if she had been defiled, what right did he have to blame *her* for it? If Two Feathers had been successful, it would have been *his* fault, *his* crime, not hers. Even if it were true, Reid had no right to blame her, hurt her.

But was Reid's reaction any different from the rest of their society's toward women they thought had been defiled? She remembered hearing stories of Indian attacks on the frontier and the whispers about the ruined, soiled women, women that no decent man would want anymore. At the time, she hadn't known what they meant, but she did now. Those women had been raped, just as Reid believed she had, just as she would have, if she hadn't unmanned Two Feathers. And like her, they were being punished by their own people for it. Why? Melissa asked herself. Why, when a woman was victimized in such a manner, did their society continue to punish her, men and women alike? If a man was attacked or abused, no one blamed *him*. But then a man didn't have to worry about purity, she remembered bitterly. It wasn't expected of him. No, there were two sets of rules, one of the man, one for the woman. It wasn't fair!

And Reid? Before he hadn't wanted her because she was a virgin. Now he didn't want her because he thought she wasn't. A profound bitterness filled her.

Reid had no sooner uttered the denial that he still desired Melissa than he regretted his harsh words, knowing that he had unfairly lashed out and hurt her again and hating himself for it. While she had been thinking her dark thoughts, he had been castigating himself severely for being so cruel. A sudden urge to take her in his arms, apologize and comfort her overcame him. Feeling contrite, he sat on the bed and reached for her.

Melissa felt the dip of the bed. Knowing Reid didn't believe her and how he felt about her, she couldn't stand being anywhere near him. She rose to flee.

Her rejection brought Reid's anger rushing to the fore again. His arm snaked out, and he caught her shoulder, pulling her back down. "Try that one more time and I'll hog-tie you to the bed!" he threatened.

Melissa glared up at him, then spat sarcastically, "Yes, master!"

Quickly, she rolled to her side in a tight ball, not seeing the look of pain that crossed Reid's face at her biting words. There she lay, nursing her battered emotions until sleep finally claimed her.

Later that night, the air turned cool, and Melissa, wrapped only in the thin sheet, instinctively moved in her sleep closer to the heat of Reid's body. She snuggled against the warmth of his back, tucking her legs behind his.

Reid had not shut his eyes all night, lying awake and feeling miserable with regret over how badly he had treated Melissa. To add to his misery, his selfish body was still aching for her, clamoring for release from the passion she had awakened in him. When he felt Melissa's soft, feminine form pressed against his back, it was too much for him. With a frustrated groan, he rose, picked up his pillow, and tossed it on the floor.

It was Reid who spent the night on the cold, hard floor.

Chapter Eight

When Melissa awakened the next morning, she was alone. She was grateful for Reid's absence. She needed time to sort out her thoughts and compose herself before she could face him again. And thinking was almost an impossibility when he was around.

In the cold light of day and out of the shadow of Reid's domineering personality, she couldn't believe Reid had been serious when he claimed she was his slave now. True, if she had been bought by another Indian or one of the trappers, she would have still been in that situation. But Reid and Nathan weren't savages like those men. They were too civilized to force a woman into white slavery. Why, they were practically family friends. No, Reid had just been angry at her for arguing with him. He had just been taunting her again, threatening her in an effort to get her to bow to his male authority.

But while she seriously doubted Reid's sincerity about his claim to own her, she had no doubts that he'd meant what he'd said about not wanting her because she had been used. That still hurt — hurt deeply. She hated herself for doing so, but she still loved him. She knew that any possibility of his returning that love was permanently lost to her now. No white man, particularly not a man as proud as Reid, wanted a woman whom he thought had been degraded by an Indian, for an Indian was considered no more than an animal. But she still had her pride, too. She would never again try to tell him the truth, that she was still a virgin. Besides, he wouldn't believe her. He'd only call her a liar again.

A knock sounded at the door. "Missy, are you awake?"

Melissa rose from the bed, hastily arranged the tangled sheet about her, and walked to the door.

As she opened it, Nathan said in a cheerful voice, "Morning. I'm sorry to wake you so early, but we have a long way to travel today." He handed her a buckskin dress and a pair of moccasins. "I don't reckon you're any too fond of Injun clothes, but this is all I could find."

Melissa accepted the tunic and moccasins. She ran her fingers over the deerskin, surprised and pleased with its softness. Her old one had been stiff with dried sweat and dirt. Apparently, this dress had never been worn.

She smiled. "Thank you, Nathan. And I'll hurry. One thing about Indian clothing, it doesn't take long to dress."

She closed the door, slipped off the sheet, and pulled the tunic over her head, thinking, no underclothes again. Well, she'd just have to put up with a drafty bottom for a while longer. She smoothed the dress down, slipped on the moccasins, and, noticing the comb still sitting on the chest, picked it up and started combing her hair.

Then, remembering Nathan at the door, she opened it. "I'll be right with you."

But when she started braiding her hair, Nathan frowned. "I wish you wouldn't do that, Missy."

"Do what?"

"Braid you hair. It looks so pretty down around your shoulders like that. Reminds me of how my ma's used to look when I was a boy."

"But it will be hot like this," Melissa objected.

"Then pull it back like you did on the steamer. It looked awfully pretty that way."

Melissa glanced around the room for something to tie it back with. Nathan took his knife and cut a string from the fringe on his tunic and handed it to her.

When Melissa had tied back her hair, Nathan looked at her admiringly. "Looks like I made a pretty good guess at the fit. I got two more buckskin dresses down in the canoe for you. I figured three would be enough until we reach the cabin and you can sew you some real dresses. Got some real pretty bolts of cloth for you. One's the same color as your eyes."

To the cabin? Then they weren't taking her

back to St. Louis? They *had* bought her to be a slave! She couldn't believe Nathan would do that to her. She was shocked by his betrayal.

Nathan saw Melissa's shocked look and said gently, "I know you were expecting us to take you back to St. Louis, but I'm afraid that's impossible at this time. St. Louis is a long way off, and winter is just around the corner. Up here, it comes kinda suddenlike. We can't take any chances on getting caught in a sudden blizzard in the middle of the prairie and freezing to death. So you'll just have to come along with us and we'll take you back next spring."

As Nathan explained, Melissa felt ashamed of herself for her thoughts. But she didn't like the idea of spending the entire winter in Reid's company, particularly knowing his low regard for her. Undoubtedly, he wouldn't be too happy about it, either. To him she'd just be an unwelcome, added burden. Well, she'd be damned if she let him throw that in her face, too.

"I understand," she replied. "But I'll only go along on one condition."

"What's that?"

"That you'll let me help. That you'll let me pull my own weight."

Nathan could understand Melissa's pride. He was a proud man himself. He scratched his sandy beard thoughtfully. "Well, I never had a hankering for cooking, housecleaning, and washing. You can do that."

The housecleaning and washing were no problem. But cooking? Melissa had never cooked a thing in her life, not even at the Indian camp. Little Crow hadn't trusted her with their meager food supply. But it hadn't looked too hard. She had just thrown everything in and boiled it.

"It's a deal," she answered.

As they walked through the trading post, Nathan wondered what Melissa would have done if he had said there wasn't anything she could do to help. Would she have actually refused to go along? Yep, knowing how stubborn she was, she would have. And that would have created problems. They certainly couldn't have left her behind, alone and defenseless.

Every time Nathan thought about how the Indians had robbed her of her family and protection and what indignities and suffering she had been forced to endure, his blood boiled. He still wished he had been the first to get to that damned Indian that sold her.

That had been the real reason Nathan had insisted Reid go with Melissa to the trading post and not him. He wanted to find Two Feathers and kill the Indian before he had a chance to get away, and he wanted to get to the Indian before Reid could. He had seen the look in Reid's golden eyes, his killing look. Nathan had seen that look before, and it always sent cold shivers up his spine. But Nathan had been determined to get to the Indian first. He had felt he could do the job quicker and cleaner.

To Nathan's way of thinking, Reid wasn't a good frontiersman. He had too many principles about killing, and he took too many chances. Reid wouldn't sneak up on a man and put a knife in his back. Nor would he take his scalp. No, his young friend would have challenged the Indian with a knife and forced him into hand-to-hand combat, risking his life unnecessarily, to Nathan's way of thinking. And when he had killed him, Reid would have left him there for the other Indians to find. And with the Indians all liquored up and just looking for an excuse to kill someone, that would have been a fool thing to do. One look at his body would have told the Indians that he had been killed by a white man, and then all hell would have broken loose. Every white man at the trading fair would be fair game.

As soon as Reid and Melissa had left for the trading post, Nathan had gone looking for Two Feathers. He had found him in the woods an hour later — dead, a knife in his back. Someone else had gotten to him first. Nathan knew it hadn't been the second buck, because he hadn't been scalped. He figured that it had been the three trappers who had killed Two Feathers, and like Reid would have, because of his aversion to scalping, they had stupidly left the white man's calling card on him. Nathan had scalped the dead man and hidden his body under some bushes.

Then he had gone looking for War Eagle. He

didn't know if he had raped Melissa, too, but he figured he had probably taken part in the raid, might have even been the Indian that killed her parents or Ellen. For this reason, Nathan planned to kill him, too. But War Eagle had disappeared. The discovery made Nathan uneasy. He hadn't looked like the kind that would give up that easily. No, that buck had had a determined look about him.

Reid was waiting for them when Melissa and Nathan stepped from the trading post. He gave Melissa a curt nod and an icy look. The look stabbed at Melissa's heart, a heart that was beginning to feel like a pin cushion from Reid's repeated barbs and hard, penetrating looks. He fell in beside them as they walked to the lake, pointedly ignoring Melissa.

Melissa looked around the trading fair warily, wondering if Two Feathers was still there. She wouldn't put it past him to sell her and then try to steal her back.

Nathan saw her look. "If you looking for that buck that sold you, you can stop worrying. He's gone," he said.

Nathan saw the sharp, oblique look Reid gave him over Melissa's head. So, Nathan thought, that had been the reason Reid had insisted he go and bring back Melissa from the post this morning. The young cuss had still been bent on finding the buck. Well, obviously Reid had found him, and now he suspected that Nathan had killed Two

Feathers and hidden his body. He'd tell him the truth later, when they were out of Melissa's hearing.

Knowing that Two Feathers was gone and that she was truly rescued and safe from further abuse, Melissa's spirits rose. She was free. Free! Her life was her own again. And she was determined she wasn't going to let Reid ruin her newfound happiness for her. Even though she knew she had lost Reid, that he would never return her love, she wasn't going to spend the rest of her life brooding about it. No, she was going to live it to the fullest. To hell with Reid!

Nathan watched Melissa as she looked around the trading fair with excited, eager eyes. She looked alive again. He smiled, knowing the healing of her spirit was already beginning. Given time, she would forget the horrors, too. Yep, she was gonna be all right.

Nathan began pointing out things of interest at the trading fair, and Melissa absorbed every bit of information hungrily. The realization that she was seeing something that few whites had ever seen only excited her more.

"See that white Injun over there," Nathan said, pointing. "He's one of those full-blooded Mandans, one of those Injuns who claim their ancestors were Welshmen who sailed to this country long before Columbus. I've heard some of them still speak Welsh."

Before Columbus? But that's impossible! Melissa thought. She looked at the Indian Nathan was pointing out. The brave's hair was so blond it was almost white, and his eyes were a startling blue. She might have attributed his unusual coloring to some lack of pigmentation, if it had not been for his thick blond beard. She knew from her own experience that Indians didn't have beards. They had so few facial hairs, they simply plucked them out. She stared at the Indian in astonishment.

When they reached the lake, Nathan indicated the canoe. "With all our supplies piled in the middle, you'll either have to sit right behind me or in front of Reid."

Melissa had no intention of sitting anywhere near Reid if she could help it. "I want to see where we're going. I'll sit behind you."

While Melissa positioned herself in the canoe, Reid whispered to Nathan, "Did you kill him?"

Nathan knew who he meant. "Nope. He was already dead when I found him. I figure those three trappers got him, since he hadn't been scalped."

"And the other one?" Reid asked.

"Couldn't find him nowhere."

Reid frowned at this bit of information. Like Nathan, he didn't think the man would give up that easily.

As the canoe glided across the lake, then up the river that emptied into it, Melissa sat back, thinking what a delightful way this was to travel after her rough, bone-jarring horseback rides. She almost felt guilty sitting back and enjoying the view while Reid and Nathan did all the work.

And the view was beautiful. The trees were a riot of color with their fall foliage. The sky overhead was a clear blue, not a cloud in sight. Occasionally, she caught a glimpse of a deer or an antelope or could even hear the coo-coo of a quail or the gobble of a wild turkey. Even the sun, her old enemy, was benign today, just pleasantly warm. Feeling lazy and contented, she dozed.

Toward noon, Melissa roused herself enough to ask, "What river is this?"

Nathan chuckled. "I'm surprise you didn't recognize it. But you would have the first drink you took. This is the Big Muddy itself."

Melissa smiled down at the river, feeling almost as if it were an old friend. "There's really no reason to drink all that muddy water, you know. All you have to do is put a cactus stem in your water-skin every morning and it will soak up all the dirt."

"Where did you hear that?" Nathan asked.

"The Indians did it."

"Well, I'll be damned," Nathan said in an astonished voice. "I've been traveling this river for over thirty years and drinking that mud. But I ain't never heard of that. Just goes to show you, you ain't never too old to learn. Next cactus I see, we're gonna stop and stock up."

Melissa smiled smugly, wishing she could see the look on Reid's face. Maybe now, he wouldn't think she was just useless baggage.

When they stopped for lunch and Melissa was out of hearing, Nathan asked Reid, "What are we gonna do about those three trappers following us?" There was no doubt in Nathan's mind that Reid's sharp eyes had also seen the canoe trailing them. Other than his scruples about killing, scruples that Nathan considered a weakness, Reid was just as good a woodsman as Nathan.

"The way I figure it, they won't try anything until tonight. They'll wait until they think we're asleep and then sneak up on us," Reid replied.

"And put a knife in our backs, just like they did that Injun," Nathan added. His dark eyes narrowed thoughtfully. "We can pad our bedrolls so they'll think it's us and wait in the trees for them. Then when they make their move, we'll shoot them."

"In the back?" Reid asked in a disgusted voice.

"You're goddamned right in the back!" Nathan retorted hotly. "If you've got some damned fool idea about having a shoot out with them, forget it! There's too much danger of that little gal being hit by a stray ball. We'll do it my way this time, whether you like it or not."

Reid had not thought about Melissa. "All right, we'll do it your way," he agreed reluctantly.

As soon as the canoe was beached that evening, Reid left to hunt for fresh meat, and Nathan started setting up camp. Remembering that her job was to cook, Melissa began collecting firewood. Nathan watched her from the corner of his eye, noting that she picked up only cottonwood branches, a smokeless wood. As she started her fire, using very small kindling and the flint he had loaned her, then banking it carefully with small stones, Nathan nodded in approval. Yep, he thought, she's learned a lot from the Injuns.

Melissa knelt on the ground beside the packs and pulled out a coffeepot and small kettle. She rummaged through the packs, but all she could find were some white and yellow chips that looked almost papery. Where were the vegetables? she wondered. She opened another sack and found some hard beans. She set the beans aside and opened another sack, this one filled with thicker, softer chips. She picked up a yellow one and smelled it. Peaches! She laughed to herself. Of course! Everything was dried. Fresh fruits and vegetables would be too bulky to carry.

She threw several handfuls of what she assumed were dehydrated potatoes, onions, and carrots into the kettle, then threw in a couple of handfuls of beans. She picked up the coffeepot and frowned down at it. Indians didn't drink coffee, and she had no idea of how it was made. She shrugged, assuming that, like the stew, it was just thrown into the pot with water and boiled. She tossed a couple of handfuls of coffee into the pot, added water to both the coffeepot and kettle, and carried them to the fire. Then she stood staring at the fire, a perplexed look on her face.

Seeing her look, Nathan asked, "What's wrong, Missy?"

She laughed and said, "I know this sounds stupid, but the Indians didn't have pots. Do I just set them down in the fire?"

Nathan chuckled. "Nope, that's what this grill is for." Pushing the stones a little closer to the fire, he placed the grill over them. "Now you put your pots on top of that."

Reid appeared from the woods a few minutes later, carrying two freshly dressed rabbits. Without a word, he handed them to Melissa, then turned and walked off.

Melissa stared down at the bloody rabbits in dismay. The Indians had roasted their rabbits in the coals, fur, guts, and all. She had no idea of how to butcher a rabbit. Sighing in resignation, she rummaged through the packs until she found a butcher knife, and then kneeling before a flat rock, she placed the rabbit on it and began chopping. When she finished, the rabbits were a pulpy mess, with splinters of bone protruding from the flesh. She scooped the pieces of meat up with her hands and threw the whole mess in the kettle. She looked down at her bloody hands in disgust, and turned to walk down to the river to wash them.

After washing her hands, she sat by the river for a while, enjoying the solitude and the peaceful woods around her. Then, realizing she had dallied longer than she intended and that her supper might be burning, she hurried back to camp to see Reid and Nathan were already spooning the stew into plates.

Nathan looked up and smiled. "This smells real good, Missy."

Melissa beamed at his praise. "Thank you."

Reid sat down cross-legged on the ground with his plate in his lap and took a big bite of stew. Then he yelped. Holding his jaw, he glared at Melissa. "What did you put in this, anyway? Rocks? I think I just cracked a tooth."

Melissa glanced at Nathan. He was pushing the stew around in his plate, eyeing it suspiciously. Then he lifted his head. "What beans did you use, Missy?"

"The ones in that sack," Melissa replied, pointing to the sack of beans.

"No wonder," Reid said in a disgusted voice. "Those beans have to be soaked for at least twelve hours to soften them before you can cook them."

"Well, I don't see as any harm has been done," Nathan said. "We'll just pick them out."

After Reid had removed the beans from his plate, he picked up a piece of meat and stared at it in disbelief. Both ends of the shattered bone protruded a good two inches. "What's this?" he asked Melissa.

Melissa glared at him. "You should know. You shot it."

"I may have shot it, but you massacred it,"

Reid retorted.

A grunt of pain from Nathan drew their attention to him. "What's wrong?" Melissa asked in alarm.

Nathan fished in his mouth with his finger and drew out a long bone splinter. "Nothing, Missy. Just a little bone splinter."

"That does it!" Reid said with a snort, tossing his plate aside. "I'll settle for jerky and coffee."

While he searched the packs for jerky, Nathan valiantly continued eating his stew. Melissa sat down, feeling miserable, knowing she made a total mess of the stew. A lot of help I was, she thought with self-disgust.

Reid sat back down, leaning against a tree, and took a bite of jerky, followed by a sip of coffee. Melissa heard a choking sound and turned to see Reid spewing coffee on the ground.

He looked up, saying in a strangled voice, "Christ! That tastes worse than rot-gut whiskey. Why didn't you put a little water in it?"

Melissa glared at him. "I did put water in it!"

Shooting him a scorching look, she deliberately picked up her cup and took a sip. Her eyes widened. The coffee tasted as bitter as her old mammy's spring tonic. To make matters worse, it was gritty with coffee grounds. She forced herself to swallow, almost gagging in the process.

Reid glowered at her, tossed the coffee from his cup, and rose. "I think I'll get a drink from the river. After that coffee, the Missouri will taste like pure ambrosia." He headed for the river, calling over his shoulder, "From now on, let me or Nathan do the cooking. Before you kill us all!"

Nathan scowled at Reid's back. "I'm sorry, Nathan. The whole meal is a disaster. I should have admitted that I don't know how to cook," Melissa said.

"Well now, Missy," Nathan replied in a soothing voice, "I should have knowed that. Little ladies like you don't know nothing about cooking. You've always had servants to do that for you. Only, when I saw you gathering wood and building a fire like a real expert, I figured the Injuns had taught you how to cook, too."

Melissa laughed harshly and said in a bitter voice, "No, Little Crow didn't trust me with their food. I guess she wasn't so dumb after all."

"Who's Little Crow?"

"She was Two Feathers' wife. Two Feathers was the Indian who captured me and sold me." Melissa looked down at her plate. "Oh, Nathan, look at the mess I made! I wanted to be so helpful," she wailed.

"Ain't no reason why you still can't do the cooking. All you gotta do is learn how to cook."

Melissa raised her head. "Would you teach me?"

"Sure. Shouldn't take long. We don't cook fancy. Why, I bet within a week you'll be as good a cook as Reid or I."

Better, Melissa thought. I've got to become a

better cook than Reid. I'll show him!

While Melissa was washing the dishes in the river, Reid and Nathan began laying their trap for the three trappers. When Melissa returned to the camp and saw the forms wrapped up in blankets, she thought Reid and Nathan had already gone to bed. Then she saw them dragging sacks to a third blanket a little farther off. She stood and stared at them in puzzlement.

Nathan rose. "We're expecting a little company tonight, Missy," he said.

"Company?"

"Those three trappers that tried to buy you yesterday," Reid explained. "They've been trailing us all day. We figure they'll attack tonight when they think we're asleep."

Melissa paled. The trappers were still trying to get their filthy hands on her? They would kill Reid and Nathan for possession of her? And she had thought the terror was over.

Nathan saw her deathly pale face. "Don't worry, Missy. We've got things under control. They ain't gonna get you."

After the bedrolls were arranged to look as if someone were sleeping in them, they withdrew to the woods that surrounded the small clearing and lay down under a cover of thick underbrush. Lying on their bellies, they anxiously watched the clearing, straining their eyes in the darkness.

An hour passed, then two, and Melissa began to feel cramped and cold. She lay shivering on the cold, damp ground, wishing she had thought to bring a blanket with her. When her teeth began to chatter uncontrollably, Reid uttered a curse and pulled her close to his side, placing one arm over her back.

Melissa tried to pull away, hissing, "Let me go!"

"You're cold!" Reid snapped back in a harsh whisper.

"Well, I don't need you to warm me," Melissa whispered back.

"The hell you don't! You're chattering like a chipmunk. They'll be able to hear you a mile away."

"Will you two stop that yapping?" Nathan whispered urgently.

Reid puller her closer, holding her in a tight grip. She knew the only way she could get away from him would be to put up a fight, and that would cause too much noise. She lay with her side pressed closely against his and his arm over her, seething silently, very aware of every inch of their bodies touching and Reid's warm breath fanning her neck. But as the warmth of Reid's body seeped into hers, she stopped shivering and, feeling like she was wrapped in a safe, warm cocoon, finally dozed.

She was awakened by the feel of Reid's body tensing. She glanced up from where her head lay on her arm and saw him watching the camp intently, a grim look on his face. The firelight danced in his golden eyes, and something else, a gleam of anticipation, the same gleam seen in an animal's eyes just before it pounces on its prey.

Her head snapped up, and she looked at the clearing, seeing the trappers crouching and creeping towards the three huddled forms in the blankets. Their long knives came as a shock to Melissa. For the first time, she realized the trappers' intention. They had planned to slip up on their victims and stab them to death in their sleep. Why, the sneaky bastards! she thought. They're nothing but cowardly murderers.

Melissa was so engrossed on what was going on in the camp that she didn't notice when Reid's arm slipped from her shoulder and he carefully sighted his rifle. And then just as the three men raised their knives, two gunshots roared almost simultaneously, deafening her and making her scream in surprise.

Two of the trappers jerked, both crying out and then slumping over the bedrolls. The third whirled, a look of total disbelief on his face. Then, as he saw Reid running toward him, he crouched, his hand holding the knife poised for battle. But as Reid flew through the air in a running leap, his lips drawn back in a snarl, his golden, feline eyes gleaming in the firelight, the last thought the trapper had was, this is no man, it's a lion!

It was over within seconds. The flying leap took the man totally by surprise. The impact, as their bodies hit the hard ground, knocked the knife from the man's hand, and before he could reach for it, Reid had buried his knife deep in the man's chest.

"That crazy, goddamned fool!" Nathan cursed. "He just had to take the risk, didn't he?"

Melissa was stunned by everything happening so fast. "What? Who are you talking about?"

Nathan glared at Reid, who was rising and pulling his knife from the dead trapper. "Him! I could have reloaded and shot that bastard before he got halfway across the clearing. But no, Reid just had to jump him!" Nathan stomped away, muttering under his breath.

Melissa followed and stood, looking about the clearing in a daze. Reid walked over to the man he had shot and stared down at the hold in the man's back. He glanced at the pistol still stuck in the man's belt, a pistol that he had never even had the chance to draw. He'd never shot a man in the back before, and it didn't set easily.

Melissa watched numbly as Nathan pushed the other trapper over on his back and gasped when the body fell away. The man's knife was buried in the bedroll, and had Nathan or Reid been lying in it, that knife would have been buried deep in either's upper back. He'd be dead! Melissa thought with sickening realization.

She stared at the knife, horrified, hardly noticing as Nathan pulled one of the bodies into the woods to bury it. Nor did she pay any attention when Reid strode over to her and glared down at her.

"How does it feel, Melissa?" he asked in a hard, biting voice. "How does it feel to know three men just died because of you? Does it please your female vanity?"

Melissa couldn't believe her ears. "You're crazy!"

"Am I? I understand you fine-bred southern ladies consider it quite an honor when two men duel over you. And I remember only too well what an accomplished flirt and tease you are, Melissa. You must have had every eligible male in the area at each other's throats. Well, you should feel quite proud of yourself tonight. You got *three* trophies out of this fiasco, instead of the usual one."

Melissa stared at him, silently seething.

Reid continued. "Maybe you should ask Nathan to scalp them for you, so you can carry your trophies on your belt." His golden eyes swept over her contemptuously. "I understand squaws carry scalps as well as braves."

The slow anger in Melissa rose until it erupted. "You bastard! I'm sick and tired of your accusations and insults!"

"Accusations? Are you denying that you shamelessly flirted with me?"

"No, I'm not! Since when is flirting a crime? And I'll even admit I tried to seduce you, but not for the reason you thought."

207

Reid's eyebrows rose at this bit of information, but before he could comment, Melissa continued, her eyes shooting sparks. "But I'll be damned if you're going to lay these men's, or any man's death at my feet. I'm tired of you blaming me for things I have no control over, Reid. I didn't ask the Indians to capture me, and I didn't ask these—these *animals* to follow me. If you think you're going to make me feel guilty about what happened here tonight, you can think again! I'm not responsible for others' crimes, even if they were committed because of me. I only answer for my own."

She turned and walked proudly out of the camp. Reid watched her, realizing that he had lashed out at her unfairly—again! She was right. You are a bastard, he thought with self-disgust.

The next morning, Nathan began Melissa's cooking lessons. She watched, feeling very foolish, as he wrapped *one* handful of coffee in cheesecloth and dumped it into the coffeepot. Then he taught her how to make flapjacks and fry bacon.

Melissa was so engrossed that she completely ignored Reid. Only when she sat down with her own plate, did she notice him watching her warily. Why, he looks like he's afraid I'm going to pounce on him at any minute, she thought. The idea was so ridiculous that she laughed. And strangely, her outburst the night before had seemingly washed away most of her resentment toward

208

him.

The days passed, with cooking lessons both in the morning and at night, and by the end of the week, Melissa was doing all the cooking. Nathan praised her lavishly, but Reid withheld comment. In fact, Reid rarely spoke, but Melissa noted with smug satisfaction that he wolfed his food down.

On the eighth day, Melissa noticed that the river had turned a paler color, looking much like coffee that had a lot of cream added to it. She commented on this to Nathan.

"It's the Milk River's influence on the Missouri," Nathan explained. "That crazy river carries so much limestone, it's almost pure white."

"Will we see it?" Melissa asked.

"Nope, it joins the Missouri much farther up. We'll be turning off at the Yellowstone soon."

The next day, they turned southwest to follow the Yellowstone River. The river was as crystal clear as the Missouri was muddy and ran much swifter.

That afternoon, Melissa gathered watercress, other greens, and wild carrots and artichokes. That night, they gorged themselves on salad, roasted pheasant, and ash cakes — small cornmeal caked baked in the fire's ashes. They topped it off with their dessert, large, dusky-blue huckleberries that she had found growing on the bushes around the river. Even Reid was forced to admit that the meal was delicious, much to Melissa's satisfaction.

When they were through eating, Nathan brought out his harmonica and began to play it. Reid and Melissa leaned lazily against two trees and listened to the music that blended with the other soft night sounds.

"Why don't you sing us a song, Missy?" Nathan asked. "You've got the prettiest singing voice I've ever heard. Like an angel's voice."

Reid remembered only too well Melissa's husky contralto. The memory of that warm, sensuous sound sent shivers of pleasure up his spine. His golden eyes locked on her in an intent, penetrating gaze.

But Melissa wasn't paying any attention to either man. Memories of her and Ellen singing their duets washed over her and, in their wake, left a painful void. A tight feeling constricted her chest.

"Missy?" Nathan asked quietly.

"No," Melissa answered in a voice so low both men had to strain to hear it. "No, I don't think I could sing without Ellen. It just . . . it just wouldn't sound right."

Quickly, Melissa rose and hurried off to the riverbank where she could be alone with her memories. Nathan and Reid watched as she faded into the dark woods, their eyes full of compassion.

"Me and my damned big mouth," Nathan muttered with self-disgust. "I just had to go and remind her."

Reid looked in the direction where Melissa had disappeared. "Don't blame yourself, Nathan. She has to face up to her loss sometime. The sooner the better."

Reid rose and strolled across the clearing, following Melissa down the hill to the riverbank. He found her staring blankly out at the water.

"Do you want to talk about it?" he asked in a gentle voice.

Melissa shook her head. "No, not now. Not yet."

He stepped closer, aching to take her into his arms, wishing she would confide in him and let him comfort her. "Is there *anything* I can do?"

Melissa swallowed hard. She felt so alone, so abandoned, so bewildered. She turned and looked up at him. "Just hold me, Reid. Please, just hold me," she said in a small, choking voice.

Reid gently enfolded her in his strong arms. Melissa had never truly grieved for her parents or Ellen. All of her energies had been expended in just surviving. As soon as she felt Reid's arms around her, she dropped her head on his hard chest, her hands clasping his tunic. And then the tears came, torrents of them, as soul-wracking sobs shook her body. Reid held her, muttering incoherent, soothing words, his hands caressing her hair and back.

For a long time, he held her as she cried out her grief. And when it was over, Melissa's soul was cleansed, and Reid's tunic was sopping wet.

211

"Are you feeling better?" Reid asked gently as Melissa disengaged herself.

"Yes." She gave a shaky little laugh. "But I'm afraid I've cried all over your shirtfront."

"It's been wet before," Reid answered in a strangely hoarse voice. He untied the bandanna he wore around his throat and handed it to her.

Melissa dried her face and muttered, "Thank you."

Reid barely nodded his head in acknowledgment.

"I'll . . . I'll wash your bandanna and give it back to you tomorrow," Melissa said, feeling suddenly very awkward. Then she turned, murmuring, "Good night," and walked back up the hill.

Reid watched her go. It had been an agony for him to hold her and not kiss her, not make love to her. Now, all his nerves seemed to be in a tight ball in the pit of his stomach from fighting to control his urges. He had known she was particularly vulnerable and he hadn't wanted to betray her trust.

Reid stood for a few minutes on the riverbank, pondering why he suddenly wanted that trust. Then his sharp, woodsman's ears heard a slight rustling sound, and all of his senses were alert. Reid's eyes darted around the darkened woods; his hand flew to the knife strapped at his waist. Then, seeing a deer emerge from the woods and dip its head to drink from the river, he relaxed and smiled. He turned and walked back to the camp.

War Eagle watched as Reid strode away, feeling the tension leave his body. For a minute, he had been afraid the trapper had discovered him. If that had happened, War Eagle would have been forced to kill him, and War Eagle didn't want to do that. He felt no hatred for the two white men. They had not harmed his woman. They had been kind to her and taken care of her, even killed the three evil trappers to protect her. To kill them was unnecessary. It would be a waste.

No, War Eagle would simply slip his woman away when they weren't around. He could wait for the right opportunity. He was a patient man. He had been taught that early in life. Nor was he in a hurry to get back to his tribe. His people had already set up their winter camp. There would be no more hunting or raiding until spring. He was not needed there. No, War Eagle would follow and watch for the right moment to take his woman.

The next afternoon, Reid, Nathan, and Melissa were forced to make camp earlier than usual. A dark line of angry thunderheads was rolling over the horizon and moving toward them rapidly. The canoe was completely emptied and pulled high up on the riverbank to prevent it from being washed away, then was turned over the supplies to protect them from the rain. The wind that preceded the approaching storm lashed at them as they worked furiously to secure the tarp that would protect

213

them from the fury of the storm. Then the sounds of Reid's and Nathan's axes blended with the cracks of lightning and rumbles of thunder as they cut branches to line the ground of their lean-to and protect the sides.

The last branch had just been set in place when the first drops of rain fell, making soft, plopping sounds on the canvas. They barely had time to duck into their lean-to before the rain came in torrents so thick that their view of the river was completely obliterated.

"Look at it," Melissa said. "I've never seen it rain so hard."

Nathan chuckled. "Well, it won't bother us. We'll be as snug as three bugs in a rug in here."

Melissa looked around the lean-to. It was so small that they would barely have room to lie down in it. But it was snug. The waterproofed canvas covered their heads and the back of the lean-to, and both sides were protected by the thick fir branches. The only side that was open was the front, and that had been strategically placed to face away from the wind so the rain could not blow in.

Their supper that night consisted of jerky and ash cakes and berries left over from the night before. But, despite the cold food, they ate ravenously, their appetites stimulated by their frantic efforts to set up camp before the storm hit.

When he had finished eating, Reid leaned back. "I'd give my eye teeth for a cup of hot

214

coffee right now," he said.

"Well, if you're looking for something to warm your innards, have a swig of this corn whiskey," Nathan said, raising the jug beside him.

"No, thanks," Reid replied tightly.

"How about you, Missy?" Nathan asked. "You want a swallow?"

Melissa was aware of Reid's feline eyes on her, his gaze so intense she felt as if he was trying to peer into her soul. The look made her uneasy. "No, thank you. Even sherry makes me nauseous."

Melissa's noticed Reid's disapproving look as Nathan took a long swig. Goodness, she thought, he really is a teetotaler. Somehow it didn't seem to fit in with his rugged frontiersman's image.

For a while, the three lay on their stomachs and watched the storm vent its fury. Then Nathan, bored with the spectacle, rolled onto his back and fell asleep. Soon, his loud snores echoed in the small lean-to.

Melissa laughed. "I never realized he snored so loud."

"Wait until you hear him in the cabin," Reid replied. "Sometimes he shakes the walls with all that noise."

Reid leaned across Melissa, who lay between the two men, and shook Nathan's shoulder roughly. The older man mumbled in his sleep and rolled over.

Reid grinned. "That's the only way you can

stop him from snoring. The only trouble is, in a few minutes he'll roll back over on his back, and you'll have to nudge him again. There's been many a night that I didn't get any sleep from having to prod him all night long."

Reid and Melissa lay for a long while, silently watching the lightning as it streaked across the night sky. Thunder rolled and the wind lashed the rain against the canvas lean-to. Outwardly, both appeared to be absorbed with the storm, but both were very aware of the other lying so close.

Reid could feel the warmth radiating from Melissa's body and smell her sweet scent. He remembered another storm when the rain had molded her wet clothes to the soft curves of her body. He glared at Nathan resentfully across her body, fervently wishing his partner was miles away instead of sleeping right beside them.

A bolt of lightning hit a nearby tree with a loud, cracking sound, sending sparks dancing down its trunk and over the ground and illuminating the lean-to in a flash of blinding-white light. Instinctively, Melissa jerked away, and found herself in Reid's arms.

Her heart beat a wild tattoo in her chest and not from her fright. "That was close," she said in a shaky voice, wishing he would kiss her.

Reid desperately wanted the same thing, but he knew he could never stop at just a kiss, and anything else was unthinkable with Nathan lying right beside them. With supreme will, he released her and lay back down. "Yes, it was. Too damned close," he replied, his answer having nothing to do with the lightning.

A few minutes later, a hard gust of wind tore a branch away from the lean-to on the side where Nathan lay. Cold rain blew in on them. Reid tried to lean across Melissa and pull the branch back in place, but he couldn't reach far enough. Muttering an oath, he knelt, straddling Melissa's hips as he leaned across Nathan and yanked the branch back in place.

Melissa held her breath, acutely aware of Reid's muscular thighs pressed against her hips. A warmth washed over her entire body, a flush that had nothing to do with embarrassment.

As Reid moved back over her to lie back down, his manhood brushed across her soft buttocks. His body's reaction to the tantalizing, brief contact was immediate. He lay down on his stomach, not wanting Melissa to see his aroused state in the lightning flashes, and then groaned in pain as he lay on the sensitive, throbbing flesh.

Hearing his groan, Melissa asked, "Is something wrong?"

"I just hit something hard," Reid answered between clenched teeth.

"A rock?"

Reid smiled grimly. "Sort of."

The position was too uncomfortable for Reid. He rolled away from Melissa, putting his back to her. "Good night," he said curtly.

"Good night," Melissa muttered, feeling very disappointed and a little hurt by Reid's abrupt dismissal.

Nathan was the first to awaken the next morning. He glanced over and saw Melissa lying with her head on Reid's shoulder, their bodies snuggled close together, Reid's arms around Melissa as they both slept. He smiled. Now, that looks right natural, he thought. Yep, those two belong together. Not wanting to embarrass them by letting them know he had seen them so intimately entwined, he silently crept from the lean-to and stole away into the woods.

When Reid awakened and discovered Melissa in his arms, he lay very still, not wanting to awaken her. He wanted to savor the feel of her soft body in his arms, the feel of their bodies touching from chest to thigh. His eyes roamed her face, feasting hungrily. He took in a long, deep breath, drinking in her sweet, heady scent, and then felt his senses swim as if he were intoxicated.

He watched as her eyelashes fluttered open and gazed down into her beautiful eyes. Then, seeing the color rise in her face when she realized where she was, he kissed her quickly on the forehead and said, "Good morning."

"Good . . . good morning," Melissa replied, still feeling half dazed and half embarrassed.

She pushed away from Reid and knelt, looking out of the lean-to. Then she gasped as her eyes beheld the wondrous sight. The raindrops on the leaves of the trees glittered in the early morning sunlight, making the whole forest around them look as if he had been sprinkled with a million diamonds.

"Oh, Reid," she cried. "Isn't that the most beautiful sight you've ever seen?"

Reid sat up, his eyes never leaving her face. "Yes, it is."

Tearing his eyes away from the lovely vision, Reid glanced around the clearing. "I wonder where Nathan wandered off to."

"He's probably looking for dry firewood," Melissa replied.

Reid rose reluctantly. "Then I guess I'd better go help him."

Melissa watched as he walked away, a thoughtful look on her face. Twice recently, he had held her in his arms, once by the riverbank when she had cried, and again last night. But he had made no effort to kiss her either time. She didn't count the little kiss on the forehead he had just given her. That had been more like a brother's or friend's casual kiss. Did he still think her soiled? Was that what held him back?

But Melissa's didn't want to be friends with Reid. She still loved him. She wanted more, much more. A small sob tore from her throat. No, she wanted all of him.

Chapter Nine

Two days later, Melissa could hardly contain her excitement. She squirmed in her seat, her sparkling eyes glued to the riverbank. Nathan had said the cabin was right around the next bend of the river, and she couldn't wait to see it.

When the canoe rounded the bend, Melissa looked around anxiously. "I don't see any cabin."

Nathan chuckled, amused at her almost childlike excitement. "It's set back in the woods. Ain't no sense in every Injun going up and down this river knowing we're here."

As soon as the canoe was beached, Melissa scurried out and hurried up the hill. Nathan and Reid exchanged amused looks and followed her. When she veered in the wrong direction, Reid ran a few yards to catch up with her.

Catching her arm, he said, "Whoa, lady. You

can get lost in these woods if you don't know where you're going. The cabin is this way." He pointed to a path off to the left.

Melissa laughed at her own impatience and allowed Reid to guide her in the right direction. The woods were thick and dark at this point. From the corner of her eye, she saw a silver blur as an animal streaked toward them from the woods. "Look out!" she cried, instinctively crouching, her heart racing in fear.

She watched in horror as the animal lunged at Nathan, almost knocking him over, and then in disbelief, as he laughed and ruffled the hair on the huge animal's head. "Howdy, boy. Did you miss me?" he said, then he looked up at Melissa. "No need to be scared, Missy. This here is my dog."

Melissa felt weak with relief and a little foolish. "When I saw him coming from the woods like that, I thought he was a wolf," she explained.

Nathan grinned, still patting the dog's head. "He is. He's half wolf and half dog."

Melissa looked down at the huge dog. He was at least six feet long from the tip of his long, pointed muzzle to the end of his bushy tail. His brown eyes were flecked with green and blue and seemed to gleam even in the daylight. But it was his mouth, with its powerful jaws and long, wicked teeth, that caught her attention. She stared at those sharp teeth, teeth that could easily tear another animal, or a man, to pieces. She shivered. Then as the large animal sat back on his haunches, his tail thumping loudly and his eyes looking at Nathan with adoration, Melissa laughed at her fanciful thoughts. Why, he looked just like any other dog. Melissa had always liked animals and, without thinking, she reached down to pet him.

"I wouldn't do that, Missy," Nathan said in a sharp voice. "Wolf don't take to strangers. Why, it took two years before he even let Reid touch him."

Melissa's hand froze in midair. Before she could jerk it back, Wolf rose and started sniffing it.

"Don't make any sudden moves," Nathan said in a low, warning voice. "I reckon if Wolf wants to take a sniff of you, you'd better let him do it."

Melissa held her breath, her heart thudding wildly as visions of Wolf's sharp teeth flashed through her brain. And then, as Wolf started licking her hand, his tail wagging furiously, she almost collapsed with relief.

She crouched before the dog, petting him. "I think you're just teasing me about him being half wolf, Nathan. Why, he's as gentle as the old hound dogs back home."

Reid and Nathan stared at the dog in disbelief. "Well, I'll be damned," Nathan said. "And here I always thought he was a one-man dog."

Melissa heard the hurt in his voice. She looked up and said, "Maybe he's a one-man, one-woman dog."

Nathan grinned. "Well, if you're the one woman, I reckon I can share him."

Melissa continued to pet Wolf. "Do you always leave him here when you're gone? Don't you ever take him with you?"

"Only when I go visiting my Injun friends," Nathan replied. "Like I said, he don't take to strangers. Besides, he can take care of himself."

"But you'd think he'd get lonely all by himself," Melissa objected.

Reid laughed. "Don't start feeling sorry for Wolf. He's got the best of two lives. During the summers, he can roam at will, as free as any wild animal. Then in the winter, while his wild brothers are struggling to survive, he can doze by the fire, getting fat and lazy on handouts."

As they resumed their walk through the woods, Melissa was glad when the big dog trotted beside his master, his nose occasionally nuzzling Nathan's hand. Melissa was no fool. Despite what Nathan had said about sharing Wolf, she knew how some men were about their dogs. If their wife left them, they'd survive, but if their dog deserted them for another, they'd never get over it.

When Melissa first spied the cabin, a surprised look came over her face. Seeing it, Nathan said, "I hope you're not too disappointed with the cabin. We did warn you it was small."

"To the contrary," Melissa replied. "It looks bigger than I thought it would be."

"Well, we just built those two little rooms on each side this past summer," Nathan replied. "One for Reid and one for me." He gave his partner a resentful look. "That was Reid's idea. He claimed my snoring kept him awake. Never saw anyone get so cranky about a little noise like he does."

Melissa struggled to keep from giggling, remembering Nathan's loud snores the night they had slept in the lean-to.

As they stepped onto a small porch covered by a low overhang, Nathan said in a disgusted voice, "This little roofed porch was Reid's idea, too."

"Damned right," Reid replied. "I got tired of having snow dumped on my head every time I opened the door to look out. Besides, during rainy weather, the porch keeps mud from being tracked in."

As Nathan opened the door, Melissa asked in a surprised voice, "You don't keep the door locked while you're away?"

"No," Reid replied. "It's considered frontier courtesy to leave a cabin unlocked when you're not occupying it. That way, anyone in need of temporary shelter is free to use it."

"You're not afraid of them stealing?" she asked.

"Ain't nothing here worth stealing," Nathan replied. "Except a little food maybe. And they wouldn't take that unless they really needed it. Anything really valuable, like our traps, we cache before we leave."

"How do you hide them?"

"Nathan and I wrap our traps in oilskins and bury them," Reid explained. "We've got over a hundred fifty traps. At sixteen dollars apiece, that's too big an investment to risk someone stealing them. A little food we don't mind. But not our traps."

The inside of the cabin was dark, and Melissa had to wait until Reid and Nathan pushed open the shutters on the window before there was enough light to see by. She looked around the room curiously. The floor was wood-planked, and in the center of the room sat a long wooden table with log benches on each side. The only other furniture was a couple of crude chairs and a smaller table in one corner of the cabin. On the walls above this table, were open shelves for storing food, pots and pans, and cooking and eating utensils.

Melissa turned to the back of the cabin and gaped at the fireplace. She had never seen such a huge fireplace. It ran almost the entire length of the room. On the floor before it lay a big bearskin rug.

She turned back around and, for the first time, noticed the small window at the front of the cabin. Hardly believing what she saw, she walked up to it and touched one of the glass panes.

"That's another one of Reid's fancy ideas," Nathan explained. "He said he couldn't stand it in here in the winter with all the shutters closed and not being able to see out. He said it gave him . . ." He turned to Reid. "What did you call it?" he asked.

"Claustrophobia."

Nathan turned back to Melissa and grinned. "Sounds like some kinda god-awful disease, don't it?"

Melissa laughed. "But the window does lighten the room and the view is pretty," she said.

While the two men were unloading the canoe and carrying the supplies back to the cabin, Melissa swept and dusted. Then, finding two big wooden buckets, she headed for the river for water.

Reid, on his way up from the river with a load of supplies, saw her. "Where are you going?"

"To get fresh water."

"There's a spring right behind the cabin." He frowned at the two buckets. "But there's no need for you to tote water. Those buckets are heavy when they're full. I'll get it for you when we're through unloading the canoe."

Melissa was surprised at his almost chivalrous attitude. Then she laughed. "You don't need to do that, Reid. If there's one thing I'm good at, it's toting water."

Reid's frown deepened as he watched Melissa walking back to the cabin. He realized she had probably toted water at the Indian camp, but he didn't feel it was right for her to do it now. After all, she was a lady, and ladies didn't do such hard work.

Melissa found the spring encircled by willow saplings. It was just large enough to form a small pool and a little stream that meandered off into the woods. The water that bubbled up from its rocky bed was crystal clear and ice cold. Melissa, after months of drinking nothing but river water, thought she had never tasted anything so delicious in her whole life.

She filled the two buckets, then bent to lift them. She staggered under their weight. Reid was right. The full buckets were much too heavy for her. But she'd be damned if she'd ask him to tote her water. She emptied half of the water back into the pool and, lifting the buckets, walked back to the cabin.

As she walked to the cabin with the water buckets, she noticed a small shed off to one side. She eyed the shed curiously, wondering what it was used for. Then dismissing it from her mind, she turned her attention to a large pile of firewood neatly stacked against the cabin. She laughed, thinking that after the Indian camp, toting water and finding firewood were going to be a lark.

On Nathan's next trip up to the cabin, she said, "I'm through cleaning the cabin. Can I help carry the supplies?"

"My God, no! Reid's already having fits about you toting water. Why don't you start cooking supper?"

Melissa looked at the big fireplace warily. "I've never cooked in a fireplace. I'm not sure I know what all those hooks and things are for."

Nathan showed her how to build a fire in the fireplace and then explained the various hooks from which her cooking utensils could be hung and the built-in spit for broiling meat. He opened an iron door at one side of the fireplace, showing her the oven.

"An oven?" Melissa cried with delight. "How wonderful!"

"Yep. No more of these gritty ash cakes. I'll have to teach you how to bake cornbread and biscuits."

Melissa's mouth watered at the thought of flaky biscuits dribbled with molasses. She hadn't had that since the inn back in Franklin. It seemed impossible that that had been only a few months ago. After all that had happened to her, it seemed like it had been eons ago.

As Nathan left the cabin again, Melissa turned back to the fire and frowned. The fire seemed to be smoking badly. She glanced around the room, realizing it was rapidly filling with smoke. Coming back in, Nathan noticed it at the same time.

"Those damned birds!" he snorted in disgust. "They've been building their nests in the chimney again. Now, I've got to climb on the roof and clear out the chimney."

Melissa stood in the smoky cabin, her eyes stinging and her nose burning from the irritating smoke. She heard the scrape of Nathan's feet as he walked across the roof, and then miraculously, as if one huge gust of wind had blown through, the cabin cleared of all the smoke. It's a good thing I didn't try to start the fire myself, Melissa thought. I wouldn't have known what to do. Why, I might have burnt down the cabin! And I can just imagine Reid's reaction to that!

After Melissa had put her stew on to simmer, she started putting the supplies on the shelves. She was busy rearranging the shelves when Nathan walked in with another armful.

"Come look at this material I bought you, Missy," he said.

Melissa walked to the table and looked at the bolts of material. Her eyes widened with surprise. There were three bolts of different-colored calico and two bolts of solid-colored cotton, and, as Nathan had said, one did match the color of her eyes. Melissa looked at the material in amazement. Then suddenly, her eyes filled with tears.

"What's the matter, Missy," Nathan asked in a distressed voice. "Don't you like what I picked out?"

"Oh, Nathan, the material is lovely. I just realized that I can have five dresses. Five! Why, I'll be dressed like a princess."

Nathan couldn't believe his ears. Why, this girl must have had a whole closet full of dresses back in South Carolina, beautiful and expensive clothes made from silks, velvets, brocades, and frothy sheers. That she could be so happy with a few bolts of cheap cotton touched him deeply—and saddened him. Poor little Missy, he thought. She had not only lost her family and clothes, but her whole way of life, too.

Melissa spied two other bolts of cloth lying on the bench beside the table. One was a pale blue flannel and the other a soft, white cotton. "What's this?" she asked, picking the bolts up.

"I thought you could make some nighties out of that blue and some of those underthings you women wear out of the white," Nathan replied.

Melissa's eyes twinkled mischievously. "And how would a confirmed bachelor like you know about women's nightgowns and underwear?" she asked in a teasing voice.

Nathan's face turned deep red with embarrassment. "Well, I do have a sister, you know."

Melissa watched as Nathan shuffled his feet awkwardly and felt a deep affection for this rough yet gentle mountain man. Impulsively, she hugged

229

him and kissed him on the cheek. "Oh, Nathan, you're wonderful. Thank you so much."

Reid picked this inopportune minute to enter the cabin. Seeing Melissa hugging and kissing Nathan, he tensed, jealousy flaring in his feline eyes. "I hope I'm not interrupting anything," he said in a hard, clipped voice.

Nathan saw the angry look on Reid's face. He's jealous, he realized. The crazy young fool! Why, I'm old enough to be Missy's father, not to even mention my ugly face.

The idea of Melissa having any romantic notions about him was so ridiculous, Nathan laughed out loud. Reid glared at him, but Nathan grinned. "Missy was just thanking me for the material that I bought her."

"Yes," Melissa said in an excited voice. "I can hardly wait to make myself some new clothes and get out of this squaw's dress." She glanced down at the dress with disgust.

The thought of Melissa dressed in an honest-to-god dress tantalized Reid's imagination, but he was still irked at Nathan, despite his explanation. Reid resented the easy companionship between Nathan and Melissa, the way Melissa directed most of her conversation to Nathan, the way she sought him out when she wanted help with something. He never stopped to consider that Melissa turned to Nathan instead of him because the older man was consistent in his attitude and manner toward her while Reid bewildered her with his sudden swings of mood from cold rudeness to warm friendliness.

Reid shrugged, dropped the armload of supplies on the floor, and walked back out without further comment. Melissa stared at his back, wondering once again what had gotten into him?

That night after Melissa had finished washing and drying the dishes, Nathan said, "You can have my room, Missy."

"Oh, I couldn't take your room, Nathan," Melissa objected.

"Sure you can. I'd rather sleep in here by the fire anyway. Like I said, it was Reid's idea to build separate rooms, not mine."

Reid glowered at Nathan. Once again, his partner had beaten him to the draw. He had planned on offering Melissa his room.

Nathan lit a candle and led Melissa into the small room that lay off to one side of the cabin. Melissa looked around at the narrow room. Compared to it, the main room was luxurious. The only furnishing was a narrow cot built into one wall and a crude wooden table just large enough to hold the candle. She glanced at the hooks that hung on one wall, assuming that was where the clothes were hung, since there was no chest or closet.

"It ain't much," Nathan said. "Reid built his room bigger, but he's got a lot more junk than I do. Books and stuff."

Melissa didn't mention that Reid hadn't offered his room to her. "It will be fine, Nathan. All I really need is a place to sleep and change my clothes."

Nathan glanced at the open doorway. "I'll nail a blanket over that. It'll give you more privacy."

231

Later, Melissa lay on the narrow cot, thinking it was much more comfortable than it looked. In fact, with its thick padding of buffalo hides and rope springs, it was sheer heaven after sleeping on the hard ground. Yes, living in this cabin wouldn't be too bad at all, she admitted. Her life would certainly be much easier and more comfortable than it had been in the Indian camp.

She was just drifting off to sleep when the noise awakened her. Nathan's loud snores echoed off the cabin's walls, the noise intensified and multiplied as it bounced off the wood. Goodness, she thought, if it's this bad in here, what must it be like in the same room with him? No wonder Reid insisted on separate rooms. She giggled, turned on her side, and buried her head beneath the small pillow.

When Melissa walked into the main cabin the next morning, Nathan had already started the fire. Determined not to be outdone, Reid had carried in two buckets of fresh water.

As she was preparing breakfast, Melissa asked, "Will you start laying your traps today?"

Nathan answered before Reid could open his mouth. "Nope, the first thing we gotta do is chop more firewood."

"But I saw a big stack of firewood outside the cabin yesterday."

Again Nathan beat Reid to the draw. "That ain't gonna be near enough wood to last us all winter. Why, that's just a drop in the bucket. Ain't unusual for the temperature to go to thirty or forty below

232

up here. Takes a heap of wood to keep this cabin warm."

"What do you use that shed out in the back for?" she asked as she poured their coffee.

"We . . ." Reid started.

"That's where we're gonna store our pelts from now on," Nathan interrupted. "That's another one of Reid's ideas. He says the pelts stink. Seems his ears ain't the only thing that're oversensitive."

Reid glared at him. "The hell I'm oversensitive! If I'd had to spend one more winter with your snores and those stinking pelts, I wouldn't have any sense of hearing or smell left!"

Nathan shrugged. "What are you gonna do today, Missy?" he asked calmly.

"I'm going to start sewing on my dresses."

"Good idea," Nathan said. "You'll find the scissors, thread and needles up on that shelf up there." He pointed to the shelves where the supplies were kept.

As soon as Nathan and Reid had left and she had finished her morning chores, Melissa had gathered her bolts of material and laid them on the table. The turquoise she set aside. That would be saved for a special dress. What she needed now was everyday clothes. She picked up the bolt of red calico, rolled it out on the table, and began cutting.

Melissa had never sewed anything in her life. All of her clothes had been made by a seamstress. Once Melissa's measurements had been taken and the style and material picked out, Melissa never saw the woman again until she appeared with the

233

finished dress. So, knowing nothing of patterns, she cut the material by estimating the size and shape of the various pieces. She cut a bodice front and back, two sleeves, a collar, and a skirt.

To make matters worse, Melissa had always shunned the embroidery work the other young ladies did to pass their time. She preferred to be out riding her horse or snuggled up with a good book. Her long, uneven stitches showed her lack of experience in plying a needle. Those pieces of material that didn't fit together, she forced to fit, putting gathers where there shouldn't be gathers and tucks where there shouldn't be tucks. She sewed day and night for the next three days, muttering very unladylike curses when she pricked herself with the needle.

On the morning of the fourth day, she finally finished the dress and held it up to view it. She frowned. It certainly didn't look like any of her other dresses had looked. But then, she hadn't expected it to be perfect. I'll try it on, she decided.

She walked into her room and quickly stripped off her Indian tunic, then slipped on her new dress. She could tell by how it felt that it didn't fit right. The waist was too long, the bust too small, and there were big, uncomfortable lumps of material in the seams. She frowned, wishing she had a mirror she could see it in. Then maybe she could figure out what she did wrong. Tears of frustration and disappointment stung her eyes.

Maybe Reid has a mirror in his room, she thought. She turned and walked from her room and into the main cabin, then froze as Reid and Nathan opened the door and walked in.

Seeing her, both men came to an abrupt halt, a look of horrified astonishment on their faces. Then Reid blurted, "What in the hell is *that?*

Melissa fervently wished the ground would open up and swallow her. She fought back tears of humiliation as she clutched the bodice where it gaped open. "It's my new dress."

Reid looked at the dress in disbelief. It was a disaster. The top of one sleeve was a puckered mass that sat midway between her shoulder and neck, the other hung to her midarm. The collar was too big on one side and too small on the other. The side seams gaped open, showing generous amounts of skin in some places. The bottom of the bodice hung at a peculiar angle two inches below her waist, and the hem dragged the floor. The gathers in the skirt were uneven, in a feast or famine fashion—either none at all or big bunches of material.

Reid shook his head with disgust. "I think you'd better stick to your squaw's dresses and forget sewing, Melissa. I've never seen such a mess."

Melissa bit her lip to keep from crying. Proudly, she raised her head and turned to walk back to her room. She took one step, stumbled on the skirt, and heard a loud, tearing noise. Horrified that the dress would fall apart right before Reid's and Nathan's eyes, she gathered up the skirt and fled to her room.

Nathan glared at Reid. "What did you have to go and hurt her feelings for? She's been sewing on that dress day and night for the past three days."

Reid was already regretting his words. "I didn't mean to hurt her feelings. I was only trying to be honest." He ran his fingers through his thick hair, then said in an exasperated voice, "What did you expect me to say? Hell, you've got eyes in your head. Did you expect me to tell her it was pretty?"

"You didn't have to say nothing."

"Like you did?" Reid said sarcastically. "Hell, Nathan, she caught us by surprise. She saw the looks on our faces, and she's no fool. Saying nothing would have been just as bad."

Reid walked to the table, snatched up a piece of cornbread from a pan sitting there. "I'll settle on this for lunch. I'm not hungry anyway. I'll see you later."

After Reid had left, Nathan walked over to the doorway of Melissa's room and peaked around the blanket that hung there. Melissa sat on the cot, once more dressed in her squaw's dress, staring at the wall, a forlorn look on her face. The calico dress lay in one corner where she had tossed it.

"Missy? Can I come in?" Nathan asked in a hesitant voice.

Melissa looked around and saw Nathan. She smiled wanly and nodded.

"Don't pay no mind to Reid, Missy. Why . . ."

"No," Melissa interjected, "he was right when he said it was a mess." She glared at the pile of calico, then wailed, "Oh, Nathan, I don't know any more about sewing than I do cooking. I'm just . . . just hopeless, that's all."

236

"Now, that ain't true," Nathan said in a firm voice. "You're getting to be a fine cook."

"I am not! I burnt the cornbread last night."

Nathan chuckled. "So did I the first few times I cooked it. Besides, Wolf liked it."

Melissa smiled despite her misery. The cornbread had been so badly burnt it was unsalvageable, and she was forced to feed it to Wolf. The big dog had gobbled it up and then sat back on his haunches begging for more.

Nathan looked at the crumpled calico on the floor. "You're not gonna give up on sewing that easy, are you?"

"What else can I do? It's different with cooking. I've had you to teach me." She looked up at Nathan, a hopeful gleam in her eyes. "Unless you can sew, too."

Nathan frowned. "Nope. Can't sew. Can't even sew on buttons."

Melissa sighed deeply.

"You're just gonna have to teach yourself. Learn by trial and error."

"Trial and error? My God, Nathan, look at that mess! Even a child could have done better than that!"

"I think you're being too hard on yourself, Missy." He looked at the calico thoughtfully. "Now, I think I know where you made your mistake. You should have started on something simple. Like one of those nighties, maybe."

"A nightgown? Why, I couldn't sew a handkerchief," Melissa said in self-disgust.

"Sure you could. There ain't much difference in one of those nighties and that squaw's dress you're wearing. You could take your squaw's dress apart and use it as a pattern."

"Pattern?"

"Yep. Saw my sister do that once. She took an old dress and ripped it apart at the seams, then laid it on the material. I asked her why she'd took her dress apart, and she said she was using it as a pattern to cut by."

Melissa sat and pondered what Nathan had said. She sensed she had made some essential mistake even before she had started sewing. She could experiment. She certainly had enough material. She had assumed she could only get one dress from each bolt of material, but the bolts held much more than she had expected. If she made them as simple as the squaw's dress, she might get two or three dresses from each bolt. And she would start out on a nightgown, as Nathan had suggested. Even if it didn't turn out too well, she'd be the only one to see it.

"Maybe I'll give it one more try," Melissa said cautiously.

That night, she carefully ripped one of the squaw's dresses apart, noting how it was sewed together before she carefully removed each seam and neck facing. The next day, she laid out the flannel, placed the pieces of the tunic over it, and cut the material. She was amazed at how much easier the sewing was when the pieces fit, and because they did match, her stitches were much neater.

Melissa was rewarded for her efforts the first time she wore her nightgown to bed. It was much more comfortable than the bulky Indian tunic, as she had refused to sleep naked. I'll make the next one floor-length, she promised herself. Then when I'm in bed I can wrap my feet up in it and keep them warm, too.

By the time she had made her third gown, her stitches were much better. Now I'm ready for my first dress, she thought. But I'll keep them simple. I'll make them exactly like the Indian tunics.

When the dress was finished, Melissa studied it critically and decided it looked good enough to wear in front of Reid and Nathan. She could hardly wait to surprise them, for she had kept her sewing a secret, not wanting them to know if she made another mess.

Because Melissa was so proud of her accomplishment, she decided her surprise called for a general celebration, a party. And today would be the perfect day, for Reid and Nathan would be gone the whole day setting their traps in preparation for winter. She'd have all day to prepare for it.

As soon as the men had left that morning, she cleaned the main cabin until it sparkled. Then she seasoned the venison haunch and slipped it into the oven to roast. After putting her beans on to simmer, she pulled on the men's jacket Nathan had brought for her and went outside.

War Eagle watched from the woods as Melissa gathered greens and wildflowers in the small meadow behind the cabin. Thus far, he had been unable to slip his woman away. She never wandered far from the cabin, and one or the other of the two trappers was always nearby.

When Melissa went back into the cabin, War Eagle looked around, wondering when the two trappers would return. Then his sharp eyes spied one of them in the far distance, walking toward the cabin. Feeling a keen sense of disappointment, he turned and walked back to the cave he had discovered. He would try again tomorrow.

Inside the cabin, Melissa arranged the goldenrod, purple-fringed gentian, and pale lavender asters in a bowl of water and set it on the table. Then she turned her efforts to herself. And first would be her bath.

She shoved and pushed until she had the heavy tub in front of the fireplace and then added the buckets of water she had been heating. Then, placing the towel and soap on the hearth nearby, she stripped and stepped into the tub. After she had washed, she sat back and sighed with contentment. She could hardly wait until Reid and Nathan returned that evening and saw her special supper sitting on the table with the pretty flower arrangement. Then she would make her grand entrance. She visioned their surprised faces when they saw her new dress and fantasized over what compliments they would give her, particularly Reid.

The door slammed open, and a gust of cold wind blew in. Melissa squealed in surprise and sat bolt upright in the tub. Then, seeing Reid standing in the doorway, she quickly covered her breasts and huddled forward. "What are you doing here?" she gasped.

Reid was stunned by the beautiful sight that greeted him. With her dark hair piled on top of her head in a mass of curls and the firelight dancing over her naked shoulders and arms, Melissa was a vision of loveliness, one that he was determined he wasn't going to be cheated of enjoying.

He shut the door and stripped off his jacket, saying in a casual voice, "I finished early."

Melissa watched in disbelief as he hung his jacket, then walked to the fireplace. "Don't let me disturb you," he said.

She crouched lower, her arms clasped tightly across her breasts, as Reid poured a cup of coffee and walked to the table. Then, as he sat down on one of the benches, she snapped, "You're not going to stay in here?"

Reid leaned both arms on the table, holding the steaming cup in both hands before him, his golden eyes slowly roaming over her shoulders and arms. "Why not?" he asked in a husky voice. "I've seen you naked before. At least, the top half."

Memories of the night by the river at Franklin rushed back, and Melissa flushed hotly. Reid saw her flush and grinned. "I see you remember."

Melissa glared at him. He chuckled, then noticed the flower arrangement on the table. "What's the occasion?"

Damn him! Damn him! Melissa thought furiously. Not only was he determined to embarrass her, but he'd ruin her surprise, too. "Nothing!" she

241

snapped.

Melissa glared at him, and Reid smiled back innocently. "You could at least go to your room until I'm finished," she said angrily.

"No, I don't think so," Reid replied in a bland voice. "You see, it's cold in my room and I'm chilled to the bone. I'd much rather stay in here where it's nice and warm."

"Then turn your back so I can get out!" Melissa demanded.

Reid took a sip of coffee, then grinned a slow, lazy grin. "Nope."

Melissa knew it was pointless to argue, and the bathwater was rapidly cooling. She carefully reached for the towel and then stood up, wrapping it around her as quickly as she could.

Reid caught a tantalizing glimpse of her entire body and then feasted his eyes on what the skimpy towel didn't cover. His breath caught in his throat. He felt a familiar tightening in his loins.

As Reid's golden eyes slid over her body, Melissa flushed, and not from embarrassment. Her knees seemed to turn watery, so weak she could barely walk to her room.

Even after Melissa had left the room, the vision of her standing practically naked in front of him continued to tease Reid's mind. His body reacted to the mental picture until he was at full arousal. Muttering oaths, he rose and walked painfully to the door. Grabbing his coat, he slammed out of the cabin.

"That was a fool thing to do," Reid muttered

under his breath as he walked, hoping the brisk air would help cool him off. Reid had been fighting his attraction to Melissa, deliberately avoiding her as much as possible. Not that that had helped any. When he wasn't around her, he was haunted by visions of her and memories of how she had felt in his arms. Now he had a new mental image to tease and taunt him and no one to blame for it but himself.

Reid wanted her more than he had ever desired any woman. But what held him back wasn't that he felt her soiled, as Melissa imagined. No, there were several reasons why Reid refused to give in to his body's demands for physical release.

In the first place, he had sworn never to fall in love again. That had happened once, and he had been badly burned. Besides, in his present position, marriage was out of the question, and over the past six weeks, he had come to admire Melissa too much to simply use her. She deserved more than just a casual affair.

The second thing that held Reid back was the look of raw terror he had seen in Melissa's eyes the day he had threatened to force her against her will. Reid feared that whatever happened to her in the Indian camp might have permanently scarred her, left her with a fear of physical intimacy with any man. The last thing he wanted to do was to add to that fear. She needed time to forget.

And time was going to be a problem. He didn't know how he was going to survive being practically isolated with her and hold to his resolve not to touch her. It was going to be a long, miserable winter. Reid scoffed at himself. Christ! That was an understatement if he ever heard one. It was going to be sheer hell.

Reid walked a long time and pondered his problem. By the time he returned to the cabin, it was dark. He opened the door and met two pairs of glowering eyes.

"Where in the hell have you been?" Nathan asked angrily from the table where he and Melissa sat and were already eating. "Missy made us a special supper tonight, and now it's turned cold."

Reid resented Nathan's tone of voice. Besides, he had asked Melissa if the flowers were for a special occasion and she had denied it. He slammed the door, jerked off his coat, and hung it on the hook by the door. "I had something to do," he said coldly.

He walked across the room and, totally ignoring Nathan and Melissa, dished up a plate of food, sat down, and began eating.

Nathan glared at him as he ate. "Missy wore one of her new dresses tonight. Don't she look pretty?" The last was accompanied by a swift kick in Reid's shin under the table.

The last thing Reid needed was anyone reminding him of how pretty Melissa was. He had just spent four miserable hours walking in the cold trying to forget that very thing. He glanced quickly at Melissa, then away. "Yeah, she looks real nice."

Melissa couldn't hide her hurt over Reid's indifference to her new dress any more than she could her disappointment when he didn't show up for supper on time. Nathan saw the look on her face, and it made him even angrier at Reid. Bastard! he thought hotly. He's always hurting her. For two cents, I'd take a whip to him.

As soon as Reid was finished eating, he rose and walked toward his room. "I'm turning in early tonight. I've got a long day ahead of me tomorrow."

Melissa watched as Reid walked across the room. She couldn't believe his rudeness. Tears stung at her eyes. A lot of good it did you to try and get his attention, she thought bitterly. Why, he's so wrapped up in himself, he doesn't even care about anyone else's feelings.

Anger came to her defense. Well, I'll be damned if I'll ever try to please him again, she thought hotly. He isn't worth the effort. I hate him!

For the next few days, Melissa, goaded by her hurt and anger, snapped at Reid anytime he came near. Reid was already riding the crest of his sexual frustration and was more than ready to lash back. Tempers flew, and the small cabin reverberated with their angry verbal outbursts.

Nathan, caught in the middle, felt like he was trapped in a cage with two snarling, spitting wildcats. He even stopped being protective of Melissa, for he discovered that when her temper was up, she was more than a match for Reid, meeting each dark, angry look, each barb, each biting insult with one of her own.

Finally Nathan had had enough. If the two young fools didn't know what was eating them, he sure did. They both wanted each other and were fighting it tooth and toenail. He decided what they needed was to be left alone and let nature take its course. They would either break down and make love—or kill each other!

When Nathan announced his plan to visit his Indian friends for a few days, Reid exploded. "You're what?"

"I said I'm gonna go visit Chief Rainwater for a few days," Nathan replied calmly. "I don't know why that surprises you. I always visit his village a couple of times each year."

"Not this early, you don't," Reid retorted. "You don't usually get randy until later in the season."

Nathan ignored Reid's remark. He'd never made any bones about the reason for his visits to the Blackfoot camp. Years ago, Chief Rainwater's daughter had taken a liking to him, and Nathan wasn't a man to turn down something so freely offered. "Well, I am this year, so I'm going."

"You're going to go off and leave me with *her?*" Reid motioned to the cabin where Melissa was.

"Missy?" Nathan said in an innocent voice. "Why, you act like she's some kinda monster or something."

"Shrew is the better word!"

"Yeah?" Nathan snapped back with a sneer. "Well, in case you ain't noticed, you ain't been so easy to live with, either."

Reid glared at him, his eyes glittering.

Nathan returned his hard look and said in a determined voice, "I've made up my mind. I'm going

246

and that's that."

Melissa wasn't happy about Nathan's announcement, either. As she watched him walking away with Wolf loping happily at his side, she wondered how she was going to stand being around Reid for the next few days without Nathan to act as a buffer.

The day Nathan left, Reid stayed away from the cabin until the cold and darkness forced him inside. Melissa placed his plate before him without a word, and as soon as he was finished eating, she snatched it up, washed and dried it, and put it away.

Then she turned, saying in a cold, clipped voice, "I'm going to bed."

But Melissa couldn't sleep. She tossed and turned, silently railing at Reid and then at Nathan for deserting her. Even after she had expended her energies, she couldn't sleep. To her surprise, she realized she was cold.

Nathan must have fed the fire periodically at night, she realized. And since he was not there, it had probably gone out. She rose and peeked around the blanket nailed to her doorway, looking at the fire. Only a few coals glowed in the fireplace. Otherwise the room was completely dark.

She peered around the darkened room and, seeing no sign of Reid, assumed he must have retired also. She walked across the cold floor and picked up a log, placing it in the fireplace. The wood sputtered, and then as the fire flared, she added a second log.

She stood before the small fire, warming her

hands and enjoying the feel of the warm heat surrounding her. The warmth felt so good she hated to leave it. No wonder Nathan preferred sleeping in here, she thought. She watched as the orange and blue and green flames in the fire flickered and danced, casting eerie shadows over the cabin's ceiling and walls.

The same cold that had chased Melissa from her bed had awakened Reid. He rose and pulled on his pants, then padded silently into the main cabin. He stopped in mid-stride when he saw Melissa standing before the fire.

With her long, black hair tumbling down her back and the firelight shining through her gown and outlining every curve of her soft, feminine body, she was a breathtaking, beautiful vision. For a minute, Reid stood and gazed at her hungrily. Then, as if drawn by some powerful, invisible magnet, he walked toward her.

Melissa didn't hear Reid until he was standing directly behind her. She whirled and, then realizing it was Reid, gasped. "Oh, you frightened me. I didn't hear you come in."

Reid didn't reply. He stood, towering over her, his golden eyes roaming over each feature of her shadowed face.

The fire cracked and popped as Melissa drank in Reid's male beauty. The firelight picked up the reddish highlights of his hair and played across his bronzed shoulders and chest. His golden eyes glowed with a warmth of their own. To her, he looked like some primeval god, dangerous and exciting.

Reid raised one hand and gently pushed a lock of Melissa's hair back behind her ear, his finger tracing that delicate shell of flesh. One slender finger trailed along her jawline and then lightly stroked her full lower lip. Shivers of delight ran up Melissa's spine.

His hand slid up her throat, those long fingers threading through her hair as he cupped the back of her head and lifted it for a kiss. He nibbled at the tiny mole that was so enticing, then the sensitive coners of her mouth before his warm lips covered hers, softly playing and coaxing. The tip of his tongue brushed her bottom lip, slowly back and forth, back and forth, sending tingles of pleasure over her and making the bones in her legs turn to water, then probed, and finally, feverishly explored the warm recesses of her mouth as he pulled her into a tight embrace, molding her soft body to his hard, muscular one.

A warmth rushed over Melissa. Her skin tingled everywhere, as if every nerve ending in her body was suddenly on fire. She leaned into him, wanting more, much more.

Reid broke the kiss and looked down at Melissa's face, his eyes searching for any sign of fear or revulsion. Her turquoise eyes were warm and hazy with passion, her lips parted in open invitation. Realizing that she wasn't averse to his touch, his fears flew out the window. The rigid control he had held over his desire shattered. A primitive groan escaped his lips as he tightened his embrace and his mouth captured hers in a deep, possessive, ravishing kiss that gave full rein to his passion.

Melissa's senses swam as Reid's artful tongue sensuously slid in and out of her mouth, mimicking the intimate act that would follow and exciting Melissa unbearably. He kissed her as if he were a part of her, bringing her to her tiptoes in a silent, eloquent plea for more, until her breath came in short, ragged gasps and a burning ache began to build between her legs.

Their lips still locked in the passionate kiss, he drew her to the floor, laying her on the bearskin rug and halfway covering her body with his own. Melissa's arms curled across his broad shoulders, and one hand tangled in his hair, drawing him closer. His tongue danced down the throbbing pulse at her throat before he buried his head in the crook of her shoulder, nipping and supping at the sensitive skin there. Melissa's hands feverishly explored his muscular back and shoulders, as if she could absorb him with her fingertips.

"Your gown," Reid muttered in a husky voice. "Take off your gown."

Dazed, Melissa sat up while Reid deftly drew the gown over her head and tossed it aside. Then laying her back on the rug, his eyes slowly roamed over every curve and hollow of her body, lingering on those delights that had been so long denied him. Melissa melted as that warm, golden gaze leisurely devoured her.

"You're beautiful, Melissa," Reid said in a deep passion-filled voice. "Every curve a perfection."

Melissa raised her arms, drawing Reid back down to her. She thrilled to the feel of his naked chest against her, the crisp hairs tickling her sensitive nipples. He kissed her mouth softly again and again, before he dropped light, nibbling kisses down her throat and across her shoulders, slowly descending inch by inch until Melissa felt she would scream with frustration before he reached his ultimate goal. Then, as his tongue lazily circled one throbbing nipple, then flicked it while he rolled the other between his thumb and forefinger, Melissa gasped, quivering all over.

She caught the back of his head as his ardent tongue and mouth played at her breasts, laving, nipping, supping. Melissa gloried in the delicious sensations he was invoking, awash in a shimmering warmth that ebbed and flowed, then, when his teeth ever so gently grazed one tender nipple, feeling as if a bolt of fire had rushed to that secret woman's place between her thighs, leaving her aching and burning with need.

His hands slowly swept down the entire length of her body in one sensuous caress that took her breath away. Then, when his hand slipped between her thighs, she arched her hips in anticipation of his touch, a strangled cry escaping her lips as his fingers slipped through the soft, moist folds and found the core of her womanhood, stroking, circling, teasing the tiny bud. Wave after wave of exquisite sensation washed over her, each more intense than the last, spasms rocking her body as a liquid fire burned clear to the soles of her feet.

Her response and the feel of her beneath his fingers, hot and wet and throbbing, was driving Reid wild. Impatiently, he tore at the lacings on his pants with his other hand and slipped them off, kicking them away. Trembling with need, he rose over her, his knee nudging her legs apart, positioning himself between her soft thighs.

Melissa was floating on a warm cloud of pure sensation. She opened her eyes and saw Reid kneeling over her. Slowly her eyes roamed over his handsome features, the breadth of his shoulders, then down to the dark hair on his chest, following that line of hair that narrowed and then flared again at his groin. Her eyes widened, seeing that bold, rigid flesh, seemingly enormous, the tip glistening in the firelight. Memories of the night Two Feathers had attacked her flashed through her mind. Her eyes filled with terror and she whimpered in stark fear.

Reid saw the look on Melissa's face. He couldn't stop, now now, not at this point. But he couldn't consummate their loving, either, not while she was so terrified of that part of him.

He leaned forward. "I won't hurt you, Melissa. I promise," he said.

Melissa jerked her eyes from him and turned her head away.

"Do you trust me?" Reid asked.

Of course she trusted him. She loved him heart and soul. But she couldn't let him put . . . *that* in her. She chewed her bottom lip, feeling torn, then muttered, "Yes, but . . . but—"

"Melissa, look at the me," Reid commanded

gently.

Melissa turned her head and looked into his eyes.

Reid shook his head. "That's not what I mean, and you know it. You know where I want you to look."

"No! I don't want to look at it."

Reid leaned forward and pulled her into a sitting position. He caught the back of her head and gently forced her head down. "Don't be afraid of it. It's not the organ that's dangerous. All it can do is get hard and rigid. It's the man using it that determines whether or not it's an instrument of pain or pleasure. It's just another part of me. Just like my hand." His hand slipped from her head, slowly caressing her back and making Melissa shiver with delight. "You're not afraid of my hand, are you?"

"No," Melissa admitted, only too aware of what wonderful sensations his hand was invoking, the fingers now stroking one breast. But she wasn't too sure about comparing his hand to his manhood. It seemed to have a life of its own. She could actually see it throbbing.

Reid sat back on his heels. "Touch it."

Melissa's face turned deathly pale. "No!"

Silently, Reid took one of her hands and guided it down, forcing it over him and firmly holding it so she couldn't pull away. Melissa was surprised at the almost velvety texture of the skin. Then, as it stirred, seeming to grow even larger in her hand, a fresh tingle of fear ran over her. Stop it! she thought. It can't jump off Reid's body and attack you.

And then, the tingle of fear was replaced with something else, a strange excitement, Reid's throbbing member seeming to set up an answering throb within her. Without even realizing it, she began stroking it of her own accord.

Reid groaned, saying in a thick voice, "Oh, God, Melissa, that feels so good. Don't stop."

Melissa knew that Reid was experiencing all those feelings he had brought her when he had touched her so intimately, and that pleased her. She wanted to return all those pleasures he had given her.

Then, as the strange excitement grew and the burning throbbing became almost unbearable, she wondered what it would feel like inside her. Suddenly, she wanted him—all of him.

She looked up and saw Reid's golden eyes on her. "Reid," she whispered raggedly, "I want . . . I want—"

Reid lowered her to the bearskin, saying huskily, "I know what you want. I want it, too. Oh, God, how I want it!"

She laced her fingers in the curls at his nape and whispered, "Then love me, Reid."

With a small, exultant cry, Reid's mouth locked over hers in a deeply passionate kiss that played havoc with Melissa's senses. He entered her slowly, fighting for control to keep from plunging in as he felt her throbbing heat surrounding him. And then he felt it, that thin membrane that obstructed his penetration. His mind flashed warning signals, and briefly he hesitated. But his body refused to obey the signals his brain was sending, refused to be denied. With a will of its own, it continued its onslaught, and as the membrane tore, Reid slid into the soft, moist void, filling her completely.

Melissa cried out as a sharp pain tore through her loins and then relaxed as Reid muttered incoherent, soothing words, his hands caressing her while he waited for her to become accustomed to the feel of him inside her. And then, as he began to move inside her, slowly and sensuously, then gaining momentum, rocking their bodies in that ancient rhythm, her eyes filled with wonder at the new sensations beginning to assault her senses. Her body became an agony of throbbing anticipation, an anticipation that grew more and more urgent. She wrapped her legs around him, holding him closer, as her senses began to spin dizzily and a roaring filled her ears. But then, as Reid groaned and stiffened above her, and then collapsed weakly over her, those sensations fled, leaving her feeling strangely disappointed and confused.

As Reid slowly drifted down from those rapturous heights, his mind, once more in control, whirled in disbelief. A virgin? That was impossible. Even if there had been any doubts in his mind, her fear of his erection earlier would have convinced him. She hadn't been shocked by what she had seen, as he would expect a virgin to react. She had been utterly terrified, behaving just as a woman who had been raped would have.

Reid rolled from her and looked down at her

thighs. Seeing the telltale blood smears, evidence beyond a doubt, the full impact of what he had done hit him.

He looked up and scowled down at her face. "You have some explaining to do, Melissa," he said tersely.

Melissa was still in a daze. "What?" she muttered.

"Goddammit, you were a virgin! You were in that Indian camp for months and yet you were still a virgin. How do you explain that?"

So, we're back to the virgin business again, Melissa thought bitterly. "What difference does it make if I was or wasn't?"

"What difference?" Reid asked in disbelief. "Dammit, a man has a right to know he's making love to a virgin."

"Then it displeased you? You didn't want me if I was a virgin?"

The outright question hit Reid like a kick in the gut. No, he wasn't displeased. He felt an exhilaration in knowing that he had been the first, the only man. But he felt guilty, too, guilty that he had taken the gift she could only give once and taken it unknowingly until it was too late to turn back.

"You're evading my question, Melissa. You led me to believe you weren't a virgin. Now explain!"

Melissa's eyes flashed. "I did not lead you to believe any such a thing! You decided *that* in your own mind. I told you I was still a virgin, that I hadn't been raped, but you wouldn't believe me — calling me a liar again!"

256

ACCEPT YOUR **FREE GIFT** AND EXPERIENCE MORE OF THE PASSION AND ADVENTURE YOU LIKE IN A HISTORICAL ROMANCE

Zebra Romances are the finest novels of their kind and are written with the adult woman in mind. All of our books are written by authors who really know how to weave tales of romantic adventure in the historical settings you love.

Because our readers tell us these books sell out very fast in the stores, Zebra has made arrangements for you to receive at home the four newest titles published each month. You'll never miss a title and home delivery is so convenient. With your first shipment we'll even send you a **FREE** Zebra Historical Romance as our gift just for trying our home subscription service. No obligation.

BIG SAVINGS AND **FREE** HOME DELIVERY

Each month, the Zebra Home Subscription Service will send you the four newest titles as soon as they are published. (We ship these books to our subscribers even before we send them to the stores.) You may preview them *Free* for 10 days. If you like them as much as we think you will, you'll pay just $3.50 each and *save $1.80 each month* off the cover price. *AND you'll also get FREE HOME DELIVERY.* There is never a charge for shipping, handling or postage and there is no minimum you must buy. If you decide not to keep any shipment, simply return it within 10 days, no questions asked, and owe nothing.

Affix
stamp
here

Reid winced, remembering the night at the trading fair when Melissa had denied she been raped. He felt like a first-class heel. "I'm sorry," he said lamely, then added in frustration, "but everyone knows the Indians rape their female captives, even if they're old and ugly as sin. Now, how in the hell did you manage to escape that fate?"

Melissa resented his question. It probed too deeply. She didn't want to tell him of her humiliating, painful experience, or be reminded of it. She pushed away from him and sat up, reaching for her gown.

Reid sat up and jerked the gown from her. His eyes glittered as he said in a threatening voice, "Answer me!"

Melissa couldn't stand being naked in front of him now. It made her feel too vulnerable. "Let me have my gown first."

Reid threw the gown over her shoulders. Melissa clutched it to her tightly. "Well?" he asked in a demanding voice.

Damn him! Why did he have to be so persistent? "All right! I'll tell you. Two Feathers did try to rape me, but I . . ."

"Yes?" Reid prompted.

Melissa refused to feel shame any longer. Dammit, it was Two Feathers' crime, not hers! "I found a knife hidden under the pallet. I cut him with it. *There.* I think I must have permanently damaged him. He never tried it again."

She had cut him so badly she had left him impotent, Reid thought in surprise. It was a terrible

257

thing to happen to a man, but he couldn't feel any sympathy for the Indian. Any man who used his sex as a weapon, to degrade and inflict pain, deserved punishment for his crime. And what could be more fitting justice than to lose the use of the very organ he had misused? And who but Melissa, with her proud spirit and fierce determination, could turn the tables on her rapist, disarming him in such an appropriate and effective manner? He sat back on his heels and laughed.

Melissa was horrified at his laugh. "It wasn't funny!"

Reid sobered instantly. "I wasn't laughing at what happened to you, Melissa. I know it must have been terrifying for you. But don't you see? You inflicted more pain and humiliation on him than he did on you. He attacked you and yet you got the best of him. I guess I was laughing because I was proud of you."

Melissa still didn't think it was a laughing matter. "It was horrible! There was blood everywhere. And then . . ." Melissa didn't want to tell him about the beating that followed. She didn't ever want him to see that ugly scar on her back.

"Then what?" Reid asked.

She looked away from Reid's penetrating look. "Nothing."

Reid frowned. He caught her shoulders and forced her to look at him. "Melissa, what were you going to say?"

Melissa jerked her shoulder and twisted away. When she did, the gown slipped, and Reid got a brief glimpse of the very thing Melissa had wanted to hide from him. Melissa saw his glance, and it horrified her. She grabbed the gown and quickly tried to cover herself.

Without a word, Reid turned her, holding her firmly while she tried to twist away. He looked down at the hideous scar and said between clenched teeth, "Did he do this to you?"

"No, his wife did," Melissa answered in a half sob. "For what I did to him."

"My God! What did she use?"

"A quirt. A leather strap of some sort."

Reid stared at the long, deep scar. It was a wonder she hadn't been crippled, and what terrible pain she must have suffered.

Melissa looked over her shoulder, tears of shame in her eyes. "Please, don't look at it. It's so ugly," she pleaded.

Reid's golden eyes rose to meet hers. "There is nothing, *absolutely nothing,* ugly about you, Melissa," he said in a quiet voice. Then he bent his head, and Melissa watched in disbelief and he kissed the length of the scar.

His surprising, tender act touched Melissa as nothing else could have. And then when his mouth trailed soft kisses up her back to her nape, she shivered with pleasure.

His warm breath fanned her neck as he whispered in her ear, "Didn't I tell you you were beautiful?"

He nibbled her earlobe and then teased her ear with his tongue, gently probing. His hands crept around her and cupped her breasts, his long fingers caressing those mounds, then teasing the rosy tips, sending delicious heat waves coursing through her body.

"Reid," she breathed.

He rolled her to the bearskin and looked down at her. "I should apologize for taking your virginity, Melissa, but I won't. Because I can't regret it." He smiled. "And now, sweetheart, I'm going to make you a woman."

"But I am a woman now," Melissa objected.

"A woman, yes. But not a complete woman. Not yet. Not until you've known the sublime ecstasy of total fulfillment. Not until you've experienced that ultimate of all sensations."

"I don't understand," Melissa muttered.

"I know you don't." His golden eyes shimmered as he said with a voice heavy with desire, "But I promise you, you will."

And that was one promise that Reid kept. He kissed her slowly, sensuously, until she was breathless, and then his lips and tongue and hands caressed and tantalized, seeking and finding all those spots on her body that brought her exquisite pleasure, until her senses were swimming, her pulses pounding, her blood flowing like liquid fire. Perspiration broke out in a fine sheen over her sensitized skin. She moaned and whimpered, then gasped as new sensations engulfed her, but still he continued his sweet-savage assault, stoking that flame of desire until it was a blazing fire that threatened to consume her.

There was no pain when he entered her this time, filling her completely. And Melissa, who thought she couldn't possibly stand any more of this exquisite torture, couldn't possibly feel any more sensations, was jolted as shock wave after shock wave traveled up her spine with each powerful, masterful stroke. The earth seemed to turn on its axis, spinning crazily, as she was thrown upward into a swirling vortex, that terrible, urgent pressure inside her building, intensifying unbearably, until it burst through, sending blinding flashes of light through her brain and rocking her body in spasms of ecstasy.

Reid hovered over her, carefully watching the expressions on her face as he carried her up that rapturous ascent. Not until he saw her eyes fly open with the wonder of it, heard her cry and felt her spasms contract his own feverish, pulsating flesh, did he allow his steely control to break. With one powerful, deep thrust, he followed her to his own shattering release.

For a long while they lay, their ragged breaths rasping in the silent cabin, still locked in that sweet embrace, Reid's head buried in the crook of her soft neck. Finally, Reid kissed her ear and raised his head to look down at her face.

Melissa looked up at him dreamily. She stroked those broad shoulders that glistened with perspiration in the firelight. She smiled, a contented, knowing smile, the smile of a woman who had just experienced total fulfillment. "And now I'm really a woman," she whispered in a wondrous voice.

261

Reid smiled back and tenderly pushed a wisp of damp hair from her forehead before he kissed her bruised mouth softly. "Yes," he muttered in a thick voice, "you're all woman."

Chapter Ten

Melissa awakened feeling like she was floating on a golden cloud. She pulled the warm blanket even closer, then stretched like a lazy, contented cat, enjoying the feel of the bearskin rug beneath her. Bearskin? Her turquoise eyes flew open. Suddenly remembering where she was, she bolted up and sat looking around the small cabin.

Seeing no sign of Reid, she glanced at the fireplace and noticed he had already stoked the fire. It burned brightly, sending delicious waves of heat out into the chilled room. The aroma of fresh brewed coffee teased her nostrils.

Memories of Reid's lovemaking the night before flooded back, making her flush hotly. Fresh tingles raced through her body as she remembered all those wonderous, exciting things he had done to to her when he introduced her to the mysteries and delights of physical love.

She stood, wrapping the blanket around her, and poured a cup of coffee. Sitting at the table, she drank the hot brew slowly, wondering what their relationship would be from now on. As much as she longed for Reid to return her love, Melissa didn't delude herself into believing he loved her just because he had made love to her. Maybe he didn't even care for her. Maybe he had just used her to satisfy his physical needs, and once they had been satiated, he would return to being the same rude, arrogant man.

Melissa winced at the thought. She couldn't stand that. After what they had shared, she couldn't go back to living under the strain of the relationship they had had, back to being the recipient of his hurting barbs and insults and his angry, hateful looks.

Another horrifying thought occurred to her. She had given herself completely, almost wantonly, that last time. She flushed with shame, remembering how she had clutched at him, begging him. What must he think of her? Surely no decent woman would behave so outrageously. And now, would he throw that in her face, too?

As the day progressed and Reid didn't return, Melissa became more and more apprehensive. She was so wrapped up with her gloomy thoughts that she didn't hear Reid when he came in, hung up his coat, and walked up behind her. Not until she felt his heat, smelled his exciting male scent, did she realize he had returned. She turned rigid with dread at what might be coming.

Reid slipped his arms around Melissa and pulled her back to him. He nuzzled her neck. "Hi, sweetheart."

Melissa knees buckled, whether from relief or the feel of Reid's lips nibbling her throat and his hand caressing her breasts, she couldn't say.

He buried his face in her hair. "That smells good."

"The stew?" Melissa asked, her voice sounding to her ears as if it came from far away.

Reid chuckled. "That, too." He turned her in his arms, and Melissa melted under that warm, golden gaze. "I've missed you today," he said in a deep, meaningful voice.

Melissa was stunned. Of all of thing she had anticipated, she certainly hadn't expected this warm, tender greeting. It bewildered her. She glanced at the table and saw the bouquet of wildflowers sitting there. "What's that?"

Reid glanced at the wildflowers and then back down at her. He grinned sheepishly. "A peace offering."

"Peace offering?"

"It's my way of apologizing for the way I've treated you. For all my insults. For my disgusting behavior."

Melissa stared at him wordlessly in disbelief.

She couldn't imagine Reid apologizing to anyone for anything, much less her.

"Don't look so shocked," Reid said in a half-angry tone of voice. "Believe it or not, I didn't enjoy hurting you."

When Melissa still stared at him, Reid turned and walked a few steps away, then ran his fingers through his thick hair. He whirled, saying in an exasperated voice, "Dammit, Melissa, have you any idea of what you've been doing to me? I've been going crazy trying to keep my hands off you."

"Oh, I can see your dilemma," Melissa said in a bitter voice. "You wanted me, and yet you didn't want me because I was soiled."

It was Reid's turn to be astonished. "Soiled?"

"You said you didn't want any man's leavings, particularly an Indian's," Melissa reminded him brutally.

"Oh, hell," Reid groaned, "this is going to be harder than I thought."

He sat on the bench and reached for Melissa's hand, pulling her to sit on his lap. She sat stiffly, staring straight ahead.

Reid cupped her chin in his hands and forced her to look at him. "I didn't mean those cruel words, Melissa. I couldn't stand the thought of another man touching you intimately. Thinking that you had been forced just made it worse. I was so furious, I didn't stop to think what I was

266

saying. I just lashed out. And unfortunately, you were the one who was hurt. That's what I'm apologizing for. That and all the other times I've hurt you because I reacted without thinking." He smiled wryly. "That's the trouble. When I'm around you, I can't think straight."

Melissa could understand that. She had the same problem around Reid. And what had been said and done was over with. It was best to bury it, try to forget it once and for all. Otherwise, it might ruin this new, fragile relationship before it even had a chance to grow. And she was wise enough to realize that's what Reid was trying to do, to start over with a clean slate between them.

She picked up the flowers and smiled. "They're lovely."

Reid's eyes searched her face. "Does that mean I'm forgiven?"

"Yes, you're forgiven," Melissa replied quietly.

Reid looked down at her beautiful eyes. He wanted her so much he ached. But he sensed this wasn't the right time. If he made love to her right now, she might think that was all he wanted from her, her body. But Reid wanted more than that. He wanted all of her.

Reid grinned. "Now that I'm forgiven, will you feed me, too?"

She laughed and rose, saying as she walked back to the fire, "You must be hungry if you're anxious to eat my cooking."

Reid frowned, then said, "I've been meaning to tell you how much better your cooking has become. Like that cornbread last night. It tasted better than mine or Nathan's ever had. What did you do to it?"

So he had noticed her little experiment with the cornbread. She beamed at his unexpected praise. "I put sugar in it."

After they had eaten, Reid helped her with the dishes, an act that surprised and pleased her. Then, while she was putting the beans in a bowl to soak for the next day, Reid went into his room and returned carrying a box.

Melissa watched curiously while he sat on the bearskin rug and opened the box. "What's that?" she asked.

"A little project I've been working on. But I'm afraid I've gone as far as I can without your help."

"My help?"

Reid grinned. "Come here," he said quietly.

Melissa knelt on the rug beside Reid and looked down at the box of colored beads and pieces of leather. Reid pulled out a long strip of leather and wrapped it around her waist.

"Perfect," he said. He looked up and smiled. "I had to guess at your size from memory. I remembered I could span your waist with both hands."

"But what would you want my waist size for?"

He grinned and reached into the box. "For these."

Melissa watched as he pulled out three beaded belts. "These are for me?"

"Yes. For your new dresses. If I remember correctly, there were three colors of calico. I made you a belt to match each color."

Melissa fingered the belts. She couldn't believe that Reid had made them for her. It must have taken hours and hours of work. Why, he must have been working on them for at least a week. She was touched by his thoughtfulness and relieved to know he couldn't have possibly made the belts since last night. Then she would have suspected they were payment for services rendered. She couldn't have borne that.

"Now, let me measure your foot," Reid said. "You're going to need some warm boots for this winter. Unless you're planning on staying inside all that time."

Melissa had no intention of staying in the cabin the entire winter. She removed her moccasin and placed her foot on the piece of leather as Reid directed her, then watched while he traced the outline on her foot. When his hand slipped up her leg, she gasped.

Reid chuckled and sat back on his heels. "I'll need your calf measurement, too."

"You could have at least warned me," Melissa

replied a little peevishly.

A devilish gleam lit in his eyes. "And spoil my fun?"

Reid's fingers sent warm tingles up Melissa's leg as he tied a leather strip around her calf and then slipped it off her leg and foot. She gritted her teeth against the sensation and sighed half with relief and half with disappointment when he sat back on his heels.

"Is that all?" she asked, shocked at her breathlessness.

"Yes," Reid answered as he gathered up his box of leather and beads. "You'll have your new boots in about a week."

As Reid started to walk back to the room, Melissa said, "Reid?"

He turned. "Yes?"

"Thank you for the belts and boots."

"You're welcome," he replied with a warm smile, then turned and walked to his room.

Melissa waited for his return for what seemed to her an eternity. What if he didn't come back? What if he had already gone to bed? His hand on her leg had lit a slow fire burning inside her, a fire that only he could quench. Damn him! Was he just going to leave her like this?

When Melissa was about to scream with frustration, Reid walked back into the room, this time carrying a blanket and two pillows. He tossed them on the rug and said in a casual voice, "Let's sleep in here by the fire tonight."

A wave of relief washed over Melissa, yet she didn't want Reid to see her eagerness. She nodded wordlessly.

Reid knelt and propped the pillows against the rolled-up blanket, then pulled Melissa down beside him and wrapped an arm around her shoulders.

Melissa was disappointed when Reid made no effort to kiss her, and then as the heat from the fire and his body surrounded her, she relaxed, enjoying the feel of just being in his arms. She sighed with contentment and looked around the cabin dreamily.

"Are all of the trapper's cabins so warm and cozy?" she asked.

"Most of the trappers don't build cabins. They spend the winter with friendly Indians or in a cave, providing they can find one that some wild animal hasn't already claimed. A few may build a temporary structure, but nothing as substantial as this because they move around from year to year. But when Nathan and his old partner found this particular spot, with its abundance of beaver and other fur-bearing animals, they figured they could trap here for years and years without the supply of pelts diminishing. That's the only reason they decided to build permanently."

"But when will you actually begin trapping?"

"We've already taken a few mink."

"Mink?" Melissa asked in surprise. "I thought you only trapped beaver."

"No, although prime beaver pelts bring the best prices. But beaver and muskrat aren't in their prime until early spring, when the ice melts and they come out of their dens. So, until then, we trap land animals." He laughed. "When I accepted Nathan's offer to become his new partner, I thought the same thing you did. We'd just trap beaver. Was I in for a surprise when I found out we'd be trapping everything—and what an education. I thought trapping was simple. I didn't know that different traps, baits, even skinning methods, were used for different animals. Nor did I realize the pelts had to be scraped and stretched on a board to dry. I never realized there was so much work involved."

Melissa laughed, remembering how hard she had labored over the buffalo hides she had scraped and cured in the Indian camp. "But at least you don't have to rub them with brains to soften them, like you do a buffalo hide."

Reid frowned, then sat up and looked down at her. "How did you know that?"

Melissa laughed, enjoying his look of surprise. "Because that's what I had to do to three buffalo hides in the Indian camp. After I had scraped them," she added, feeling a little twinge of pride in her accomplishment.

Reid laughed. "Well, I be damned. If I had known that, I wouldn't have had to sneak out into the woods to tan your buckskin. I thought you would be repulsed if you knew brains were used to tan them and refuse to wear them."

"What buckskin?"

"The buckskin I've been tanning for you to make a new skirt from."

"A skirt?"

"Sweetheart, you can't run around outside in the snow in just a jacket and boots and a thin cotton dress in between. That would leave a lot of skin without proper protection. I thought you could wear a long buckskin skirt over your dress when you went out."

Melissa was astonished. She had thought he didn't care a thing about her, while all along he had been secretly working on things that would please her or add to her comfort.

"Do you think you can do it?" Reid asked.

"What?" Melissa asked, still distracted by her thoughts.

"Make a skirt from the buckskin."

Melissa thought about it. She had more confidence in her sewing skills now that she had made a few garments successfully. But first she'd experiment on a piece of calico. She wasn't going to make that mistake twice. Then a new though occurred to her. "But what will I sew it with? I can't use a needle and thread on buckskin."

"We have a special needle and heavy thread we use to sew the nail holes in our pelts. You can use them."

A minute of silence passed. Then she looked at Reid. Somehow, "thank you" seemed inadequate for all of his thoughtfulness. She muttered, half to herself, "About the buckskin, I don't know what to say."

"Then don't say anything," Reid replied. He lay back down on the bearskin rug beside her and folded his arms under his head. Looking up at the ceiling, he said, "Of course I wouldn't be averse to you showing your appreciation in another way."

"What way?" Melissa asked suspiciously.

He turned, a wide grin on his face, a teasing look in his eyes. "A kiss would be nice."

Melissa's heart hammered in her chest at the thought. But she had never kissed a man. Been kissed, yes. But she had never initiated a kiss.

"You don't have to if you don't want to," Reid said when he saw her hesitancy.

Oh, but she did want to. She ached to feel those warm, sensuous lips of his against hers. Gathering her courage, she leaned over him and placed her lips on his, moving slowly, testing. A low groan rose from Reid's throat, a groan she felt rather than heard. His arms slipped around her, drawing her closer as he began to kiss her

274

back. The kiss grew warmer and warmer, until Melissa finally pulled away, her hands on Reid's chest as she looked down at him.

Reid smiled up at her. "Sorry, that was supposed to be your kiss, but I couldn't resist. Besides, I think it was a mistake. It only whetted my appetite. Now I want more of the same."

Melissa looked into those shimmering golden eyes and melted. The kiss had only made her hungrier, too. She said in a shaky voice, "I know what you mean," then more boldly, "What do you propose we do about that?"

His look turned smoldering as he answered in a husky voice, "This." He rolled her to her back as his lips covered hers.

Reid's lips moved over hers softly, sensuously, then possessively as he deepened the kiss, his tongue probing, demanding entrance. Melissa needed no urging. She opened to him gladly. Their tongues touched and danced, teasing, then eager, their hearts pounding in unison as their excitement grew.

Melissa whimpered in protest as Reid's lips moved away to tease the corners of her mouth, then scattered fiery kisses over her cheeks and eyes and temples. He nibbled at an earlobe, then traced the throbbing pulsebeat down her throat with his tongue, groaning in frustration when his exploration was impeded by the neckline of her dress.

With a growl of impatience, he quickly and deftly undressed her, ripping off his own clothes before rejoining her with another deep, passionate kiss that seemed to suck the air from her lungs and left her senses staggering.

He looked down at her, his golden eyes drinking in every inch of her, lingering on her rose-tipped breasts and the dark triangle between her thighs. "You have the body of a goddess," he muttered thickly.

He dropped his dark head, his tongue drawing lazy circles around one soft breast until his lips covered the rosy crest, his teeth gently pulling and nipping. Melissa moaned throatily, pulling him closer, wishing he would never stop this delicious torment. She whimpered when his mouth moved away, then gasped in renewed pleasure as his tongue brushed the other nipple, then flicked, sending hot waves washing over her body and curling her toes. Slowly his head descended, leaving a blazing trail of fire across her abdomen until he stopped to leisurely explore her navel.

Melissa felt the brush of his manhood against her thigh, the brief touch thrilling her, her body quivering in anticipation. Instinctively, she arched her hips, vaguely aware of him hovering over her, then kneeling between her thighs. She looked up to see those eyes of molten gold watching her intently and then gasped in shock as he dropped his head, burying his mouth in the soft curls that surrounder her womanhood. "No!" she cried.

But Reid was not to be denied. He was determined to taste that honeyed sweetness, explore with his lips and tongue what his fingers had already mapped out. He held her twisting hips in a firm grip, cupping her buttocks in a vise as he lifted her to him, his mouth devouring that hot, throbbing flesh, his tongue teasing the hard bud before seeking and plundering her inner secrets.

Melissa trembled as new, tumultuous sensations swept over her. Then as the sweet, powerful undulations began, she moaned, her hands tangling in his crisp curls to pull him closer, vaguely hearing his soft chuckle as she arched her hips, her thighs gripping his head, begging for more. Over and over, the waves of pleasure crested and fell away, only to rise again, until she was writhing, her breaths coming in ragged sobs, fearing she would go out of her mind if he didn't stop and yet not wanting him to stop.

Reid plunged into her with one smooth, powerful movement as his mouth came crashing down on hers. Melissa tasted herself on his lips, then his tongue, exciting her even more. She locked her legs around his slim hips, hungrily pulling him deeper, squeezing until Reid clenched his teeth, fearing he would lose all control, his body trembling with excruciating need.

He jerked his mouth from her, whispering in

an urgent voice, "Easy, sweetheart, easy."

Melissa's only answer was an anguished sob as she ground her hips against his and her nails raked his back.

Reid began his movements then, his own need becoming as urgent as Melissa's. He strove in bold, powerful strokes, driving deeper and deeper, increasing in momentum as he swept them both up that rapturous ascent, higher and higher, spinning dizzily, then hovering with breathless, agonizing anticipation at the crest, their bodies shuddering. Then they hurled into oblivion, his hoarse, triumphant groan blending with her small cry of ecstasy.

They lay in total exhaustion, bathed in their own sweat, floating in that warm afterglow. Finally, Reid lifted himself from her and lay on his back, pulling her to his side and laying her head on his shoulder.

For a long while they lay that way, silent in their contentment. Melissa watched, fascinated with the steady rise and fall of Reid's chest, the bronzed skin covered with a fine sheen of perspiration glistening in the firelight. Her fingers ran through the damp chestnut curls on his chest, stopping over his heart to relish the feel of that powerful muscle thudding against her hand. He's beautiful, she thought dreamily as her hand swept lower, then brushed the crisp hairs at his groin.

Hearing his sharp intake of breath as her hand briefly touched him there, Melissa smiled and boldly took him into her hand, feeling a thrill when she felt him stir beneath her fingers, then harden. She was amazed at how like her own flesh his was, hot and throbbing, even moist at the tip, except it was on the outside and hard, while hers was hidden and soft. Even its shape was sculptured to fit hers, although it seemed almost impossible that something that large could fit inside her. She wondered how she could ever have been terrified of it, when it gave them both so much exquisite pleasure.

"You know where this is leading," Reid said in a ragged voice, his hands sweeping over her back.

"I know," Melissa whispered with a smug smile, a little pleased with her power over him. Then she gasped as his hand cupped her between her thighs, his fingers moving with tantalizing purpose.

Then his warm lips covered hers, and Melissa was swept up in yet another whirlwind of passion.

The next two days and nights passed in a haze of utter happiness for Reid and Melissa, both discovering that they enjoyed each other's company as well as their rapturous lovemaking. It turned out that they were both avid chess players, and Melissa laughed out loud when she saw the shocked expression on Reid's face when she soundly beat him the first game they played. They discovered a mutual love of reading, and Melissa was delighted when Reid led her into his bedroom and showed her his bookcases crammed with books.

Melissa stared at the books in amazement. Nathan had told her Reid had books, but she had expected to see dime novels, and certainly not this splendid collection of classics. She was filled with curiosity about this man she knew so intimately and yet didn't know at all. Obviously, Reid was a well-educated, well-read man, yet another contradiction that didn't seem to fit in with his tough frontiersman's image.

That night, she gathered her courage and asked, "Reid, who are you?"

Reid frowned. "What do you mean, who am I?"

"I mean, frontiersmen don't read Homer and Shakespeare. You've been well educated and that usually speaks of privilege."

"Yes, I came from a well-to-do family," Reid admitted. "My father was one of the wealthiest bankers in Savannah. And you're right, I was well educated. I had the best tutors money could buy."

"Then what are you doing way out here, trapping furs?"

"No person or thing forced me away, Melissa,

if that's what you're thinking. It was my own decision. I ran away when I was sixteen."

"Ran away? But why?"

"My father was determined that I go into the banking business with him. Banking just didn't suit my nature. I like being out in the open, preferably being my own boss. The thought of being locked up in a stuffy bank all day and being told what to do by a board of directors who thought they owned you body and soul went against my grain. The West had just opened up and I was anxious to roam and explore. The call of adventure, I guess. Anyway, I ran away."

"Have you ever regretted it?"

"No. I'm still not banking material. I never will be. Maybe I won't be a trapper the rest of my life, but one thing is for sure. City life isn't for me. I like working outdoors and I don't like being crowded."

"But did you have to run away? Surely, if you had explained, your parents would have understood."

"My mother died when I was twelve. And I did tell my father how I felt," Reid replied with a hint of bitterness in his voice, "but he was a stubborn man. It was his way or not at all. We had a violent argument, and I left the next day for parts unknown."

"But, Reid, he was your father. He must have

regretted what happened, worried himself sick over you."

Reid sighed. "I was young and impulsive at the time. About five years later, when I was . . . when I was more mature, I wrote him, thinking it was time we mend our fences. He sent my letter back, still in the envelope unopened, with a curt note saying he no longer had a son named Reid."

"Oh, Reid," Melissa said, her heart breaking at the hurt look on his face.

"Like I said, he was stubborn. And I guess I had it coming. I don't think about it much anymore. And I sure don't worry about him. He's got my younger brother, and Tom won't disappoint him. He'll make a great banker."

And who do you have? Melissa wondered sadly. You have me, Reid! her heart cried out. We have each other. We don't need anyone else.

On the evening of the fourth night, Melissa and Reid sat down to eat, both very aware of each other and anticipating the joys to come later. But neither was really hungry. Finally, Reid put his fork down and took hold of Melissa's hands, saying in a husky voice, "We'll eat later."

As they rose from the table, the door slammed open and Nathan strolled in, saying in a loud, jovial voice, "Howdy."

Two shocked pairs of eyes stared at him. Oops, bad timing, Nathan thought, seeing the fleeting look of disappointment in Melissa's eyes and the scowl Reid shot him. Well, they must have made up, considering he'd caught them holding hands. And his sharp eyes hadn't missed that telltale bulge in Reid's pants, either. Nathan could hardly contain his delight.

Melissa was the first to recover. She smiled wanly. "Welcome back, Nathan. We were just . . . just sitting down to eat."

Nathan shut the door behind him. "That smells mighty good."

While Nathan hung up his coat, Melissa dished up another plate and set it on the table. Then they all three sat down to eat. Melissa was miserable, torn by conflicting emotions. She was glad to see Nathan, but she didn't want to give up her nights of delightful lovemaking with Reid, which they would certainly have to do now that Nathan was back. She hardly listened as the two men exchanged news.

As she washed and dried the dishes, her misery just grew. By the time she was finished, her disappointment was so keen that she was afraid she would break down in tears. She started for her old bedroom. "It's been a long day. I'll see you two in the morning," she said in a low voice.

Reid rose and caught her arm as she passed, pulling her back to him. Putting his arm around her possessively, he gave Nathan a hard look.

"You can have your bedroom back now, Nathan. Melissa and I will be sharing mine from now on."

Melissa was shocked speechless by Reid's blunt announcement. The only sigh that she even heard him was the red flush that slowly crept up and colored her face.

Nathan could hardly keep from jumping up and down for joy. He had to bite his lips to keep from laughing with glee. "Sure thing," he managed to mumble before he turned back to the fire, a wide grin spreading across his face.

Reid took Melissa's arm firmly and led her to his room before she could object. It wasn't until he had lit the candle that she finally reacted.

Her eyes glittered with fury. "How dare you!" she hissed. "How dare you so blatantly announce our relationship to Nathan that way."

Reid caught her shoulders, shaking her lightly, saying in a determined voice, "If you think I have any intention of letting go of what we've been building between us the past few days, you're crazy. Things are *not* going back to the way they were before Nathan left. And if you'll be honest with yourself, you'll admit you don't want that, either."

The words were like a bucket of cold water in her face. No, she didn't want to go back to that, either. She wanted to be with Reid, lie in his arms, but still . . . "But what must he think of us?" she wailed.

He drew her into his arms. "He'll have a hell of a lot more respect for us if it's out in the open, instead of us sneaking around behind his back." His voice took on a hard tone again. "And make no mistake about it, Melissa. I'm not letting go of you, not now, not after what we've shared." Then he chuckled, adding, "Besides, I suspect that's exactly what the old coot wanted to happen when he left the way he did. He wanted us to become lovers and he knew we'd never do it with him around all the time."

Melissa pondered Reid's words. Was that why Nathan left so abruptly? He certainly didn't look the least bit surprised when Reid made his announcement. In fact, unless she was imagining things, there had been a devilish, almost smug look in his eyes.

Then all thought fled as Reid pulled her down on the cot, his lips soft and persuasive as his hands worked their magic.

A few minutes later, she surfaced, objecting breathlessly, "But he'll hear us."

A few seconds later, the sound of Nathan's loud snores filled the cabin. Reid chuckled. "Over that? Sweetheart, a tornado could go through here and he'd never hear it with all racket he's making."

Melissa giggled and pulled his head back down.

The next morning, however, Melissa was having second thoughts. She dreaded going into the main cabin and facing Nathan. She was afraid she would see disappointment or, worse yet, disgust, in his eyes. She didn't think she could bear for Nathan to think badly of her. When she could delay no longer, she squared her shoulders and walked into the main cabin.

"Good morning," Nathan called in his usual cheerful voice.

Melissa searched his face closely, but could see no sign of disapproval. In fact, as she prepared breakfast and they ate, Nathan acted as if nothing unusual had even happened. Under Nathan's matter-of-fact, casual attitude, Melissa relaxed. Her only moment of embarrassment came when Reid carried the wood to enlarge his cot with into his bedroom and started hammering away. She blushed beet-red and could have sworn she saw Nathan's lips twitching.

A few days later, Reid met Melissa as she was heading down the hill toward the river. "Where are you going?" he asked.

"For a walk." She looked around at the trees, rustling in the dry, warm breeze. Multicolored leaves drifted down and littered the ground beneath them. "Can you believe this weather? Why, just a few days ago it was cold, and now it's just as warm as summer."

"It's Indian summer," Reid replied. "But it

won't last long. A day or two at the most. Then the real winter will begin. Better enjoy it while you can."

"I intend to." She looked around. "Where's Nathan?"

"He and Wolf have gone hunting."

"Then you're through for today?" she asked, obviously pleased.

"Nathan is. I still have a few more traps to set. Shouldn't take me long, though." He smiled, his golden eyes promising sensual delights. "When I'm through here, would you care for some company?"

Melissa's heart beat a crazy tattoo at the look in his eyes. She smiled back. "I'd love it."

"I'll meet you down by that big rock by the river in about thirty minutes. You know the one I mean?"

Melissa had never ventured far from the cabin, but she remembered the day they had arrived seeing the huge boulder about a half a mile downstream. "I know," she answered, nodding her head.

Reid turned and loped away, calling over his shoulder, "See you in a little while."

Melissa walked down to the river and followed it downstream until she reached the big boulder. Then she stood at its base, admiring the woods all around her, totally unaware of the dark eyes watching her intently.

War Eagle smiled. He knew his patience would be rewarded, if he only waited long enough. For a brief minute, he gazed at her hungrily, his heart pounding in anticipation. And then he stepped from behind the tree, where he was concealed, and into the clearing by the river.

"War Eagle!" Melissa cried in surprise. She glanced about her in disbelief. "What are you doing here?"

He stood before her, tall and proud, just a hint of a smile on his lips, his eyes as impassive as always and showing nothing of the excitement he felt. She was finally his. They would be gone before the white men even noticed she was missing. He would make her his wife, and the Great Spirit would smile down on their union, blessing them with much happiness and many children. He held out his hand and motioned for her to come with him.

Melissa stared at him in disbelief. He had come for her, trailed her all this way? And now, he expected her to go with him? Just like that? Was he insane?

Then she saw his muscular body tense and his dark eyes narrow. His hand flew to his knife as he rushed toward her. Thinking he meant to take her away by force, Melissa screamed. And then he shoved her to the side so hard she tumbled to the ground and rolled away, seeing a flash of gold from the corner of her eye, the sound of a horrible animal scream in her ears.

She looked up just in time to see the huge mountain lion, his teeth gleaming in the sunlight and his wicked claws bared, flying down from the top of the boulder and bearing War Eagle down with him, the ground shaking from the impact of their bodies. Melissa watched in terror as the monstrous cat and War Eagle rolled over, first War Eagle on the top, then the cat, sending the dry, crisp leaves beneath them scattering everywhere. The cat snarled and bit and lashed out with its razor-sharp claws as War Eagle struggled to subdue it, his grunts and labored breathing mixing with the cat's furious snarls and growls. They rolled, faster and faster, this way and that, until they were a mere blur. And then, Melissa's eyes caught a glimpse of the flashing arch of War Eagle's knife as he plunged it into the cougar's body.

Then they were perfectly still, the silence all the more ominous for its suddenness. Cautiously, Melissa rose and crept to the man and the huge cat.

The mountain lion lay on its side next to war Eagle, a knife handle protruding from its chest, the blade sunk deep in its heart. Her eyes flew to War Eagle. He lay on his back, his buckskins ripped to shreds. Deep, bloody lacerations crisscrossed his broad chest. But it was the sight of his neck that made Melissa's knees buckle, her heart rise to her throat. In typical animal fashion, the cat had gone for the jugular vein, the muscles, tendons, and big blood vessel totally laid open on one side by a deep gash, the blood pouring out like a fountain. She collapsed on her knees beside him and stared down at him.

As War Eagle felt his life draining away, he was pleased that the Great Spirit had given him an honorable warrior's death. He knew he had fought the big cat bravely and slain his enemy. That he had given his life to save the life of the woman he loved pleased him even more. He wanted only one more thing before he died. He turned his head and looked up at Melissa, allowing his eyes to speak in death what he had never told her, never let his eyes betray in life. He told her silently and eloquently of his love.

Melissa watched as War Eagle's eyelids fluttered down and his breath stilled. She had seen the look in his eyes, and she knew a dying man's eyes never lied. It was true. He *had* loved her!

She had felt no remorse when Reid and Nathan had killed the three trappers. They had been cruel men, bent on murder and driven by animal lust. They had deserved their fate. But War Eagle had loved her, not just lusted after her, and he had been a noble man, a man admired and respected by his people, a man destined for great things. And now, because of her, he was dead. He hadn't just given her his love, but the greatest gift he could—his life. A profound sadness, mixed with a strange guilt, filled her, overwhelming her.

"No!" she shrieked, the blood-curdling scream echoing through the woods. She threw herself over War Eagle's bloody chest, tears streaming down her face, sobbing, "You can't die! You can't!"

Reid had heard Melissa's first scream and come running, terrified at what might be happening to her. He had entered the clearing just as Melissa had knelt beside War Eagle, had stood right behind her and seen the look of love in War Eagle's dark eyes. And now, seeing her crying over the warrior as if her heart was breaking, raw jealousy rose in Reid, and with it, anger. He jerked her to her feet and shook her. "Who was he? Your Indian lover?"

Reid's accusation shocked Melissa from her almost hysterical state. She pulled away from him, hissing, "You know better than that. You know I was a virgin until *you* took me."

"All right, so he wasn't your lover," Reid conceded, his golden eyes still flashing. He pointed to War Eagle's body, saying, "But that's the same Indian who tried to buy you at the fair. He followed you from the Indian camp there, and now here. And I saw the look in his eyes before he died. He was in love with you!"

"I know," Melissa replied in an anguished

voice, her guilt a heavy burden on her soul.

Reid could hardly force the words from his mouth. "Did you love him?"

Melissa had felt some feelings for War Eagle, a profound respect for the man himself, a gratitude for the way he had treated her. But she had not loved him. "No, I didn't love him."

"Then why was he in love with you? Did you flirt with him? Did you lead him on?"

Melissa's head shot up, her eyes blazed. "You're never going to forget I flirted with you, are you?"

"Dammit, Melissa, that man was in love with you! He followed you all this way. Are you telling me you didn't give him any encouragement at all?"

Melissa remembered the young men back in South Carolina whom she had deliberately encouraged and then tossed aside. Now she was ashamed of her childish but hurtful game. But she had never led War Eagle on. "No, I didn't!" she denied hotly. "I never did anything to encourage him. I was too busy just trying to survive. I didn't realize until today, when he was dying, that he *was* in love with me."

"Then if you didn't love him and you didn't encourage him, why are you crying over him?"

"You wouldn't understand," Melissa replied in a brittle voice, turning away from him.

Reid whirled her around to face him, his eyes

blazing. "Try me," he ground out.

Melissa looked up into his face and saw the determined glint in his eyes. She knew he'd hound her until she gave him some explanation. And yet how could she explain what she couldn't understand herself?

"It's hard to explain, Reid. I hardly understand it myself. You see, War Eagle was the only one who showed me any kindness during my entire captivity. He was the one who loaned me his knife when Ellen was bitten by the rattlesnake. And when she died, the other Indians wanted to leave her to the vultures, but War Eagle made them wait until I'd buried her. He even let me have his buffalo hide to wrap her in. And once he stopped Little Crow from beating me, then helped me up. I know that doesn't sound like much, but at the time those small acts of kindness meant a lot to me. And now I feel like I've betrayed his kindness. He's dead now—because of me. He pushed me aside when the cat jumped me. He gave his life for me."

She looked down at War Eagle for a minute, then said in a low voice, "He was a noble man, a cut above most men. They said, at the camp, that he would have been the next chief, and he would have done great things, good things for his people. He could have had any Indian maiden he wanted, but he wanted me. Why, I don't know. And now I've brought him to his

death. He deserved better than that from me."
Fresh tears glittered in her eyes. "I feel so unworthy."

Reid understood better than Melissa thought. She had unknowingly and unwittingly lured the Indian to his death, and because she couldn't return his love, she felt guilty and unworthy of his sacrifice. Now that his anger and jealousy were gone, he, too, felt a profound sadness over War Eagle's death, for when he had seen him at the fair he had sensed a kinship with the proud, fierce warrior.

He took her into his arms, cradling her, saying in a gentle voice, "Don't blame yourself. It was something you had no control over. And nothing just happens in life, sweetheart. There's a reason for everything, although we mortals often can't see it. A being higher than all of us chooses our time to die and the circumstances. It's all part of his master plan."

At that minute, Nathan came tearing through the woods, Wolf running and barking at his side. As he broke into the clearing, he yelled, "What happened? I heard Missy screaming." Then he saw the dead mountain lion and War Eagle's body and stopped dead in his tracks. "Well, I'll be damned. It's that Injun from the trading fair. What was he doing here?"

"He came for Melissa," Reid answered.

Nathan's eyes flared with anger. "That bastard!"

"No, it wasn't like that!" Melissa cried, not wanting anyone to think badly of War Eagle.

"No, it wasn't," Reid agreed. "He was in love with Melissa and saved her life when the cat jumped her." He looked at Melissa with eyes filled with emotion. "I'll always be grateful to him for that."

Nathan was stunned by their words. He looked down at War Eagle thoughtfully. Yes, he could understand War Eagle loving her. She had all the attributes an Injun admired: courage, spirit, strength. That she was beautiful was only an added attraction. He glanced back at Melissa, seeing her tear-streaked face. And what had she felt for the Injun, he wondered. Love? No, he knew she loved Reid with her whole heart and soul. Some other emotion was upsetting her.

A low growl attracted Nathan's attention. He turned to see Wolf sniffing the dead mountain lion, the ruff on his neck standing on end. "I wonder what that cat was doing this far east?" Nathan asked, half to himself. "Don't usually see them around these parts. They stick mostly to the mountains. Must be one of the rogue cats." He looked down at the huge cat, its length almost as long as War Eagle's. "Ain't never seen one that big, either. I'm surprised that buck managed to kill him."

Melissa shivered in remembrance of the fierce

fight. Reid turned her to lead her away. "I'll take you back to the cabin."

She jerked away from him. "No! Not until he's buried!"

Reid and Nathan were surprised by her fierce words. Reid frowned and started to object to her staying to watch them bury War Eagle, then seeing the determined gleam in her eyes, decided against it. "All right. I'll get a shovel from the cabin."

As he turned, Melissa caught his arm. "No!" Reid turned to her, a puzzled look on his face.

"Please, can't we bury him the Indian way? On a burial platform?" Seeing Reid's frown, she continued. "He let me bury Ellen my way—the white man's way. It's the least I could do in return."

"Yes, I suppose it is," Reid agreed. He turned to Nathan. "Come on. Let's get our axes and some rope."

When they were out of Melissa's hearing, Nathan asked, "What's she talking about, burying Ellen?"

Reid related to Nathan what Melissa had told him as they walked. When he had finished the story, Nathan said in a sad voice, "So that's how Ellen died. And poor little Missy had to bury her herself." He shook his head. "I wonder if we'll ever know everything that happened to that little gal while she was their captive. The story

296

seems to be coming out in bits and pieces."

Yes, and all of it ugly, Reid thought bitterly. But he had no intention of telling Nathan about Melissa's night of terror at Little Crow and Two Feathers' hands. If she wanted to tell Nathan, that was her decision, but Reid would never betray what he felt had been told to him in confidence, not even to his best friend.

Melissa sat and watched silently while Reid and Nathan built the burial platform, then wrapped War Eagle's body in a buffalo hide and tied it securely with rope. Her heart felt heavy with remorse, knowing she had led this proud, brave warrior to his death. And now he was buried far away from his people, with no one even to mourn him properly, no one to honor him. She knew there was no way she could bring back his life, but there was something she could do.

After Reid and Nathan had lifted the body on the platform and laid it out, they jumped down and looked back up to survey their work. Neither noticed when Melissa picked up the knife that Nathan had left on the ground.

Melissa looked up at the shrouded body on the platform with tears in her eyes. I'm sorry I couldn't love you, War Eagle, she said silently. But I did respect you. She placed the little finger of her left hand on a rock and raised the knife. "And now — I honor you," she whispered.

Reid and Nathan heard the thud as the knife hit the rock and Melissa's gasp of pain. They whirled, then froze in horror. One third of Melissa's little finger lay on the ground, and blood poured from the amputated digit. The stared in shocked disbelief at the bloody knife in the other hand.

Reid was the first to recover. He rushed to her, yanking his bandanna from his neck as he ran, then wrapping it tightly around her hand. He gathered her to him and looked down at her ashen face.

Melissa looked up and saw the shaken look on Reid's pale face. She smiled, whispering, "Now War Eagle has had a proper burial, too. Just . . . just like Ellen." And then she gave in to the excruciating pain, allowing the welcoming blackness to claim her.

Reid crushed her limp body to his and looked up at Nathan. "Why in the hell did she do a crazy thing like that?" he asked in an anguished voice.

Nathan was still shaken himself. He had always suspected Missy's emotions ran deep, but he never dreamed she would go that far to repay what she had felt was a debt of honor, and somehow he sensed it was that more than gratitude for saving her life that had motivated her. "That's . . . that's the Injun's way of mourning. That's how they honor their dead. She must have seen them doing it at the Injun camp."

"Self-mutilation?" Reid said in horror. "That's disgusting!"

"It's their way of showing their respect to their dead. And Injuns value respect even more than love."

Reid picked Melissa up in his arms and stood, holding her fiercely to him. "That's the goddamnest thing I've ever heard! It's crazy! Just plain crazy!" He turned and strode to the cabin, still crushing Melissa to him in that tight, fierce grip, as if he was afraid War Eagle, even in death, would claim more of her.

Nathan turned and gazed back up at the body on the platform, his look pensive. Yep, he thought, to the white man self-mutilation did sound crazy, but it was the Injuns' way. Reid didn't understand, but Missy did. She had given War Eagle the only gift she could, a token of her respect, knowing that he would value it even more than her love. And he had a feeling deep in his gut that War Eagle knew what Missy had done and was mighty proud of her and very pleased.

Chapter Eleven

Reid helped Melissa recover from the self-inflicted injury, snarling any time Nathan came near her to help, shocking the older man with his fierce possessiveness. And so Nathan stood by, feeling useless, while Reid, after giving Melissa a hefty dose of jimsonweed to kill the pain, shaved the shattered finger bone clean, sewed the protective flap of skin over the stump, then bandaged it.

For the next few days, Nathan watched from the sidelines as Reid patiently and gently cared for Melissa's every need—spoon-feeding her, bathing her, changing her bandages, keeping her heavily sedated the whole time and never leaving her side. The mountain man was amazed at his young friend's tenderness, and wondered if Reid realized that he was blatantly exposing the depths of his love for Melissa to Nathan or whether he was even aware of that love himself.

On the third day, Melissa emerged from her foggy world and stubbornly refused to take any more jimsonweed, despite Reid's pleading, or, when that failed, his threats. To add to Reid's frustration, Melissa insisted on getting up, arguing that the longer she stayed in the bed, the weaker she would become.

After a heated argument, Reid finally compromised. "All right! I'll carry you into the main cabin and you can sit and watch Nathan prepare supper. But you're not getting on your feet yet."

Before Melissa could argue further, he wrapped her in a blanket and carried her into the main cabin, a deep scowl of disapproval on his face.

As he sat her in the rocking chair by the fire, Melissa looked at the new piece of furniture in surprise. "Where did this come from?"

Nathan grinned. "I made it for you. Ain't nothing as pretty as a woman sitting in a rocking chair by the fire." Unless it's a woman rocking a baby by the fire, he added silently. He glanced meaningfully at Reid and then at Melissa, his grin growing even wider at that pleasing thought.

Melissa was touched. She smiled, blinking back tears. "Thank you, Nathan. That was real sweet of you."

Nathan flushed, then glanced at Reid, who was scowling even deeper. Nathan shuffled his feet nervously before muttering, "You're welcome."

Melissa sat back and rocked while Nathan prepared supper, aware of Reid's golden eyes watching her closely. He probably expects me to faint any minute, she thought, then giggled to herself. And if he isn't careful, he'll spoil me rotten. Why, he's worse than my father, my old mammy, and Ellen all rolled up into one. I've never felt so safe and secure, so loved and cared for.

Love. The word came as a shock to her. Did he, could he possibly love her? Her heart soared at the thought. But then she remembered that he had never told her he loved her. Don't get your hopes up, she warned herself sternly.

To get her mind off that unsettling thought, she forced herself to look about the cabin. She smiled, thinking of how cozy and comfortable it was, how at home she felt. And that itself was amazing. Back in South Carolina, she had slept in feather beds, walked over plush carpeting, ate beneath crystal chandeliers, and had known every comfort money could buy. Yet, this small cabin with its crude furnishings seemed more like home than the other ever had.

Her eyes drifted to the small window pane and widened with surprise. "It's snowing!"

Nathan chuckled. "Yep, it has been for two days."

Melissa rose, intending to walk to the small

302

window and look out. The room spun dizzily.

Reid pushed her gently back down, admonishing her in an angry tone of voice, "Didn't I tell you you were too weak to be up?"

Melissa was shocked at her weakness, but she wasn't about to admit that to Reid. "I just stood up too suddenly."

"The hell you did!"

"I just wanted to look outside," she replied irritably.

Reid scooped her up in his arms and walked toward the window.

"For heaven's sake, Reid, there's nothing wrong with my feet," Melissa compiained. "I'm not sick. I just injured my finger and it doesn't even pain me anymore. You don't have to carry me everywhere."

"You've lost a lot of blood and you're weak."

"I'm weak because I've been in bed too long."

"And that's exactly where you're going back to if you don't stop arguing with me," Reid threatened. "Never have seen such a stubborn woman in my life," he grumbled.

But Melissa wasn't paying any attention to him. Her eyes were glued to the snowy scene outside the window. "Oh, Reid, it's beautiful."

"It is now," Reid admitted. "But you're going to be sick and tired of snow by the time spring comes."

Melissa watched the snowflakes as they drifted

down, some so large she could actually see their delicate patterns. "They say no two snowflakes are exactly alike," she said in a wondrous voice. "That seems incredible, doesn't it?"

Reid nodded.

"I wish I could touch one," she said, half to herself.

"Never satisfied," Reid grumbled.

Then to her amazement, he walked to the door, stopping to catch the door handle while he still held her in his arms. A gust of cold wind surrounded them as Reid stepped out into the small porch, sending the snowflakes swirling around them.

"Just one," Reid said in a stern voice. "And hurry, before you catch your death of a cold."

Melissa reached out and caught a snowflake in her hand. She looked down at it in amazement, studying its lacy form before it melted.

"That's all," Reid said in a gruff voice, carrying her back into the small cabin and sitting her again in the rocking chair.

"Thank you," Melissa said as he knelt before her and tucked the blanket about her.

He looked up, his golden eyes warm with emotion. He picked up one hand and kissed the palm, his tongue licking sensuously.

Melissa shivered at the brief contact, feeling her desire rise. Goodness, I must be well if I can think of *that*, she thought.

Reid smiled knowingly, then picked up her injured hand and gently kissed it. "Later," he said in a husky whisper, his promise sending Melissa's heart racing with anticipation.

Within a week, Melissa was up, stubbornly resuming her household chores despite Rcid's almost-violent objections. War Eagle was never mentioned between them. To Melissa, her debt of honor was paid, her strange guilt appeased, and Reid could never find the courage to ask Melissa for an explanation of her self-abuse. Just thinking about it left him shaken; he wasn't prepared to delve deeper. He secretly feared that Melissa might have been driven by an emotion deeper than respect, an emotion that she may not have been aware of herself. And if that were true, Reid didn't want to know.

The first time Melissa saw Reid dressed to go out in the snow to check his traps, she stared at the strange oval contraptions on his feet. "What are those?"

"Snowshoes," Reid replied. "The Indians originated them. They keep you from sinking down in the snow."

Melissa looked at the open-weaved strips of leather in disbelief. It looked to her like the snow could sift right through them. Besides that, they looked awkward. "But aren't they hard to walk in?"

"They take some getting used to," he replied

with a twinkle in his eyes. "As you'll soon find out."

"Me?"

"Yes, if you intend to go out into this deep snow, you'll have to wear them, too."

The next day, Nathan volunteered to take the trapping run himself so Reid could stay home and teach Melissa how to walk on snowshoes.

Warmly bundled up, Melissa waited patiently while Reid strapped the snowshoes to her feet. He stepped back and grinned. "Okay, let's see you walk."

Seeing the devilish gleam in his eyes, Melissa looked at him suspiciously. Cautiously, she raised one foot and took a step, then, pleased that nothing disastrous had happened, took another. But with the second step, she stumbled on the first snowshoe and tumbled to the ground.

Reid threw his head back and laughed lustily. Melissa glared up at him, saying hotly, "You knew that was going to happen!"

"Yes, I did," Reid admitted, his lips still twitching with amusement. He offered her his hand.

Melissa slapped his hand away. "I'll get up by myself, thank you."

After she had finally struggled to her feet, Reid said, "Point your toes out. That way you won't trip on the other snowshoe."

Melissa glared at him. "You could have told

306

me that in the first place."

Melissa took a few cautious steps. She felt ridiculous, like a big, awkward duck. As long as she walked in a perfectly straight line, she was all right, but if she veered even the slightest, she lost her balance and fell.

After falling the sixth time, she sat in the snow, her legs sprawled in front of her. She stared at the snowshoes, saying in disgust, "It's hopeless. I'll never learn."

"Sure you will," Reid replied, helping her up. "All it takes is practice."

"It seems to me they're more trouble than they're worth," Melissa grumbled. "It would be easier to crawl."

"Nope. Once you get used to them, you can even dogtrot in them. Nathan and I can cover thirty or forty miles a day that way."

After another hour of Melissa's struggles, Reid finally called a halt. Melissa was relieved. Her buckskin shirt was wet from falling in the snow, and her legs and backside were numb from cold. As soon as they were in the cabin, she rushed to the fire to warm herself.

Reid frowned, noticing her damp skirt for the first time. "Better get out of those wet clothes."

"I will as soon as I get warmed up," Melissa replied, her teeth chattering.

"What you need is a nice hot bath to warm you up. Now, you get out of those wet clothes while I warm some water for you."

Melissa was reluctant to give up the warmth of the fire, but the promise of a hot bath overrode her reluctance. She hurried into their bedroom and stripped off her wet clothes. Wrapping herself in a blanket and grabbing a towel and a bar of soap, she walked back into the main cabin.

While Reid poured the steaming water in the tub, Melissa tied her long hair on top of her head and stood by the tub impatiently while Reid tested the water temperature.

Reid grinned and made a slight bow to her. "Your bath, m'lady."

Melissa started to drop the blanket and then, realizing Reid was still standing beside her, asked, "Aren't you going to leave?"

"Nope."

Melissa remembered another bath and Reid's stubborn refusal to leave. Besides, after their intimacy it did seem a little late to be worrying about modesty. But she couldn't hide her deep flush of embarrassment when she dropped the blanket and stepped into the tub.

When she was settled, Reid said, "Where's the soap?"

"Here," Melissa answered, holding out her hand with the soap in it.

"Give it to me," Reid said, taking it from her before she could object. "I'll wash your back for you."

Melissa wasn't too sure about that. She was afraid it would lead to other things. But as Reid started washing her back, she relaxed, enjoying the feel of his hands briskly soaping and massaging her tired muscles.

"Oh, that fccls good," she sighed.

"Well, enjoy it. But just remember, my turn is coming."

"Your turn?"

"Yep. As soon as you're through, I'm going to climb into the tub, too." His eyes twinkled. "If it wasn't so damned small, I'd be in there with you right now."

Reid handed the bar of soap to Melissa over her shoulder. The slippery sliver slipped through her fingers and dropped between her legs.

Reid grinned. "I'll get it."

"Oh, no you won't!" Melissa retorted, fishing frantically for the elusive soap.

Reid chuckled and went to the fire to put more water on to heat. Melissa hurried her bath, not wanting the water to get too cold for Reid. Besides, she still didn't trust him not to start something before her bath was through. When he turned his back, she took the opportunity to climb out, quickly dry off, and don the blanket. She smiled smugly when she saw the look of disappointment in his eyes as he turned and saw her already wrapped in the blanket.

But her smug smile faded as he casually undressed right in front of her and walked past her in all of his naked, masculine glory. Despite herself, she couldn't take her eyes off him, feeling her pulse quicken as her eyes swept over his magnificent male physique. Well, he certainly turned the tables on me, she thought, feeling her frustration rise as he calmly stepped into the tub and sat down, denying her hungry eyes of everything but his broad shoulders and half of his muscular chest.

He grinned and handed her the soap. "Your turn."

Melissa took the soap and began washing his back, marveling at the feel of those powerful muscles rippling and bunching beneath her fingers. Her hands slipped up to his broad shoulders and massaged, then absently stroked as her eyes fell on his nape, the damp chestnut hair curling invitingly. She fought the urge to kiss him there, as he had done so often to her.

Reid chuckled, and Melissa flushed, suspecting he was reading her mind. That devil! she thought. He knows exactly what he's doing to me, and he's enjoying it.

She stood up and handed him the soap. "Wash your own back!" she snapped.

Reid made no comment. He took the soap and began lathering his chest and arms. When he saw Melissa heading for the bedroom door, he called, "How about adding some of that hot water for me?"

Melissa turned and glared at him.

He gave her a lopsided grin that tugged at her heartstrings. She walked back to the fireplace, thinking, oh, he's smooth all right. One little smile, and you melt like so much butter.

While Melissa was busy with the warm water, Reid hurriedly soaped himself all over. By the time she returned to the tub, he was covered with lather.

"How hot is that water?" he asked.

"Just warm, I'm afraid," Melissa answered, trying very hard to keep her eyes from wandering from his face.

"Then how about pouring it over me?"

Melissa frowned. It would take both of her hands to pour the water, and one was already busy holding the blanket closed over her breasts.

"Come on, sweetheart," Reid coaxed. "You can see this tub is too small for me to dunk in."

"Oh, all right!" Melissa snapped. She put the bucket of water down and quickly wrapped the blanket around her, tucking it in at her breasts. Then she lifted the bucket of water over him and poured.

She turned, but before she could put the bucket down, Reid yanked the blanket away and pulled her into the tub. She shrieked as she fell back over him, her shapely legs dangling over the edge of the tub, her bottom sitting on his

311

lap. Grasping one of Reid's knees with one hand
and the rim of the tub with the other, she struggled to rise, sputtering impotently, but Reid held
her firmly around the waist, chuckling at her
futile efforts.

She gave him a murderous glare. "Let me go!"
she demanded.

Reid smiled. "Nope."

Melissa was only too aware of what she was
sitting on. She could feel him, hot and throbbing
at the back of her thighs, so close and yet . . .
It was maddening.

"Relax, sweetheart," Reid muttered as he nibbled her shoulder, then buried his head in the
crook of her neck, mouthing the sensitive skin
there. One hand held her firmly on his lap while
the other caressed her breasts, then dipped lower.
She gasped, feeling those sensuous, intimate
strokes.

Hearing her gasp, he laughed. "You've been
wanting this, sweetheart. You can't deny it."

Melissa was already reeling with the sensations
his skillful fingers were evoking. She moaned,
then murmured in a weak voice, "Yes, but not
here."

Reid looked down at the small tub as if he
had forgotten it was still there. Then he nodded.
"You're right. Besides, the water's getting cold."

He pushed her up gently, and when Melissa
was standing, he rose and stepped out of the

tub. Before she could head for their bedroom, he pulled her down on the bearskin rug before the fire.

"Nathan might come back," she objected.

"Nathan is gone for the day. We have all afternoon. And I've missed making love to you before the fire. I like to watch your face while I'm loving you."

He reached up and tugged at the rawhide thong that held up her hair, and it came tumbling down around her shoulders and down her back. One long raven strand hung over one breast, curling enticingly around one rosy nipple. Reid stared at it, fascinated, then bent and kissed the rigid bud before he took the strand of hair and curled it around his hand, pulling her with him as he lay back on the rug.

His golden eyes glowed. "You little witch!" he said in a roughened voice. "Teasing me . . . acting so innocent sitting in that tub . . . traipsing around here with only that blanket covering you . . . deliberately taunting me."

"You accuse *me* of taunting?" Melissa retorted. "What about you? Walking around here stark-naked, flaunting your body before my eyes and then . . ."

"Then what?" Reid asked in a quiet voice.

Melissa flushed deeply.

"Then what?" Reid persisted, nibbling the corner of her mouth.

"Then leaving me hanging while you . . . while you bathe!"

Reid chuckled, then whispered in her ear, "Hungry, sweetheart?"

Tears of frustration glittered in her eyes. "You devil! You know I am."

He rolled her on to her back. "Then you shall be satisfied, my hungry lady."

His mouth covered hers in a long, searching kiss, his tongue exploring the sweetness of her mouth before darting around hers, drawing a moan from deep in her throat. He bathed her face with featherlike kisses, then moved to her breasts, lazily tracing one rosy nipple, then the other. His fingers stroked her soft breasts as he nibbled at the tender flesh of her abdomen, then circled the enticing dimple there, his tongue flicking erotically.

Melissa shuddered as the delicious waves washed over her. She reached for him, only to discover that he had moved lower, dropping fiery kisses up the soft, sensitive skin of her inner thighs. Then he began slowly inching upward, until she whimpered in anticipation, trembling when he buried his mouth in that dark triangle. His tongue was an instrument of exquisite pleasure, flicking and teasing, exploring her thoroughly, driving her wild with excitement.

He hovered over her, his warm breath fanning her face, whispering against her lips, "Still hun-

314

gry, sweet?"

Yes, she was still hungry, but hungry for the taste of him. Catching him by surprise, she rolled him to *his* back, her lips nibbling down the long column of his throat and across his broad shoulders. She ran her fingers through the dark, crisp curls on his chest, then licked the hard male nipple, smiling in satisfaction at *his* groan of pleasure. A feeling of power filled her as she continued her tender assault, nipping across his taut abdomen, the muscles jumping reflexively at the feel of her soft, teasing lips. She stopped, playing havoc with his senses as she tantalized his navel, surprised at how much pleasure she was deriving from his pleasure.

Bolder now, she moved lower, dropping a trail of fiery kisses over his lower abdomen, deliberately brushing his groin. Reid groaned, and Melissa delighted in *his* frustration. She nibbled at his thighs, her tongue flicking, feeling the powerful muscles tense. Then she sat back on her heels, her hand wrapping around him, sensuously stroking his immense, throbbing hardness that stood so proudly before her.

Reid's blood was surging through his veins like liquid fire, his senses reeling, his body trembling with delicious agony from Melissa's sensual movements. But when he saw her lowering her head, every muscle in his body went rigid with shock. She wouldn't! he thought in utter disbelief. Surely, she wouldn't make love to him *that* way! And then, when he felt her feathery kisses, followed by her tongue swirling around him, he gasped.

His hands tangled in her hair as he jerked her head upward. His eyes searched her face. "Do you even know what you're doing?" he said in a ragged voice.

Melissa smiled down at him, a soft, mysterious smile. Her eyes were warm and glowing with emotion. "Yes, my darling," she whispered. "I'm showing you how much I love you."

Reid was shaken to the core by her words, and fast on its heels came another shattering revelation. He realized that he loved her, with an intensity that he had never dreamed possible. He loved her deeply and profoundly, with all of his fierce heart and passionate soul. He knew that there was no future for them, that he could offer her nothing. But he couldn't turn back. He couldn't give her up. Not now.

His mouth took hers in fierce possession, and Melissa responded mindlessly to that deep, passionate kiss. The fire that had been smoldering between them flared to new heights. Melissa felt the hot, moist tip of him against her womanhood. She feverishly arched to meet him, welcoming him with a glad cry, sheathing him as he drove deeply inside her, her muscles rippling about and caressing each inch of his long length.

316

Their union was a fierce coming together. Melissa met each powerful, searing stroke with one of her own. Their bodies rocked, their mutual passion blazing as they grew frenzied in their urgency. Then they lay poised, momentarily suspended in time, before they climaxed in a white-hot, tumultuous eruption that shook them both with its intensity and sent brilliant fireworks flashing through their brains.

They lay, shuddering with aftershocks from their soul-shattering experience, their breathing ragged, too exhausted even to move. Finally, Reid kissed her temple, relieved her of his weight, then nuzzled her neck. "Satisfied, my sweet temptress?" he whispered.

She muttered incoherently, her tongue being occupied with licking a line of sweat from his tanned neck. His salty taste excited her all over again. She smiled seductively up at him, a warm gleam in her eyes. She rubbed her knee against his thigh, an act made all the more erotic by the slickness of their perspiring bodies. Then, deliberately, she brushed against his inert manhood in open invitation.

Reid sucked in his breath, his eyes widening in surprise as he felt himself responding. He shook his head in disbelief, then chuckled. "Little witch! You'll be the death of me."

Melissa smiled and purred, "Oh, I doubt that."

He lifted her in his arms and stood. As he walked toward their bedroom, Melissa nestled against his hard chest. "What about the tub?" she asked in a dreamy voice.

"I'll get it later," Reid muttered.

But Reid completely forgot about the tub. He loved her slowly, with a tenderness and agonizing sweetness that was a stark contrast to their fiery union earlier. Afterward, completely satiated, they both fell into an exhausted sleep.

They were awakened by the slam of the front door as Nathan came in.

"Oh, my God," Melissa whispered. "What time is it?"

Reid looked about the darkened cabin, realizing they had overslept and let the fire burn down. They could hear Nathan stumbling about in the dark cabin, muttering curses under his breath.

Reid jumped from the bed and pulled on his pants. But before he could go into the main cabin, they heard a sudden crash, followed by a distinct splash of water.

And then Nathan's roar filled the cabin. "Who in the hell left this goddamn tub in the middle of the room?"

Reid laughed, then called, "Hang on, Nathan. I'm coming."

Melissa could hear Nathan's angry sputters as Reid helped him from the tub, where he lay in an undignified sprawl. She rolled about on the bed, giggling helplessly.

Two days later, Melissa heard a call coming from outside the cabin. Drying her hands on a dishtowel, she walked to the window and looked out.

Two trappers stood in the snow, their heavy packs strapped to their backs. It was impossible to determine their age or even what they looked like, for their faces were covered with thick beards, and their hair hung in long, stringy masses around their faces. Even their eyebrows were thick and bushy.

"Hello in there? Anybody home?" one of the trappers called.

For the first time, Melissa realized her precarious position. She was alone. Reid and Nathan wouldn't be back from checking their traps for another hour or two. Memories of the three trappers who had tried to buy her flashed through her brain. Her heart raced in fear.

"Hey! It's mighty cold out here! Can we come in?" the trapper called.

Melissa remembered what Reid had said about the frontier code of hospitality. Their cabin was open to any seeking refuge from the elements. She knew that if Reid or Nathan were here, they would open the door to these strangers.

She peered out the window again, trying to decide what to do. The two men looked freezing cold, shivering and huddling, with their hands buried in their armpits. And they looked exhausted. She studied their eyes, looking for any sign of cruelty, but all she could see was total misery.

Well, she thought, who was she to break the age-old frontier code? If she was going to live in this wilderness, she'd have to learn to live by their rules. Gathering her courage, she walked to the door and opened it.

If Melissa hadn't been so frightened herself, she might have laughed out loud at the dumbfounded looks on the men's faces when they saw her. One, as if disbelieving what he saw, rubbed his eyes and looked again.

"A white woman!" the other trapper gasped. They stared at her as if she were some apparition, and Melissa was relieved to see no signs of lust in their eyes.

Finally, one of the trappers recovered enough to stammer, "Sorry, ma'am. We . . . we weren't expecting no white woman. We'll . . . we'll be on our way."

They turned and started walking wearily away, one casting a last look of admiration in her direction. Melissa watched for a minute as the trappers trudged away, then frowned as she realized that it was starting to snow again. Surely, they couldn't be dangerous if they were willing to leave without asking for even a brief respite from their misery, she thought. Why, that could be Reid and Nathan out there.

"Please, come in for a cup of hot coffee," Melissa called to their backs.

They turned, a surprised look on their faces. Then one frowned, yelling back, "Your husband may not like that, ma'am."

Husband? Yes, naturally they would assume she was married, since she was white. A little thrill ran through her at the thought of being Reid's wife. She smiled, calling, "He and his partner will be back any minute now." Might as well play it safe, she thought. Surely, if they thought Reid and Nathan would be returning any minute, they wouldn't try anything.

The two men hesitated, looking at the cabin with longing eyes. Finally one called, "If you don't think they'd mind, a cup of coffee would taste mighty good right now."

"Then come in, before your hands are too frozen to even hold it," Melissa called back.

Melissa watched as they eagerly tramped back to the cabin and unstrapped their heavy packs, dropping them in the snow. As soon as they had slipped off their snowshoes, she opened the door wider for them to enter.

While they removed their coats, she walked to the fireplace and poured two cups of coffee, placing them on the table. She turned to see the two trappers looking about the cabin with admiring eyes.

The older of the two men, his eyes fixed on the calico curtains she had made, said in a wistful voice, "You sure have a purty cabin, ma'am. Reminds me of the old homestead back in Tennessee."

Melissa heard the longing in his voice and felt ashamed of herself for even hesitating to invite them in. Why, they were nothing but two hardworking trappers, half-frozen, exhausted, and now looking a little homesick. Tantalized by the smell of Melissa's simmering stew, one of the trapper's stomachs growled loudly. He shuffled his feet in embarrassment. And hungry, too, she added.

"Please be seated, gentlemen," Melissa said, almost laughing when she saw their startled looks at being called "gentlemen."

Apparently, the unaccustomed address reminded one of his manners. He flushed. "Pardon me, ma'am. We should have introduced ourselves. I'm Pete Masters and this here is my brother, Mike."

Melissa wondered just how she was supposed to introduce herself. She was hesitant to say Mrs. Forrester. Reid might not appreciate that. Why, he might even accuse her of trying to trick him into marriage again. And yet, if she used her maiden name and Reid turned around and referred to her as his wife, that might be awkward. She decided to keep it simple. She smiled and said, "I'm Melissa."

The two men sat down and drank their coffee, their looks of gratefulness tearing at Melissa's heart.

When they had finished drinking their coffee, Pete rose. "Well, Mike, I reckon we'd better be on our way. This here lady's got chores to be tending to." He said to Melissa, "Sure to thank you for the coffee, ma'am. Best damned . . ." He winced, then said, "Excuse me, ma'am. Best danged coffee I've ever tasted."

"But you're not going yet? Surely, you'll stay for supper," Melissa said, surprising even herself.

Pete and Mike exchanged astonished looks. Then both their stomachs growled. Pete flushed in embarrassment. "Well, that's right neighborly of you, ma'am." Then he grinned. "Can't say we ain't hungry, with our bellies growling like they are. And that there stew sure does smell mighty tempting."

"Then have another cup of coffee while I add more vegetables to the stew," Melissa said with a smile.

The two trappers sat silently while Melissa prepared supper, their eyes following her every move. But Melissa wasn't worried; she knew they were no threat to her. If anything, their looks were adoring. Now I know how a saint feels, she thought, laughing to herself.

An hour later, when Reid and Nathan walked in, they stared in disbelief at the two trappers sitting at the table. Reid shot a quick look around the cabin, then saw Melissa standing by the fireplace. A brief look of relief passed through his eyes before he turned them back to the two trappers.

Pete and Mike had jumped to their feet when the two men walked in. Now, feeling themselves under that fierce, golden gaze, a gaze that reminded them too much of a dangerous mountain lion, they shuffled their feet nervously.

Melissa broke the tension in the small cabin. "Reid, Nathan, this is Mike and Pete Masters. I've invited them for supper."

A brief look of surprise passed over Reid's face before he turned his glowering look on Melissa.

Pete saw the look and knew Reid was displeased. He sure didn't want the little lady getting into trouble because of him. "Sure was neighborly of your wife."

Melissa saw Reid's eyebrows rise at the word "wife." Oh, God, she thought, now he'll think I told them I was his wife, and I'm sure he'll have some scathing remark to make to that.

But to her surprise and relief, Reid said nothing. He turned back to the trappers, eyeing them suspiciously. Even Nathan's look was distrustful.

"If you want us to leave, just say so," Pete

said.

Melissa waited for Reid and Nathan to say something. But when they remained grimly silent, Melissa couldn't believe their rudeness. "You'll do nothing of the sort!" she said hotly.

Four pairs of astonished eyes turned toward her, then Reid's narrowed dangerously. *If he thinks he can intimidate me with that look, he's got another thought coming,* Melissa thought, still furious at his and Nathan's rudeness.

She glared back at Reid. *"I'm* the cook around here, and *I* extended the invitation!"

She turned and walked to the fire, but hearing no response, she whirled back around. The four men were eyeing each other warily, their bodies tensed with expectation.

Melissa's eyes glittered dangerously. "Stop eyeing each other like a pack of hound dogs itching for a fight. I'm putting supper on the table, and you'd damned well better eat it before it gets cold!"

Pete's and Mike's bushy eyebrows shot up in shock at Melissa's language. Nathan chuckled at their look. "Well, I reckon we'd better do what she says. Once Missy gets her temper up, it don't pay to argue."

Pete and Mike laughed nervously.

"Come on, sit down," Nathan said, taking off his coat and hanging it on the hook by the door.

The two men hesitantly sat back down at the

table, and Nathan joined them. Reid hung up his coat and then, giving Melissa a hard look, reluctantly joined them.

Melissa placed the eating utensils on the table and then the food, ignoring Reid's angry scowl. After pouring their coffee, she sat down to join them.

The trappers eyed the food with obvious hunger. "Been a long time since we've sat down to a home-cooked meal," Pete said. "We sure appreciate this."

"Where you from?" Nathan asked as Melissa dished them all a big plateful of food.

"Tennessee," Pete answered, his mouth watering as his eyes devoured the food.

Seeing his look, Nathan said, "Well, dig in. We'll talk after we're through eating."

And dig in they did. From the way they ate, Melissa thought they must be famished. When they finally finished, there wasn't a scrap of food left.

Pushing back from the table, Nathan looked at the two trappers. "Are you freemen?"

"Nope," Pete answered. "We work for the Missouri Fur Company. We're on our way up the Yellowstone to Fort Manuel."

Melissa was surprised at this bit of information. She hadn't realized there was a trading post even farther west than they were.

Hearing the scratching on the front door that

was Wolf's signal he was ready to come in for the night, Nathan rose. "Excuse me."

He walked to the door and opened it. Wolf came in, stopping to shake the snow off his fur before he trotted to the fire and lay down, totally ignoring the strangers.

Nathan chuckled as the two trappers' eyes widened when they saw the big dog. He'd been assessing the two men while they ate and figured they were innocent enough. But when Wolf ignored them, he knew they weren't in any danger. Wolf had an animal's instincts about people, instincts that made him a better judge of character than any man.

"That's my dog," Nathan said proudly. "He's half wolf."

Pete gave a shaky laugh. "You could have fooled me. I could have sworn he was *all* wolf."

Nathan chuckled and launched into the story of how he had found Wolf. Soon he and the two trappers were swapping tales about dogs they had owned, then arguing about which breed of dog made the best coon dog. Reid sat by, saying nothing.

Melissa listened to their tales while she washed and dried the dishes, aware of Reid's eyes on her and wondering why he couldn't relax and act more friendly, like Nathan was doing. She saw him frown when Nathan pulled out his keg of corn whiskey and offered the two trappers a drink. She shook her head in disgust, thinking that Reid was as bad as a straight-laced school-teacher when it came to drinking. For heaven's sake, all Nathan and the two trappers were doing was enjoying a companionable drink.

As soon as Melissa was finished with the dishes, she walked to the rocking chair, intending to sit and listen to Nathan and the two brothers, who were exchanging stories of the experiences on the frontier.

But before she could lower her body, Reid slipped his arm possessively around her waist. "We'll be saying good night now."

Melissa glared at him. How rude could he be? Was he asking their guests to leave?

"Sure thing," Nathan said. "We'll try to keep it quiet out here so we don't disturb you."

Pete and Mike, who were already rising to leave, looked surprised by his words.

"Sit back down," Nathan said to the trappers. "Ain't no sense in your leaving now. You can sleep here tonight and get an early start tomorrow."

The two brothers smiled their appreciation and sat back down. "Much obliged," Pete said.

Reid glared at Nathan behind the trappers' backs, and the older man glared back. Then Reid practically dragged Melissa across the cabin, saying curtly, "Good night."

Melissa jerked her arm free. She turned and

328

smiled at the two trappers. "I probably won't see you before you leave in the morning, so I want to wish you good luck."

Pete and Mike stumbled to their feet and smiled back. "We sure want to thank you for your hospitality and that fine supper, ma'am," Pete said. Mike nodded his head in hearty agreement.

"You're welcome, gentlemen. Good night."

" 'Night, ma'am," they answered in unison.

Melissa turned, gave Reid an icy look, and walked into their bedroom. As soon as Reid shut the door that he had built for added privacy, he whirled her around. "You crazy little fool! What do you think you were doing, inviting them in?"

"I believe it's called frontier hospitality," she whispered back angrily. "You said no one was denied shelter from the elements out here . . . or food!"

"My God! Nathan and I weren't even here. Don't you realize you could have been raped and killed?"

"Oh, for heaven's sake," Melissa said in a low, exasperated voice. "Do you think I'm stupid? I knew they wouldn't hurt me before I even invited them in."

"Oh? And how did you know that?" Reid said in a biting voice.

"By the look in their eyes."

"The look in their eyes?" Reid said in an incredulous voice. "Christ, they haven't taken their eyes off you all evening. I've never seen such hungry looks."

"Hungry, yes, but not lustful. And believe me, I should know the difference. I've been there, remember? I'm the one who was almost raped."

Reid paled at the memory of what had almost happened to her. "You were lucky that time, Melissa. Lucky that you got your hands on a weapon. But you've got to remember this isn't the East. Out here, some men go for years without seeing a woman, much less a beautiful woman. And they get hungry, damned hungry. Even a man who's basically decent can lose control. A man's animal need can be mighty powerful. How long do you think they can fight off their baser natures before they finally give in to that need? Particularly with someone flirting the way you were with them."

"Flirting?" Melissa gasped.

"Yes, flirting! Dammit, I saw the way you were smiling at them."

"There you go again! Accusing me of flirting. For your information, I was just being friendly," Melissa replied hotly.

Reid sighed in exasperation. "To a hungry man, there's no such thing as a friendly smile. There's just one kind of smile, a smile that invites. And in your case, you were inviting trouble."

Melissa couldn't believe her ears. Despite everything Reid had said, she knew she hadn't misjudged the two brothers. They were hungry, but only for the sight of a woman, as they were for anything that reminded them of civilization and home.

And they had shown her the utmost respect. But she knew it would be useless to argue with Reid. She sighed and started removing her dress.

"Thank goodness you had the presence of mind to tell them you were my wife," Reid said. "Otherwise, they may have gotten the mistaken idea that you were up for grabs. Then Nathan and I would have had a fight on our hands."

Melissa realized what Reid said was true. She knew the only reason the trappers were so gentlemanly was because they thought she was Reid's wife. But if they had known she was only Reid's . . . Reid's what? Why, Reid had never once told her he loved her, not even after she had so foolishly blurted out that she loved him. And what would the two brothers think if they knew Reid had bought her from an Indian? That she had been an Indian captive for months. No, if they had known the truth, they wouldn't have respected her. They would have thought her dirt, fair game for any man strong enough to take her—if they wanted her. A bitterness filled her, not only for the things she had no control over, but for giving herself so freely to Reid. Suddenly she felt used.

"I didn't tell them I was your wife. They only assumed it," Melissa said in a bitter voice. She laughed harshly. "They thought I was a lady. Isn't that ridiculous?" Her voice rose to a hysterical pitch. "They didn't know I was your whore!"

Reid felt the ugly word like a kick in the gut. He caught her shoulders roughly. "Don't you *ever* call yourself that!"

"Why not? Isn't that what I am?" Melissa retorted, fighting back tears.

"Hell no!" Reid roared, then looked about nervously. Hearing the loud voices and laughing coming from the main cabin, he realized the three men couldn't hear anything he and Melissa were saying, provided they kept their voices down.

"Then what am I?" Melissa demanded.

"You're the woman I love, goddammit!" Reid ground out. "And I won't have you demeaning yourself."

"Love?" Melissa scoffed. "You never told me you loved me."

"You crazy little fool! What do you think I was saying every time I loved you?"

"You don't have to love someone to make love," Melissa pointed out.

"I wasn't just making love. I was loving you! My God, do you think a man goes to all the trouble arousing a woman just to find release for himself? No, sweetheart, if you think that's what goes on between a man and a whore, you're sadly mistaken."

His word were slowly sinking into Melissa's brain. "Then you really *do* love me?" she asked in a small, wondrous voice.

Reid pulled her into a fierce embrace, "Yes, you little witch, I love you." He pulled her even closer, until Melissa could barely breathe. "When I walked in and found those men here, I was terrified. I must have died a thousand deaths before I saw you and realized you were unharmed. If anything should happen to you—"

He lowered her to the bed and kissed her, an urgent, desperate kiss. Then he pulled away and groaned.

"What's wrong?" Melissa asked.

He smiled wryly at her. "When a man tells a woman he loves her, he should be able to follow it up with showing her how much. But I don't dare, because once I start loving you, everything else ceases to exist. Someone has to keep an eye on things with that going on in the next room."

The noise from the next room was getting steadily louder. What Melissa had thought was going to be one or two sociable drinks was turning into an out-and-out drinking binge, for obviously the three men were getting roaring drunk. And Reid had a point. Sober, Pete and Mike were nice enough men, but what if they got mean and ugly when they were drunk, as she knew some men did? She remembered the night at the trading fair and how wild the Indians had become. She shivered and moved closer to Reid.

They lay for a long while, listening to the lusty laughter and ribald jokes, jokes that made Melissa blush and Reid clench his teeth because he knew she was hearing them. Finally Reid had had enough. He jumped out of bed, a thunderous look on his face.

"Where are you going?" Melissa asked.

"I'm going in there and tell them to shut their filthy mouths!" Reid said angrily. "There's a lady present."

"No, Reid, I don't think that would be a good idea. They've completely forgotten I'm here or they wouldn't be talking that way. And isn't that what you're worried about? That one of them might try something because of me?"

Reid hesitated. Reminding them that Melissa was around might not be a good idea.

"They're not hurting anyone," she continued. "If you go in there bellowing like a bull, they might get angry and no telling what might happen. Besides, they're so drunk they don't even know what they're laughing at."

Reluctantly, Reid lay back down on the bed and took her back into his arms. As the noise gradually died down, Melissa drifted off to sleep. But Reid stayed awake and listened closely.

It wasn't until he heard the two trappers whispering good-bye to a half-asleep, grumbling Nathan, and the sound of the door opening and closing, that he finally allowed himself a brief nap.

When Melissa awakened the next morning, she was alone. She lay smiling and hugging herself with happiness, savoring the knowledge that Reid really loved her. Then she jumped from the bed and dressed quickly, feeling marvelously alive.

She walked into the main cabin, practically bouncing with happiness. Nathan sat at the table with his head in both hands. Reid was pouring his partner a cup of coffee.

"Good morning!" she cried brightly.

Nathan winced and clutched his head tighter. "Don't scream, Missy," he groaned.

Reid laughed. "Don't pay any attention to him. He's having to pay the piper for his little party last night."

"Oh God, I'll never take another drink," Nathan moaned. "I must have three heads and all of them are pounding."

While Melissa fixed breakfast, Reid plied Nathan with coffee. By the time they were finished eating, Nathan was beginning to look human again.

Reid sat back, nursing a cup of coffee, and eyed his partner thoughtfully. "You feel up to taking the run by yourself today?"

"Sure I can," Nathan answered. "You got something planned?"

Reid's eyes turned to Melissa. "Yes, I was thinking I'd stay home and teach Melissa how to shoot a gun."

Melissa turned from where she was washing dishes. "Shoot a gun?" she asked in a horrified voice.

"Yes, shoot a gun," Reid replied firmly. "We were lucky yesterday that nothing disastrous happened. With you alone here so much, you need to know how to protect yourself."

"But I couldn't shoot anyone," Melissa objected.

"Dammit, Melissa!" Reid said in an exasperated voice. "Don't think just because Pete and Mike acted decent enough, that's the way any stranger wandering through here is going to behave toward you. You're a beautiful woman, and white. And that's too much temptation for most of these women-hungry men out here. Do you realize what a prize you are? Why, you're probably the only white woman west of the Missouri."

"Not the only one," Melissa replied, "There was another woman captured with Ellen and me. Hannah Jones. She was the one who cut Ellen's snake-bite wound and sucked out the poison, then helped me bury her."

Reid frowned. "And she's still back at the Indian camp? Still alive when you left?"

Alive and kicking, Melissa thought with a smile as she remembered her friend. "Yes."

Nathan shook his head, saying in a voice full of pity, "That poor woman. She'll be stuck out there with those Injuns the rest of her life."

Melissa wondered if she should tell the men how Hannah felt about her captivity, that she felt it no worse than the life she had lived, that she even preferred her Indian captor to the white man she had been married to. No, even Nathan, who had Indian friends himself, would be outraged at that. The thought of a white woman preferring an Indian to any white man would be too much for their male egos. Their pity for Hannah would turn to scorn. Only another woman, particularly a woman who had been abused by one of her own, would understand.

"But Reid's right, Missy," Nathan said, breaking into her thoughts. "Any woman who lives in the wilderness should know how to shoot a gun. You need to protect yourself, not only from strangers that might harm you, but Injuns and wild animals, too."

The mention of Indians was all it took. She had no intention of being captured a second time.

As soon as Nathan left, Melissa's shooting lessons began. Reid started by showing her how to load the muzzle-loaded rifle, then positioned it against her shoulder, showing her how to aim and fire.

They stayed out most of the day, coming into the cabin just long enough to warm their hands. Reid pushed her unrelentingly, determined that she should learn and learn well, for he knew her life could well depend on it.

When they finally returned to the cabin, it was almost dark, and Melissa was bone tired, her shoulders and arms aching from the powerful recoil, her head pounding from the noise. She collapsed into the rocking chair, wondering where she would find the strength to prepare supper.

"You have a good eye," Reid remarked, adding another log to the fire. "Most people have a tendency to pull to one side or the other, but your aim is true."

At that minute, Melissa could have cared less about her aim. All she wanted to do was go to bed.

"Go lie down, sweetheart," Reid said in a tender voice. "I'll wake you when supper is ready."

"You're going to cook supper tonight?"

"Yes, tonight I'm the chef."

Melissa was vastly relieved. She walked wearily to their bedroom and was asleep the minute her head hit the pillow.

Reid's supper was delicious, and Melissa ate ravenously, her appetite stimulated by her strenuous exercise and being outdoors. As soon as the dishes were washed and dried, she headed back to the bedroom.

She was just stripping off her dress when Reid walked into the bedroom. "Don't get undressed. There's something outside I want to show you."

"Can't it wait until tomorrow? I'm so tired."

"I know you are, sweetheart. But this is something you don't see often and I don't want you to miss it."

"What?"

"You'll see. I don't want to spoil the surprise."

As Melissa slipped her clothes back on, she thought, This had better be worth all the trouble. She gave Reid an irritated look and walked to the door.

Reid grabbed his coat and slipped it on. Then he opened the door, and they stepped out onto the small porch.

Melissa looked around, then snapped, "I don't see anything unusual."

"Look up there," Reid said, pointing to the sky.

Melissa's breath caught in her throat. Shimmering bands of pale green and rose lights spiraled and waved over the dark sky. "It's beautiful," she whispered. "What is it?"

"The Northern Lights," Reid answered. "It's a natural phenomenon that we don't see too often at this latitude. I understand the farther north you go, the more spectacular they are."

Melissa stood for a long time watching the lights in a mixture of fascination and awe.

"Aren't you cold?" Reid asked.

"A little bit. But I don't want to go in yet. I've never seen anything like it."

Reid opened his jacket and pulled her against his warmth, then closed it over them both, wrapping his arms around her. Melissa felt a deep contentment as she stood wrapped in Reid's warm embrace and watched the awesome, beautiful panorama of lights. Knowing that Reid shared the sight with her only added to her happiness. This is what love is, she thought, sharing things, big and small.

A few days later, Reid returned from checking his traps early, and he and Melissa went for a walk in the snow. Melissa was so intent on walking carefully on her snowshoes, in order not to trip herself, that she paid little attention to where she was walking.

"Watch out," Reid said, pulling her back. "You don't want to step in that." He pointed to a blackened area on the snowbank in front of her.

Melissa stared at the darkened area. "What is it?"

"Snow fleas."

"Fleas? Out here in the snow?" She looked closer, seeing the thousands of small jumping and twitching bodies. "You'd think they'd freeze to death."

Reid laughed. "Sweetheart, the flea can live in the snow or in the desert. He must be the hardiest, most ornery creature on earth. Hell, he'll probably be the last creature on earth. When all else is gone, there will still be a flea."

Melissa remembered the insect that had tormented them back in South Carolina, one that seemed capable of surviving anything nature or man could throw at it. "Or a cockroach," she said.

"No. The flea will outlast the cockroach."

"Why do you say that?"

"If you'd ever had a flea on you, you'd know the answer to that. All that jumping around drives you crazy. No," he said in a decisive voice, "the flea will be the last creature on earth, because the cockroach will commit suicide just to get away from him."

Melissa laughed. "That's ridiculous."

"You think so, huh?" Without warning, he scooped her up in his arms and pretended he was going to throw her covered with fleas into the snowbank. Melissa shrieked and hung on to his neck for dear life.

Reid's golden eyes shimmered. "You have a choice. You can have either them crawling all over you—or me."

Melissa cocked her head thoughtfully. "I don't

341

know. That's a difficult decision to make."

His dark eyebrows rose. "Oh? In that way?"

A mischievous gleam appeared in her eyes. "Well, you sort of drive me crazy, too."

Reid smiled down at her, his golden eyes warm with promise. "Sweetheart, you haven't seen anything yet."

He turned and walked back to the cabin, still carrying Melissa, a determined look on his face.

Chapter Twelve

Nathan sat back and stretched his long legs out before him on the bearskin rug. With his belly full and the warmth of the fire, he felt as contented as a big, lazy cat. He rolled on his side and absently scratched Wolf's ear. Then his eyes drifted to where Melissa was standing and washing dishes. He smiled when he realized she was humming.

His eyes widened in surprise when he heard her start to sing quietly. He glanced over at Reid, standing before the fire. The two men exchanged knowing looks, neither saying a word for fear they would break the spell.

Reid sat down on the hearth, relishing the sound of Melissa's rich contralto voice. The sound washed over him like a loving caress. God, how he loved her, he thought, his eyes watching every tiny movement she made, as if he was trying to imprint her in his mind for eternity.

Nathan studied Reid silently. He sure ain't the same he used to be, Nathan thought with satisfaction. I've never seen him look so happy, so content. That Missy has made a new man out of him, just like I figured she would.

Nathan's eyes drifted back to Melissa. And she was happy, too. So happy she was bursting with joy. Even singing now. Yep, if there were ever two people made for each other it was these two. The only trouble was, being around all that happiness made him feel kinda left out sometimes. And knowing what was going on in that bedroom was beginning to give him an itch.

When Melissa came to sit down beside them, Nathan said to Reid, "Ain't been much in the traps the last few days. What do you say to us taking a little vacation? I've been hankering for a little visit with my Blackfoot friends."

Reid's lips twitched with amusement. Like hell, he thought. What Nathan was hankering for wasn't just visiting. But he certainly wasn't going to object. The thought of having Melissa completely to himself and knowing they'd be able to make love any place or any time of the day sounded like sheer heaven to Reid. "Sounds good to me," he replied.

Two nights later, Reid and Melissa lay sprawled out on the bearskin rug before the fire playing chess. Melissa lay on her stomach, propped on her elbows, her hands cupping her face as she frowned at the chessboard. Reid lay on his side, his head propped on one hand, watching her with a smug smile. He knew he had her where he wanted her. This was *one* game he was going to win.

Then he cocked his head, listening intently.

"What's wrong?" Melissa asked.

"I thought I heard something," Reid said, rising and walking to the window to peer out.

Melissa followed him and looked out, too, but she couldn't see anything in the darkness. "Maybe it was a limb breaking under the heavy snow," she suggested.

"No, it was a different noise."

He listened a minute, then said, "There! Did you hear that?"

Melissa didn't have Reid's sharp woodsman's hearing. "I didn't hear anything."

Reid picked up his gun and opened the door. He stepped out on the small porch and looked around. Melissa joined him.

"Stay here," he said firmly, then walked a few yards into the clearing that surrounded the cabin.

The light from the cabin poured through the open door and illuminated part of the clearing. All Melissa could see was the swirling snow drifting down and the white blurs of the snow-covered trees at the edge of the clearing. The silence was heavy, almost eerie.

Reid stood and scanned the woods, every instinct razor sharp. Something was out there. He could feel its presence. But was it man or beast? Whichever, it was menacing, dangerous. The hairs on his nape rose. He started backing slowly toward the cabin, his eyes glued on the woods, saying to Melissa, "Get back to the cabin."

"But I . . ."

"Now!" Reid yelled.

But before Melissa could even move, it came charging out of the woods, its speed incredible for something so large and massive. And then the grizzly reared, standing on his hind legs and towering a good three feet above Reid, his teeth gleaming in the light, his eyes glowing like two red-hot coals. A roar filled the air, a blood-curdling sound that shook the earth and sounded as if it had come straight from hell itself.

A horrified scream tore from Melissa's throat at the same time Reid raised his gun and fired. The grizzly grunted and staggered back a step or two. Blood poured from the wound in its huge chest and dropped onto the snow at its feet, but the shot was not a killing blow. The pain served only to enrage the huge, shaggy beast.

"Run! Get into the cabin!" Reid yelled, but before he could turn and run, a thousand pounds of animal fury lunged at him, one huge paw knocking his gun from his hand as the other swiped at his leg. A razor-sharp claw tore through his buckskin pants and left a long, deep laceration in his thigh.

Holding his thigh with one hand, Reid tried

346

desperately to get away from the bear, stumbling backward while he groped for the knife at his waist. The grizzly swiped at him again, this time hitting him across the chest. The blow knocked the wind out of him and brought Reid to his knees.

Melissa had been watching in horror. When the grizzly knocked the gun from Reid's hands, she turned and ran back into the cabin, grabbing her gun. Reid had insisted she keep it loaded at all times, arguing that she was still too slow and awkward at leading, and now she was grateful for his foresight. She ran back outside just as the bear swung again, the powerful blow knocking Reid off his feet and backward in the snow. Reid lay on the ground, perfectly motionless.

Melissa didn't know whether Reid was dead or just knocked senseless. She only knew that she had to kill the bear, or Reid would be killed for certain. The huge beast loomed over Reid, growling and snarling, still swinging its massive paws.

If I shoot now, the bear might fall on Reid and crush him under all that weight, she thought. I'll have to lure the grizzly away from him. She spied a piece of firewood that Reid had dropped in the snow that afternoon. She picked it up and threw it at the bear, yelling at the same time to get his attention.

The firewood hit the huge beast on its shoulder. It looked at Melissa, then back down at Reid, as if trying to decide which to attack.

"Come here, you bastard! Come and get me!" Melissa yelled, waving her rifle at the bear.

Then the bear turned, taking a few lumbering steps toward her. Her breath caught in sheer terror. She raised the gun, struggling to control her trembling hands. The animal towered over her, raising both massive paws, those weird red eyes glittering. Then it roared, and Melissa felt the heat and smelled the stench of its breath as she looked up into the immense, gaping chasm that was its mouth. She aimed right into that black void and fired.

She stared at the bear in disbelief as it just stood there. My God, how could she have missed? Then, like a huge tree that had been felled, it toppled to the ground, the earth shaking from the impact. Melissa just had time to jump back to keep from being crushed by its awesome weight.

Melissa slumped, weak with relief, and then gasped as she saw the bear struggling to rise. She had just stunned it. My God, what did it take to kill it?

She had to kill it while it was still down. But with what? She was too slow at loading her gun, and Reid's was empty, too. She looked about for some more powerful weapon. The glitter of metal just inside the door caught her eye. Reid's ax! She dropped the gun and ran to the ax, staggering under its weight as she carried it outside. She watched as the bear struggled to all fours and swayed, then flopped back down on the ground.

Just as the bear raised its shaggy head to try again, Melissa lifted the ax and, with all the strength she could summon, slammed it down. The sickening crunch of bone shattering filled her ears as she buried the ax deeply into the back of the bear's thick neck.

The momentum of the blow brought Melissa to her knees beside the bear. She knew that she had finally killed him. Then the horror of it all came rushing in on her. She struggled to her feet, her legs feeling like rubber. A violent trembling came over her. And then, as the sickening smell of fresh blood and the animal's fetid odor filled her nostrils, she gagged. She lurched away, half gagging and half sobbing, then again fell to her knees as she stumbled over Reid.

The sight of him lying on the ground brought her to her senses. She stared at him, her heart in her throat. Then, seeing the rise and fall of his chest, she cried out, "Oh, thank you, God! Thank you!"

She leaned over him and shook his shoulder. "Reid! Wake up! You've got to try to stand so that I can get you into the cabin."

Reid's head rolled to one side.

Melissa rubbed snow on his face, hoping to revive him. Then she shook him again. "Damn it! Wake up! You'll freeze to death if you stay out here."

She stared down at his limp body, his deathly pale face. "Don't you dare die on me," she sobbed. "No! No, I'm not going to let you die!" she cried fiercely.

With a will born of desperation, she shoved and tugged and pulled, slowly inching him toward the cabin. Her fear of losing him poured adrenaline into her bloodstream, giving her a strength she had never known she possessed. But even then, it was a slow, agonizing ordeal.

When she had finally dragged him into the cabin, just far enough to shut the door, she collapsed, her breath coming in deep, painful gasps. She was exhausted. All she wanted to do was close her eyes and sleep.

As her breath finally slowed, she became aware of a stickiness on her fingers. Raising her head, she saw that her hand was lying in a puddle of blood — Reid's blood.

A new flow of adrenaline rushed through her veins. She sat up and quickly examined him. His buckskins were shredded. There were multiple scratches over his chest and arms. But she knew from his blood-soaked pants that it was the wound on his leg that was life-threatening.

She ran to their room and brought out her sewing basket, then quickly cut away his pants leg. A long, deep gash ran down his thigh, from a few inches below his groin almost to his knee, and Melissa knew that the only way to stop the bleeding was to stitch it closed.

She gathered her supplies, Nathan's jug of corn whiskey, a pot of boiling water, and bandages. She placed her scissors and needle in the pot of boiling water, picked up a spool of thread, then tossed it aside. Reaching up to Reid's head, she pulled out several long strands of hair and threw them into the boiling water, too. She splashed whiskey over the wound and washed her hands in it, then poured off the boiling water and threaded the needle with a strand of Reid's hair. The sewing was slow and tedious, but when she had finished, the gaping wound was closed and just oozing blood. She bandaged it carefully and then cut away his shirt to examine his other wounds. None were deep enough to require stitching, so she cleaned them with whiskey and bandaged the largest one on his arm.

Melissa tried to pull Reid closer to the fire, but could only manage to drag him another foot or two. She placed a pillow under his head and spread blankets over him. Only then did she give in to her exhaustion. She lay beside him, her hand on his chest. Feeling the reassuring beat of his heart, she finally dozed.

She was abruptly awakened when the door slammed open and Nathan rushed in, stumbling over them. Wolf was right on his heels.

"Godalmighty!" Nathan cried. "When I saw that dead bear out there and all that blood, it scared the hell out of me. Thank God, you're both alive."

Melissa couldn't believe her eyes. Somehow, miraculously, Nathan was back. He wouldn't let Reid die. An immense wave of relief washed over her, relief so overpowering she threw herself in Nathan's arms and sobbed uncontrollably.

Nathan rocked and soothed her until she finally calmed down.

"I'm sorry," Melissa sobbed. "But I'm so relieved you're here. I've been so worried about Reid."

"There, now, don't you worry no more." He gently pushed her back. "Now, let me take a look at him."

Nathan lifted the blanket and examined the wounds on Reid's chest and arms, then removed the bloodstained bandage and looked at his thigh.

"You sewed him up like the Injuns do? With his own hair?" he asked in a surprised voice.

Melissa looked down at the wound and frowned, wondering if she had done the right thing. "Do you think I should have used thread, instead?"

"Nope. I reckon you did the best thing. For some reason, wounds sewed up with the same person's hair don't fester as bad as those sewed with cotton or silk. Don't rightly know why, though. He looked down at the minute stitching. "You sure did a fine job."

Melissa was relieved to know Nathan approved, but she was still worried about Reid.

"How much blood does a person have to lose to cause unconsciousness?"

"A good bit. Why do you ask?"

"Because Reid's been unconscious ever since it happened?"

"Unconscious? You mean you ain't drugged him yet?"

"No."

"But if he was unconscious, how in the hell did you get him in here?"

"I just kept pushing and tugging until he was here."

Nathan stared at her in astonishment. It seemed impossible that a little thing like her could pull a man the size of Reid any distance, much less from outside.

"Do you think he's unconscious because he lost so much blood?" she asked.

Nathan shook his head as if to clear it, then looked down at Reid. "I doubt that. His color is too good." He felt at his wrist. "And his pulse is good and strong."

Melissa watched as he examined Reid more closely. He looked up. "Reckon I've found the problem. Feel back here on the back of his head. He's got a good-sized goose egg back there. He must have hit his head on something hard."

Melissa felt the knot. "Yes, he must have hit his head on a rock buried beneath the snow the last time the bear knocked him down."

Nathan frowned. "Wait a minute, Missy. If Reid was knocked out, who put that ax in the bear's neck?"

"I did," Melissa said calmly, then wailed, "Oh, Nathan, it was horrible! Reid shot the bear, but it just kept coming. Then the bear slapped his gun out of his hands and did that to his leg. Reid kept trying to get away from it, to get his knife out, but the bear kept knocking him down. Then I shot the bear in the head, but I must have missed its brain. I just stunned it. So, while it was down, I hit it with the ax."

Again Nathan was dumbfounded. He stared at her. It seemed incredible that she would fell an animal the size of a grizzly bear. With an ax, no less! Every woodsman knew the female guarding her young was the most dangerous animal in the world, much more so than her male counterpart, but he had never realized that human females had the same fierceness when it came to protecting their loved ones. And he'd never understand where she found the strength.

Melissa continued. "I'm so glad you decided to come back earlier than you had planned."

"Reckon you have to thank Wolf for that." He ruffled the fur on Wolf's neck as the big dog trotted up to them upon hearing his name. "You see, all of a sudden, he started acting real strange. Damndest thing I ever saw. Barking at me and running out of the tepee, over and over. Then he grabbed my sleeve and yanked on it, like he was telling me to come on. Well, I finally got up to see what he was having such a fit about and he took off like a bat out of hell in this direction. I figured he must have known something was wrong here, so I put my snowshoes on and dogtrotted back here as fast as I could."

Melissa was amazed. How could the dog have sensed danger from that far away? It was uncanny. She hugged the dog. "Thank you, Wolf."

The big dog thumped his tail on the floor. She could have almost sworn he was grinning with self-satisfaction.

She looked back down at Reid, chewing her lip in her anxiety.

"Now, don't you be worrying none. He's gonna be fine," Nathan assured her.

"I don't know, Nathan. I've heard of people hitting their heads and never regaining consciousness."

A look of stark fear filled Nathan's eyes. Quickly, he hid the look from Melissa, not wanting to frighten her even more. But he couldn't hide his look of deep concern.

"Do you think we should move him closer to the fire?"

"Nope, not until he wakes up and we know he's gonna be okay. He can't be uncomfortable, since he can't feel nothing." He looked down at the exhausted girl. "I tell you what. You stay here by him and I'll fix us a pot of hot coffee."

Nathan turned toward the fire. Goddamn, after this shock, I need a drink, he thought. And it won't hurt to slip a tot into Missy's coffee, either.

After Nathan had added more wood to the fire and fixed coffee, he handed Melissa a cup of coffee and hunkered beside her, drinking his own. A few minutes later, Reid groaned and opened his eyes.

"Christ, my head hurts," he mumbled. "Who slugged me?"

Melissa and Nathan were so relieved, they both laughed.

Reid looked around the cabin with dazed eyes. "What happened?"

Nathan chuckled. "Seems you and a grizzly had a little disagreement."

Suddenly remembering, Reid's eyes flew open. "Melissa?" he asked, trying to sit up. Then he groaned, holding his head.

"I'm here, darling," Melissa sobbed with happiness. She hugged him. "Everything is going to be all right."

"Thank God," Reid mumbled, holding her tightly to him. "Thank God you're safe."

A few minutes later, Nathan broke the couple up. Pulling gently on Melissa's shoulder, he said, "Better give him some of this jimsonweed for the pain." He handed her a cup.

Reid drank the bitter painkiller gratefully, and when he dozed back off, Melissa said, "Maybe we shouldn't have given him anything to make him go back to sleep just yet."

"Nope, that's just what he needs. With that blow he took, he needs to rest and not get excited. He's gonna be all right now. Of course, I reckon he'll have a hell of a headache for a day or two. Maybe it's a good thing he's got that bad leg. Probably the only way we'll keep the stubborn cuss down."

Nathan peered out the window. "I'd better get out there and skin that bear before it's frozen. If it ever gets completely frozen, I'll never get it butchered."

"It can rot out there for all I care," Melissa spat.

Nathan chuckled. "Now that wouldn't be very smart. I don't reckon we want every wolf within a hundred miles at our door." He turned and pulled on his coat. "If you need me, you just holler."

Later that morning, Nathan built a cot beside the fireplace for Reid. Since he was still drugged, it was necessary for Nathan and Melissa to carry him to it. Nathan lifted his shoulders while Melissa took his feet. The older man was shocked at how heavy Reid was, and wondered again how Melissa had managed to drag him in from outside.

By this time, Reid's chest and arms were covered with ugly bruises from where the bear had mauled him. Because of the pain from them, combined with that from his wounded leg and headache, it was necessary to keep him drugged that day. By nightfall, the meager supply of jimsonweed was gone, since Reid had used most of it on Melissa when she was injured. When Nathan tried to get Reid to drink some of his whiskey for the pain, Reid refused.

"Goddammit, I know how you feel about drinking, but you're hurting and this will help the pain," Nathan argued.

"No!" Reid hissed.

"But, Reid, this isn't the same as drinking," Melissa joined in. "It's like taking medicine."

Reid clenched his teeth with pain. His golden eyes glittered. "I said no! Now, Dammit, leave me alone."

Melissa turned and walked angrily back into the kitchen in the other corner of the cabin. Furious at Reid's obstinance, she started banging pots and pans.

When Nathan joined her, she snapped, "What's he trying to prove? How brave he is? Well, he won't get any sympathy from me."

"Don't be so hard on him, Missy," Nathan said in a low voice.

"I'm not being hard on him! He's being hard on himself. It's stupid to hurt when it's unnecessary. He's just being stubborn."

"No, he ain't. He's got his reasons for how he feels about drinking. Good reasons."

"What reasons? Religious convictions?"

"Nope. Don't have nothing to do with religion."

"Then what?"

"Ain't my place to say," Nathan said in a tight voice. "Just take my word for it."

Nathan looked over at Reid, who was bundled in the blanket with perspiration from pain beading his brow. "He needs you, Missy."

Melissa glanced over at Reid. Tears glittered in her eyes. "I know, Nathan. But I can't stand to see him in pain."

"Then don't make it harder than it is for him. He's already miserable enough without knowing you're mad at him, too."

"You're right, Nathan," Melissa answered, feeling ashamed of herself. She walked over to Reid and sat down beside him, taking his hand. He smiled at her gratefully and closed his eyes, then eventually slept.

The next day, Reid was alert and much more comfortable. Nathan sat talking to him as Melissa prepared their supper on the other side of the cabin.

"Thank God you came when you did, Nathan," Reid said. "Otherwise that bear would have killed me and probably Melissa, too."

"I didn't kill that bear," Nathan replied. "Missy did."

Reid couldn't believe it. Bears were one of the hardest animals in the world to kill. It took multiple shots to bring one down, unless you were lucky enough to put a ball through his heart or brain. And considering how massive a bear's chest was, and how small his brain, that would be a hundred-to-one shot.

"Melissa shot him?" he asked in a shocked voice.

"Yep, she shot him," Nathan replied. "Her ball missed his brain by a fraction of an inch, just like yours missed his heart. It wasn't her ball that killed him. It was the ax."

"Ax? What in the hell are you talking about?"

"Well, apparently that shot of hers stunned him. While he was down, she hit him with your ax." Nathan grinned. "Neatest piece of work I've ever seen. She severed his spine and bashed in the back of his skull. Hell, she damned near chopped off his head."

"Are you telling me she killed that bear with an ax?"

"Sssh, keep your voice down," Nathan cautioned, glancing at Melissa. "Missy don't like no one talking about it."

Reid stared at Melissa, his look incredulous.

"I know what you're thinking," Nathan remarked. "It doesn't seem possible a little thing like her could even pick up that ax, much less swing it. She's like one of those warrior women. You know, the ones that are supposed to be so strong."

"An amazon?"

"Yep."

Reid grinned. "Well, I don't know about that, but one thing is for sure. She's one hell of a woman."

"She sure is," Nathan agreed, then he chuckled. "That poor old bear didn't know what it was getting into when it tackled our little Missy. Now," he said, pulling back the blanket that covered Reid's leg, "let's have a look at that leg."

Nathan unwrapped the bandage, and Reid looked down at the wound curiously. Then he frowned. "What did you sew it up with?"

"I didn't sew it up. Missy did. I didn't get here for several hours after it happened. By then, she had you in the cabin and had sewed you up with your own hair. That's how the Injuns do it."

"My own hair?" Reid said in a disgusted voice. "Why in the hell didn't she use thread?"

"Now before you start complaining, take a look at that leg. It's mending right smart."

Reid looked down at the wound. It was healing remarkably well. There was none of the puffiness or redness around the stitches that was usually seen with thread-stitched wounds. And there was certainly no sign of infection.

Nor was there the next day, when Nathan and Melissa bathed Reid.

After they had finished, Reid smiled up at them. "I have to admit I feel better." He rubbed his beard. "Now if I had a shave, I'd feel almost human again." He grinned at Melissa. "How about it, sweetheart. Will you give me a shave?"

"Me? Why, I don't know anything about shaving. Why don't you ask Nathan?"

"Not me," Nathan said. "Hell, I don't even shave myself."

"Why don't you just grow a beard, like Nathan?" Melissa asked. "It would protect your face from the freezing weather."

"No, to the contrary," Reid replied. "Wearing a beard and mustache isn't too smart in this cold weather. The moisture from your breath freezes in the hair and causes frostbite."

Melissa's look was dubious. She turned to Nathan. "Is that true?"

"Yep."

"Then why don't you shave your beard in the winter."

Nathan shrugged his shoulders. "Because I'm too damned lazy to shave everyday. Besides, if I shaved my beard, everyone will see all those ugly frostbite scars I got on my face."

Reid and Melissa laughed at Nathan's logic.

"If you bring me my shaving stuff, I'll do it myself." Reid said.

"No, I'll do it," Melissa relented. "But don't complain if I cut you."

"I'm not worried," Reid said. Then he grinned. "Besides, I've still got a whole head of hair left. You could sew up a lot of cuts with that."

Melissa glared at him and then flounced away to get his shaving equipment.

She discovered that shaving someone was not

an easy task. By the time she was finished, Reid's face was nicked and scraped in several places. But, despite that, Melissa couldn't help but admire his handsome face. It would be a shame to cover that with a beard, she thought.

Her eyes drifted across his broad, naked shoulders and chest as she tucked the blanket closer around him. Those familiar feelings stirred in her. Goodness, she thought, shocked at herself, how can you think of *that* at a time like this?

Two days later, after he had helped get Reid settled, Nathan went out to check the traps. Reid watched Melissa with hungry eyes as she went about her chores. Finally, when she passed by him, he caught her hand and pulled her down to sit on the cot beside him.

As he lifted her hand and kissed her palm, she laughed shakily. "Stop that, Reid. I've got work to do."

"What's more important? Me or your chores?" he asked as he nibbled the soft skin of her inner wrist.

A shiver of pleasure ran up Melissa's spine. "Why you, of course."

Reid smiled, his warm golden eyes drifting over her. "In that case," he whispered. He pulled her into his arms, his lips moving slowly as he leisurely kissed her, savoring her taste.

Melissa struggled for reason, but as the kiss deepened and his searing tongue slid into her mouth, flicking and teasing, all thought fled. A low, throaty moan escaped her lips as she caught his head, threading her fingers through his thick hair, kissing him back hungrily.

Reid's long fingers slipped inside her dress, cupping one soft breast, rubbing the rosy tip with his palm. His lips left hers to lavish lingering kisses across her face. His warm breath stirred the hair by her ear. "Take off your dress."

"Reid, we've got to stop. We can't . . ." She gasped as his hands slid under the dress, his long, skillful fingers burning a trail of fire along the length of her legs and across her back as he slowly pulled it up.

The dress was tossed aside as Reid impatiently buried his face between her breasts, nuzzling and bathing them with soft kisses. Melissa arched her back to give him better access, her arms circling around his broad shoulders as she dropped kisses on his thick hair.

Melissa was spinning under the intoxicating feel of his warm, searching mouth against her breasts, his lips nibbling, then rolling one sensitive bud, then the other, sucking gently. His manly scent filled her nostrils, exciting her more.

"Reid, we . . . we've . . . we've got to . . . we've got to stop," she whispered in a ragged voice.

"No, it's too late to stop," Reid muttered hoarsely, his hand drawing hers to his erection, the rigid flesh throbbing with anticipation. Then his own hand found and searched her femininity, his subtle, deft fingers taunting with soft savagery.

Her senses swimming, Melissa sobbed, "This is madness. You can't . . . Your leg."

"We can . . . You can," he whispered back, his warm lips once more softly torturing her breasts. He pulled her gently over him. "You do the work."

Melissa looked at him in confusion.

"Ride me, sweetheart," Reid muttered, pulling one of her legs over him to straddle him.

Carefully, she shifted her weight over him. Feeling the hot, moist tip of him against her, she swiveled her hips, bathing him with her own moisture, drawing a gasp from Reid. As she slowly lowered herself over him, enclosing him inch by inch, and Reid felt her velvety heat surround him, the muscles rippling and clutching, he sighed with a long shudder of exquisite pleasure.

Melissa's eyes widened with wonder, feeling his long length buried deep inside her, more aware than ever before of her own throbbing, swollen flesh. She moved tentatively at first, seeking those movements that gave them both the most pleasure—slow, sensuous movements—then, feeling those rhythmical waves engulfing her, surging and ebbing, she drummed her hips against his.

Reid watched her above him, his eyes drinking in her beauty, his hands stroking her thighs, her hips, her breasts. And as she moved more wildly, he nipped at her shoulders and soft breasts, and then, feeling that unbearable pressure building to its crest, he pulled her down to him, his mouth covering hers in a deep, searing kiss as he arched his hips, thrusting deeply. He exploded inside her as the universe shattered into a million glittering pieces.

Melissa collapsed weakly over him. As soon as she could, she tried to rise and relieve him of her weight.

Reid held her tightly, whispering, "No, sweetheart. Stay with me. I've missed feeling you in my arms, my body against yours."

"But I'm too heavy," Melissa objected.

"You're as light as a butterfly."

Melissa snuggled closer, nuzzling the strong column of his throat, tasting his saltiness there. She really didn't want to leave him, either. She loved holding him closely, with her legs as well as her arms. If it were possible, she would take all of him inside her, absorb him completely, body and soul.

But when she felt him hardening and growing inside her, her concern for him overrode all else. She tried to rise. "No, Reid. No more. You'll hurt your leg."

Reid's hands twisted in her hair, pulling her back down. "Sweetheart, you're a worry-wart," he whispered against her lips before his mouth claimed hers masterfully, quickly dissolving all resistance.

When Nathan returned that evening, Melissa was busy cooking supper. He glanced over at Reid and frowned. What's he looking so smug about, he wondered.

"Everything go okay here?" he asked, eyeing Reid suspiciously.

"No problems," Reid answered.

"Well, let's have a look at that leg," Nathan said, walking over to Reid and tossing back the blanket. Seeing the fresh bloodstains on the bandage, he said, "Just what I figured. You're bleeding again."

Melissa whirled at Nathan's words. Her face turned ashen.

"You've been up to something, haven't you?" Nathan accused. "Something you shouldn't have been doing."

Melissa blushed furiously, horrified that Nathan would guess what they had done.

"What did you do? Get out of bed when Missy's back was turned?"

"Yes, I had a bit of exercise," Reid admitted, leaving Nathan to draw his own conclusions.

"Damn fool! Trying to walk on that leg. I hope you're satisfied."

"Yes, I am," Reid remarked candidly. His eyes met Melissa's over Nathan's shoulder. He grinned. "It was worth it."

Despite his setback, Reid was soon able to hobble to a chair and back with Nathan or Melissa's assistance. A few days later, when Nathan was again gone from the cabin, his golden eyes followed Melissa around the room.

Melissa was very aware of his warm, ardent gaze on her and very careful to stay out of his reach. As much as she wanted him, too, she felt guilty over his setback and was determined it wasn't going to happen again.

"Come here, Melissa," Reid commanded quietly.

Reid's deep, husky voice washed over Melissa like a caress. She fought back her rising desire and turned away from him. "No, Reid. No more until you've completely healed. I won't have that wound opening again."

Reid frowned. "You're a hard, cruel woman, Melissa. Are you just going to leave me like this?" He motioned to the bulge straining at his pants.

"I certainly am," Melissa replied. Then she laughed to herself, seeing the expression that came over his face. He looks like a little boy who just had his candy taken from him, she thought. "And you can stop that pouting. That won't do you any good, either."

Reid chuckled. "You just wait, sweetheart. In a few days, when this leg of mine is better, you won't be able to run from me. I'll catch you if I have to chase you all over the cabin."

If I keep getting hungrier, in a few days you won't have to chase me, Melissa thought wryly. I'll be chasing you.

Within a week, Reid was limping around the cabin on his own steam.

One night, Nathan asked Melissa, "What are you going to do with your bearskin?"

"*My* bearskin?"

"Yep," Nathan replied. "You killed the bear, so the skin belongs to you. You want to put it somewhere here in the cabin?"

Melissa was willing to eat bear meat. Living with the Indians had taught her not to waste food. But she certainly didn't want to look at the skin of the animal that had almost killed Reid. No, she didn't want any reminders around of that horrible night. "I don't ever want to see that bearskin again! Not ever!"

Nathan gazed thoughtfully into the fire for a few minutes, then said to Reid, "If I went to visit my Blackfoot friends for a few days, do you think you two could manage to stay out of trouble?"

Reid laughed. "I suppose we could."

Nathan looked back at Melissa. "You sure you don't want that bearskin?"

"I'm positive," she answered.

"Well, in that case I think I'll take it with me. Injuns are real big on bearskins. Think I'll take the sled and take them some of the meat, too. We've got more than we can possibly eat."

That was fine with Melissa, too. She was sick and tired of bear meat. She longed for some elk or deer or even rabbit for a change.

A few days later, Reid dropped the snowshoes he was rewebbing and limped to the window to look out.

"What's wrong?" Melissa asked.

"I thought I heard something."

Melissa's heart leapt in her throat, remembering the last time they had had this conversation.

Reid continued staring out the window. "Do you see anything?" Melissa asked.

"Yes, but I don't believe it. Come here and look at this."

Melissa looked out of the window. Nathan was coming toward the cabin, dogtrotting beside Wolf, who was pulling the sled. Behind him were seven Indians on horseback, each pulling a sled behind them.

"Who are they?" Melissa asked.

"Some of his Blackfoot friends, I assume. I recognize that first one. He's Chief Rainwater."

They watched as the strange procession stopped before the cabin. As Nathan released Wolf from his harness and the big dog ran off chasing a snow rabbit, the Indians dismounted, pointing to the cabin and chattering amongst themselves.

As Nathan led the Indians up to the cabin, Reid muttered, "What in the hell is he up to?"

The door opened, and Nathan entered, the trail of Indians right on his heels. Nathan grinned, saying to Melissa, "This is Chief Rainwater and some of his tribal council. The chief insisted on seeing the woman who killed a bear. He doesn't believe it's possible. Injuns think only the strongest and most skillful warriors can kill a bear. It puts them in line to become chief."

The Indians stared at Melissa mutely. She recognized those curious looks. She had seen the same looks at the Indian camp when they had first ridden in. Apparently these Indians had never seen a white woman, either.

Her heart pounded in fear as Chief Rainwater stepped forward and took her hand, looking at her skin closely, then rubbing his finger over her arm. He reached up and fingered her face, then ran his hand over her hair in wonder. Melissa forced herself not to flinch at his touch. She stood proudly, her eyes bravely meeting his dark eyes as he stepped back and scrutinized her again. Finally he grunted and said something to Nathan.

Nathan smiled. "He says not only is the white woman beautiful, but she is brave and bold, too. Now he believes she could kill a bear."

The Indian chief said something else to Nathan. Nathan shook his head and pointed to Reid, talking in a stern voice.

"What did he say?" Reid demanded.

"He wanted to know if he could buy Missy. He said such a brave woman should be a chief's wife. I told him no, that the woman belongs to you." Nathan grinned. "I also told him that you were a great warrior. That you had counted coup

371

on the bear."

"Counted coup on a bear?" Reid asked in disbelief. "I never heard of such a thing."

Nathan shrugged. "Neither have I. But they consider touching their enemies as counting coup. I reckon they consider a bear a worthy enemy." Nathan's black eyes twinkled. "Of course, if I were to tell the truth, that bear did a heap more counting coup on you than you did him."

Reid glared at him. Melissa fought back a laugh.

"Reckon you can scare up some vittles for our guests, Missy?" Nathan asked, ignoring Reid's hot look.

Melissa was stunned. She had never cooked for this large a crowd. "I suppose so."

"Better put on a couple of pots of stew and bake a heap of cornbread. These Injuns eat like horses," Nathan said.

Trying to prepare a meal with a houseful of curious Indians turned out to be quite a chore. They were everywhere, all over the small cabin, fingering things, poking into the cabinets and opening sacks and canisters. Every time she turned around, she was bumping into one of them. They were particularly fascinated with the oven, and Melissa clenched her teeth every time one of them opened the door to peek into it. At this rate, her cornbread would never get done. She sighed in relief when they discovered the rocking chair, standing in line like children to wait for their turn to sit and rock in it while the others laughed uproariously.

Reid sidled up to her. "How much longer before that stew is ready" he asked.

"It should simmer another hour or two," Melissa answered. "The meat is still tough."

"Hell, go ahead and serve it, so they'll leave. Otherwise, we're liable to be stuck with them all night."

When Melissa announced the meal was ready, Nathan said, "Just set the pots of stew and pans of cornbread in the middle of the floor, like they do in their camps."

Wisely, Melissa made no effort to join the men while they were eating. She knew that Indian women never ate until the men were finished. She didn't even care when there wasn't a spoonful of stew or a crumb of cornbread left. She was just glad to be finished cooking for them.

As soon as the Indians had finished eating, they rose and, without a word, walked out of the cabin. Nathan followed them.

Melissa looked at the mess in the middle of the cabin. Not only would she have to wash all the dishes, but the floor would have to be scrubbed, too. She shook her head in disgust, then made her way through the clutter and joined Reid at the window.

"Now what in the hell are they doing?" Reid asked, half to himself.

Melissa peered out the window. The Indians were unloading their sleds and stacking big piles of furs in the snow.

"I'm going out there and see what's going on," Reid said, pulling on his coat.

Curious herself, Melissa said, "Wait for me." She and Reid walked out just as the Indians were riding away, pulling their empty sleds behind them. Reid and Melissa stared dumbly at the stacks of furs the Indians had left behind.

Melissa had seen big stacks of furs on the wharves in St. Louis, but she had never seen such a variety of furs. There were the brown pelts of beaver, muskrat, mink, and otter; the gray pelts of wolf and wolverine; the russet peels of marten; the orange-brown pelts of red fox, the black pelts of sable; and the white pelts of ermine, their tails tipped with black.

Nathan walked up to them. "Well, Missy, what do you think of the trade I made for your bearskin?"

Melissa looked at him with astonishment. "You traded one bearskin for all these furs?"

"Yep."

"What the hell!" Reid exclaimed, looking at the stacks of furs in disbelief. "What's wrong with those Indians? Are they crazy?"

"How good a look did you get at that bear?" Nathan asked Reid.

"Not very good," Reid admitted. "I was a little busy at the time," he added ruefully.

374

"Didn't you notice his color?" Nathan asked.

"Yes, he was gray. One of those silvertip grizzlies."

"Nope, he wasn't no silvertip." Nathan grinned. "He was an albino."

"An albino?" Reid asked in astonishment. "Are you sure?"

"Hell yes, I'm sure," Nathan snapped. "I skinned him, didn't I? I'm telling you, he was a pure albino. His fur and skin didn't have a bit of coloring. His claws were colorless, not black like other bears. His snout was just a pale pink. Why, even his eyes were pink."

Melissa remembered those eyes glowing red in the firelight. She shivered.

"Well, I'll be damned," Reid muttered. "I've never heard of an albino bear before."

"Neither have I," Nathan answered. "And neither had Chief Rainwater. Now you know why he was willing to trade all those furs for that bearskin."

"But that's ridiculous!" Melissa cried. "All these furs for one bearskin?"

"Albinos are rare in any animal, Melissa," Reid said. "With his head and claws still attached, that bearskin would have bought a good price anywhere. And I assume that's the way you skinned him," he said to Nathan.

"Yep. Didn't want no one saying he was a polar bear," Nathan answered. "Course I had to sew up that hole in the back of his neck." He turned and looked at the pile of furs. "There must be eight thousand dollars worth of furs there."

"Eight thousand dollars!" Melissa gasped. "Why, that's highway robbery!"

"No, it ain't," Nathan replied in a defensive voice. "Like Reid said, albinos are rare. But Injuns value them even more than white men. They think any albino is big medicine. And since that's a bearskin, the animal they consider the most fierce of all creatures, they think it's really powerful medicine. Besides, all those furs didn't come from one Injun. The whole tribe chipped in. From now on, that albino bearskin will be their tribal talisman."

Melissa still thought the price ridiculous, even if the bear had been an albino.

"What are you gonna do with all your money, Missy?"

"My money?"

"Yep. Those are your furs now. I reckon you'll be wanting to sell them."

"Well, I may have killed the bear, but you skinned it and made the trade. I think we should split the money those furs bring."

"Split it?" Nathan said in surprise. "Naw, Missy, I couldn't do that."

"I insist. I won't take a cent unless you agree to split it," Melissa said in a determined voice.

Reid laughed. "You might as well save your breath, Nathan. You know how stubborn she

376

can be when she's made up her mind."

Melissa glared at him. Then remembering how he had almost lost his life to the bear, she said, "On second thought, I think we should split it three ways. Reid deserves a share, too."

"Me?" Reid asked in surprise. "Why should I get a share?"

"Because you played the most important part. Without you, I couldn't have killed the bear, and then Nathan wouldn't have been able to skin him and to make the trade."

"I still don't understand," Reid said. "What part did I play?"

Melissa's eyes twinkled mischievously and grinned. "You were the bait."

Chapter Thirteen

The second week in February, the warm, dry chinook winds blew down from the Rockies and melted the snow. The warm air was a welcome relief after the howling blizzards of January.

Water dripped from the eaves of the roof as the snow melted in the daytime, then froze again at night, leaving long icicles hanging from the roof. The steady, nerve-racking drip, drip, drip filled the cabin. To this was added the soft plopping and dull thudding sounds as the snow fell off the tree limbs and dropped below.

The snow on the ground melted in irregular patches, leaving the larger snowbanks honeycombed with pockets of air from the warming winds. The water ran down the gullies, joining the melted water at the river's edge. The ground turned to oozing mud. Patches of purple and lavender appeared as the crocuslike pasqueflower raised their heads, seeking the warmth of the sun.

Melissa was awakened one morning by a new

sound, a noise that sounded as if scores of guns were being fired. She bolted up in bed, her eyes full of fear. "What's that?"

"It's the river breaking up," Reid said in an excited voice. "Hurry and dress. This is something you've never seen in South Carolina."

The three of them rushed to the riverbank, Reid holding Melissa's arm to steady her as they splashed through the slippery mud puddles. And then they stopped and watched with awe.

The noise was deafening as the ice cracked with loud retorts, echoing over the woods. Then it began to move, grinding, crushing, bucking, and heaving, as huge blocks of ice tilted, pitching every which way, gouging the river bottom until the normally placid, clear river was frothy and muddy.

"I've never seen anything like it," Melissa yelled over the din.

"If you think this is bad, you should see the Missouri when it breaks up," Nathan yelled back. "Then it really does have more mud than water."

"And now the spring floods will begin," Reid added.

And the spring floods did come. The river turned into a rampaging monster, sweeping uprooted trees and huge chunks of ice along with it. But that was not all the water carried: Huge buffalo carcasses bobbed and dipped in the swirling water, buffalo that had wandered out onto the river and frozen to death during the winter. Many of the carcasses were already putrifying, the flesh bloated and turning green. For days, the stench of these half-rotten animals fouled the air.

Reid and Nathan began trapping in earnest as the ice melted and the beavers began to come out of their lodges. The men went from dawn to dusk as they made their rounds, setting their traps in the shallow water of the river or in the water by the runways leading to the beavers' dams. After the traps were set and their chains staked, a small twig was positioned to project over the trap. On this twig, the bait, castorum, was placed.

As the season progressed, there were furs everywhere. Stretching frames with drying pelts were scattered all over the cabin, and when all the frames were full, the pelts were nailed to the cabin's walls, many of them the prized blanket pelts taken from beaver weighing over fifty pounds. As if looking at the pelts everywhere she turned wasn't bad enough, they also had a steady diet of beaver meat. Melissa became just as sick and tired of it as she had once been of bear meat.

Where Reid and Nathan were busy with their trapping, Melissa was often bored and restless. She took to taking long walks through the woods. Since Wolf was no longer needed to pull the sled, he often accompanied her, trotting beside her until he spied a squirrel or a butterfly to chase. And then he was off, barking furiously.

She delighted in the sights nature unveiled each day as spring lavished her gifts upon the earth. Even before the other trees put out their tender buds, the wild cherry and plum trees burst into bloom, their white flowers perfuming the air. And then the earth seemed to explode in a mass of color as the meadows were covered with the pink shooting stars, the showy white blossoms of the trillium, the purple dogtooth violets, the yellow snapdragons and buttercups, and the sweet-smelling lavender sweet peas.

Melissa enjoyed watching the abundant wild-life as much as the colorful flowering, amazed that the animals and birds seemed to have no fear of humans. She chuckled as she watched a harried prairie hen herding her brood of curious, darting chicks through the woods and then held her breath as a family of skunks passed her with their distinctive waddling gait. With a tender pinecone, she lured a squirrel to eat from her hand, admiring his thick, bushy tail as he ate, but taking care to keep her fingers away from his sharp teeth. She stopped to watch a beaver preening itself by the river, using the two pecu-liar toes with split nails on each of its hind legs to comb its hair and then oil its coat, and then laughed as she viewed the beaver's kits cavorting in the water near their lodge. She crouched and watched a rabbit nibbling daintily on a fern, and when it stood on its hind legs to eye her back, she wiggled her nose, mimicking it.

At the end of April, Reid and Nathan called a halt to their trapping. The beaver and muskrat were beginning to molt from the heat. Many other trappers would continue taking these inferior pelts, but the two men felt taking anything but prime pelts was wrong. To them, killing an animal for a fur that would only bring a few dollars was wasteful, an abuse and an insult against nature. So they collected their traps, oiled them, wrapped them in oilskins, and buried them for the next trapping season.

When they tallied the furs they had taken, Nathan said to Reid, "We'll never get all these furs and those we got from the Blackfeet into our canoe. We're gonna have to build a raft to get them down to St. Louis. It's a good thing you've got keelboat experience."

Again, the sound of axes biting into wood rang through the forest. Even in the cabin, Melissa could hear the steady thwack, thwack, thwack and then the loud crack before the tree toppled to the ground with a swoosh, followed by a deafening thud.

When the logs were trimmed to an even length, they were lashed together with ropes and the cracks between the logs caulked with river mud. A small lean-to and mast were added. Finally the raft was pushed into the river, where it sat rocking gently as the last and most important addition was made—its steering oar.

Then the pelts were loaded on the raft. This was a long, grueling task, for the furs had to be carried from the cabin, through the woods to the river. It was Melissa who finally suggested making a travois so Wolf could help. From then on the work went much faster, for the big dog could pull twice as much as the two men could carry, in half the time. When all of the furs were finally loaded, they were covered with oilskins and firmly lashed down.

The next day was declared a holiday, a day to rest up before they finished their final packing. Melissa and Reid decided to spend the day in the woods, but when they invited Nathan to join them, he declined, saying he'd lounge around the cabin and keep an eye on the raft.

Early the next morning, Reid and Melissa left the cabin, carrying Reid's fishing pole, a blanket, and a lunch, just in case Reid didn't catch any fish. They walked leisurely, intent on enjoying their day to the fullest, meandering through the woods and meadows that were covered with wild strawberries blooming in profusion.

They walked down to the river. Melissa sat down on a flat rock that jutted into the river and watched Reid as he fished, laughing when he muttered curses as the fish he had patiently coaxed to take the bait got away at the last minute. After Reid had caught four perch, they built a small fire and cooked them, then sat on their blanket and hungrily ate the tender, flaky fish.

They dozed for a while, and then Reid made slow, lazy love to her. With sensuous caresses and tender, aching kisses, he slowly stoked her fires. Even after he had slid into her moist warmth, his movements were unhurried, deliberately drawing out the exquisite lovemaking so they could savor each delicious sensation to the fullest.

And Melissa felt no embarrassment at making love in the wide open. To her, the feel of the warm sun and gentle breeze on her naked skin, the sound of bees droning and birds singing in her ears, the smell of crushed grass and honeysuckle in her nostrils, only made the intimate act more natural and beautiful.

Later, when the sun grew hotter, they took a swim. Melissa gasped as the ice-cold water rushed over her. Then, once she had become accustomed to the cold, they splashed and cavorted like children.

They took turns diving from the flat rock. Melissa stood in the river and watched as Reid climbed on the rock for yet another dive. As he stood, her breath caught in her throat at his sleek, animal beauty. My magnificent lion, she thought as her eyes feasted on his naked body. Then, realizing he was watching her in return, she looked up into those golden, feline eyes. He smiled, as if he knew her thoughts, and then a look of purpose came into his eyes before he dove, heading straight for her.

Melissa shrieked and turned, heading for the bank. He caught her, his laughter a low rumble in his chest as they wrestled and he pulled her to the mossy ground, straddling her.

He sat back on his heels, his eyes riveted to the rise and fall of her breasts glistening in the sunlight. They drifted lower, then locked on the dark hair between her thighs, the water drops glittering like diamonds. He lifted his head, his gaze like molten gold, watching her as his slender fingers slipped into her dewiness, sweetly probing, his thumb gently massaging the small bud, sending shivers of yearning coursing through her. He dropped his head, his mouth replacing his fingers, his tongue invading, tasting her honeyed sweetness, then moving closer and closer to that throbbing center. Melissa heard a roar in her ears as the sweet tremors shook her.

Only when Reid had brought her to that peak again and again did he finally raise his head, slowly trailing featherlike kisses over her stomach, stoping to pay homage to each breast before his tongue played in her ear, leaving her dizzy and breathless. His lips captured hers in a deep, fierce, consuming kiss, stamping her as his possession.

Melissa moaned, filled with an unbearable aching, a need to have him inside her. She dropped one hand over his erection, guiding it to her. Her voice was low and throaty. "Now, Reid.

I want you now."

"No, not yet," he whispered back.

He rolled to his back, bringing her with him. His voice was husky with emotion. "Love me, sweetheart. Taste me."

Melissa didn't hesitate for a second. Her hands stroked his belly and thighs as her mouth fluttered downward. He trembled with anticipation as her lips closed over his throbbing hardness, her tongue swirling about the hot tip, then flicking erotically, ravishing tenderly. As his arousal surged to a powerful, almost unbearable peak of excitement, he moaned a husky growl, caught and rolled her to her back, then plunged deeply into that inviting heat, feeling as if he was drowning in that sweet, tight warmth.

He took her with a tender savagery, as if he were determined to place his brand on her, his hips grinding, his stokes fierce and demanding, his kisses devouring. They rode that white-hot crest of passion, and then, as he heard her rapturous cry, he stiffened, then he erupted in a fiery burst deep inside her.

"I love you, sweetheart. God, how I love you!" he whispered raggedly in her ear. He raised his head and looked down at her, then framed her face in his hands. "Do you have any idea of how much joy, how much happiness, how much contentment you have brought me over the past months? If I should die tomorrow, I'd die feeling I had led a rich, full life because of you, because of what we have shared. No man could ask for more in this life."

Melissa wrapped her arms around him as he buried his face in her breasts. Something about his words, the intensity of his voice disturbed her. Was it because he had mentioned death? But that was silly. Reid was a healthy young man. Surely they would have many, many years of happiness. But still, she clutched him fiercely to her.

As their special day came to an end, they hated to leave their spot by the river. Finally they gathered their blanket and fishing pole and walked back to the cabin, strolling along the river's edge with their arms around each other's waists.

When they rounded a bend in the river, Melissa's breath caught. A huge dark cloud loomed over the entire eastern horizon, and an enormous rainbow arched across the darkened sky, its bands of brilliant colors shimmering in the sunlight. "Look, Reid! A rainbow!"

"Yes. It must be raining over there."

Melissa admired the spectacular sight. "I've never seen such a big rainbow. Or such a beautiful one."

The rainbow was a fitting ending to a perfect, special day, a day each would remember for the rest of their lives.

Before they left, two days later, Melissa stood at the edge of the clearing and looked back at the cabin. Despite her excitement at returning to civilization, she felt a sadness at leaving, even if it was for only a few months. So much had happened to her here. Here, she had become a woman, had come to know the real meaning of love between a man and a woman, a love that had only grown with time. With her personal accomplishments, big and small, she had proved herself no longer a spoiled, helpless girl, but a self-sufficient, self-assured woman, a fitting mate for a rugged frontiersman.

There was no doubt in Melissa's mind that she and Reid would be married, particularly since his passionate vow of love by the river. And Reid was an honorable man. In her heart and soul, she was already his wife. All that was needed was the ceremony to make it official, and that would have to wait until they reached civilization.

"Melissa!" Reid called from the river. "It's time to leave!"

"Coming!" Melissa called back. She hugged Wolf. "Now you be a good boy and we'll see you in the fall."

Reid stood at the back of the raft to steer, and Melissa and Nathan stood at each side to pole if necessary. But the river was still running high from the spring floods, and the current was strong. They raced down the Yellowstone and entered the Missouri—muddy as always. As they swept down the river, the prairie around them became flatter, the grass taller, the trees more sparse. The pungent odor of blue sage filled the air.

They passed a Minnetaree Indian Village, its earthen huts looking like huge ant hills, and then went past the burned ruins of Fort Mandan, where Lewis and Clark had wintered before their famous westward trek. They stopped at Fort Pierre, an American Fur Company trading post, and restocked for the rest of the trip, buying their supplies with pelts.

When the Missouri turned eastward toward the Mississippi, Melissa began to watch the banks, wondering if she could see the wreckage of the keelboat the Indians had attacked, but she could see no sign of it. Either it had burned completely, or the wreckage had been swept away by the spring floods. She felt a deep sadness, knowing she would never know where her parents' bones lay.

When they passed Franklin, Melissa gazed up at the river bluff, remembering the night she and Reid had lain under the big oak. Their eyes met across the raft, and Reid smiled, telling her that he remembered, too.

It was almost a month from the day they had left the cabin on the Yellowstone when they arrived at St. Louis. The river port was even busier that it had been the past summer. Steamboats, keelboats, flatboats, pirogues, and canoes were lined all along the crescent-shaped bank, each jockeying for a position by the wharves. Tempers

389

flared under the hot sun. French and English curses flew across the water. The roustabouts of two keelboats clashed, jumping across the water from one boat to the other with fists and poles flying. One man, knocked from the deck where the fight was going fast and furious, was almost crushed between the two boats.

After hours of struggling through the river traffic, they finally managed to dock at the levee on Market Street. Nathan quickly hired a wagon, and as soon as their furs and possessions were unloaded, sold the raft to a man who would break it up and sell the logs for firewood. A minute later, the man was on his hands and knees, hacking away at the ropes that held the raft together.

Nathan turned to Reid. "Why don't I sell the furs while you take Missy to the hotel? Ain't no sense in her having to stand around in a hot, smelly warehouse." He added to Melissa, "That is, if you trust me to sell your furs for you?"

"Trust you? Why, what would I know about selling furs?" Melissa replied. Her eyes twinkled. "Besides, if you do half as well at selling as you did trading, I should be a wealthy woman."

"Well, I don't know about wealthy," Nathan said, scratching his beard.

"You can be assured that Nathan will get you the best price, Melissa," Reid said. "He'll haggle until the fur broker gives him what he wants just to get rid of him."

Nathan chuckled and climbed into the wagon. "I'll see you two at the hotel."

After Nathan drove off, Reid said, "Let's walk this way and see if we can find a carriage for hire."

As they walked across the levee, Melissa became very self-conscious. She had been aware of being stared at as they traveled down the river and had assumed it was because she was white. But white women were no novelty here in St. Louis. Then she became aware of what they were staring at—her bare calves and ankles. She realized that no white woman, even a prostitute, appeared on the street with part of her lower limbs showing. Mortified, she flushed deeply.

"Reid, I can't go into a hotel dressed like this."

Reid had become accustomed to seeing Melissa's lower legs bared. "Like what?"

"My legs! They're bare!" she answered in acute embarrassment, wishing she had a hole to hide in.

Reid glanced around the levee and saw the men's lecherous stares. He gave them a hard, warning look. One look at the dangerous glint in those feline eyes was enough to make even the boldest of them reconsider. The offending eyes magically found other things to occupy them. No one wanted to tangle with this fierce-looking man.

"We'll stop at a dressmaker's and see if she has

any ready-to-wear," Reid said, placing a protective arm around her.

Melissa was relieved when they sat down inside a carriage. At least there, no one could see her lower legs. And after the look Reid gave the driver, she knew *he* wasn't about to turn around, not even for a quick peek.

"Do you know a dressmaker's shop?" Reid asked the driver when they were settled. "Preferably one that caters to ladies of quality."

The driver's eyebrows rose at the last words, but he wasn't about to question the dangerous-looking man. If the trapper said she was a lady, then that was fine with him. "Yes, sir," he replied, his eyes staring straight ahead.

"Then take us there," Reid said.

After a short drive, they stopped before a shop on Rue de la Missouri. Reid paid the driver, who drove off in a hurry. Reid took Melissa's arm and guided her toward the shop. "Don't expect to find anything stylish here in St. Louis. The clothes will be serviceable, but not particularly pretty."

"I don't care what they look like, just so they cover my legs."

When they entered the shop, the small bell over the door announced their arrival. The proprietress and her two customers turned and gasped loudly, staring at Melissa's bare legs. Then, seeing the outraged looks that came over her customers' faces and fearing they would leave in a huff, the proprietress hurried to where Melissa and Reid stood, saying in a haughty voice, "See here, you can't come in here. This shop is for ladies."

Melissa's face blanched at the insult.

Reid turned and gave the woman a murderous look. "Maybe you'd better look again, ma'am. This *is* a lady!" he answered in a low, deadly voice.

The proprietress was no shrinking violet. She had had dealings with these rugged frontiersmen before. But she was no fool, either. One look at the gleam in those strange, golden eyes told her she had better tread carefully.

"Excuse me, sir," she said nervously. "I . . . I didn't realize."

Melissa almost felt sorry for the woman. She knew how intimidating and frightening Reid could be, and she could understand the woman's attitude if she was trying to uphold her shop's reputation for catering to ladies of quality. After all, I do look no better than a street urchin, Melissa admitted to herself. She stood proudly and said, "I'd like to look at some ready-to-wear, please."

The proprietress's eyes widened in surprise. The woman's voice certainly sounded like that of a true-bred lady. She studied Melissa under lowered lashes. And she certainly couldn't find fault with her bearing. If anything, it was regal. But what was she doing dressed in that horrible calico rag?

"This way, madame," the proprietress replied, walking toward one corner of the shop.

Melissa flushed at the address. Naturally the woman would assume she was Reid's wife. Well, Melissa certainly wasn't going to correct her. Undoubtedly, she wouldn't consider a mistress a lady, and the whole thing would start all over, with the woman being shocked and insulting and Reid being defensive and protective.

When they came to a rack of dresses, the woman stopped. "Take your time looking. I'm Mrs. Wright. When you've made your selections, just call and I'll show you the dressing room."

Mrs. Wright turned and almost ran into Reid. She looked up at him in shock, surprised that he had followed them across the shop.

Reid glared at her, as if daring her to ask him to leave. Goodness, Mrs. Wright thought, he's certainly protective. But didn't he realize he was out of place in this strictly feminine shop? She glanced nervously at her other customers, who were staring at Reid in disbelief.

Melissa saw the woman's nervous glance and knew what was worrying her. "I won't be long, Reid. Do you want to meet me outside?" she asked, hinting that he should leave.

Mrs. Wright sighed in relief and moved away.

Reid glanced around and said under his breath, "Are you sure you'll be all right?"

Melissa laughed. "For heaven's sake, what do

you think they're going to do, eat me?"

Reid grinned, his golden eyes turning warm. "Sounds like a good idea to me."

Melissa flushed under that warm look. Then she regained her composure. "If I can kill a bear, I can certainly hold my own with these women. I'll meet you outside in about an hour."

Reid fished in his pockets and brought out a wad of bills. Handing her the money, Reid said, "Buy just enough to get you by until we reach New Orleans. Then you can have some pretty clothes made."

Melissa watched him as he left the shop. So that was their destination. New Orleans. She'd been hesitant to ask him. He'd been acting strangely for the past few days, withdrawn and brooding. Nathan had said something about him having heavy debts. Was he worried the furs wouldn't bring a good price?

And would they be married in New Orleans? The thought thrilled Melissa. Of course, what could be more perfect than to be married in that exciting, romantic city?

She turned back to the dress rack, the thought of marriage drowning out the memory of Reid's peculiar behavior. To her surprise, the dresses were much more stylish than she had expected. She made her selections quickly: three dresses, an assortment of underwear, a pair of shoes, and a nightgown. The last was made for the benefit of the stuffy proprietress. She wondered what the woman would think if she knew Melissa slept in the nude? The poor woman would probably have a stroke, she thought, laughing to herself.

Mrs. Wright led her to the dressing room and then turned to leave. Melissa flushed and said, "I'm afraid I'll need some help with lacing my corset."

Mrs. Wright stared at her in horror. She wasn't even wearing a corset? Why no lady would be caught dead without her corset.

Melissa guessed her thoughts. Her mind sought frantically for some kind of explanation, but she didn't want to admit she had been captured by Indians. She knew Mrs. Wright would not only pity her, but undoubtedly scorn her, too, assuming she had been violated and was now a ruined woman. She couldn't stand being looked at like that.

"The steamboat my husband and I were traveling on hit a snag farther downriver and sank," Melissa lied. "We lost all our clothes. The accident occurred at night and I was only in my nightdress. Fortunately we were rescued by a Kentucky family on a flatboat, and they loaned me one of their daughter's dresses. We just docked in St. Louis."

Mrs. Wright didn't question the story. Boat accidents were a common occurrence on the river. The whole Mississippi was littered with debris from these accidents.

"Why, you poor dear," Mrs. Wright said in a sympathetic voice. "I had no idea. Please, forgive me for the way I behaved earlier."

"That's quite all right," Melissa answered.

But Mrs. Wright's reaction would have been quite different if she knew the truth, Melissa thought. The victim of a steamboat accident was one thing, the victim of an Indian raid and subsequent capture quite another. A fresh wave of bitterness washed over her.

"It must have been a terrible experience," Mrs. Wright said as she pulled the laces of Melissa's corset tighter.

"Yes, it was," Melissa answered, feeling the stays biting into her sensitive flesh.

Melissa fought for breath in the constrictive garment as Mrs. Wright pulled the laces even tighter. After months of wearing the loose tunic, she couldn't stand the tight corset and wondered how she had ever borne the silly garment. Why, it was an instrument of pure torture.

"Take it off!" she gasped.

"Off?" Mrs. Wright asked in a shocked voice.

"My ribs. I can't stand it!"

"But, but . . ." Mrs. Wright sputtered.

"My ribs were injured in the accident. Please, it's killing me."

"Oh, you poor dear," Mrs. Wright crooned, unlacing the garment.

As soon as the corset was removed, Melissa sank in a chair, still gasping for breath.

"Are you all right?" Mrs. Wright asked in a concerned voice. "Maybe you should see a doctor."

"No, no they're just bruised, that's all," Melissa said quickly. "I'll just have to settle on a size larger dress until they've healed."

Once Melissa was dressed, Mrs. Wright looked at her critically. "Well, I'll have to admit, with your small waist you certainly can't tell you're not wearing a corset."

No, you can't, Melissa thought, viewing herself in the mirror. And I'll be damned if I'll ever wear one again, she vowed silently. I'd rather wear a size larger dress than be put through that torture.

After the soft moccasins, the shoes pinched her feet, too. But she knew she couldn't walk around in moccasins for the rest of her life. She would just have to endure until her feet became accustomed to shoes again.

"You'll need a bonnet, reticule, and gloves, too," Mrs. Wright reminded her.

Melissa suppressed a groan. As it was, she felt overloaded with all the petticoats, and now she would have to wear a bonnet on her head and gloves on her hands? She nodded glumly.

Once Melissa was dressed, Mrs. Wright stood back and admired her. Goodness, what a beautiful young woman she was when she was attired properly, the woman thought.

Melissa's thoughts were vastly different. She

was miserable in all the clothing. Already, the heat beneath the long skirts and petticoats was making her legs perspire. The fitted bodice felt constrictive, and the bonnet ribbon beneath her chin was driving her to distraction. She wondered at the wisdom of her society. They dressed for appearances, the women squeezing their insides together and swaddled in so many layers of clothing they could barely walk, the men wearing coats and ties even in sweltering weather. The Indian might adorn his garments with beads and quillwork, but his primary concern was for comfort and protection from the elements. And whites had the audacity to call the Indians stupid!

After Mrs. Wright had wrapped Melissa's purchases, she stepped out onto the boardwalk in front of the shop. Reid was waiting for her, pacing the street like a caged lion. When he heard her call, "Reid," he turned and his expression changed from annoyance to outright admiration.

He smiled warmly. "You look beautiful, Melissa."

"Thank you." As he took the packages from her, she said, "I'm sorry I took so long."

"It was well worth the wait," Reid replied, his eyes drifting appreciatively over her.

When they reached the hotel, Nathan was waiting for them in the lobby. He eyed Melissa's new clothes. "Well now, Missy, don't you look pretty."

"Thank you," Melissa replied, resisting the urge to scratch her neck, where the stiff ribbon was beginning to make her itch.

"Have you sold the furs already?" Reid asked.

Nathan beamed. "Yep, and I got a good price, too. Missy's furs brought nine thousand dollars and ours got six. That means we each get five thousand."

Melissa did some quick figuring. "Wait a minute. I thought we agreed we were going to split my profits in thirds."

Nathan and Reid grinned at each other. "And Nathan and I agreed we'd split *our* profits in thirds, too," Reid said. "You see, we decided to make you our partner."

"Partner?" Melissa asked in an astonished voice. "But I didn't do any trapping."

"But you worked as hard as we did," Reid replied. "You did all the cooking, cleaning, and washing, releasing us from those chores we hate so much so we could concentrate on trapping. And don't forget all those nail holes you sewed up in our furs."

"But that's still not fair," Melissa objected. "I didn't go tramping out in the snow and rain. You and Nathan did all the hard work."

"It's just as fair as you splitting with us because Nathan skinned and traded your bearskin and I acted as bait. We either go thirds on the whole thing or not at all," Reid said in a firm voice.

Melissa knew it was pointless to argue. "All right. But only if you let me pay you back for what you paid Two Feathers for me."

Reid and Nathan grinned even broader at each other.

"Well, I reckon we'll agree to that, Missy. Let's see now," Nathan said, scratching his beard thoughtfully, "I think you can pick up one of those St. Anne medals for about a dime."

Reid's eyes twinkled. "And I'd say my hand mirror cost me about a quarter and the kettle cost another dollar." His lips twitched as he looked at Melissa. "That means you owe us a dollar thirty-five."

"A dollar thirty-five!" Melissa cried in an outraged voice. "Are you telling me you bought me a medal and a mirror and a kettle that was only worth a dollar and thirty-five cents?"

Reid and Nathan laughed heartily, much to Melissa's chagrin. Then they told her how they had tricked Two Feathers, and she laughed, too.

But as they walked to their rooms, Melissa couldn't help feeling a little insulted. Trick or no trick, no woman liked to admit that her market value had been a mere dollar and thirty-five cents.

Chapter Fourteen

The next day, the three of them boarded the steamer for their trip downriver. Melissa was excited at the prospect of returning to New Orleans, but as the day wore on she became more and more puzzled by Reid's strange behavior.

He was more withdrawn than ever, gazing out at the water, his look pensive. Several times, she caught him gazing at her strangely, an almost hungry look in his eyes, but, oddly enough, there was nothing sexual about it. His demeanor disturbed her, but she couldn't complain about his lovemaking that night. There was certainly nothing distracted or withdrawn about that. Never had his lovemaking been so fierce, so demanding, so urgent, or so achingly sweet. And when Melissa finally fell asleep, near dawn, she was totally exhausted and satiated.

After Melissa had fallen asleep, Reid rose and dressed. He stood for a long time, looking down at her as she slept, his eyes slowly moving over each feature, committing them to memory.

Then he turned and left the cabin, walking down the deck until he reached Nathan's cabin. Then he knocked on the door.

"Who is it?" Nathan called sleepily from inside the cabin.

"It's me," Reid said in a low voice. "Can you come out for a minute? I need to talk to you."

The door opened a minute later. "Is something wrong with Missy?" Nathan asked in a concerned voice.

"No," Reid answered. "But it concerns her. Walk down the deck with me, I don't want to take any chances on her overhearing us."

Nathan frowned at his words and the solemn tone of his voice. He followed Reid down the deck until they stood at the stern of the boat.

For a few minutes, Reid stared silently down at the river flowing past them. Then he looked at Nathan, his eyes fiercely intense. "I'm leaving."

"Leaving? What in hell are you talking about?"

"When we dock at Cape Girardeau for firewood an hour from now, I'm getting off this boat and walking away—alone."

"You're walking out on Missy?" Nathan said in a shocked voice. "Why? Did you two have a fight or something?"

"No."

"Then why in the hell are you leaving her? You love her and she loves you."

"And that's the problem. I should have never let it happen in the first place. It's wrong."

"Wrong? Loving each other is wrong?" Nathan asked in a loud, disbelieving voice.

"Sssh, keep your voice down," Reid hissed. Then in a hard voice, he said, "Have you forgotten I'm a married man?"

"Hell no, I ain't forgotten that! But you could get a divorce. No one would blame you after all this time. Considering what happened—"

"No!" Reid interrupted in a firm voice. "Divorce is out of the question. It always has been and it always will be."

"What about Missy? What does she have to say to that?" Nathan asked angrily.

Reid paled, his eyes shifted. "She doesn't know I'm married."

Nathan was stunned. "Doesn't know? You mean you ain't told her about Valerie? After all this time?"

"No, I haven't," Reid admitted.

Nathan stared at him, too shocked even to speak.

"Dammit, I tried not to fall in love with her," Reid said in a pained voice. "I fought it tooth and toenail. And then after it happened and I knew she loved me too, I couldn't force myself to tell her. It was selfish, I know, but I wanted that brief time of happiness. I wanted it like I've never wanted anything else. But I never wanted to hurt Melissa."

Nathan could understand. Reid had gone through hell with his marriage. From the very first, it had been a disaster. Nathan could understand a man grabbing at his chance for happiness, even if it was for only a few months. "Then tell Missy how things are with Valerie. She loves you. She'll understand."

"And offer her what?" Reid said bitterly. "A place in my life as my mistress? Oh, I thought about setting her up in New Orleans, but I realized I can't do it to her. I love and respect her too much."

"But she's already been your woman for months," Nathan argued.

"It was different up on the Yellowstone. You were the only one around. You understood. But here? No, making her my mistress would demean her, humiliate her in front of others. I can't do that to her. I just realized that yesterday."

"Why don't you let her make that decision?" Nathan snapped.

"Because I think I know what she'll decide, and she deserves better than what I can give her. She deserves a man who can give her more than love, a man who can give her everything—his name, his home, his . . . his children."

Nathan had never felt so frustrated in his entire life. He knew this was tearing Reid up, and he knew Missy was going to be hurt, too. And for what? "Then dammit, divorce Valerie!" Nathan said angrily. "Why should you ruin your and Missy's chance for happiness over a woman who's incapable of even caring, who's—"

"No!" Reid said in an emphatic voice. "No divorce! That's final! I made the promise till death do us part, for better or worse. I made a commitment, and I intend to keep it."

Nathan knew by the tone of Reid's voice and the determined set of his chin that it was pointless to argue with him. Reid had made the decision, and he'd stick by it, come hell or high water, regardless of whether he hurt Missy and himself in the process. Him and his goddamned principles, Nathan thought angrily. And yet, it was Reid's determination to stick by his principles, regardless of the price he himself had to pay that made Nathan respect him so much, that set him a cut above other men in Nathan's eyes.

Reid looked back down into the water and sighed heavily. "I have a big favor to ask of you."

"What's that?"

"I want you to help Melissa through this. I had thought I'd take her to New Orleans, see her safely settled, then just disappear. But I can't do that to her. She'll need someone, and you're her friend. That's why I'm doing it now, before you get off the boat at Cairo."

"You mean you're actually gonna walk off, no

explanation, no nothing?"

"It's the only way I can do it," Reid replied in an agonized voice. "Do you think I can stand there and say, 'I love you, but I'm leaving you?' She'll demand an explanation. And then I'm afraid she'll try to talk me out of it, or worse yet, stick with me because she pities me. I couldn't stand that."

"Then leave her a note or something," Nathan argued.

"No. I've got to end it once and for all. I've got to kill her love for me. Make her hate me. And what better way than just to walk out on her with no explanation? Make her think I callously used her. Once she hates me, then she can forget me and go on with her own life. I'd rather that than have her pitying me or clinging to false hope."

"And what in the hell am I supposed to tell her?" Nathan asked in an exasperated voice.

"Nothing, absolutely nothing. And you've got to promise me you won't tell her about Valerie. No matter what, she's not to know my real reason for leaving."

Nathan hesitated.

"Promise me," Reid demanded, forcing Nathan to look him in the eye.

"All right!" Nathan snapped. "I won't tell her nothing."

"Take her to Jeanette in Natchez. She'll take care of her. She'll see her safely back to Charleston, if that's what Melissa wants. Or if she decides to stay in Natchez, Jeanette can introduce her into society. She'll have her pick of plenty of eligible bachelors. She'll fall in love again and eventually . . . eventually marry."

"Jeanette? You're gonna send her to Valerie's aunt?"

"Jeanette is my friend. She'll help me. I'm sending a letter with you, explaining everything and asking her not to tell Melissa the real story. She'll understand. She won't let me down."

"I'm supposed to walk in with Missy and a letter from you?" Nathan asked in a dumbfounded voice.

"Hell, no!" Reid retorted in exasperation. "Melissa must never know Jeanette is a friend of mine, much less a relative by marriage. You know how proud Melissa is. She'll never accept Jeanette's help. Tell her Jeanette is a friend of yours, and then take the letter to Jeanette before you take Melissa to meet her. That way, Jeanette will be prepared for her."

Nathan laughed harshly. "Do you really believe Missy is gonna fall for that? What would an old mountain man like me be doing with a high-class lady like Jeanette Woodward for a friend?"

"Tell her you did business with Jeanette's husband before he died. Hell, you'll think of something. Just be sure Jeanette knows your story, and whatever you do, don't let Melissa know Jeanette's my friend. If she finds that out, she's liable to take off on her own, and there's no telling what kind of trouble she'd get herself into."

Nathan thought of the white slavers, who captured unprotected women and supplied the bordellos in New Orleans and Natchez-Under-the-Hill with unwilling victims. He shuddered to think of Missy coming to that end. No, Reid was right. With Jeanette, she'd be safe and have someone to look after her.

Nathan's concern turned to Reid. "What about you? How are you gonna make it without Missy?"

Reid smiled ruefully. "I'll survive."

"Sure you will," Nathan said sarcastically. "Just like you have all these years? Hell, if you think you were miserable before, it ain't nothing to how you're gonna be hurting from losing Missy."

"I can't regret what happened for myself, Nathan. I only regret that I'm going to have to hurt Melissa. She gave me more happiness in just a few months than I've known in my entire lifetime. At least now, I have pleasant memories to sustain me."

Drive you crazy you mean, Nathan thought. He ached for his friend. Melissa would have Jeanette to help her get through the bad time, but who would Reid have in the long, lonely months ahead?

He looked at Reid hopefully. "You want to

join me this summer in Kentucky? You know how highly my sister and her family think of you. They'd be tickled to death to have you."

"No, but thanks anyway. I'll do what I do every summer."

"Go up and down the river gambling?" Nathan asked in disgust.

Reid shrugged. "It's not a bad life. I win a few, I lose a few, but I always manage to make a fair profit. It's a hell of a lot more profitable than keelboating or hiring out for manual labor."

"Yeah, and one of these days you'll land up getting yourself killed, too."

"I don't cheat," Reid replied in a tight voice.

"Hell, I know that!" Nathan snapped back. "But one of these days some hot-blooded, sore loser is gonna get it in his head that you did and pull a gun on you."

"I can take care of myself."

Nathan glared at him, but Reid smiled. "I appreciate your concern, Nathan, but don't worry about me."

They turned and walked back down the deck, each man brooding on his own dark thoughts. Finally Nathan asked, "We gonna meet in the same place next September?"

Reid turned, a deep frown on his face. "I can't go back to the cabin on the Yellowstone, Nathan. I'm sorry, but that place is too full of memories of Melissa."

Yeah, it's just like I thought, Nathan thought bitterly. Talking about his memories sustaining him and already they're haunting him. "We don't have to go back there. We can find another spot."

"No, that wouldn't be fair to you. You've already bought trapping rights from the Indians and you've been going there for years. Besides, you knew my joining up with you was only temporary, until I could buy my land back. Well, with this year's profits, I'll be clear of my debts."

"Yeah, but that's just getting the land out of hock. What are you gonna do about buying slaves? You can't run a plantation without them."

"Like I said, I'll travel the river this summer and gamble. With any luck at all, I should be able to double my stake. Who knows, maybe I'll even hit it big."

"Again? Don't count on it," Nathan said glumly.

"Either way, I'm going back to the plantation next spring and start putting in a crop. Cotton's going to grow on that land next year, even if I have to plant it, hoe it, and pick it all by myself."

Nathan couldn't hide his disappointment. "I'm gonna miss you."

Reid smiled at the mountain man's admission. For all of his rough, tough exterior, Nathan had a tender heart. "And I'm going to miss you, too. Why don't you take that nephew of yours in with you? He's been badgering you for years."

"Hell, he's just a green kid."

"So was I when you took me on."

Memories came flooding back to Nathan. He grinned. "Yep, you sure were. Green and sassy as hell. Guess if I can make a man out of you, I can make one out of him, too. Just hope he don't turn out to be so damned bull-headed."

Knowing there was nothing more to be said, both men turned and walked back to Reid's cabin. Nathan waited while Reid went inside to pick up his belongings. When he returned, Reid handed Nathan the letter addressed to Jeanette Woodward. Nathan took it grimly and silently slipped it into his pocket. Then the two men walked to the gangplank just as the landing at Cape Girardeau came in view.

"When am I gonna see you again?" Nathan asked, feeling a lump in his throat.

"You know where my plantation is. Why don't you spend next summer with me?"

"Hell, you'll probably have me hoeing and picking cotton, too."

Reid grinned. "It'll keep you in shape. That way you won't get fat and lazy."

They watched as the gangplank was lowered. The sun was just rising in the east, the horizon a pale line of rose. The silence hung heavy between them, the only sound the lapping of the

412

river against the steamer.

Finally Reid turned and said, "Thank you, Nathan. I realize I'm leaving you in an awkward spot."

"Hell, forget it. After all, what're friends for?"

Reid's eyes drifted across Nathan's shoulder to the cabin where Melissa still slept. The look of pain and longing in his face tore at Nathan's heart.

"Take care of her for me," Reid muttered in a half-choked voice. Then, abruptly, he turned and walked down the gangplank.

Nathan felt a sudden moisture in the back of his eyes, and a tightness constricted his chest. Why does living have to be so damned painful? he wondered. He watched as Reid disappeared in the swirling, early morning fog. Angrily, he swiped at the tears in his eyes. And why did the two people he loved most in this world have to have more than their share of that pain?

Because Melissa was so exhausted from Reid's lovemaking the night before, she slept late the next day. It was almost noon when she came on deck. She glanced around, but could see no sign of Reid. Then, spying Nathan standing at the rail, she walked up to him. "Good morning," she said cheerfully.

"Morning," Nathan mumbled, staring down at the water glumly.

Melissa looked at him curiously. It wasn't like Nathan not to return her greeting with equal cheerfulness. And he looked pale and drawn. Had he drunk too much the night before, causing another hangover?

"Have you seen Reid?" she asked.

Nathan had had a lot of hard things to do in his lifetime, but never anything as difficult as this. He took in a deep breath. "He's gone," he said bluntly.

"Gone? What do you mean?"

"He got off the boat early this morning."

"Are we supposed to meet him somewhere later?" Melissa asked in confusion.

"Nope. He ain't coming back."

Slowly the words began to penetrate Melissa's brain. "You mean he's gone—for good?" she whispered.

"Yep," Nathan replied grimly.

Melissa stood silently for a minute, stunned by Nathan's words. Then she cried out, in an agonized voice, "But why would he leave me? Just walk out like that? I know he loves me."

"Damned if I can figure him out," Nathan mumbled in all honesty. Then seeing the look of pain on Melissa's face as Reid's desertion slowly dawned on her, he stepped forward. "Missy . . ."

"No! Don't say anything!" Melissa interjected. Tears glittered in her eyes as she backed away from him, mumbling, "I've got to be alone. I've got to think."

She whirled and ran for the cabin. Once there, she sat on the bunk and stared out vacantly, still bewildered, a million questions swirling in her mind.

Why had he left her? She knew he loved her. Not only had he told her so with words, but in his actions, too. But then she remembered that he had never made a commitment. Telling someone you loved them wasn't a lifetime promise. In fact, he had never mentioned marriage, except that night by the river in Franklin. What had he said then? No one could force him to marry her. It was out of the question.

Was that it? Was Reid one of those men who were afraid of marriage? Was that why he had left so abruptly? Because he was afraid she would expect him to marry her, push him for it? But that didn't make sense, either. Men who feared marriage were usually men who were afraid of responsibility. And that wasn't Reid. Besides, he had no qualms in refusing to marry her earlier. Then why would he now?

Was he reluctant to marry her because he felt she wasn't suited to the role of a trapper's wife and life on the frontier? But that was ridiculous. She had already proven she could keep up with his rugged way of life.

Maybe he hadn't really loved her after all. Both times he had said the words, he had been emotionally charged, once when he was angry at her for letting the strange trappers come in the cabin, the other after making love. Had it only been passion talking?

Her mind flew back to that special day by the Yellowstone River. Had she imagined his impassioned words? Had she read a deeper meaning in them because she wanted him to love her as totally, as completely, as she loved him. Had it been no more than an illusion, like that beautiful rainbow she had seen? Like it, was Reid's love not real? Did it exist only in her eyes?

Perhaps that's what her whole time with Reid had been, an illusion. Had she misled herself? Had she created her own beautiful rainbow by convincing herself that he really and truly loved her, only because she desperately wanted it to be true?

For a long time, the questions flew through her mind, questions that had no answers. And then, as she realized that he was gone for good, that he had walked out of her life, this time forever, she was filled with an aching sense of loss, much more profound and powerful than any other she had felt before. She cried, long and bitterly.

And when there were no more tears left, she tried to build up her anger at him, to blame him for using her, to hate him. Oh, how she tried to hate him! But she couldn't. Her love was too strong.

Wisely Nathan left her alone, knowing that there was nothing he could do or say that would ease her pain. When she emerged from the cabin two days later, she had again undergone a metamorphosis. She was a woman who had loved and lost, and because of it, she was a much deeper, wiser person. Physically, there was no change, except for the hint of sadness in her eyes, a sadness that spoke of a maturity beyond her years, a sadness that gave her beauty an even more haunting quality.

Chapter Fifteen

Nathan glanced down at Melissa as the two of them stood at the rail of the steamboat. She had certainly surprised him. He hadn't expected her reaction to the shock of Reid leaving her to be what it had been. He had anticipated that she would behave like any other woman who had just been deserted by the man she loved. But there had been no hysterics, no crying, no ranting or raving, no avowals of hatred. If she had done any of these things, she had done them in the privacy of her cabin and spared Nathan the pain of having to witness it. And other than those first few questions, she had asked for no further explanations. In fact, she had never mentioned Reid's name since that fateful day.

Nathan was relieved. He hadn't relished the thought of having a raving, hysterical woman on his hands and wasn't too sure he would have been up to handling it. In fact, he would have preferred to tangle with a mountain lion; at least then he would have been in his element.

He was also relieved by her silence. He doubted that he could have stood too many probing questions without breaking down and telling her the truth, thereby breaking his promise to Reid. Nor would he have been able to stand by and listen to Melissa falsely accuse Reid of misusing her without defending his friend and letting the cat out of the bag. If she felt any bitterness, any hatred toward Reid, she had hidden her feelings well. And he thanked God for that, for Nathan felt there was nothing worse in this world than a bitter, vindictive woman, spewing out her hatred like so much poison. No, in Nathan's opinion, Melissa had handled the crisis well, which only increased his admiration for her and verified his original estimation of her character. She had real grit.

She surprised him again when he announced his plans for taking her to Jeanette Woodward in Natchez. Nathan had half expected Melissa to balk and, knowing how stubborn she could be, had dreaded the confrontation, fearing she would argue with him until it became a contest of wills. But she had accepted his plans gracefully, asking only a few calm questions and revealing her new maturity. His mind flashed back to the conversation between them that morning.

"Missy, you know how much I think of you, but you can't stay with me. I'm just an old mountain man, a drifter, and you belong with your own kind. I know a fine woman in Natchez. Jeanette Woodward. She's the wife of one of my old business partners, and like you, a real lady. I'd like to take you to her."

"But don't you think that would be an imposition on her?" Melissa asked.

"Nope. You see, her husband died about ten years ago and she's all alone now. I think she gets kinda lonely rambling about in that big, old plantation house all by herself. She'd probably enjoy the company."

"Plantation house? I thought you said her husband was one of your old business partners?"

Nathan was prepared for this question. He'd already figured out his story. "He was. A lot of these here plantation owners have their fingers in more than one pie. Her husband backed me and my first partner when we first went into trapping. It was kinda a side business for him. Anyway, we all got to be friends of sorts."

Nathan watched Melissa anxiously to see if she would swallow the story. When she stood silently pondering, he added, "Missy, it ain't safe for a pretty young woman like you to stay all by herself with no protection. There's all kinds of skulduggery going on out there. White slavery and stuff like that. I'd never forgive myself if anything else happened to you."

The mention of "white slavery" was all Melissa needed. She had no intention of being captured again and forced to submit to some man's lust.

No, she was never going to be in that position again. From now on, she was going to have complete control over her life.

"I suppose that would be the wisest thing to do," she answered thoughtfully. "At least, for a few days. Until I can decide what I'm going to do."

Wisely, Nathan didn't push. Getting her to Jeanette was his job. Keeping her there was Jeanette's problem. He'd just have to trust Reid's judgment about the woman's ability to look out for Missy.

The shuddering of the boat as it changed course brought Nathan back to the present.

The engines of the small sidewheeler labored as the boat struggled to cross the strong river current. The paddles spun, thrashing wildly at the water as if they were intent on beating the river into submission. Water flew, the drops glistening like jewels in the sunlight.

As the boat steamed toward the river landing at Natchez, Melissa curiously scanned the city below the bluffs, the infamous Natchez-Under-the-Hill. Squatting on a narrow, muddy table of land by the river was a huddle of tin-roofed, weatherbeaten shacks that covered every square inch of ground right up to the river's edge, where they perched on stilts.

Nathan was also eyeing Natchez-Under-the-Hill, his expression wary. Hell-Under-the-Hill, as it was known by its river name, was the sin city of the Mississippi and talked about all up and down the river. It was said, "whatever way you like it, mister, you can get it in Natchez-Under-the-Hill." It was a hell-raging, roaring, raunchy, wide-open sin spot. Here a man could buy raw whiskey and rawer women. Here he could gamble on racehorses, cockfights, fistfights, and cards. Dance halls, saloons, peep shows, gambling dens, race tracks, and cheap hotels sat side by side. And intermingled in and all around were the countless houses of prostitution, high class and low class.

Crime thrived in the rowdy sin spot squatting in the stinking mud flats by the river. It was a brawling, loud, violent city where elegantly dressed planters and businessmen from above the hill and out for an evening "down the line" brushed shoulders with the loud, boisterous, hot-tempered boatmen and rugged frontiersmen out for a last fling. All came to taste the delights of the wicked city, and waiting to prey on them were the scum of the earth—river rats, cardsharps, pimps, murderers, pickpockets, thiefs, harlots, and fugitives. No sane man walked through its dark, twisted dank-smelling streets without a gun or a knife for protection.

On the sunny bluff above this brawling, violent hellhole sat the other Natchez. Here, beside the wide esplanades and the peaceful, tree-lined streets were the elegant homes. Here was the well-bred Natchez, the scene of lavish balls and sedate dinner parties. The women were ladies, soft-spoken and graceful; the men were gentlemen, well mannered and courteous. Here was the seat of gracious southern living.

Natchez was a paradox, with her two distinct parts—her upper and lower cities. There was darkness and sunlight, dreadful stench and the sweet smell of magnolias, boisterous, drunken laughter and soft music, shanties and elegant homes. There were those who said Natchez was a lady with her head in the clouds and her feet in the mud. Others said she was a woman with a split personality, half lady and half whore.

When Melissa and Nathan departed from the steamboat on the noisy, busy river landing, Nathan flagged down a carriage. As they drove past the wharves and through the narrow, crisscrossed streets, Melissa looked about the notorious city with a mixture of fascination and disbelief.

They turned down Silver Street, the main thoroughfare and toughest street on the Mississippi River. Drunken men, white and red, staggered past them. Prostitutes of every color, fat and skinny, young and old, beautiful and ugly, many of them naked to the waist, hung from the windows touting their charms or mingled with the crowds below, some openly fondling a man in their eagerness to entice a customer. Dance-hall girls with brief, gaudy costumes and painted faces stood before the saloons where drunken laughter, tinny music, roared obscenities, and the

423

clatter of games could be heard.

Violence seethed and exploded all around them. The doors of a saloon slammed open as two boatmen rolled from the brawl going on inside and out onto the wooden boardwalk, their fists flying as they yelled curses at one another. Farther down the street, two frontiersmen fought a deadlier battle, their wicked bowie knifes glittering in the sunlight as they crouched and circled and slashed with murderous intent. A pistol shot resounded from one gambling den, and seconds later, a cardsharp ran from the building, his derringer still smoking. Once, Nathan and Melissa's carriage was forced to a stop. In the street before them, two harlots fought, kicking and gouging, their naked legs flashing as they rolled in the mud. From a dark alley, a boatman stumbled, yelling that he'd been robbed. In another dark alley, sprawled in a scum-covered mud puddle, another unfortunate lay, the knife still protruding from his back.

The city reeked with odors. The smell of cheap perfume, sour liquor, stale smoke, sweat, sex, vomit, blood, and death mixed with the smell of dank mud, decaying vegetation, and rotting wood to create an unbelievable, sickening stench.

As their carriage climbed the steep, twisting road up the bluff to the city above, Melissa looked back down at the city below with horror. Now she knew why they called it a hellhole, for she felt as if she had just emerged from the depths of hell itself. She had survived an Indian attack, an attempted rape, a cruel captivity, even fought a raging bear, but never in her life had she been as terrified as she had been during that brief ride through Natchez-Under-the-Hill.

When the carriage rolled over the bluff and down the sunny, cobbled street, Nathan took a deep breath of blessedly fresh air and muttered, "Thank God, that's over."

Melissa laughed shakily. She glanced at the beautiful homes flashing by. "Will you take me to the plantation today?"

"Nope, not today. I think I'll go visit Jeanette tonight and feel her out. Just to be polite, you know," he added quickly.

"Of course," Melissa agreed. "I can't just go barging in without an invitation. Besides, that will give me more time to make myself presentable."

Melissa was impressed with the hotel Nathan checked them into. After the hotel in St. Louis, the Steamboat Hotel was sheer elegance and luxury. She bathed and then climbed into the first featherbed she'd seen in a year.

But it was a long time before she slept. Memories of Reid flooded over her, bringing silent tears and leaving her feeling empty. She wondered if she would ever feel whole again.

* * *

Jeanette Woodward walked to the window and looked out at the circular drive. Despite her middle age, she was still an attractive woman. There wasn't a gray strand to be seen in her reddish-blond hair, and her eyes were as vivid a blue as they had been when she was sixteen. Only her figure was changed, fuller and more voluptuous.

Seeing no sigh of an approaching carriage, she turned and walked back to a chair. She sat and pulled Reid's crumpled letter from her pocket, staring down at it. She didn't need to open it. She had already memorized the words.

Reid had told her everything. He had explained how he had met Melissa and her family on their trip to St. Louis, about Melissa's capture by Indians and her captivity, at least as much as he knew, and how he and Nathan had found her being sold at an Indian trading fair. He had been perfectly candid about their love affair and his deep feelings for Melissa. What surprised Jeanette was his refusal to get a divorce. Even after Nathan had explained Reid's reasons, she didn't understand. Did Reid blame himself for what had happened? After all these years? God knows, he had done everything a man could possibly do. She wished she could have talked to him personally. Maybe she could have convinced him that his decision to stick by Valerie was futile, utterly senseless.

Jeanette had always like Reid, even before he married her niece. When he had first settled in

Mississippi, after he had acquired his plantation, everyone had been impressed with the intense, dynamic young man. The way he had worked so hard in his determination to make his plantation one of the best in the area had earned everyone's admiration and respect. His exceptional good looks, his intelligence and charm, and his magnetic male sensuality had only added to his appeal. No wonder he had had such a devastating effect on the female population. Every belle in Mississippi and half of those in Louisiana had pursued him.

Jeanette knew in her heart that the reason Valerie had wanted Reid was simply because all her friends were pursuing him. Jeanette's niece had always taken pleasure in snatching up what someone else wanted and then, half the time, because she hadn't really wanted it in the first place, she would toss it aside or destroy it. There was no doubt in Jeanette's mind that Valerie had never loved Reid. Her niece had been incapable of the emotion. The only person she had ever loved was herself. No, she had married Reid to spite her friends and then once she had him had seemed bent on making his life miserable. Well, she had certainly succeeded. And now, she was still succeeding.

Jeanette gazed up at the portrait of her niece that hung over the fireplace. The painting had been done the same year Reid had met her. Jeanette had to admit that Valerie had been an exceptionally beautiful girl. Blonde, blue-eyed, dimpled, petite, she was the epitome of southern beauty—until you looked at her eyes. The artist's paintbrush hadn't lied; it had caught not only that flirtatious look but more—that hard glint as well. Jeanette had always been aware of that malicious glint in Valerie's eyes. She had never been able to understand why Reid hadn't been able to see it, too, why such a sensible, intelligent man hadn't been able to see past her niece's glittering facade. But unfortunately, Reid had not found out her true character until it was too late. Only after the marriage had Valerie dropped her pose. Then Reid had discovered what an utterly selfish, destructive, essentially weak woman he had tied himself to for life.

And what of this woman Reid was sending her? Had he fallen in love with the same type of woman again? She had heard that people had a tendency to do that. She shuddered. She couldn't stand living with another one like Valerie. After her parents had died of yellow fever, Valerie had come to Jeanette's to live; she had disrupted the whole household with her demands and temper tantrums and had managed to make everyone around her miserable.

But Valerie would have never survived what this Melissa had gone through, Jeanette reminded herself. Melissa had lost her entire family, endured a degrading captivity, and then coped admirably in a wilderness where no white woman had ever been, much less survived. Why, Reid had written that she had even killed a bear, thereby saving his life. How amazing!

But regardless of what the young woman was like, Jeanette knew she had to do this for Reid. Even if she wasn't his friend, she owed him that much, considering the hell he had gone through with her niece.

Jeanette was jerked from her musing when her majordomo stepped into the drawing room. She looked up at the gray-haired Negro. "Yes, Samson?"

"Dey's here, Miz Jeanette."

Jeanette rose, pushing the crumpled letter back into her pocket. "Goodness, I didn't even hear them driving up. Show them in, please."

When Melissa and Nathan stepped into the drawing room a moment later, Jeanette's breath caught in her throat at Melissa's beauty. Quickly, she looked into the young woman's eyes. Thankfully, they held no malicious glitter, only a hint of sadness that made them even more startling. Gracious, Jeanette thought, this one was going to rock Natchez's exclusive society to its very roots. She'd need a whip to beat the men away from her door.

Nathan shuffled his feet awkwardly. He had no idea of how to introduce two high-class ladies to each other. He cleared his throat nervously and said in a stiff voice, "Mrs. Woodward, may I introduce Miss Randall."

Both women looked at him as if he was crazy. Then Jeanette laughed. "Oh, no, there'll be none of that foolishness in this house, Nathan." She smiled at Melissa. "Please, call me Jeanette."

Melissa had been watching Jeanette's eyes, too. She didn't know how much of her story Nathan had told her, but the woman was bound to know she had been an Indian captive. But she saw no signs of pity or scorn in the woman's eyes, only kindness and warmth. She relaxed and smiled. "I'm Melissa, and thank you for welcoming me into your beautiful home."

All of Jeanette's doubts fled when she saw Melissa's dazzling smile. She liked this young woman and sensed that they would become good friends. "My dear, I'm thrilled to death to have you. Sometimes, I get so restless and bored rambling about in this big house all by myself."

Memories came flooding back to Melissa. "I think I know what you mean. I lived on a plantation much like this one back in South Carolina. I had every luxury a girl could possibly want. And yet sometimes I felt I would scream with boredom."

"Yes, plantation life is rather restrictive, especially for women," Jeanette remarked.

Their eyes met. They both sensed a kindred spirit. Then Jeanette laughed. "But you can hardly complain about this past year of your life being boring. Why, you've been places and seen things few white men have ever seen, much less a woman. My gracious, the stories you'll be able to tell your grandchildren! Someday, you will have to tell me all about your adventures."

Melissa was surprised at Jeanette's enthusiastic words. She had never stopped to think about it, but she *had* had quite an adventure. True, she had had some bad experiences, but she had had some exciting ones, too. During the past year, she had traveled over thousands of miles of wilderness and had seen fascinating things, things that a white woman like Jeanette, stuck on a lonely plantation, would never imagine. And she knew that Jeanette's interest didn't stem from morbid curiosity. No, Jeanette was just like Melissa had been when she had begged Reid and Nathan to tell of their adventures. She hungered for something new, something exciting, something to relieve her boredom.

"Yes, we'll do that one day," Melissa replied. She glanced at the portrait above the fireplace. "What a beautiful girl. Is she your daughter?"

Jeanette paled, and Nathan squirmed in his seat. Why didn't I think to take it down before she arrived? Jeanette asked herself. "No, she's my niece, Valerie," Jeanette replied, in what she hoped was a calm-sounding voice. "She came to live with me when her parents died. She's married now."

"Does she live near here?"

"No, she's in New Orleans."

"You must miss her terribly."

"I'm lonely, my dear, but quite frankly, I don't miss Valerie," Jeanette replied in all honesty. "She was the most selfish, most spoiled, most demanding person I've ever had the misfortune to live with. I don't even like discussing her."

Melissa was shocked at Jeanette's blunt words. She wished she hadn't even mentioned the girl, and that was exactly what Jeanette had hoped for. She wanted no more questions about her niece.

Jeanette deftly turned the conversation away from Valerie, telling Melissa about all the events that had happened around the world during the past year. Nathan sat by, watching and listening in silence as the two women talked, amazed that women could be interested in such a variety of things. Why, they hadn't even mentioned new styles of clothing one time. Reid had certainly known what he was doing when he sent Missy to Jeanette. They were as alike as two peas in a pod. From the way they were acting, you'd think they'd been friends all their lives.

By the time he was ready to go that night, Nathan had no reservations about leaving Missy with Jeanette. He knew she was where she belonged. He rose. "Well, I reckon I'd better be going."

Melissa's heart sank at Nathan's words. She had been dreading this all day. As comfortable as she felt with Jeanette, Nathan had become so much a part of her life that she didn't know if she could bear to let him go.

Jeanette saw the look on Melissa's face. "Can't you stay for a few more days, Nathan?"

Nathan was feeling just as miserable as Melissa, but he knew delaying his departure wouldn't make it any easier on either of them. "Nope, 'fraid not. My sister's expecting me and I'm already running late. She might be getting worried."

"You could send her a letter," Jeanette suggested.

Nathan grinned. "Nope. Can't do that. I can't write and she can't read."

Both women laughed at his candid admission.

At the door, Jeanette said, "You're free to come visit any time, Nathan. You know that, don't you?"

Nathan looked at her with surprise. He knew she wasn't extending the invitation for just as long as Melissa was in her house. She *did* mean anytime. He was shocked and deeply touched that she would open her doors to a coarse, old mountain man like himself. "Thank you, ma'am," he muttered.

Jeanette left them to say their good-byes in private. Melissa and Nathan looked at each other, both blinking back tears.

"Will I see you again?" Melissa asked.

"Well, Missy, I reckon that depends upon what you decide to do. If you go back to South Carolina, I doubt it. But if you decide to stay in these parts . . ." His voice trailed off. He didn't want to influence her in her decision for his own selfish reasons.

Melissa wasn't sure just what she wanted to do with the rest of her life. Up until a week ago, she had assumed she would spend it with Reid. But she was sure of one thing. She wasn't going back to Charleston.

"I'm not going back to South Carolina," she said in a decisive voice. "Maybe I'll stay out here someplace." Her eyes brightened. "Maybe New Orleans."

Nathan beamed. "Well, if you settle there I can visit you every summer."

Melissa's spirits lifted. "Regardless of where I settle, it will be somewhere near the Mississippi." She laughed. "I've got river water in my blood now."

Nathan nodded in understanding. Men who made their living on or by a river became as attached to it as sailors did to the sea. Like their sailor cousins, they felt uncomfortable if they got too far away from the water.

"You be sure and leave directions with Jeanette on where I can find you," Nathan instructed.

"I will," Melissa answered. She hugged him fiercely and kissed him on the cheek. Then she stood back. "Thank you for being such a wonderful friend."

Nathan grinned. "Friendship works two ways,

Missy. I figure I've gotten a heap more happiness from you than I ever gave." He touched her face in a surprisingly tender gesture, then mumbled, "I'll see you next summer."

Melissa blinked back fresh tears. "Yes, next summer."

Wisely, Jeanette left Melissa much to herself the next week. She knew the girl needed time to recover from her long, exhausting trip down the river and from the shock of Reid's desertion.

One night when they were sitting in the drawing room, Jeanette asked in a gentle voice, "Have you been thinking about your future?"

"I'm glad you brought it up," Melissa answered. "I've been wanting to talk to you about it. I'm not going back to Charleston. I have no family left, and even if I did, I wouldn't want to go back."

"Because you're afraid of how they will treat you if they knew you had been an Indian captive?"

"How did you know how I felt?"

"Because I'd feel the same way if I were you. You forget, Natchez is a frontier town. I've seen how people treat women who have returned from Indian captivity. They either pity them, look down on them, or stare at them like they're some oddity. It's disgusting."

Jeanette looked thoughtful. "You could make

up a story, you know. Tell them your family was killed in an accident of some sort," she offered.

Melissa laughed, then related her experience with the dressmaker in St. Louis.

Jeanette laughed. "See, she never even questioned you. You could use that story again. Why, boat accidents are so common out here, no one even bothers to ask where or when."

"But still, I don't want to go back to Charleston. I was bored to death before I ever left. I want to be independent, and I want to stay somewhere in the West. Maybe New Orleans."

Jeanette's breath caught. New Orleans? Why, she couldn't let her move there. That's where Valerie was. She might hear stories or, even worse, run into Reid. "Why New Orleans?"

"In the first place, I fell in love with the city. In the second place, business seemed to be thriving there. I have five thousand dollars from the sale of my furs. I thought I might invest in a business."

"From selling furs?" Jeanette asked in an astonished voice. "Do you mean that you trapped, too?"

Melissa laughed. "No, but it's a long story. I'll tell you about it some other time."

"But don't you think you're rushing things?" Jeanette asked. "Why don't you wait until you've received your inheritance? Then you'll know how much you have to invest."

Melissa chewed her lip. "I'm not too sure there

is an inheritance. You see, my father sold everything before he left South Carolina, and I know he was carrying a lot of money on him at the time we were attacked."

"Melissa, I can't believe your father would carry all his money on him. Perhaps the down payment for the plantation he was thinking about buying, but not all. No, that money must be in a bank somewhere."

"But I wouldn't know where to begin looking for it. That money could be anywhere. In South Carolina, in New Orleans, maybe even in St. Louis. And I don't even know if he left a will."

"Then you'll need a lawyer. They have ways of tracking down all those things. Besides, due to the unusual circumstances of your parents' deaths, you'll probably need affidavits, some kind of legal proof of their deaths. A lawyer can handle the whole thing for you. In the meanwhile, you can stay here with me."

"But that might take months! I couldn't impose on you that long."

"My dear, the people of Natchez are known for their southern hospitality. Friends come and stay for months, even years. Why, there was one family whose guest landed up staying with them permanently. They even built him his own personal quarters."

Melissa knew what Jeanette was proposing made sense. She would be foolish to rush into an investment before she even checked out the possibility of an inheritance. But would Jeanette open her doors to her if she knew the truth? And if she was going to stay for any length of time, she'd have to tell her. In a few months, the truth would become all too obvious.

Melissa looked Jeanette straight in the eye and said, "Before we discuss my staying with you any further, there's something you need to know. I think I'm going to have a baby. My monthly is almost two weeks late, something that has never happened to me before."

A baby? Jeanette *was* shocked. Reid had said nothing about a baby. But then, he must not have known. Melissa had said she thought she was pregnant. If she was only two weeks late, then Melissa hadn't realized it herself when Reid left her. Surely if Reid had known, he wouldn't have deserted her, and now Jeanette had no earthly idea of where to find him. He could be anywhere between New Orleans and St. Louis. God, she wished she had known before Nathan had left. He could have found Reid for her. Jeanette didn't know what to do. This certainly put a different light on the whole situation.

Melissa watched the emotions playing across Jeanette's face. At first, she had looked shocked, but now she appeared more perplexed and flustered. Melissa felt she owed Jeanette some explanation. She sighed deeply. "I think it's time to tell you my story."

Melissa told Jeanette everything, from the

minute she had seen Reid standing on the river-landing until he walked out on her. She spared herself nothing. She even divulged everything that had happened during her captivity, telling Jeanette things she had never told Reid. By the time she finished relating her story, the sun was rising.

What a remarkable story, Jeanette thought, and for it to end so sadly. There was only one thing she was curious about. "And how do you feel about this baby? Do you want it?"

Melissa's head snapped up. "Of course I want it! It's Reid's baby."

"Then you don't hate him. You still love him?"

"Yes, I still love him," Melissa admitted. "Oh, I tried to hate him, but I couldn't find it in me. I still love him. I always will."

"It will be hard raising a child by yourself, you know," Jeanette pointed out.

"I know. But I intend to," Melissa said in a determined voice.

Jeanette smiled. "If any other woman had said that, I'd think she was foolish. I'd strongly urge her to put the baby up for adoption. But after everything you just told me, I have no doubts in my mind that you can do it."

Jeanette rose and stretched. "Now let's have an early breakfast and get some sleep. Then this afternoon we can drive into Natchez and get you a lawyer. The sooner he can get to work on your inheritance, the better. With the baby coming, you're going to need it."

It was Melissa's turn to be shocked. "You mean, you still want me to stay? Knowing that I lived with a man I wasn't married to? That I'm going to have an illegitimate baby?"

"I not only want you to stay, Melissa, I insist upon it."

Melissa was relieved, but she realized she would be placing Jeanette in an awkward position. If the elite Natchez society should ever find out the truth of her harboring a woman of such low morals, as they would undoubtedly look upon a pregnant unmarried woman . . . "But—"

"My dear," Jeanette interjected, "you're a strong and determined young woman, and I admire you for it. But let me warn you. I'm a stubborn woman myself. If you try to walk out my door before this baby is born, I swear I'll personally hog-tie you to your bed!"

Chapter Sixteen

Melissa sat back in the carriage and carefully arranged the black skirt around her. The dress belonged to Jeanette, part of her old widow's weeds, a very necessary garment for Melissa now that she was supposed to be in mourning.

She and Jeanette had decided on the story they would tell Natchez. Melissa was now a relative of Jeanette's late husband, and had just recently lost her own husband in an unfortunate hunting accident. Her family had sent her to Natchez, feeling Charleston was too full of memories that would remind her of her husband.

Once they had settled in the carriage, Jeanette said gently, "You realize you'll have to tell the lawyer the truth, though."

Melissa felt sick. She hated to relate her story to a complete stranger. The fact that he would be a man would only make it more embarrassing. She shuddered to think of what his opinion of her would be.

Jeanette saw the look on Melissa's face. "Don't worry, my dear. I've picked the perfect man. Not only is he one of the best and most-respected lawyers in Natchez, but he's also one of the most compassionate human beings I've ever known. You can be sure he will be very discreet and anything you tell him will be held in utmost confidence."

Melissa nodded grimly. She knew there was no way to get out of it. She wouldn't submit to it if it was just for herself. But if there was an inheritance, she owed it to her baby.

When they reached the city proper, Melissa looked around her with new appreciation. She hadn't paid much attention to the city when she and Nathan had driven through it before. At that time, she had been worried about her meeting with Jeanette.

They drove along the old, jasmine-lined streets and passed houses and stores, many of them stuccoed and with wrought-iron balconies in the Spanish manner of architecture. They turned into a wide, sunny esplanade that ran into the plaza where huge oaks and magnolias grew. Below them, Melissa could see the Mississippi stretching like a yellow ribbon into the horizon. The air was filled with the scent of magnolias, jasmine, and roses.

Melissa looked around her. "Your city is beautiful."

Jeanette smiled. "Thank you, my dear. We in Natchez are very proud of our city and our history. Natchez dates back even further than St. Louis or New Orleans, if you consider the first white settlement. The French built a military post here in 1700, but it was almost wiped out by the Natchez Indians and abandoned."

At South Wall and State streets, they passed a half block of small quarters and then stopped. "This is Lawyers Row," Jeanette said with a laugh. "I think every lawyer in Natchez has an office here."

Melissa swallowed hard and, with the help of Jeanette's coachman, stepped down from the carriage. She looked about the busy, crowded street nervously. Her anxiety increased when they entered the small office. Clerks were rushing about everywhere. It didn't look very private to her, and she certainly wasn't anxious to tell her story within hearing range of all these ears.

"Is Mr. Roberts in?" Jeanette asked one of the clerks.

"Yes, ma'am, I believe he is," the clerk replied, looking at them curiously.

"Will you tell him Mrs. Woodward would like to see him, please?"

"Yes, ma'am." The clerk gave them a penetrating look and then turned away, walking to one of the office doors and opening it before he disappeared behind it.

Melissa turned and looked about the busy office, very conscious of the men's eyes on her.

"Jeanette," a deep, masculine voice said. "What are you doing here? Don't tell me you've taken to delivering your invitations to your balls personally?"

Melissa realized that the voice belonged to the man they had come to see. Gathering her courage, she turned. Her heart sank when she saw the man. She had hoped he would be a gray-headed, kindly, *old* man.

Quickly she scrutinized him. She judged him to be somewhere between his mid-thirties and forty. He was tall and slim, his dark hair tipped with silver over his ears, giving him a distinguished air. His face was turned slightly away from her, but from what she could see, he was attractive looking. But what disturbed her was the vital aura that seemed to surround him. No, she couldn't bare her soul to this dynamic stranger.

Jeanette laughed. "No, Aaron, I'm afraid I'm here on business." She was all too aware that every eye and ear in the office was on her. "Is there someplace we can talk privately?"

Aaron was surprised at Jeanette's words. He knew old Judge Hamilton handled her legal affairs, as he had her late husband's. Was the woman thinking of changing lawyers? But why him? He wasn't even old Natchez. And if she did wish to switch to him, it would be awkward, and he certainly didn't want everyone in this office knowing it.

"I have to appear in court shortly," Aaron replied smoothly. "Perhaps I can drop by the plantation this evening."

Jeanette was relieved. She had never been in a law office before. She had no idea they were such crowded places. "That will be fine, Aaron. We'll expect you for dinner."

Aaron turned, for the first time aware of Melissa standing off to the side. His dark eyes swept over her in quick appraisal. Then he turned to Jeanette, a questioning look on his face.

Jeanette smiled. "Dear me, where are my manners?" She pulled Melissa forward. "Melissa, this is Aaron Roberts. Aaron, Mrs. Randall is a relative of my late husband who just arrived from Charleston. She just recently lost her husband in an unfortunate accident. She'll be staying with me for a while."

Jeanette was aware of every ear listening. By tonight, all of Natchez will know of Melissa, she thought. Well, it's just as well they hear the story this way as any other.

Aaron turned back to Melissa. She found herself looking into a pair of deep liquid-brown eyes, the kindest eyes she had ever seen. The tension that had been building in her seemed to melt under that warm, compassionate gaze.

"How do you do, Mr. Roberts," Melissa managed to mutter.

"May I offer my profoundest sympathy, Mrs. Randall," Aaron said quietly.

My God, what a beauty, Aaron thought. And so young to be a widow. He looked into her eyes and saw the sadness there. He recognized that look. It was the look of someone who had lost one they loved deeply. Yes, he could certainly empathize with her.

Melissa was flustered by Aaron's sympathetic manner. She knew it was because he thought her to be a widow. She felt like a hypocrite. She could hardly force herself to look him in the eye.

"We're keeping you from your business, Aaron," Jeanette said. "We'll see you this evening. Around seven?"

"I'll be there," Aaron replied.

As soon as the carriage rolled away, Melissa said, "Jeanette, I can't tell that man my story. He's too young. Can't we find another lawyer? An older one, perhaps?"

Jeanette was alarmed. She didn't want to take Melissa to any other lawyer in Natchez. She had a reason why she had picked Aaron Roberts, a reason other than all the good reasons she had given Melissa earlier. Aaron wasn't old Natchez. He hadn't been born and raised in the vicinity. By Natchez standards, he was a newcomer to the city. He had never known Valerie or Reid. By the time he had arrived in the city, the gossip about them had died down. She didn't know whether

Melissa would even mention Reid by name, but if she did use his name to any other lawyer in town, they would recognize it and might let the cat out of the bag. And Reid had been emphatic that he never wanted Melissa to know about Valerie.

"My dear, he's one of the most capable lawyers in town," Jeanette assured her. "As I said, everything you tell him will be kept in strictest confidence."

"But any lawyer would keep what I tell him in strictest confidence," Melissa countered.

Jeanette laughed. "My dear, if you really believe that, you are naive. Why, I wouldn't trust half of them as far as I could throw them. After all, look at how many of them become politicians. No, Aaron is the best man for the job. Besides, we've already contacted him. How would I explain that I've changed my mind?"

That would be embarrassing, Melissa realized. Besides, she'd hate to insult the man. After all, Jeanette had assured her he was capable.

But Melissa was still very nervous when Aaron arrived that evening. Jeanette was aware of Melissa's tension, so she kept the conversation light at the dinner table, hoping to give Melissa time to compose herself and become more at ease in Aaron's company.

After discussing the usual mundane subjects, Melissa felt more relaxed and asked, "Were you born here in Natchez, too, Mr. Roberts?"

The liquid-brown eyes turned to her. "No, I'm from the East. I'm surprised you didn't notice my Yankee clip. I moved here four years ago."

"Drawn by the excitement of the West?" Melissa asked.

A flicker of sadness passed through Aaron's eyes. Then he smiled. "Yes, you might say that."

"Well, Aaron is one of us now," Jeanette said.

Aaron's dark eyebrows arched. "You mean I've finally passed the test?"

"What test?" Melissa asked.

Jeanette laughed. "Aaron has always had some silly idea in his head that the people in Natchez didn't trust him."

"Because you're a Yankee?" Melissa asked.

Aaron chuckled softly. "No, because of my first name."

"Aaron? What's wrong with that?" Melissa asked in confusion.

"Aaron has always thought the people in Natchez associated him with Aaron Burr," Jeanette answered. "After his grand scheme for his empire of the Southwest was found out, Burr fled to Natchez. Society here welcomed him with open arms. After all, he had been vice president, would have been President even if it hadn't been for one vote. But when General Wilkerson turned on him and Burr was arrested for treason, the people here were shocked—and terribly embarrassed."

"And very wary of anyone with the name

448

Aaron," Aaron added.

"Oh, Aaron, that's just your imagination," Jeanette said.

"Perhaps," Aaron admitted. "But let's face it. Aaron isn't a very common name. The fact that I was born in New Jersey, graduated from Princeton, served in the army, and practiced in New York just like Burr didn't help my case any. No, Jeanette, Natchez was definitely leery of me when I first arrived. And I can't honestly say I blame them." He laughed. "I even considered changing my first name."

Melissa and Jeanette laughed.

After dinner, Jeanette led them into the drawing room and then turned to Aaron. "I'm afraid I deceived you this afternoon. Melissa is the one that needs your professional help."

"Oh?" He looked at Melissa. "You need a lawyer to help settle your husband's estate?"

Melissa flushed at the word "husband." "No, it concerns my inheritance from my parents. You see, I'm not sure there is one."

"Not sure?" Aaron asked, a frown crossing his face.

"It's a long story, Aaron," Jeanette said. "Would you like me to stay?" she asked Melissa.

Melissa dreaded what she had to do, but asking Jeanette to stay would be cowardly. She was a big girl now. She had to stand on her own two feet. "No, I don't think that's necessary."

After Jeanette had left, Melissa sat down in a

chair, and Aaron settled his long frame down in one opposite her. She twisted her handkerchief nervously. "I don't know where to begin."

Aaron felt sorry for the young woman. She looked as if she might bolt at any minute. He was accustomed to seeing clients behave in this manner, as if they thought their lawyer was judge, jury, and executioner all rolled into one.

He leaned forward. "Relax, Mrs. Randall. I promise you, I don't bite. And I'm not here to interrogate you. I'm here to help you. Now, you just talk and I'll listen. If I have any questions, I'll ask them when you're finished."

Melissa nodded and took a deep breath. "A year ago, my father sold all of his property in South Carolina and moved our family west. His tobacco crop had failed for the past three years, and my father was determined to buy land in the West and start a new plantation."

Aaron nodded. Since the Louisiana Territory had been opened to the public, people had been flooding in from both the North and the South, poor farmer and wealthy planter alike, all seeking the rich fertile ground around the Mississippi, and Aaron was knowledgeable enough to know tobacco was one of the most soil-depleting crops there was. More than one tobacco plantation had failed for this very reason. Yes, he could understand Melissa's father seeking new land.

"When we reached New Orleans," Melissa continued, "he met a man who was selling a tobacco plantation on the Missouri River, past Franklin. My father was interested, so we traveled up the Mississippi and then the Missouri to have a look at it. The keelboat we were traveling on was attacked by Indians about ten days out of Franklin. Everyone but my sister, myself, and another woman were killed. We were taken captive, but before we reached the Indian camp, my sister was bitten by a rattlesnake and died."

Melissa hesitated. She absolutely refused to tell Aaron anything about her humiliating captivity. "In the fall, the Indian who had captured me took me to a trading fair to sell me. There were two trappers there who had traveled on the same steamer with my family as far as Franklin, and they recognized me. They bought me from the Indian, but it was too late in the year for them to bring me back to St. Louis, so I stayed with them all winter. Six weeks ago, they brought me back to St. Louis. One of the trappers knew Jeanette and he brought me here."

Aaron was stunned. He hadn't expected to hear such a shocking story. There were a lot of gaps in her story, deliberate gaps, he knew. Was she ashamed because she had been an Indian captive? Because she had lived with two men in the wilderness? But there was no reason for her to feel that way. The first circumstance she had no control over; she was the victim. And the second had been out of necessity for survival.

451

What about her husband? There had been no mention of him. Had he been killed in the raid, too? Or had he stayed behind in South Carolina? Or had she married one of the trappers?

"And you need help with your inheritance," Aaron said in a calm, matter-of-fact voice. "You said you weren't sure there was one. Why do you think that?"

Melissa was shocked by Aaron's calm attitude. She searched his face. If he was shocked by her story, he certainly showed no signs of it. And she didn't see any signs of pity she had dreaded, either.

"I don't know where my father's money was. He was carrying a great deal of money on him at the time of the attack, but Jeanette said she thought that was probably just the down payment for the plantation. She thinks the rest of the money from the sale of his property must be in a bank somewhere. But I have no idea where it is, nor do I know where his will and legal papers might be."

"I see," Aaron replied. "I agree with Jeanette. Your father was a planter, a businessman. I doubt very seriously that he'd carry the entire sum with him. No, most likely, both the money and his legal papers are in a bank somewhere. Where did you say you were from in South Carolina?"

"Charleston."

Aaron nodded. "We'll try there first. It's got

to be either there or in New Orleans or St. Louis. But don't worry, we'll find it."

Melissa sighed, feeling as if a great weight had been removed from her shoulders.

"Now, I need some information," Aaron said, slipping a small notebook from his pocket. "First of all, I need your father's full name."

Melissa froze. Jeanette had introduced her as *Mrs.* Randall. This was the part she had been dreading the most. She hated to tell him the truth.

She squared her shoulders and said, "Mr. Roberts, I'm afraid there's something else I must tell you. Randall is my maiden name. I've never been married, much less a widow. Jeanette and I made up that story for appearances' sake. You see, I'm going to have a baby."

That's why she never mentioned a husband, Aaron thought. There wasn't one. The lawyer part of him told him it didn't matter, it had absolutely no bearing on his case, but the man in him was curious. Who was the father? One of the trappers? And if so, had she loved him? Yes, he suspected she had. The look he had seen in her eyes, that look of deep sadness, wasn't from losing her parents and sister. No, it came from the loss of a much more profound love, a once-in-a-lifetime love. He knew. He had been there himself.

Aaron forced his mind away from the disturbing questions to the business at hand. "From the standpoint of your case, Melissa, not being married is to your advantage," he said in a calm voice. "If you were married, your inheritance would go into your husband's estate. This way, collecting your inheritance will be much less involved."

Melissa couldn't believe it. Why, he had shown absolutely no shock at all. She stared at him.

"Melissa," Aaron said gently, "I'm your lawyer. Your personal life is none of my business. If you're worried about your true marital status leaking out by way of your claim on your inheritance, forget it. I assure you, it will be handled discreetly. No one will know that the Miss Randall I'm representing and the new widow Mrs. Randall are the same person. And you need not worry about me personally divulging that information. I would never betray a client's trust."

He turned and walked to a small desk. Sitting down at it, with pencil poised, he said, "Now, what was your father's first and middle name?"

As Aaron asked questions and Melissa answered, she began to relax. She was ashamed that she had almost refused to talk to him. Why, no one could have been kinder or gentler. And not once had she felt he was invading her privacy. By the time they had finished, they both had a healthy respect for the other, Aaron for Melissa's courage and she for his competence.

Aaron rose and slipped the notebook into his pocket. "I'll get an investigator on this tomorrow.

Personally, I don't think tracking down the will and money will take all that long. It's getting the will probated that will be the problem. With no death certificates or witnesses to testify that they saw your parents die, it might take a little time. But don't worry. If there is an inheritance there, I'll get it for you."

"Thank you, Mr. Roberts."

Aaron smiled. "I think under the circumstances you should call me Aaron. I'll be needing to ask more questions and you're going to be seeing a lot of me. I'd feel less like an interrogator if you'd call me by my first name." He grinned. "That is, if you feel you can trust someone whose first name is Aaron."

Melissa laughed. "Only if his last name isn't Burr."

Melissa started to rise. "Don't bother," Aaron said. "I'll have Jeanette show me out. I'm sure you're exhausted after all those questions."

Before Aaron opened the door to leave, he turned to Jeanette and said, "There's one thing I'm curious about. Why did you bring Melissa to me, instead of taking her to your own lawyer?"

Just as Jeanette had had a reason for taking Melissa to Aaron, she also had a good reason for not using her own lawyer. She said in all honesty, "I may trust Judge Hamilton with my legal matters, but I would never trust him with a young woman's reputation. You know how he drinks. I wouldn't put it past the old sot to get drunk and blab the whole story."

Aaron knew exactly what Jeanette meant. The old judge was sharp, but he did drink too much, and he *was* a blabbermouth when he got tipsy. Several times, Aaron had heard him telling things about his clients that he had no business divulging. Such a breach of ethics disgusted Aaron. No wonder people didn't trust lawyers.

Deliberately, Aaron withheld comment. To do so, would be just as bad as blabbing about a client. Besides, the old man never did it intentionally. "Good night, Jeanette, and thank you for the lovely dinner."

As Aaron drove away, Jeanette thought, He *is* special. If she had made that remark about Judge Hamilton to any of her other lawyer friends, they would not only have agreed with her, but would have promptly launched into a verbal attack on the old man. She wished there was some graceful way she could change lawyers, but felt that she couldn't do that to the old judge. He'd been good to her over the years. Still, when he died, her business was going to Aaron.

She walked back into the drawing room. Melissa was waiting for her, a bright smile on her face. "Well, you certainly look like you're feeling better," Jeanette remarked.

"I am. I feel like I've had a tremendous burden lifted from my shoulders. I haven't felt this relaxed in almost two weeks. And you're right about Aaron. He's the most understanding man I've ever met. Why, he didn't act the least bit shocked by my story or my pregnancy."

"I think lawyers are like priests, my dear. They've heard so much they're past being shocked. And I expected Aaron to be understanding. He lost his own family just before he moved out here. Many think that's why he moved here, to get away from his memories."

"Was it his parents?"

"No, his wife and baby. She died in childbirth. I understand he was deeply in love with her, and I believe it's true."

"Why?"

"Because he's a very attractive man. Maybe you didn't notice, but you can be sure every belle in Natchez has. When he first came here, they were all chasing him. But he never looked twice at any of them. Oh, he was always polite, but very aloof. Rumor has it that he's suffering from a broken heart and will never remarry."

"But that would be a shame. He's still young and so . . . vital."

"Yes, he is. It seems a waste, doesn't it?"

Melissa nodded, but she thought she understood. If Aaron had loved his wife as deeply, as profoundly, as completely as she had loved Reid, then he knew he could never love that strongly again. Any other love would be a mere shadow, an imitation of the real thing. After that kind of love, could any man or woman settle for less?

As soon as Natchez heard that Jeanette Woodward had a guest, her friends flocked to her door, curious to see the newcomer. When they carried back the fact that the visitor was a beautiful young widow, a new bevy of curious arrived—the eligible bachelors. And having seen the stunning beauty, they continued to come.

Jeanette was alarmed at first. She had been glad she would not be expected to introduce Melissa into Natchez society because the "widow" was in mourning. Jeanette kept hoping that Reid would realize his mistake and come back. She was still convinced that if Reid knew of the baby, he'd forget his foolish principles and divorce Valerie. The last thing she wanted was for Melissa to become interested in another man. But as the men came and Melissa was coldly indifferent to them, Jeanette began to relax.

In truth, she began to find the situation humorous. Since she hadn't taken Melissa to Natchez, the men had come to her. Of course, they didn't come openly courting. With Melissa still in mourning, that would have been socially inappropriate. No, they all came on the pretext of visiting their friend Jeanette, but all for the same actual purpose. Each hoped to get a jump on the other when Melissa was out of mourning. As time wore on, the excuses they gave became more and more outlandish. Jeanette would chuckle for hours after they had left at their ridiculous explanations.

On one such day, Melissa snapped, "It's not funny, Jeanette! I feel like someone has declared open season on me. There seems to be a man behind every potted plant, every shrub, every tree. Why, one of those idiots actually serenaded me the other night."

"Yes, I heard," Jeanette said, chuckling louder. "He sounded like a bullfrog with a cold. Only two men around here could possibly have such a terrible singing voice. Who do you suppose it was? Henry Beauchamp or John Thaller?"

"Probably Henry," Melissa replied in disgust. "He fancies himself quite the Casanova."

The sound of a buggy coming up the driveway caught their attention. "Not another one," Jeanette said in exasperation.

"That does it!" Melissa cried. "I'm going upstairs. She hurried out of the room, and without even looking down the hall to see who was coming in the front door, she started up the stairs.

"Melissa?"

Melissa recognized Aaron's deep voice. She turned, saying in a pleased voice, "Aaron! It's good to see you."

"Where are you going in such a rush?"

"Nowhere, now," Melissa replied, walking back down the stairs and taking his arm. "Come into the drawing room."

After Jeanette and Aaron had exchanged pleasantries, Aaron said to Melissa, "I have good news. We tracked down your father's old lawyer in Charleston, and he had your father's will. He also knew the name of the bank your father had used in Charleston. We contacted the bank and they've confirmed that the rest of your father's money is there. The lawyer in Charleston has agreed to handle everything from that end, and I'll take care of things from this end. He sent you a letter, explaining what you might expect."

"Oh, Aaron, that's wonderful!" Melissa cried.

Aaron handed Melissa the letter, and she read it quickly. Her inheritance wouldn't make her a wealthy woman, but it would be a substantial sum. If she invested it wisely, she should be able to live comfortably on the profits.

"Thank you, Aaron."

"Whoa, lady," Aaron said. "We're not finished yet. It may take a year or more before you see that money. The probate courts move pretty slowly."

Melissa wasn't surprised. He had warned her it might take some time.

"Can you stay for a while, Aaron?" Melissa asked.

"Why, yes, I can. I don't have any appointments this afternoon."

"Good. Then you can stay for dinner, too," Jeanette said.

They had just settled down when the sound of another carriage came from the driveway.

Melissa got up and looked out the window. "Oh, no! It's Harry again," she wailed.

460

"Is something wrong?" Aaron asked.

Jeanette laughed. "Melissa is being hounded to death by all the young swains in Natchez. Harry Beauchamp has already been here three times this week."

"Forgive me, Aaron," Melissa said. "I don't mean to be rude, but I can't stand one more minute of that arrogant bore. I'm going upstairs."

"Well, I don't see why you should have to go upstairs just to avoid him," Aaron said. 'If he's making a pest of himself, just ask him to leave."

"Oh, I couldn't do that," Melissa objected. "He's the son of one of Jeanette's best friends. I wouldn't want to cause any hard feelings."

"Then I've got a better idea," Aaron said. "Why don't you and I go for a drive? I'll pretend I'm leaving. In the meanwhile, you go out back and I'll swing my buggy around and pick you up. When Henry walks in the front door, we'll be driving away."

Melissa looked doubtful.

"That sounds like a wonderful idea to me," Jeanette said. "Now, hurry, before he gets here."

A few minutes later, Aaron and Melissa were driving away, laughing like two conspirators. To Melissa's delight, Aaron didn't drive down the main rutted road, but chose instead a small trail through the countryside.

"You can drive a one-horse buggy places you can't take a bigger carriage," he explained.

461

"That's why I prefer them."

Melissa enjoyed the drive through the country-side immensely. The cotton fields stretched for miles and miles, the pink and white blossoms fluttering in the breeze. They drove through a thick pine forest, the buggy wheels making a crunching noise on the heavy carpet of pine needles. Some of the trees were covered with honeysuckle and grapevines, the fruit just beginning to ripen. The air was pungent with the smell of pine, honeysuckle, and damp earth.

The trail circled around, then followed the high bluff above the river. Melissa gazed at the fluffy white clouds racing across the sky and then across the river at the lush, green lowlands of Louisiana stretching endlessly into the horizon. From the river below, Melissa heard a cannon boom, announcing the arrival of a packet.

The wheels of the buggy clattered when they drove onto the cobbled streets of Natchez. As they were passing through the business district, Melissa's eyes widened. On the street before one of the shops, a bright yellow carriage stood. The Negro who sat proudly on the driver's seat was clothed in bright yellow livery. Even the horse's harnesses were yellow. As they passed, a blond-headed woman, wearing a yellow dress and carrying a yellow parasol, stepped out of the shop and walked to the carriage. The driver scampered down from his perch and helped her into the carriage. Melissa had never seen so much yellow. All that bright color was glaring in the sunlight and almost hurt her eyes to look at it.

Aaron saw the astonished look on her face. "Your visit to Natchez has been complete, Melissa. You've just had the honor of viewing Katherine Lintot Minor, the Yellow Duchess. She never wears any other color. I understand even her pantaloons are yellow. Her entire home is decorated in yellow. Yellow walls, yellow carpeting, yellow upholstery and drapes. Even the flooring is made of yellow flagstones."

"Is she really a duchess?"

"No. She's married to Steven Minor, a wealthy land owner. He was an American who drifted down here during the Spanish period, a soldier of fortune. Katherine is the leader of Natchez's high society. To be invited to a ball at their home, the Concord, is every Mississippian's dream come true."

"Have you been invited to a ball at the Concord?"

Aaron grinned. "Yes, I have. And I shouldn't have sounded so critical. Actually, they're nice people. Steven Minor, especially. He's a natural-born diplomat.

"I know a little inn where they sell ice-cold watermelon," Aaron said a few minutes later. "Would you be interested in a slice?" His eyes twinkled. "Or is eating watermelon beneath your dignity?"

Melissa wondered what Aaron would think if

he knew some of the things she had eaten over the past year. Undoubtedly, he'd be a little shocked. "That sounds delightful," she answered.

The gentleman callers continued to descend on Jeanette's home. In their eyes, Melissa's aloofness made her appear mysterious, only adding to her allure. In an effort to discourage them, Melissa spent much of her time in her room. Therefore, when Aaron arrived a few days later and asked her to go on another ride, she was delighted.

They drove to the bluff overlooking the river and walked on the promenade there. From this lofty vantage point, the river could be seen for miles and miles.

Melissa glanced down at the city beneath the hill. The tin roofs on the shacks flashed in the sunlight, sending up shimmering heat waves. The stench and raucous sounds of the city drifted upward. One hawker had a particularly penetrating voice, and Melissa blushed as he described in lurid detail the delights of the flesh to be found in one brothel.

She walked to the edge of the bluff and looked down at the river, then said to Aaron, "Look at those two steamboats."

"Yes, they're racing to see who can get to that empty space by the landing first."

Melissa watched as the two boats steamed side by side toward the river landing. Their paddles were spinning so fast they were a mere blur, the water a yellow froth behind the wheels. Even from where she stood, she could see the boats shuddering from the engine's vibrations. Loud hoots and calls of encouragement came from the crowd watching the race below the hill, urging the two boats onward.

"Those damned fools!" Aaron said angrily. "Those engines weren't built to take that kind of abuse. Their boilers can explode at any minute. Look at that smoke!"

Melissa saw what Aaron said was true. The smoke coming from the smokestacks had turned from the usual grayish-white to a dark, angry black, boiling up in the sky and casting a dark shadow over the river, fouling the crystal-clear air. Red-hot cinders flew through the air and drifted across the bluff, a few falling on Melissa and Aaron and burning their exposed skin.

But despite the hot cinders, the two stood rooted to the spot and watching the sight below, terrified that any minute they would see a flash of light, hear a roaring explosion, and then see pieces of debris and bodies hurling through the air. They gritted their teeth as the first boat darted into the empty landing space, scraping against the wooden wharf and shaking it precariously, and then gasped as the second boat veered sharply, just missing colliding into the first one by mere inches.

Melissa leaned against the railing, feeling weak with relief at the near disaster.

Aaron glared down at the boats, gripping the railing so tightly his knuckles were white. "Those goddamned fool captains! Didn't they realize they were jeopardizing every life on their boats? They should be tarred and feathered."

Aaron's outburst shocked Melissa. She had never seen him be anything but calm. She could have sworn that he would never lose his cool composure.

Aaron saw her look and apologized. "Forgive me, Melissa, but that kind of incompetence infuriates me. What right do those captains have to gamble with the lives of their passengers? And for what? To save a little time? And those fools down on the landing, encouraging them. The whole thing is sheer insanity."

"It was foolish," Melissa agreed.

Aaron looked back down at the river. "I feel very strongly about this. I don't usually talk about my clients, but in this particular case, one of my clients and I both agree that the public should be made more aware of what's happening on that river. The death rate from boat accidents is appalling. It's true, some of the disasters can't be helped. There are accidents — a boat hitting a snag or a planter, a collision in the dense fog. But too many deaths are unnecessary. They're caused by the kind of stupidity we just witnessed."

He turned, facing Melissa. "My client and his wife were on a steamboat whose captain pushed

466

the boat beyond its engine's endurance. The captain's only excuse was that he was running behind on his schedule. The boilers exploded. My client's wife was killed outright and her husband maimed for life. He was horribly burned. His hands are just a mass of scar tissue. He'll never be able to work again. So he came to me. We're suing the steamboat company for compensation, but I know that we won't get a cent. The steamboat companies are too powerful."

"What about the captain? Can't your client sue him?"

"The captain has already paid the price for his foolish mistake. He was killed in the accident, too." He turned and looked back down at the river. "As if we don't have enough problems on this river, I've heard of several instances where the steamers raced just for the sport of it. People were placing bets just like they do at a racetrack. I shudder to think what will happen on this river if that becomes a common practice."

"But surely the steamboat companies don't approve of that."

"To the contrary. I suspect they encourage it. They think if they can prove they have the faster boats they can get more business."

"But that's terrible!"

"Exactly. And that's why the responsibility lies at their door. They could stop this whole business immediately by making it a policy that their

467

boats don't travel beyond the speed the engines were built for, and by firing on the spot any captain that goes against that policy. If a captain knows his job is on the line, he'll think twice before he jeopardizes his passengers' lives. But I'm afraid the steamboat companies won't do this until the death toll gets so appalling that the public finally cries out in outrage. And how many innocent people will die in the meantime?"

Melissa was impressed, not only by his words but by his tone of voice and the look of concern on his face. He cares about people, she thought. He really cares. Not just his loved ones and his friends, but all people.

They went back to the buggy. Riding through the tranquil streets, Melissa soon forgot the upsetting scene on the river.

As they drove down one tree-lined residential street, Melissa asked, "What's that noise?"

Aaron slowed the horse and looked around. Then he pointed to the top of a huge tree. "Look up there. It's a kitten."

The little gray kitten was high up in the branches, clinging for dear life and mewing pitifully. Aaron and Melissa climbed down from the carriage and tried to coax the kitten down, but the small cat was too terrified. He only howled louder.

Aaron took off his coat and tie and handed them to Melissa.

"What are you going to do?" she asked as he

slipped off his shoes and socks and rolled up his pants legs.

"I'm going after him."

"You? You're going to climb that tree?"

"Well, I'll admit it's been a long time since I've climbed a tree, but somebody has got to bring him down."

Melissa looked up at the tree. "But it's so tall."

Aaron grinned. "Relax, Melissa. I've climbed much taller trees than this one back in New Jersey."

Melissa watched as Aaron shinnied up the tree trunk and then climbed toward the kitten. His agility was surprising for a man his age. For the first time, she became aware of his broad shoulders, his excellent physique.

But as Aaron climbed toward the kitten, the frightened animal climbed even higher. Melissa's breath caught as the limb Aaron was standing on swayed precariously. My God, she thought, he must be at least fifty feet up. If he fell, Aaron could break his neck.

Aaron finally coaxed the kitten down far enough to catch him. Then, holding the kitten close to him with one hand, he climbed back down and jumped to the ground.

He set the kitten on the ground, saying with a laugh, "Now, off with you, you little scamp. And don't be climbing any more trees until you're big enough to get back down."

Melissa looked at Aaron as he watched the kitten bounding off. He certainly didn't look like the distinguished-looking lawyer she was accustomed to seeing. With his hair tousled and falling over his forehead, he looked much younger. He *is* very attractive, she thought, as if seeing him for the first time. And how many grown, mature men would take the time and trouble to rescue a kitten? Her respect for him grew.

From that day on, Aaron was a frequent caller at Jeanette's plantation. A week later, he escorted the two women to the theater.

Melissa had been reluctant to go, feeling it was not in keeping with her state of mourning. But Jeanette, backed by Aaron, had convinced Melissa to attend the theater. "The people of Natchez are not as strict about mourning as they are in the eastern section of the South. Our heritage may be English, but we have absolutely no puritan in us."

"But still, I'd hate to shock any of your friends," Melissa countered.

Jeanette laughed. "Melissa, many of Natchez's leading families are descendants of pirates and slave traders. Do you really think you're going to shock them? Besides, I have a private box. I doubt if anyone will even notice you."

But Natchez did notice. At some time or another, every eye in the audience was on the box where the lovely young widow sat, not because they disapproved, but because everyone was fascinated with the beautiful woman with the sad eyes. During intermission, many of Jeanette's friends visited the box. They all agreed with Jeanette's opinion—balls and parties might be in bad taste for someone in mourning, but not the theater. One elderly woman declared that the theater was not just entertainment, but was educational, too. The comment brought a few raised eyebrows, but no one corrected her. The matriarch of Natchez's high society had spoken. Natchez had given its approval.

And so, when Aaron invited her to the theater the next week, Melissa accepted enthusiastically. Jeanette declined, saying she had seen the play in New Orleans the year before, but insisted that it was perfectly acceptable for Aaron to accompany Melissa alone.

This time, Melissa enjoyed not only seeing the play, but the audience as well. The women were dressed beautifully, their lavish gowns showing every color of the rainbow. And Melissa had never seen so many glittering jewels dangling from throats and ears and wrists. Even the men were dressed elegantly, in their white frilled shirts and dark evening suits.

That night when Aaron left her at the door, instead of giving her a friendly peck on the cheek, as had become his habit of late, he pulled her into his arms and kissed her warmly. At first, Melissa was too surprised to object. Then as his kiss deepened and became more passionate, she shocked herself and pleased Aaron by responding eagerly, embracing and kissing him back, her body straining against his.

After Aaron had left, Melissa paced the floor, deeply disturbed by the way she had responded to his kiss. What in the world had possessed her? She didn't love Aaron. Oh, she had a deep affection for him, she admitted. But that was all. No, she was still deeply in love with Reid. Then how could she have possibly behaved so shamelessly?

Melissa was apprehensive the next day when Aaron came to call. But he behaved so naturally she soon relaxed, enjoying his company as she always had. When he made no further advances, she decided she had put too much emphasis on the kiss, had only imagined their brief flare of passion.

A few days later, Aaron took Melissa for another ride. As they drove to their favorite spot on the bluff, Melissa looked about at the cotton fields. Some of the fields had been picked clean, the plants looking rather forlorn without their ornamentation. In others, the puffy cotton was so thick the whole field appeared white. In some places, the cotton was just being picked, the slaves' dark bodies glistening with sweat as they trudged down the rows and pulled their long white bags behind them.

When they climbed from the carriage, they walked to the edge of the bluff and looked down. Below them, the grapevines twisted over the chalky ground, the branches picked clean of their fruit by the birds. At the river's edge, two boys sat fishing with long cane poles. A third lay beside them, sunning himself lazily.

"Come over here where it's cooler, Melissa," Aaron said, guiding her to a small bench under a huge spreading magnolia. "I want to talk to you."

Melissa wondered why he sounded so solemn. "Is something wrong?" she asked.

Aaron smiled. "No, I just think it's time we had a serious talk."

"About what?"

Aaron looked her directly in the eye. "About us."

"Us?"

"I realize I'm a great deal older than you, sixteen years to be exact, but I really don't feel that there's that much of an age gap between us. Your experiences during the past year have matured you beyond your years."

Melissa was frankly confused. What in the world was he talking about? What did their ages have to do with anything?

Aaron saw her puzzled look and smiled ruefully. "For a lawyer, I'm doing a lousy job of presenting my case. I'm asking you to marry me, Melissa."

Marry? Melissa was shocked.

"We enjoy each other's company," Aaron continued. "We like the same things. We—"

"Aaron! I can't marry you! I'm fond of you, but I don't love you."

Aaron smiled and replied in a patient voice, "I know. And I don't love you, either, Melissa. At least, not the way you're talking about. I've only loved one woman that way. My wife. I loved her totally, completely, passionately, and I'll never love that strongly again."

"Then why are you asking me to marry you?"

"Because I suspect you've experienced the same kind of love and, like me, have lost it. We both know we'll never love that strongly again. Which is why we'd work out well together. Neither of us expects a grand passion. Our marriage would be based on friendship, deep affection, and mutual respect. We're both lonely. I don't think either of us wants to go through life without a companion. On the other hand, neither of us wants to get involved with a partner who would expect more than we can offer."

"Haven't you forgotten something? I'm going to have a child. Another man's child."

"Which is another good reason for us to marry," Aaron said calmly. "Raising a child alone would be very difficult. Besides, every child deserves two parents, and I think I have the qualifications to make a good father."

And would Aaron love her child, she wondered. Yes, if he didn't love her, he'd have no reason to be jealous of the other man and hold it against the baby. Besides, Aaron would never do that. A man who cared as much about people as Aaron did would have no reservations about loving a baby. And he'd be gentle, too, she thought, remembering how he'd rescued the kitten. And her baby did deserve a father.

"And I think we would do well together sexually, too," Aaron continued. "That kiss the other night proved that."

Melissa flushed furiously, remembering how eager she had been.

Aaron smiled, amused at her blush, then said, "Oh, we'll probably never have sublime happiness or reach the greatest heights of ecstasy, but we'll never know bitter disappointment when the bubble bursts, either, since we're not marrying because of physical attraction. All and all, I think we'd be quite content."

Aaron was making some very good points. She knew of many successful marriages that had started out with a less substantial foundation. But if he was willing to take on another man's child, he had a right to know the circumstances.

"Aaron, I'd like to tell you about my baby's father."

"That's not necessary, Melissa."

"Maybe not for you, but it is for me."

They sat on the bench and Melissa told Aaron everything about her and Reid's tumultuous love affair. She didn't try to color the story in her favor, either. She admitted that she had chased

475

Reid, even deliberately tried to seduce him. She made it perfectly clear that Reid had never offered her marriage, even though he had told her he loved her. How ironic, she thought bitterly. One man loved me, but never wanted to marry me. Another offers marriage, but doesn't love me.

Aaron listened quietly, but when she told him about Reid's desertion, he was puzzled. He had assumed the man had left her because he didn't love her. But from what Melissa had said, the trapper must have loved her just as deeply and completely as she loved him. Then why hadn't the man asked her to marry him? A suspicion entered Aaron's mind. Was the man already married? If he had been, Melissa had obviously never suspected it, and Aaron certainly wasn't going to suggest it. It would only make her feel used.

Melissa ended with, "And I still love him. I know it's foolish, but I can't help myself. I'll always love him."

"Do you think he'll come back?"

Melissa had secretly clung to that hope. But by this time, Reid was undoubtedly on his way back up the Missouri. "No, he won't be back," she answered in a dull, lifeless voice.

"Then think about what I said for a few days. But if you decide the answer is yes, I see no reason to wait. I think we should be married right away."

476

"Right away?" Melissa said in shock. "But I'm in mourning."

"Melissa, you need a husband's support now. You need it during your pregnancy and at the time of your baby's birth, not a year from now."

"But what will everyone in Natchez think?"

"When you blossom the next month or two, everyone will know you were pregnant when your husband died. I think they'll agree that there was no point in our waiting. If we're already married, it won't be necessary for you to make up a name to put on the baby's birth certificate. Mine can go on it. Once we're married, you can stop this pretense of being another man's widow. You'll be my wife."

As they drove back to the plantation, Melissa thought hard about everything Aaron had said. Reid was gone from her life, and she knew she would never love that deeply again. Yet she didn't want to raise her baby alone, didn't want to go through life alone, either. And if she was ever going to marry, what better man than Aaron? He would never expect her to give him something she could never give to another man.

As Aaron drove up the circular driveway, she said, "I'll marry you, Aaron."

Aaron stopped the carriage and looked down at her, his warm brown eyes searching her face. "You're sure? Don't you want more time to think it over?"

"No, I'm sure."

Aaron kissed her tenderly. "I think, in view of the circumstances, we should have a simple, quiet ceremony. A friend of mine, Judge Bennington, could marry us. How does a week from today sound? Is that too soon?"

Melissa was amazed at the calmness of her voice. "That will be fine."

Aaron smiled and kissed her more warmly. Then he helped her from the carriage and, putting an arm around her, said, "Let's go in the house and tell Jeanette our good news."

Chapter Seventeen

Jeanette heard the knock from where she sat, alone, in the drawing room. Who could be calling at this late hour of the evening? she wondered irritably. Well, at least that was one good thing about Melissa and Aaron's marriage. After the ceremony tomorrow, she wouldn't be having every eligible man in Natchez at her door. Yes, the young men were going to be in for quite a shock.

She was vaguely aware of the sound of Samson's shuffling gait in the hallway as the old man went to answer the door. Her mind was occupied with more pressing thoughts. She had been shocked at Melissa and Aaron's announcement that they were going to get married. She had never dreamed they were anything but friends. At first she had been disturbed, feeling a sense of betrayal for Reid. But then she remembered that it was not Reid who had been betrayed, but Melissa. He had walked out on her first. For days, she had struggled with herself, trying to decide whether or not she should tell Melissa the truth. But Jeanette was afraid that Reid would never return, and if she were right, Melissa would have missed the chance for a secure marriage to an exceptional man.

Hearing the sound of footsteps outside the door, Jeanette glanced up and frowned. What was wrong with Samson? She had told him she would accept no callers tonight.

And then, as a man stepped into the room, her breath caught. "Reid!"

Reid smiled, "I didn't mean to startle you, Jeanette. I told Samson I could see myself in."

Jeanette was shocked by his appearance. He looked terrible. There were dark circles under his eyes and deep lines of fatigue on his face, and he was much thinner than she had ever seen him.

"It's all over, Jeanette." he said in a weary voice. "Valerie is gone."

For a minute, Jeanette was silent, then said, "I can't say I'm surprised, Reid. I've been expecting it for years." She shook her head. "And I can't say I'm sorry, in all honesty. It's for the best," she said in a sad voice.

Reid nodded grimly and walked farther into the room. Jeanette looked at him with concern. "And you, Reid? Are you all right? Are you still blaming yourself?"

Reid walked to a window and looked out. "I never blamed myself, Jeanette. That's not why I stuck by her. I know that I wasn't responsible for what happened, and that I did everything that was humanly possible. I stuck by her because it was the right thing to do, the only thing I could do. And I don't regret it. All I feel now is relief that it's finally over."

Suddenly he whirled, his look one of intense anticipation, the golden eyes that had seemed so lifeless just minutes before glittering with excitement. "Where is she? Did she go back to Charleston?"

Jeanette was torn by indecision. Now she wondered if she should tell *him* the truth. She didn't want Aaron to be hurt, either.

"I said, did she go back to Charleston?"

"I heard what you said, Reid. But there's something you should know. Melissa's getting married — tomorrow."

Reid was shocked by Jeanette's announcement. Then his eyes filled with pain as he said in a bitter voice, "She didn't lose any time finding another man, did she?"

"It's not what it sounds like, Reid. Remember, you walked out on *her*. The man she's marrying is a friend of mine. He's a good man. And that's what you wanted me to do, remember? You wanted me to introduce her to other men."

"Then she's here? In Natchez?"

"Yes."

"Where?"

"Reid, she's getting married tomorrow."

481

Reid's golden eyes flashed. "You're damned right she's getting married tomorrow! But not to him. She's marrying me! I love her and I won't give her up."

Jeanette was just a little frightened by Reid's fierce possessiveness. But the decision was Melissa's. "No Reid, I don't think . . ."

"No?" Reid roared. "Don't tell me no! I've gone through hell these past months, telling myself no. No, Reid, you can't have her. No, Reid, give her up. No, Reid, forget her. Well, I'm free now. Free! And I'm not going to give her up again. Not ever!" His eyes glittered dangerously. "Now, for the last time, where is she?"

Jeanette had never seen Reid look so fierce. She swallowed hard. "Upstairs, in the green bedroom."

Reid whirled and tore from the room. He took the stairs three at a time, his heart pounding in anticipation. He hesitated briefly at the door, then opened it and stepped into the dimly lit room.

Melissa was standing at the window and looking out at the moonlit night. Her back to him, she was unaware of anyone entering the room. Reid stood for a minute, his eyes hungrily drinking in the sight of her, feeling an incredible exhilaration at just being in the same room with her.

Sensing someone staring at her, Melissa turned. Her breath caught, her heart raced. The room seemed to spin dizzily before the floor finally became the floor and the ceiling the ceiling again. Was she hallucinating? Had he come back to haunt her? Why this night of all nights? Why was her memory of him so strong that she felt she could almost reach out and touch him?

Reid's tawny eyes drifted over her, taking in each lovely feature of her face. In the prim, full-gathered nightgown, with the moonlight from the window behind her making a halo around her hair, she looked like an angel stepped down from heaven.

"I thought I had committed every inch of you to memory," Reid said quietly. "I can't believe how incredibly beautiful you are."

Melissa tingled as the sound of his deep, rich voice washed over her. This was no delusion. He was real! "What are *you* doing here?" she whispered.

Reid's eyes shimmered with the intensity of his emotion. "I've come for you, Melissa. I love you. I want you to be my wife."

To Melissa it seemed that she had waited a lifetime to hear those words, and now it was too late. She had promised herself to another man. "You're too late," she muttered. "I'm going to marry another man."

"No! You're *not* going to marry another man!" He crossed the floor in three quick strides and caught her shoulders in a fierce, hurting grip. "You don't love him. You love me!"

Suddenly, the memory of all the pain she had

suffered when he had left her surfaced, and with it came anger. She jerked away from him, her turquoise eyes flashing. "Don't touch me!" she hissed.

She backed away from him, glaring at him. "Who do you think you are? My lord and master? Do you think you can walk in and out of my life at the drop of a hat and still find me waiting for you with open arms? No, you walked out of my life. Now you stay out of it!"

"There were reasons why I left you, Melissa," Reid said in a tight voice.

"Reasons?" Melissa shrieked. "Excuses, you mean. No, I don't want to hear any of your excuses, any of your lies. Get out!"

"Not until I've explained," Reid ground out.

"No! Get out!"

Reid caught her shoulders again and shook her lightly. "Listen to me, Melissa," Reid pleaded. "I love you."

Melissa's eyes glittered with unshed tears. "Love me?" she spat. "Do you think those are the magic words? That all you've got to say is 'I love you' and I'll fall at your feet? No! You're lying!"

Reid's look was thunderous. "If you won't believe my words, then maybe you'll believe this."

One hand caught her nape as he snapped her head back and his mouth covered hers in a fiery, demanding kiss. Melissa tried to struggle, but was helpless under those warm, questing lips, lips that commanded her to respond. He pulled her closer, molding her soft curves to his hard body.

Melissa's mind screamed in outrage, but her body recognized its mate, and her heart knew its love. She was powerless against the onslaught of sensations and emotions that flooded her. Against her will, she melted against him. And then she was kissing him back, hungrily, feverishly. It was a long kiss, a kiss of such intensity she felt he was drawing her very soul from her body.

When Reid finally lifted his head, he said in a ragged voice, "I never lied to you, sweetheart. I love you more than life itself. I know I hurt you. I hate myself for that, but it couldn't be helped. I couldn't ask you to marry me — because I was already married."

Melissa was stunned, the words like ice water on her feverish body. Married? No, he couldn't be. He said . . . Then Melissa realized that Reid had never said anything explicitly, one way or the other. It was Nathan's words that had led her to believe Reid was unmarried. What had he said? "And Reid has nothing to hold him here." And Reid had once told her it would be impossible to force him to marry her, that it was out of the question. Buy why hadn't he just come out and told her the truth?

As the full impact of the words hit her, she felt sick with shame. "My God!" she whispered, "I'm an adulteress."

Reid flinched at the ugly word. "You have

485

every right to hate me, Melissa. I should have told you the truth. I didn't tell you at first because I had no intention of falling in love with you. I fought against it with everything I had. And then, after it happened, I loved you too much to let you go. I needed your love — desperately."

"And your wife? What of the pain we've caused her?"

"I hurt you, Melissa. I even hurt myself. But I never hurt my wife with my infidelity. I know what I did was wrong, but I didn't cheat her of anything."

"How can you say — "

Reid silenced her with a finger on her lips. "Don't say anything until you've heard me out. Let me explain, and then if you still want me to, I'll leave."

Melissa was emotionally exhausted. She had had too many shocks in one night. She nodded numbly.

"Let's sit down," Reid said. "This is a long story."

Reid sat on a chair and Melissa on the bed. Reid began. "As you know, I joined up with Nathan about a year after I came out here. Every summer, Nathan went back to his family in Kentucky and I traveled the river, gambling. I'd always been fairly lucky at cards, and then one summer I got into a poker game with a Creole down in New Orleans. By the time the game was over, I'd won a plantation on the Yazoo River here in Mississippi. I told Nathan I was quitting trapping and going into raising cotton."

He continued. "The plantation had good, rich soil, but it was in sad condition. It had been neglected for years. The Creole had left an overseerer in charge, who had spent most of his time drinking and wenching. I fired him and weeded out the lazier slaves. Then I started getting the land back in shape, one field at a time.

"There was an old slave on the plantation. He'd been working cotton all his life, as had his parents and grandparents before him. Cotton was in his blood. There wasn't anything he didn't know about growing cotton. He taught me, and I worked in the fields right along with my slaves.

"We made a good showing that first year. I bought more slaves and cleared more land. The second year, my profits were even better. I was on my way. But every plantation needs a family. So I headed for Natchez, looking for a wife. That's when I met Valerie."

Melissa's head snapped up at the last word. Valerie? The vision of the beautiful girl in the painting downstairs flashed through her mind. Of course, it had to be the same Valerie, and that explained how Reid had found her. He had known where she was all along, had probably told Nathan to bring her here. Reid's wife was Jeanette's niece. She felt sick, remembering how she had told Jeanette everything about herself

487

and Reid.

"How could you?" she cried in outrage. "How could you send me to one of your wife's relatives? How could you humiliate her and me that way?"

"Melissa, you promised to hear me out. Please, let me finish, before you judge me."

Melissa sat back, her eyes glittering with resentment as Reid continued his story. "Valerie was a beautiful girl. I was attracted to her from the very beginning. And from the way she flirted with me and teased me, I thought she wanted me, too. I proposed, she accepted, and we were married."

A bitterness crept into Reid's voice. "I found out how my wife really felt about me on our wedding night. My lovemaking repulsed her. She said she couldn't stand for anyone to touch her body intimately. It belonged to her. She barely tolerated me. Every time I made love to her, it left me feeling dirty, as if I'd committed some crime. Needless to say, I didn't go to her bed often, only when my need became so great it was either that or go to another woman.

"I brought her back to my plantation, determined to at least try to make a success of our marriage. The plantation was isolated, and certainly nothing as luxurious as what she had been accustomed to. She complained constantly, about everything. I tried to explain that I was trying to get the plantation back on its feet, that the luxuries would come in time. But she wanted everything—right then. She met me at the door everyday with her demands.

"After a few months, she started badgering me about going back to Natchez. She was bored. She missed the parties, the balls, the gay social life. She wanted to come back and live with Jeanette. I refused. She was my wife, my responsibility. She belonged with me.

"And then she got pregnant. I was ecstatic. In the first place, I wanted children badly. In the second, I thought that if she had a baby to occupy her time, she wouldn't be so bored. She'd be more content, maybe even grow up. One day when I was out in the fields, the house slaves sent for me. Valerie was miscarrying. God, I felt so guilty. My first thought was that I should have sent her back to Natchez where she could be close to a doctor."

A pained look came into Reid's eyes. "She couldn't wait to throw in my face what she had done. She hadn't miscarried. She had deliberately aborted herself. She didn't want that *thing* in her, she said. *Thing!* That's what she called our baby. She had deliberately murdered it. *My* baby! I think that was the day I stopped loving her, if I ever did in the first place. I never went back to her bed after that."

Unconsciously, Melissa's hand flew protectively to her abdomen where Reid's child lay, the child she already loved. He had wanted a child desperately, but his wife had deliberately killed it. Her heart filled with compassion for him.

"Then it started, the drinking." Reid said in a dull voice. "At first it was one too many glasses of wine at dinner, then a few before. When she started drinking, I stopped. I thought that if I gave it up, she would, too. But she didn't. When I came home and found her drunk in the middle of the day, I locked up the liquor. But she still managed to get it. I broke every bottle I could find, and told every slave that if they brought it for her, I'd sell them."

And that's why he's so against drinking, Melissa realized. Nathan was right. He did have a good reason.

"She told me the reason she drank was because she was bored. So I relented and brought her back to Natchez, but it was too late. She still drank. At home, every party we went to, she got stinking drunk. We were an acute embarassment to Jeanette. Jeanette and I decided it was time for drastic measures. I took her to a doctor, who put her in a sanitarium. When she was supposedly cured, we brought her back to Natchez. By that time, it was planting season. I had to go back to the plantation or lose everything. Jeanette told me to leave Valerie with her for a few months. A month later, Jeanette sent word for me to come get her. Valerie had started drinking again, this time worse than before. To make matters worse, she was often violent and Jeanette couldn't handle her. By the time I got to Natchez, Valerie had disappeared. I searched a month before I found her. She was in a whorehouse in Natchez-Under-the-Hill—selling her body to any man who would buy her a drink."

Melissa gasped. Valerie had been repulsed by her husband's lovemaking. She had refused Reid, who made love so tenderly, so beautifully. Yet she had sold her body, prostituted herself for liquor? Melissa was horrified.

Reid didn't notice Melissa's reaction. He was too caught up in his memories. "I took her back to the plantation and put her under guard, but she still managed to get the stuff. This time it was corn whiskey, the raw, potent poison. Some river rat must have been selling it to her. It became a game of hide-and-seek. You wouldn't believe how cunning she became. She found the most incredible places to hide it.

"She started accusing me of infidelity." Reid laughed bitterly. "She didn't want me, but she didn't want anyone else to have me, either. When I pointed out there wasn't a white woman within fifty miles, she accused me of sleeping with my female slaves. The whole idea was totally groundless, ridiculous, but it was useless to argue with her."

Reid walked to the window and stared out at the moonlit scene below him for several minutes. When he turned, Melissa was shocked at the tortured look on his face.

"I came home one night and she was stinking drunk, as usual. She met me at the door, screeching accusations. God, you wouldn't believe how vile her language could be. It would have shocked a riverboatman. I was exhausted. We had spent all day trying to drain a swamp, and I was in no mood for her ugly language or her hysterics.

"I decided the best thing to do was to ignore her. I walked up the stairs, intent on only one thing—to get to bed and try to get some sleep. She followed me, still hurling her accusations. When we got to the top of the landing, she attacked me, clawing and slapping at me. She was a wild woman. I couldn't do anything with her. Somewhere in the struggle, she pulled away from me and tumbled down the stairs. I tried to catch her, but she just slipped right through my fingers."

Melissa waited, her heart in her throat. The silence was unbearable. She thought she would scream if he didn't say something soon.

Reid sat weakly back into the chair and let out a long sigh. "She hit her head when she fell. She never regained consciousness. That was six years ago."

Six years ago? She had been unconscious for six long years? Melissa was horrified.

"I took her to doctors in Natchez, New Orleans, then back East, and finally to Europe. They all told me the same thing. She had suffered massive brain damage. She would probably never regain consciousness. She might live for a month, or for years. I brought her back to New Orleans and placed her under the care of the Catholic sisters at Charity Hospital in New Orleans.

"By that time, I was deeply in debt. I'd sold my slaves, practically every stick of furniture, and the land was heavily mortgaged. Jeanette wanted to help me out, but I refused. Valerie was my wife and my responsibility. That's when I went back to trapping with Nathan.

"When four years had passed and there had been no change in Valerie's condition, the doctors advised me to divorce her quietly and go on with my own life. But I couldn't do it. I won't be a hypocrite and claim I loved her, because I didn't. She had killed that emotion long before, but I did pity her. She had been a beautiful young woman, and I felt that no one deserved to have to lie for years, locked in some vacuum between life and death. I couldn't bring myself to walk out on her. To me, that would have been wrong, like kicking someone when they were down."

Reid looked deeply into Melissa's eyes. His voice was anguished. "Even after I fell in love with you, I couldn't do that to her. As desperately as I loved you, as much as I wanted you, I couldn't turn my back on her. But, Melissa, my loving you never hurt her. I hurt you, myself even, but I never hurt her. She was beyond hurting."

Reid was silent for a few minutes, his look far away. The minutes ticked away with agonizing slowness.

"She died last week," Reid finally said in a voice so low Melissa had to strain to hear him. "It was pneumonia that finally killed her. I was with her at the end, and I'm glad I was. It's strange, but there at the end, I think she knew what was happening and my being with her comforted her. There was something in her eyes, a spark of life I hadn't seen in six years. And I think she knew that by her dying she was releasing us both from our misery."

Melissa's eyes were shimmering with tears. She was glad he had stood by his wife to the end, too. She wouldn't have wanted it any other way. Buy why had he waited until it was too late to tell her?

"Why didn't you tell me?" she sobbed.

"To what purpose, Melissa? So I could ask you to be my mistress? No, I couldn't shame you that way. I loved you too much."

"I would have waited for you to be free."

"For how long? Another six years? A lifetime, perhaps? No, I couldn't do that, either. That would have been burying us both alive. And I would have always wondered whether you were waiting for me because you loved me or because you pitied me. I could have never stood that."

Melissa couldn't answer. She was sobbing uncontrollably. She cried for Reid, for all the years he had lived with no one to console him, no one to love him. She cried out of pity for Valerie, and she cried for herself, because she couldn't marry Reid now. It was too late. She had promised Aaron she would marry him. She had never seen him as happy as he had been this past week. She feared he had fallen in love with her after all, and she couldn't hurt him. She *wouldn't* hurt him.

Reid pulled her gently into his arms, whispering, "Sssh, sweetheart, it's all over. It's all behind us now. We have the rest of our lives together."

No we don't, Melissa thought sadly. But we do have tonight. And she wanted this night desperately. One night to fill her with memories, memories to last her a lifetime. Yes, she thought fiercely, this was one night fate was not going to cheat her out of. This was *their* night, hers and Reid's.

Her hands framed his face, her eyes searching, caressing each feature, etching it upon her memory. Then she pulled his head down to hers. As their lips met, Reid groaned and pulled her into a tighter embrace, kissing her with a feverish intensity. Still locked in that kiss, he scooped her up and carried her to the bed.

Laying her on the soft mattress, he raised his head and looked down at her, "I thought I would never hold you in my arms again." His groan was a cry that came from the depths of hell. "Oh, sweetheart, I love you. You have no idea of what I've been through these past months." He buried his head in the soft crook of her neck, muttering, "I felt like I had left a part of me behind. That I was only half a man."

Tears glistened in Melissa's eyes. Oh, my darling, if you only knew how close to the truth your words are, she thought. You did leave a part of yourself with me, and now your child is growing inside me. But I can never tell you. No, if you knew of it, you'd never let me go.

"Sssh, my love," Melissa whispered against his temple. "Just love me."

And love her he did. His mouth, his lips, his body said the words so eloquently. And Melissa loved him back. They were hungry for each other, a hunger that couldn't seem to be satisfied. Their kisses were feverish, their hands eager as they explored and stroked and caressed each other.

Reid's clothes and Melissa's gown were tossed to the side. Their eyes roamed over each other, he admiring her beauty and feminine curves, she his superb muscular masculinity. They came together like two young animals, frenzied, their kisses wild and fierce and savage. Their hands and mouths roamed at will, loving each inch of each other. He tongued her, and she tongued him. He growled his pleasure, she purred hers, and they both moaned and gasped and sighed. They took and gave freely with all the strength in their young, eager bodies and all the love in their souls.

And when they were both trembling with intense excitement, their bodies joined and became one. As Reid plunged into her moist, soft warmth, burying his long, rigid length deep inside her, they both exhaled a rapturous sigh at the exquisite sensation.

"Oh, God, Melissa," Reid muttered huskily against her lips, "you feel so good. I had forgotten how warm and tight and sweet you are."

They lay savoring the feel of their closeness, their naked, feverish bodies straining even closer, his hard, masculine flesh pressing against her soft, feminine flesh, chest to chest, hip to hip, thigh to thigh, the dark hairs surrounding their joining tangling and intermingling.

Reid bent his head and hissed her, softly, tenderly, as he began his strokes — slow, sensuous movements that stoked the fires of their passion. The tempo of their lovemaking increased as they rocked and swayed in the oldest, most sensuous, most intimate dances of all time.

They were locked in their own world now, a wondrous, rapturous world of their own making, climbing steadily up that glorious, lofty height. Breaths quickened, hearts raced, lips met with heated abandon, sweat-dampened bodies strained with urgency as they moved closer and closer to that pinnacle of passion. Deliberately he held them at that quivering zenith, until the exquisite pleasure became unbearable, their bodies feeling as if they would explode and shatter into a million pieces if they didn't reach their release soon. And then, with one powerful, deep thrust, they were hurdled over that rapturous crest, soaring, spinning through space and time as blinding lights flashed in their brains and a roaring filled their ears.

Together, they drifted on that warm, glorious cloud of utter fulfillment, slowly descending, still locked in that sweet embrace, murmuring endearments and exchanging soft kisses. Reid rolled from her and laid her head on his shoulder, his hands smoothing her tangled hair and caressing her back.

"We're going to have a wonderful life together, sweetheart," Reid said quietly. "I'll have to start all over at the plantation, but it will be much easier than before, with you beside me. We'll build it together, and someday it will be the finest cotton plantation in Mississippi."

He sat up, leaning on one elbow, and looked down at her. His eyes drank in her beauty from head to toe, and Melissa tingled under that warm, golden gaze.

He stroked her arm. "You know, I still can't believe how beautiful you are. I thought I could never forget your body, and yet I don't remember your skin being so incredibly soft and silky."

His hand cupped one of her pregnancy-swollen breasts. "I even forgot what full, beautiful breasts you have. Somehow, I remembered them as being smaller."

As he bent his head and nuzzled the soft mounds, bathing them with soft kisses, Melissa's breath caught. Oh, no, please don't let him guess, she prayed.

His hand strayed across her abdomen. Melissa sucked in her belly, hoping he couldn't notice the little bulge there. She sighed in relief when Reid's fingers moved lower and tangled in the soft curls between her legs.

"I've gained weight," she muttered, hoping he would accept that explanation for the changes in her body.

He raised his head, his lips dropping soft kisses over her shoulders and up her throat. "It's most becoming, sweetheart. Just more for me to enjoy and love."

Oh, why did he have to keep saying those things, keep reminding her of their baby. The words tore at her heart; she ached for him.

"Hush," she whispered, pulling him closer. "Let me love you."

Reid never wondered at her fierce, abandoned lovemaking, her almost desperate urgency. He couldn't. He was drowning in sheer sensation. And then he was too busy loving her back, delighting in the taste and feel of her, his blood coursing through his veins like liquid fire and pounding in his ears as he carried them back up those spiraling, dizzy heights to yet another searing burst of sweet, fiery fulfillment. And when their torrent of lovemaking was spent, he slept, exhausted and blissfully content.

But Melissa didn't sleep. She wasn't going to waste what was left of her time with Reid doing that. She pressed closer to him, as if trying to imprint him on her own body. Her hands caressed him, trying to commit each muscle, each hollow to memory. Her eyes studied the features of his face, hoping to burn the vision of him into her brain. Oh, God, how she wished she could just absorb him, take him into her body and carry him with her the rest of her life.

And finally, when the sun was just beginning its slow ascent in the sky, she kissed his sensuous lips softly and turned to leave the bed.

The soft kiss awakened Reid. He caught her arm. "No, stay here beside me," he said in a drowsy voice.

Melissa's heart hammered in her chest. She couldn't bear to look at him then, not yet. "I can't. I've got to get dressed for my wedding."

Reid smiled and sat up. "One more day won't matter. Come back to bed, sweetheart.

Melissa rose, slipped on her gown, and turned to him. "No, Reid. Not our wedding. I've got to get dressed for my marriage to Aaron."

The shock of her words had the same impact on Reid as a kick to the belly. "You can't be serious," he breathed.

"Last night didn't change anything, Reid. I'm

still marrying Aaron."

Reid bolted up from the bed, towering over her. "After what we shared last night?" he asked in disbelief. "How can you? What kind of a woman are you?"

Melissa's eyes flashed. "I'll tell you what kind of a woman I am! I'm the same kind of woman you are a man. Do you think you're the only one who has principles? Keeping a commitment is just as important to me as it is to you."

"You haven't made the commitment yet."

"Haven't I? What do you call making a promise? I promised Aaron I would marry him. I gave my word. My word is just as important to me as yours is to you."

"You're trying to pay me back for walking out on you. You're trying to hurt me back," he accused.

"No, Reid, I'm not trying to hurt you. I'm trying to keep from hurting Aaron. He's a good man, a trusting man. He doesn't deserve to be tossed aside like he's some used rag. I can't hurt him. I *won't* hurt him!"

"You're making a mistake, Melissa. You don't love him."

"Yes, I do love him, Reid," Melissa replied, realizing for the first time the truth of her words. "But not like I love you. It's a quieter love, a gentle love, perhaps a better love."

Reid's face blanched of all color at her words. He stared at her in stark disbelief.

Melissa turned and walked to the window. Staring out of it, she said, "Now, please leave, Reid."

Reid stared at her back for long minutes. He couldn't believe he had lost her. He refused to believe he had lost her. He couldn't go through that pain again. No, she was just threatening him. She wouldn't go through with it.

While Reid dressed, Melissa kept her back to him. He walked to the door, opened it, and then turned. His golden eyes bored into her back. "You won't do it, Melissa. In your heart, you know you love me. I'm leaving Natchez today on the *River Queen*. The boat leaves at two o'clock this afternoon. I'll be waiting for you."

"I won't come," Melissa replied, staring out the window.

"You'll come," Reid said in a determined voice.

Melissa heard the door close behind her. She slumped weakly, leaning her head against the windowpane. A tear trickled down her cheek. "No, Reid," she whispered, "I won't."

Aaron watched Melissa as she walked down the staircase. His eyes searched her face carefully. He wasn't surprised when he found what he was looking for. He would have been disappointed in her if he hadn't.

He smiled as she stepped down the last step. "You look beautiful, Melissa."

"Thank you, Aaron," Melissa replied. She was glad Jeanette had talked her into wearing something other than black for the wedding. She knew that she looked pretty in the new turquoise dress, and she needed all the self-confidence she could muster to bolster her courage. And she was glad they had decided on a simple wedding at the judge's office with only Jeanette and one of Aaron's friends as witnesses. As nervous as she was, she couldn't have stood a crowd's curious eyes on her.

As they walked to the door, Melissa said, "I thought Jeanette was coming with us?"

"No, she changed her mind. She said she'd meet us there," Aaron replied.

When they reached the outskirts of Natchez, Aaron turned the buggy toward the bluff, instead of taking one of the streets that led into the city. "I thought Judge Bennington's office was in the other direction," Melissa said.

"It is, Melissa. But I want to talk to you first."

They stopped on the windswept bluff, and Aaron helped Melissa down from the buggy. He led her to the bench under the magnolia tree, the same bench she had sat on when he proposed.

When she was seated, he looked down into her face. "He's come back," he said quietly.

It was a statement, not a question. "How did you know?" Melissa asked in surprise.

"Jeanette came to see me this morning. She felt that I should know what's going on. She told me everything about Reid's wife. But even if she hadn't told me, I would have known. I could see it in you eyes."

"It doesn't matter, Aaron. I'm going to marry you."

"Why?"

The blunt question stunned Melissa. "Why . . . why because I love you."

Aaron shook his head. "Don't, Melissa."

"But I do! I really do love you!"

"Yes, I think we do love each other, in a way. But there are all kinds and degrees of love. And we both know you don't love me the way you love him."

"I don't want that kind of love. It's too powerful, too consuming. It's too painful."

Aaron cupped her chin and lifted her head, looking deeply into her eyes. "Melissa, you don't mean that."

"He deserted me!"

"And now you're trying to punish him? Hurt him back? No, Melissa, I think that young man has suffered enough."

Reid had accused Melissa of trying to punish him the night before, and she had denied it. But when Aaron accused her of the same thing, she realized for the first time that she *was* trying to spite Reid, to hurt him back. Her desertion had caused a deep wound in her soul. She still loved him, but the bitterness had been there all along, buried deep inside her. "He should have told me. He should have trusted me."

"Melissa, there's nothing you can say that will

turn me against Reid. I can't help but admire him. He stood by his wife until the bitter end. He gave up his only true love, his chance for happiness to stick to his beliefs, to stand by a woman who had never loved him."

"You would have done the same thing," Melissa snapped.

"Yes, I would have," Aaron admitted. "But I loved my wife deeply, so my devotion wouldn't have been remarkable. But Reid didn't love his wife. It's a wonder he didn't hate her, considering what she had put him through. No, he did it because he felt a deep moral conviction that it was the right thing to do. And a man who sticks to his convictions, regardless of the pain and unhappiness it brings him, is a rare man in this world today."

Melissa knew what Aaron said was true. Reid was a remarkable man. And she did love him—with her whole heart and soul. What she felt for Aaron couldn't even begin to compare with what she felt for Reid. But, still she hated to hurt Aaron. Her eyes shimmered with tears as she reeled with indecision.

Aaron's voice was gentle. "Melissa, I won't marry you. I still think if things had worked out differently, we could have had a contented life together. But there's a big difference between contentment and sublime happiness. I know. That's the kind of happiness I had with my wife. We had ten wonderful years together. I've had more happiness than most people have had in a life-time. But what have you and Reid had? A few months? A brief season of happiness?"

Melissa was silent, misery written all over her face.

"And don't worry about hurting me, if that's what's bothering you," Aaron continued. "You can't hurt me, because I don't love you deeply. I told you in the beginning that I've only loved one woman that way, with my whole heart and soul. I've had my grand passion, my once-in-a-lifetime love. Now it's your and Reid's turn."

An immense wave of relief washed over Melissa. Her eyes danced with happiness. Aaron had given her his blessing and her freedom. She hugged him and kissed his cheek. "Thank you, Aaron. If my baby is a boy, I'm going to name him after you."

Aaron's eyebrows arched in mock horror. "God forbid! In that case, I sincerely hope it's a girl."

They both laughed, then Aaron said, "Now, we'd better get you to that steamboat before it leaves. Otherwise, you might have to search the entire West for your young man."

Melissa nodded eagerly, her heart pounding with anticipation.

As they started down the road on the bluff toward the river landing, Melissa spotted the *River Queen*. The crew was just starting to pull in the gangplank. "Look, Aaron! The boat is ready to leave!"

Aaron glanced down. "Hang on, Melissa!" he said as he whipped his horse.

It was a wild, crazy ride down the steep, narrow road. The small buggy bounced over the deep ruts, jarring their teeth, and then tilted precariously as they rounded a bend in the road on one wheel.

Melissa gasped as she saw a lumbering wagon, loaded high with cotton bales, blocking the road before them.

"Get out of the way!" Aaron yelled, then sawed on the horse's reins.

The buggy flew past the wagon, one wheel on the very edge of the steep road. Melissa glanced down and saw the sharp drop to the river below. She sucked in her breath and held on for dear life.

They passed the wagon at breakneck speed, leaving the black driver wall-eyed with fright and sitting in a flurry of choking dust. They tore through the narrow, dank streets of Natchez-Under-the-Hill. The people in the streets scattered out of their way in fear, many yelling angry curses at their backs. They clattered onto the wooden landing and came to a screeching halt.

Reid had stood at the railing as the *River Queen* was being loaded, his eyes on the road above him, willing Melissa to come to him. Every muscle in his long body was taut as he strained his eyes. The knuckles on his hands were white as he clenched the railing. His pulse drummed in his ears. It was an agony, the waiting, the wondering. She had to come! She had to!

And then when he saw the gangplank being pulled in, he let out a long, ragged sigh. She had meant what she said. She wasn't coming. He had lost her, this time for good. A pain like none he had ever felt before swept over him and, in its wake, left an aching void. He turned and stumbled blindly away.

On the wharf, Aaron jumped down from the buggy, then swung Melissa down. "Hurry!" he urged her.

Melissa needed no urging. She gave him a quick kiss and then ran, weaving through the crowd. Her bonnet flew off, the pins in her hair scattered, and her dark, long hair tumbled down. She picked up her skirts to run even faster, totally oblivious to the men whistling and ogling her shapely calves and trim ankles. The wind rushed past her face as she flew down the pier, and her long hair trailed behind her. Melissa's heart pounded, feeling as if it would burst in her chest. Her breath came in ragged gasps, but still she raced to the man she loved.

Reid heard the commotion on the wharf and turned to see what was happening. His tawny eyes filled with wonder when he saw Melissa racing through the crowd, pushing aside anyone who got in her way. A feeling of unbelievable happiness filled him and exploded. He laughed with sheer joy.

Then, seeing the boat pulling away from the landing, he turned and yelled up at the captain, "No! Stop the boat!"

But it was too late. The paddles were already turning. The boat was slowly pulling away, the gap between it and the wharf steadily widening.

Melissa was racing beside the steamboat now, directly across from Reid. He held out his arms and yelled, "Jump!"

Reid could have told her to jump off the end of the earth and she would have. This was Reid who was waiting for her with wide-open arms, the man she loved. Nothing, certainly no small small expanse of water, was going to keep her from him. Without the slightest hesitation, she took a running leap and flew through the air.

The crowd on the river landing who had been watching the drama held their breath in fear as the young woman flew from the wharf and across the yellow water. Then, as Reid caught her, plucking her from the air and swinging her around, they cheered loudly.

Reid put her on her feet, his strong arms still around her. They stared at each other for along minute. Then Reid kissed her, warmly, deeply, thoroughly.

The rowdies in the crowd on the river landing whistled, hooted, and gave loud catcalls. The more polite smiled their approval. But Reid and Melissa were oblivious to it all. For them, the rest of the world had ceased to exist.

Finally Reid lifted his head and gazed down at her, his golden eyes shimmering with emotion. "You came. You came after all," he said in a gentle, disbelieving voice.

"Yes, my love, we're here. We're both here." Reid's brow furrowed. "We?"

Deliberately, Melissa arched her back, pressing her abdomen against him so he could feel that slight bulge that she had so carefully hidden from him before. "Me—and our baby."

The look of surprised wonder, then pure joy on Reid's face brought tears to Melissa's eyes. He embraced her fiercely, saying in a voice choked with emotion, "Oh, my love, I'll never let you go again. Never!"

Melissa's eyes filled with tears of happiness. She looked up over his shoulder into the sun and, through the moisture in her eyes, saw the rainbow. But she knew that this rainbow was no brief illusion. It would never disappear. Like their love, it would always be with them.

ZEBRA HAS THE SUPERSTARS
OF PASSIONATE ROMANCE!

CRIMSON OBSESSION   (2272, $3.95)
by Deana James

Cassandra MacDaermond was determined to make the handsome gambling hall owner Edward Sandron pay for the fortune he had stolen from her father. But she never counted on being struck speechless by his seductive gaze. And soon Cassandra was sneaking into Sandron's room, more intent on sharing his rapture than causing his ruin!

TEXAS CAPTIVE   (2251, $3.95)
by Wanda Owen

Ever since two outlaws had killed her ma, Talleha had been suspicious of all men. But one glimpse of virile Victor Maurier standing by the lake in the Texas Blacklands and the half-Indian princess was helpless before the sensual tide that swept her in its wake!

TEXAS STAR   (2088, $3.95)
by Deana James

Star Garner was a wanted woman—and Chris Gillard was determined to collect the generous bounty being offered for her capture. But when the beautiful outlaw made love to him as if her life depended on it, Gillard's firm resolve melted away, replaced with a raging obsession for his fiery TEXAS STAR.

MOONLIT SPLENDOR   (2008, $3.95)
by Wanda Owen

When the handsome stranger emerged from the shadows and pulled Charmaine Lamoureux into his strong embrace, she sighed with pleasure at his seductive caresses. Tomorrow she would be wed against her will—so tonight she would take whatever exhilarating happiness she could!

Available wherever paperbacks are sold, or order direct from the Publisher. Send cover price plus 50¢ per copy for mailing and handling to Zebra Books, Dept. 2375, 475 Park Avenue South, New York, N.Y. 10016. Residents of New York, New Jersey and Pennsylvania must include sales tax. DO NOT SEND CASH.

ZEBRA ROMANCES FOR ALL SEASONS
From Bobbi Smith

ARIZONA TEMPTRESS   (1785, $3.9█

Rick Peralta found the freedom he craved only in his di█
guise as El Cazador. Then he saw the exquisitely allurin█
Jennie among his compadres and the hotblooded ma█
swore she'd belong just to him.

CAPTIVE PRIDE   (2160, $3.9█

Committed to the Colonial cause, the gorgeous and ind█
pendent Cecelia Demorest swore she'd divert Capta█
Noah Kincade's weapons to help out the American rebel█
But the moment that the womanizing British privateer fir█
touched her, her scheming thoughts gave way to burnin█
need.

DESERT HEART   (2010, $3.9█

Rancher Rand McAllister was furious when he became t█
guardian of a scrawny girl from Arizona's mining countr█
But when he finds that the pig-tailed brat is really a volu█
tuous beauty, his resentment turns to intense interes█
Laura Lee knew it would be the biggest mistake in her li█
to succumb to the cowboy — but she can't fight against gi█
ing him her wild DESERT HEART.

Available wherever paperbacks are sold, or order direct from t█
Publisher. Send cover price plus 50¢ per copy for mailing an█
handling to Zebra Books, Dept. 2375, 475 Park Avenue Sout█
New York, N.Y. 10016. Residents of New York, New Jersey an█
Pennsylvania must include sales tax. DO NOT SEND CASH.